KILLING
ABEL

Fratricide

M. TIEMAN

TABLE OF CONTENTS

ABOUT THIS BOOK

K illing Abel is a novel based on a few thousand words from the Book of Genesis in the Old Testament of the Christian Bible. From "In the beginning . . ." to the Flood, God provided us with only two-and-one-half words a year of history, so there is much left open to the imagination, and the way I imagine it is what you have in *Killing Abel*. In *Killing Abel*, God is a loving Father, and that is not an easy role, as many fathers would regrettably admit.

Being a good father is the most important, most difficult, and without exception, most consequential obligation a man has. The woman who rocked the cradle of the progeny whose descendants would one day rule the world, rocked the cradle with a foundation from her parents——or lack thereof. The foundation of her progeny will largely determine whether the ruler will be a good leader or a cruel dictator.

Any foundation for a coherent worldview must start at a logical place, and there is only one choice available for where to begin. If the underlying context is not Genesis 1:1 "In the beginning . . ." then it is a pretext. If you cannot trace your worldview back to a beginning, then what is it based on? If it has no beginning, then it has no foundation. Of all the tasks a man could face in life, the one I would least like to undertake is that of trying to deny a beginning.

As the cradle is rocked, the wisdom of the person's hand can only be seen in the future actions of the child, and therein lies the rub. Looking back at men's actions is humanity's only way to find a context for those actions, and only with a true context will a coherent foundation for their own lives be assembled.

Understanding history is wisdom. Wisdom is by far the most precious asset there is as it leads to a truly fulfilling life. Trying to change the future is like trying to change the past: it can't be done without looking very closely at what cannot be undone. Not understanding history is a recipe for repetition, despair, poor government, errant philosophy, and bad theology. *History exists apart from religion.* And it can be kept separate with the discovery of the true, logical, and/or the likely context of each historical event.

Theology and philosophy, regardless of the price of admission or the heritage and prestige of the institutions where they are taught, have no bearing on the night sky in all its glory, awe, and wonder. Each night as the sky is viewed ever closer, the contents of the heavens never fail to confirm the Word of God, "In the beginning . . ." The skeptics and the scholars alike would fail even the slightest audit of their lives while God's tinkering is the context for every truth.

Killing Abel is written with the premise that God is free-and that neither you nor I can force God's hand; that neither you nor I can bear up against what is true in an attempt to make God out to be something that fits our own misconceptions–conceptions that are not based on God's actions.

Most religious dogmas object to an animated and dynamic view of God the Father. Their leadership will reject a God who can learn, a God who can adjust, a God who takes risks and a God who is on occasion, sorry. Killing Abel embraces "God's openness." All the while the prideful deep church, and their leaders won't even consider the idea–as their attendance wanes.

In the truest sense of the word, I believe that *Killing Abel* is a very novel interpretation of the events of Genesis from Adam to

Noah. This is not meant to be theology——it is a story of a loving Father and His children based on what little is known, and to a very large extent it is fiction.

Some biblical references are noted. The references are intended to give the reader the biblical text I used to base the fictional accounts on. All of the fiction is added in an attempt to bolster the biblical text with fictional but logical context. In Killing Abel, I embrace the concept put forward in Occam's Razor, that the "simpler explanation is most likely the right one."

Perhaps God decided not to reveal much about the first seventeen hundred years of man's history so that man would think more about those early days. Or maybe God believed that a small, firm foundation would be best for man to look back on.

My experience thus far in life is that thinking is a chore that is avoided by far too many people——but it is my favorite thing to do. I encourage you to take this opportunity to think more than you usually do while you consider my novel view of the killing of Abel.

—— M. Tieman

— 1 —
GUILTY

E ve stood and watched a large snake eat from the tree of the knowledge of good and evil——the reptile reminded her of someone.

"Lucifer, is that you?" Eve questioned the large serpent. Lucifer was an angel, a created being that was different from Eve in that he was only spiritual, and was lacking flesh. The angel was the same as Eve in that he had free will. He was the most beautiful being in all of creation, a being who, after much forethought and debate within the Godhead, had been sent to assist man in the Garden of Eden.

Lucifer was informed by the Trinity of Their desires for the man, the woman, and their progeny. He was then given dominion over the garden and its contents. He was there to provide guidance, answers about daily life and a degree of protection for the created son and daughter. (KJV Eze. 28:13)

This strange serpent acknowledged Eve but didn't speak a word to her. He was content with his knowledge of Eve, the intended mate for Adam, with her ability to procreate, and her uncertainty as to who he was. He watched her and waited. He was in a fig tree, the tree of knowledge, in the midst of the beautiful Garden in Eden, and

Eve was watching the serpent intently from below as he ate freely and pleasurably from the tree.

Eve was both conflicted and tempted by what she was seeing. She was conflicted because the serpent seemed unaffected by the fruit of the tree that Adam had told her to stay away from, and she was tempted by the fig because it looked so delicious as the juice dripped from the mouth of the serpent. She was suddenly very hungry, too. What harm could there be in taking a bite of something that looked so delicious, she did not consider. As she continued to justify her desire, she looked around for the man, but Adam was nowhere to be seen.

The serpent spoke. "Adam doesn't need to know what we know, now does he?"

She recognized his voice, his manner; the angel was now talking out of the mouth of the large snake. While that seemed strange to Eve, who had only been alive for seven days, it was not unthinkable to her that an angel could occupy the body of a reptile. Eve didn't know much about Lucifer. She only knew that he was an angel, a being unlike her or Adam, a being that was above her in some ways but beneath her in importance to her Father.

"How did you know I was looking for the man?" Eve asked the snake.

"Eve, come and enjoy the knowledge with me. You won't surely die," said the serpent in an attempt to deceive the woman. (KJV Gen. 3:1)

Eve's mind raced with all the possibilities. *Perhaps Adam was confused or mistaken when he told me not to go near this lovely tree,* she wondered. *Lucifer is clearly enjoying the fruit, and something so good to eat and so nourishing to the body couldn't be bad, could it? Knowledge doesn't seem to hurt Lucifer; how could it hurt me?* She continued to watch him. She found it simply fascinating that the fruit didn't seem to hurt Lucifer.

Lucifer was the angel that God had sent to answer Adam and Eve's basic questions about daily life. The angel would cover them from physical harm as they learned about their physical limitations. The knowledge of good and evil was not something they needed for daily life.

"Lucifer, why do you try to disguise yourself as a serpent?" Eve wondered aloud. The serpent unwound itself slowly and disappeared behind one side of the tree, reappearing on the other side as the angel Lucifer. Now he was a fleshless but clothed spiritual being. If the being had a sexual nature to it, male or female, it was not readily discernible to Eve. Though different than Adam, this being had a definite feminine side that showed itself to Eve, making the angel more approachable. The now less apprehensive Eve, listened.

"Is this better?" he asked.

"Neither Adam nor I am to eat from this tree. We are not even to touch it," Eve said. (KJV Gen. 3:2–3)

Lucifer began to gently examine the hanging figs one by one until he came to one that was hanging just above his head. It was the ripest of the ripe fruit. With his angelic hands, he grasped the fig, seizing the attention of Eve. As he squeezed the fig, the juice slowly dripped into his open mouth. Eve watched . . . Drip, drip, drip as the angelic being was clearly savoring each drop. She watched as the nectar went into the being's mouth, down his throat, and then disappeared into his clothing. (KJV Gen. 3:6)

Unbeknownst to her, Lucifer had now begun to ponder his own desires, departing far from his given dominion, as he savored Eve's attention far more than the fig's sweet nectar.

Eve's eyes, now gazing directly above her head at a ripe fig, *this fruit is good . . . why is it forbidden? It must be the source of Lucifer's knowledge?* Eve now believed that this tree in the midst of the garden must possess some special knowledge: the knowledge that she didn't have, the knowledge that she wanted, the knowledge that she thought she deserved.

That knowledge had to be a very powerful tool, a tool that could help her understand so many things. Eve was a child, a grown child, a fully endowed woman-child only seven days old. *I need more knowledge, I want more knowledge, and this knowledge of evil, alone, will be liberating. I won't need Lucifer or anyone else to guide me; I will be able to guide myself.*

Slowly, Eve walked closer and closer to the low-hanging fruit on the tree.

"You won't surely die," repeated Lucifer. (KJV Gen. 3:4)

Slowly, she reached out her hand to the fruit——and then stopped.

As the moment hung, like the dangling fruit that was now tempting Eve, Lucifer became uncontrollably anxious. With her fingers one hand-length away from her temptation and his desires, Eve turned her focus on him. His diamond eyes were shining as if he knew something that she did not. But Eve saw only what she wanted to see: that he was clearly enjoying the knowledge. He took a deep breath and gave her a reassuring nod, and she looked back at the fruit of her desires.

With great anticipation, her eyes tightly closed and her head slightly raised, she plucked the fig from the tree and embraced it— first with a deep inhalation to savor its aroma, then with her lips as she partook of it. The juice dripped from her mouth to her breast, and her eyes remained closed.

Lucifer stood behind Eve while they both savored the moment, with his eyes also tightly shut. Slowly, in sync, they opened their eyes. They were now heading down the same path. They were of one mind with a mutual goal. They had their knowledge—now they needed the man to join them.

The man, suddenly, had become Lucifer's only obstacle to his desires. Lucifer wanted to go in a different direction, away from the Father. *Now Eve follows me, if I can convince Adam to do as well, they will procreate for me.*

Eve now saw Lucifer very differently than she had moments before. Now they were allies on a mission. Now the two of them had a sense of family, a common goal, a corporate destination that was inspired by the prideful heart in the *now* evil Lucifer.

The knowledge she had gained was not specific in nature. It was about being able to discern how very different the aspects of life could be from each other—left and right, God and Lucifer, good and evil. It was not satisfying; the knowledge did not satiate her desires in any way. *Something is missing*, as she looked to her guide Lucifer yet again.

Below the tree of knowledge, they searched together for the man. Their conspiracy was a silent one but well understood. They had different motives but the same goal—seducing Adam. Eve wanted the man to join her in her newfound freedom of choice and to hopefully satiate her newfound lust for knowledge; and Lucifer believed that Eve's womb was of no use to him without the man. They didn't have to wait long. Within a few moments, as if it had been planned, Adam appeared, walking towards them.

Unlike Eve, Lucifer was not naïve or misguided. He was interested in only one thing—fulfilling his ambitions to move away from God, to do his own thing apart from his creator. He envisioned having subjects of his own, the offspring of Adam, who would worship him as he believed he deserved.

Lucifer ignored Eve's beauty, even though there were no females to be found among the angelic beings. He did lust for something though, something eternal—children of his own. He was not aware of any abilities he might have to procreate. But Adam and Eve could procreate, and he wanted them to procreate for him. After all, there was power in numbers. Their offspring would follow him and he would rule over them. They would worship him, and live under the tree of knowledge.

As Eve and Lucifer watched Adam approaching, they could tell from his slow pace that he sensed danger and that he knew that Eve had at least touched the tree, in direct disobedience to him. No one said a word. The tension grew as the silence continued until Eve could wait no longer.

"We have been looking for you, Adam. Where have you been?"

We? thought Adam. *Is Lucifer now her mentor, her partner? But partner in exactly what?*

"Eve, how do you feel? Are you okay?" asked Adam.

Adam was more confused than annoyed, as Eve actually seemed to be fine.

"I am fine. I don't feel doomed," said Eve. "Please come and join us." But Adam was still contemplating the situation. He could see the remains of the eaten fruit on the ground, and he could see the juice drying on Eve's hands, face, and bare breast as she reached for yet another fig.

"Eve, that's not a good idea. We were told not to eat from this tree. (KJV Gen. 2:17) This is the tree in the midst of the garden, is it not?"

"Of course it is. Look at it. It is good for food. It is nourishing, remember Lucifer told us that our flesh needs nourishment. If you want to know Lucifer as I now know him, you will need to join me. You won't surely die," said Eve.

"Do I not know Lucifer now?" Adam replied.

"Well, yes, but not the way I know him. I know him, and I now also know good. Don't you want to know the difference between what is good and what is not?" asked Eve. "The only way to know that difference is to eat from the forbidden tree."

Sensing that timing was important, Lucifer grabbed yet another fig and moved towards Eve. He looked at her; she looked back at him. They were still of the same frame of mind. Their conspiracy need not be spoken, and this would become the modus operandi for like-minded evildoers for millennia to come. The only goal Eve and Lucifer had at that moment was the seduction of Adam. They needed him to join in their rebellion——their lust to go a new way——in opposition to their creator.

Lucifer understood that Adam had the wherewithal to stop him. He could either convince Eve to withdraw, or he could simply choose not to partake and then admonish Eve for what she had clearly done. Eve, on the other hand, did not understand and was not even concerned with what the eternal consequences of Adam's decision might be.

"Join us, Adam," invited Lucifer. With a nod of his head, he encouraged Eve to hand Adam a fig.

Eve had not yet known Adam as a husband. Though they were both fully mature physically, they were very childlike in mind. They had only possessed awareness for seven days now, and for the moment, their thoughts were far away from the formidable inner desires that God placed in both of them to ensure procreation—their thoughts were centered only on the forbidden fruit on the tree——a force more powerful than had originally been envisioned by Adam. (KJV Gen. 2:25)

On the other hand, Lucifer and Eve's like desires had brought them together in mind, body, and spirit. Not so unlike what God had envisioned for the coming together of men and women.

"Adam, here is the fruit. You can touch it," Eve said as she held out a fig to Adam, tempting him again and again with the tasty fruit.

Still wary, Adam pondered his next move as he walked slowly towards Eve. She held the fig out from herself, then slowly brought it towards her chest as Adam approached. Adam felt a desire for Eve that he had never experienced before. He had never before seen her with such a look in her eyes. She wanted him to come closer to her. She wanted him to be with her, to come with her to the knowledge of good and of Lucifer.

All of Adam's attention was now on Eve and it seemed to him as if the world was standing still. He could perceive no sound, no movement, and for the moment, no Lucifer—to him there were only the two of them. Now Adam's mind was in turmoil. *What did she want? What did she need?* She still held the fig that she had offered to Adam and now she caressed it with her open mouth and took a big bite.

"That was mine," Adam said.

Eve's heart quickened and Lucifer bowed his head, knowing he had secured his victory.

Slowly, Adam reached out to Eve. She was resting her head against the tree and her hair was draped gracefully over her shoulders. Juice from the fig dripped down her neck and onto her bare breasts as she slowly pushed herself away from the tree and picked another large, ripe fig. Holding one fig in each hand, she crossed her arms tightly over her chest. Then she slowly uncrossed her arms and offered the second fig to Adam. Adam took the fig. Without understanding why, he turned his attention away from the seductive Eve to the fig in his hand.

Unseen behind them, Lucifer was gaining in size and strength. He sensed that his moment was at hand, that they would soon follow him, that they would bear children that would be his.

Adam accepted the fig from Eve and raised it to his lips. Behind them, the previously beautiful Lucifer transformed into a monster, arching over the scene to cover them as they consummated his rebellion.

For what seemed like an eternity to Eve, Adam stared at the fruit more intensely than he had ever looked at the naked woman. Unlike Eve, he very purposefully and calmly made his decision to partake of the fruit. With his eyes closed, he embraced the fruit with his lips and his tongue. Then, with a crushing bite into the fig, he delivered a crushing blow to the future of mankind.

Adam noticed a palpable feeling of separation from God as he willingly ate of the fig and enjoyed it, just as Eve had enjoyed it. Surprising to Adam, the sensation of gratification from eating the fig lasted but a few moments. Adam's lust for the fig was quickly satiated as he began to realize what had just happened. Just looking at his sticky fingers coated in the dried juice of the once tempting fig was annoying him. Adam was looking around while trying to rub off the fruit's dried remnants from his hands. At first, he sensed it, then he saw it, things were changing and would never be the same.

His first clue was Lucifer's new look, which was not at all pleasing, as it had previously been. Now Adam truly knew Lucifer, and this was not pleasant knowledge. Now that Lucifer had successfully orchestrated the fall of man, Eve too could see the fallen angel, the deceiver, his former beauty having been replaced by the ugliness of the now beastly looking angel. Lucifer's actions alone created his fall, his new look, and his new demeanor; that of a demon.

"What have I done?" she screamed. Adam was also looking up at Lucifer as Eve screamed again, "What did I just do?" But Adam did not hear her. He was consumed by his new knowledge of the now beastly Lucifer. Eve looked down at her hand in which she still held a half-eaten fig then dropped the fruit to the ground. With her other hand, she wiped the juice from her face and then she spat the remaining taste of the fruit at the ground. "Adam!" she screamed in horror. (KJV Gen. 3:7)

This shook Adam from his stupor. He didn't fully understand what Eve was experiencing, but he assumed that she was seeing what he was seeing——an all-new Lucifer, a Lucifer who was now terrifying.

Lucifer, savoring this moment of man's torment, paid no attention to the man or to the woman; his pride enveloped him, and his plans for the future consumed his every thought and inspired him to speak to his adopted children.

"You shall worship me now; I and I alone have given you your freedom." Lucifer was lost in his pride and his pride guided his every thought now.

Their guilt will guide them to the tree of knowledge, where they will kneel in worship of me and I will never let them depart, as they live in fear of its judgment. They will live in fear!

Adam embraced the naked Eve, hoping that this would calm her fears, which it did. He held her protectively and shielded her from the sight and the sound from the growing demonic presence of Lucifer. With his head beside hers, but not looking at her, he spoke.

"You're okay. I'm here. I will protect you." Eve trembled in his arms and cried. When she began to calm down, her crying subsided and she pushed herself away from Adam. "Thank you for coming to my aid," she said, "I was just so shocked at——" But then she looked at Adam and saw him differently in his nakedness, very differently than she had before. Then she looked at her own nakedness next to his and pushed him even farther away.

"What are you looking at?" she said to Adam. Adam was staring at her with wide eyes. "Adam, cover yourself," she said, as she quickly gathered leaves from the fig tree and handed some of the leaves to him. "Take these. Hold them over yourself and I will do the same. Let's leave this place, now," said Eve. She smashed one of the figs that had fallen to the ground and smeared the pulp and juice on her body, using the stickiness to sew fig leaves to her skin, hiding her nakedness. (KJV Gen. 3:7)

As Adam and Eve fled from the area, they found a place to hide from the view of the tree and they hoped from their Father's view as well. Eve asked, "Adam, why? Why did you eat that fig?" For Eve now realized that she hadn't actually wanted Adam to eat the fruit of the tree.

"You offered me the fig, but now you're saying . . . What are you saying? You didn't want me to eat it?" Adam asked, as he struggled to keep his fig leaves in place.

"Adam, cover yourself, now," Eve said again as she too struggled to keep her fig leaves in place. She felt the urge to cover herself more strongly than did Adam and she wanted to cover more of herself as well. As she continued to adjust her fig leaves, she answered Adam. "Well, no, I didn't. Not really. You had a choice, and you didn't have to eat. I didn't want you to eat. You are the one who told me not to eat from that tree. What are we to do now?" Eve was distraught. She could sense a separation from the Father; she sensed distance and condemnation from the Father. Adam was a man that she didn't know anymore and perhaps could never trust again. *If the man won't heed the words of his own Father will he ever do what I ask of him?*

Eve was confused and afraid. She had gotten what she thought she had wanted; but, in the end, it was not what she had wanted at all.

Adam could also feel a separation from God and from Eve. When he had come to Eve under the tree to protect her from Lucifer, he had felt a connection with her, however brief, but now that connection seemed to be broken.

"Eve, it's not my fault. I thought you wanted me to join you in your knowledge of Lucifer. Didn't you want me to share the knowledge of evil with you? You did offer me the fig." Adam shook his head in confusion and felt something new——fear. But fear of what, he did not know; nor did he know where it came from. It seemed to be in the wind.

"Lucifer wanted you to eat as I ate. He convinced me to help him seduce you, but I didn't really think you would succumb. You are the one who told me not to eat from that tree," said Eve, confused. Each of them was dealing with a spectrum of thoughts, feelings, and meanings that were not easily understood by them. In addition, their Father fighting His significant grief, looked through the Holy Spirit to see what might lie ahead for His beloved creation. He could only see the general outline of the unknown future that was now forced upon Him.

THE TRINITY AFFIRM THEIR DECISION TO PROCREATE

"We made man in Our image; as I love my Son, mankind has the ability to love Us and to love themselves," God reminded the Others. The three of Them knew that giving fleshy beings the ability to love would limit Their Triune essence in ways not yet seen or understood. (KJV Gen. 1:27)

"With the ability to love comes an unknown future, unknown to all. Love cannot be otherwise," said the Son. The Holy Spirit peered into the rocky road ahead for mankind, as far as He could possibly look and said, "Learning will be dynamic, challenging, and at times very painful for Us to endure."

"Wisdom will come to Us in time and hopefully to many men as well," God said. "We shall strive forward."

They All agreed.

God, still lamenting the new course of His Creation, watched as the man and the woman both struggled to keep their fig leaves in place in a vain attempt to hide their shame. Adam and Eve found themselves lost in Paradise. They needed——they *wanted*——their

Father. While their fear of meeting with Him was influencing their reactions at the moment, they were far more worried about the possible return of Lucifer. God was relieved to sense that His children feared Lucifer, and He would bless His children by removing that fear from them. Removing their fear would mean restricting Lucifer's dominion, an easy enough task for the Father. But dealing with the children's fear of their Father would be a much more difficult challenge, for God and for all fathers to come. Lucifer's fall meant that he would no longer have unfettered access to man. God would now allow him access to the tree of knowledge only, and only there would he be free to entice men unto rebellion.

Lucifer's plan and actions on that day had forever and irrevocably condemned him and all the beings who would follow him. The previously mighty angelic being was no longer the bright and morning star among angelic beings, and God changed his name accordingly. The once magnificent and now fallen creation of God would now be called Satan. He was also prophetically titled the Prince of Darkness, as he would come to rule a very dark place.

God spoke, "Lucifer, We contemplated your failure long before your fall. Your pride has caused you to tempt My children into rebellion and now We lament that the humility of the Son will be needed. Your weakness has now become Our strength. The tree of knowledge is now yours." With that, Lucifer was tethered and fettered to the tree. From then on, it would be his only tool for tempting others into rebellion. "You see yourself as a snake. Then a snake you shall be. You will crawl on your belly for all your days," said God. (KJV Gen. 3:14)

After Adam and Eve had eaten the forbidden fruit, the knowledge they had obtained from the fruit had quickly become guilt. This guilt had caused them to hide themselves from their Father and to hide their nakedness from each other.

Lucifer felt no such remorse. In fact, all he felt was anger and rage against God——and against his newly adopted children, Adam and Eve. Lucifer had opened their eyes. But now they shunned him and wanted nothing to do with his demonic ways. This enraged him. God had now limited and linked Lucifer's power to the tree where guilt had been conceived and born, and the tree would now be the tabernacle of guilt——for those judged guilty——for eternity.

"I will use this tree, and I will use its roots that have spread far and wide," Lucifer cried out, not knowing if God could hear him, or if God was even listening. Again, far louder and far more intensely, he challenged, "I will use this tree; I will use it again and again and again until I possess all of Your progeny, all of procreation will know me by my tree!"

Every leaf of the tree fell to the ground as the tree resonated with the thunder of Lucifer's voice. Looking up through the branches, now barren of leaves, he announced to the Heavens, "I will entice every person who ever lives to live under this tree——my tree——and to serve me and serve my tree. All that do live under it will be mine. You have agreed."

Then Lucifer turned his anger towards Adam and Eve and just as he did his voice suddenly became audible to them. "How dare you turn your backs on me?" The startled couple looked around but could not see him and the voice continued. "I am the one who gave you what you wanted. I gave you your freedom." They knew that voice and they were afraid, and once again felt ashamed for what they had done. Those were the last words they would ever hear from their deceiver.

So that was the great fall of Lucifer and he didn't go alone. The angels, who followed him, fell alongside him. But Lucifer had no intention of going down alone with his angelic brethren–He would work hard every day using his only tool, the tree of knowledge, to try to bring each and every guilt filled human spirit down to him. Guilt was of the strongest human emotions and Lucifer was its author.

So God cast down the disgraced angel out of Heaven, along with the one third of all angels who had followed Lucifer in his rebellious ways——from above the earth——into the earth He cast them. God used the prideful, fallen angel as an example to demonstrate the consequences of rebellion and betrayal while residing in Heaven. Lucifer was irrevocably exiled into darkness inside the earth, away from God and only available to men who worshiped his tree of guilt.

In the Godhead, the Holy Spirit spoke out to the Father and to the Son. "We had hoped for a different outcome, but now I can see only a difficult and sorrowful path ahead for the Father. Let Us now turn Our hopes towards a less painful path for the Son." The Father looked to His only Son in Heaven and expressed His love and His hopes for Him, unspoken but entirely understood and appreciated by the Son. Words alone will always fall short–as all loving fathers struggle to express their love for their children.

With Lucifer sufficiently restrained for now, God turned His attention to the much more problematic issue of being a Father to His children and made the first of the many difficult decisions with which a new Father is faced.

"Adam, why do you hide from me?" God inquired with great disappointment. (KJV Gen. 3:8–9)

"I was naked, and when I heard You walking through the garden I was frightened and I hid," said Adam.

"How did you know that you were naked?" God asked. "Did you eat any fruit from that tree in the midst of the garden?" (KJV Gen. 3:11)

"It was the woman You put here with me," the man said. "She gave me some of the fruit, and I ate it." (KJV Gen. 3:12)

God then asked the woman, "What have you done?"

"The serpent tricked me," she answered, "and I ate some of that fruit."

"You must leave the garden." God made this clear to them with the fearful wind that now began to blow. "Go with the wind and don't look back," God said to them.

The wind ushered them away from the center of the garden. Whichever way they turned, they found themselves pushed away from the center. If they veered to the left, the wind moved them back; if they moved to the right, the wind guided them back——and so it went. As they went on, their path became narrower and narrower.

The wind finally stopped moving, and so did they. They somehow knew that they were no longer in the garden. Now they could see where the river that flowed from the garden split into four rivers. (KJV Gen. 2:10) It was very beautiful here, with many a fragrant flower and many a fruit for eating. It was still a paradise in many ways.

The two adult-childs were content with the beauty of the scene they saw before them——but then they looked back and realized that the loveliness of the earth they had just been exiled to was eclipsed sevenfold by the beauty of the garden from which they had just been forbidden.

It now seemed to them that the center of the garden had been the source of the wind. What they were looking at was a vision framed in a way that would not easily be forgotten, and in the center of that frame they could see the smaller tree. That tree standing in the center of the garden, God had given a name that was apparently indicative of its great power: the tree of life. God's intentions regarding the tree of life had never been explained to them by Him or by Lucifer. Now, neither Adam nor Eve were ever likely to know exactly what powers the small tree held. (KJV Gen 2:9)

As their eyes focused on the small tree in the center, they heard, "You will not enter the garden again." (KJV Gen. 3:22–23) With those words, the one and only entrance to the garden was forever blocked to Adam and Eve by cherubim——beings that were very different from man and from angels, too——that had been sent by God and the Son. *We shall block the entrance to the garden with an image for the benefit of man, should man choose to look. Two cherubim with swords of fire will convey the message man will need. A message of signs and wonders to assist man in realizing creation's capabilities, in what can be achieved.*

Only seven days before these events, God had put the final touches to His creation by creating Eve for the purpose of procreation with Adam. Then He had looked upon the totality of His creation and said, "It is good." (KJV Gen. 1:31)

It was a wonderful creation, created just for man to enjoy abundant life. Now it had become, in one sense, a complete and utter failure. With a heavy heart, God mourned the loss of His good creation and set about strategically cursing it.

God knew that any curse He handed out would cause millions of future human beings to misunderstand Him, even to hate Him——especially those who would be reactionaries, those who would never even consider the difficult choices that all fathers must make——but ultimately, in order to bless His creation, it was absolutely necessary to now curse His creation——an action that had been forced upon Him by the choices of His son Adam.

After He had created the universe and all that was in it——for man——God had rested for a day. (KJV Gen. 2:2) The week would now be seven days long instead of six so that man could also rest. Because man, as a blessing, would now have to work. There would be no more help from angels and no more largely carefree gardens for man.

God's earthly creation was good, but now it needed to be intentionally marred by His own hand. The Holy Spirit's view of the future was limited by the very few events that had transpired thus far in creation. The Holy Spirit gathered as much wisdom as could be discerned and conveyed to God that this would not be the last time that strategic adjustments would have to be made to Their creation.

"Father, does it grieve You to curse Your handiwork, the creation?" asked the Son.

"Yes, and more so than I would have expected it to. I have been a Father to You, but being a Father to man is going to be as dynamic, if not more so, than We had anticipated."

"Many difficult decisions, not unlike this one, lie ahead for the Father and for the Son," said the Holy Spirit.

God, having only one Son in Heaven, was now discovering just what it meant to have a rebellious child and how difficult a Father's duties can often be.

God began with Eve's curse. "Eve, because of what you have done, your gestation time in bearing children will be multiplied. The size and the age of all children to come will be increased to ensure their survival in this new, harsher, fallen world. You have brought this upon yourself," God told Eve. Then He said, "Your desire shall be for your husband, and to the extent that he uses that desire for himself, he will rule over you." Adam was listening as God placed this curse upon Eve. (KJV Gen. 3:16)

Adam and Eve were still reeling with the shock of their exile from the garden when they saw two lambs walking towards them, one from the left and one from the right. Eve went over to one of them. Her instinct was to pet the beautiful, furry creatures, a welcome distraction from the recent events.

"Adam, are those the same animals that were with us when we first met?" Eve asked.

"Why, yes, that is the animal that God seemed to have a special——" Adam stopped speaking mid-sentence as he saw the two animals being lifted up by a powerful whirlwind.

Adam and Eve shielded their eyes from the dust, smoke, dirt, and red liquid in the air. When they sensed that the whirlwind had ceased, they let out huge sighs of relief and opened their eyes . . . and saw that they were no longer naked. (KJV Gen. 3:21)

"Wow, look Adam. Look at me," Eve said, looking down at her new and perfectly fitted garments. "These are beautiful. I love them." Eve wasn't looking at Adam as he slowly walked over to where the whirlwind had been.

"Eve, look at this. I don't think you're going to want to pet these ewes any longer," Adam said, and he motioned to Eve to come over to take a closer look. Eve looked at her beautiful clothes, and then she looked at the bodies of the slain ewes. She didn't know what to think as she and Adam stood side by side looking at the bloody flesh at their feet.

"At least we aren't naked anymore," Adam said, while Eve remained silent.

Above the bloody ewes, at the point of egress from the garden, God and the Son had placed some curious multi-sided guards that could see in all directions without having to turn or move. They looked intimidating, yet they appeared to be unaware of their surroundings. They were large and angelic-looking but perhaps were not any type of being, moving yet not sentient. They were very advanced creations of some kind, very curious and intentionally so. They had been made especially for guarding important or possibly dangerous items while providing man with signs and wonders. These two guards seemed to control two fiery swords that moved, apparently at random, from one side to the other of the narrow access point to Eden. (KJV Gen. 3:24) There was a smell of burnt flesh in the air, and smoke could still be seen coming from their swords.

God continued by cursing Adam. Adam's curse was that he must struggle to live and to provide——keeping his hands, his mind, and his spirit occupied with the daily problems that all human life would now enjoy. As a result, man would now have to work much harder just to survive each day. (KJV Gen. 3:17–19) This would have the fortunate effect of keeping him tired, thus limiting to some extent the guilt that Adam was responsible for by having caused the fall. These hardships would be real, but God believed that they would help guide mankind back from the abyss. The hardships were a blessing that a fleshless being such as Lucifer would never know.

Lucifer's curse was very different from Adam's curse or Eve's curse. God would reserve the right to change Lucifer's dominion from time to time as a means of teaching men the ramifications of rebellion. Lucifer, because of where he had rebelled, had no chance of redemption. Man, on the other hand, though cursed, was still loved by God-so much that He would move Heaven and earth if it would save even one of His beloved. Because of this love, God would allow man to choose which tree to live under——Lucifer's tree of knowledge, or His tree of life.

—— 2 ——
MARRIAGE AND SACRIFICE

After their fall and their expulsion from the garden, life became difficult for Adam and Eve. Their memories of the garden began to fade, obscured by the day-to-day struggles of life in exile. Their memories of the Father Himself were also moving further and further away from their thoughts, as everyday life consumed them. This was an aspect of the curse that neither they nor the Father had anticipated.

The curse and the cascading consequences of their rebellion were separate and distinguishable results of their fall. One consequence was that Adam was not able to sleep through the night. He would fall asleep, exhausted from his day of hard work, only to wake up a couple of hours later unable to go back to sleep. This problem grew worse and worse for Adam as he felt increasingly burdened by his tremendous guilt over the part he had played in Lucifer's rebellion. Adam was so ashamed of this that he couldn't bear to even think about talking with his Father about his problems. He knew he was to blame and he felt that he would have to deal with it as best he could.

Adam became desperate for relief from this guilt, and as the burden became ever more debilitating, he sought to find an answer.

He didn't believe that he could live, or would even want to live, if a cure for his guilt could not be found. Adam became determined to find a remedy.

In desperation, he searched everywhere for something to relieve his suffering. The answer was not in the food he ate nor in the drinks he drank; it was not in the counsel he received from his wife, Eve; nor could he find it in his work or in his relaxation. Adam loved his wife and would sacrifice everything for her and their marriage; but, as Adam suffered, so did the marriage. Adam even had problems performing his marital duties.

Then, one day, Adam came upon a large snake and remembered that he had heard God cursing the serpent to forever crawl upon the ground. Adam wondered if he might get some answers from this serpent. *I remember Eve telling me that Lucifer occupied the serpent.* He reached out to it in desperation.

"Lucifer," he called softly to the snake. "Are you there?"

Wow, that felt really bad, Adam realized, and he looked around.

"Eve. Eve," he called out, suddenly fearful that she might have seen or heard what he had just done. He felt relieved when she did not answer, and that caused him to ponder for a moment. He had just done something wicked, and he felt relief that Eve had not caught him. *Why would that be so?*

Eve had first been Adam's companion, and now she was his wife. At this point, Eve's opinion of him was far more important to him than was his now distant Father. Her standing in his life was influencing Adam's conscience in the place of his Father's.

If I feel relief because of Eve not knowing my wicked thoughts, then that must mean that my wife would have been further burdened and disappointed if she did know them. If this is true, then does my Father need shielding from my wicked thoughts and deeds as well? How can one shield one's actions or thoughts from God? Am I constantly burdening Father with my wicked thoughts?

Like everything else in Adam's life at the time, this was a clue. One thing did seem to be true——Lucifer and the tree of knowledge were the source of his guilt and therefore could surely not be the cure. So he discarded the idea of seeking out Lucifer and repented that he had even tried. Again, in this repentance, he felt a tinge of relief and saw this as another clue.

Seeing the snake had brought Adam's thoughts back to the garden, and he began to sort through the events that had occurred there. *Maybe these memories will bring me more clues for finding a cure for my guilt.* The first thing that came to his mind now, as it had many times before, was the tree of life.

God had never really explained anything about the tree of life to them. Knowing the name of the tree had seemed sufficient at the time, and neither Eve nor Adam had questioned God or Lucifer any further about it. Looking back now on the tree of life, it took on a new meaning for Adam. *The tree of life might be a cure for guilt?*

So, time and again, Adam's memory took him back to the garden and to the tree of life. Adam had no other context for his life other than those first few days in the garden. He had no memory and no experience prior to that time. With no history, he had no wisdom to speak of other than the understanding that he existed——and a very painful existence it was at the moment. The only thing that gave him strength to keep going was his faith that a loving Father would provide a way for him.

Closing his eyes in despair, Adam's mind would often quietly turn to the image of His Father, not in prayer but in wonder. With his eyes closed, he felt, he sensed, he believed unto somehow knowing that he was made in the image of God and that God did love him. This sense of his Father's love seemed innate and was a real source of comfort to him.

Adam wondered if what he needed was to get back to the Garden in Eden and eat the fruit of the tree of life. If he did, perhaps he would be rid of the chronic guilt that was dragging him down and making him feel less than alive. It was the only solution he could think of, but it was extremely problematic——even if he could find his way back to the garden, the two large cherubim standing guard would surely keep him from entering. He came to realize that if the tree of life held any answers for him, those answers could only be discerned from outside the garden.

So Adam thought back to his foundation, to the beginning, and reasoned that if his Father wanted him to find a remedy for his guilt, a loving Father would have made it discoverable. His foundation gave him no room to consider any other possibilities. This convinced Adam that there was a remedy and that it was discoverable. The only thing left to do was to discover it.

Adam searched for clues everywhere. Hundreds, maybe thousands of times, Adam thought back to the moment when God realized that Adam had aligned himself with Lucifer. He considered everything from the memory of that moment as a possible clue, but nothing more could he discern.

Adam also asked Eve many times about her memory of the events surrounding their fall, hoping that her recollections would help him gain some further understanding.

Both of them thought about the moments that had followed their eating of the fruit from the tree, when they had felt the separation between them and God. Adam first recalled feeling the presence of God in the breeze that had come out of nowhere and how that was when both of them had sensed their creator distancing Himself from them because of their guilt.

On one occasion, Adam asked Eve, "Remember the breeze at the tree of knowledge, just before Father confronted us over our rebellion?"

"Yes," Eve said.

"That breeze——what did you feel at that moment?" asked Adam.

Eve thought about this and said, "I felt fear, but it was not my own fear. It was God's concern for us. It was His fear."

"Wow," said Adam, as he realized he'd thought the same thing. This was something new to think about——God could be fearful. "Is it possible for God to be afraid?" Adam asked Eve.

"I don't know," she said.

"I don't know either," Adam agreed, as he continued to consider this new revelation.

They had not yet acquired much experience or wisdom, but what they had was all they had to work with. So they searched their memories and their experiences, hoping to discover more that would lead them to a remedy for the guilt that plagued Adam far more than it did Eve. The two of them agreed it was Adam's failure to protect Eve in the garden, and that was now his major burden.

THE FIRST MARRIAGE

One year had passed since Adam and Eve had been ushered out of the garden by a fearful wind that had come from its center.

"Adam, do you remember our first fight?" Eve asked him, hoping for a light-hearted moment to help comfort her stressed-out husband.

"Yes, yes I do," he said with a chuckle.

This is working, Eve thought and continued. "We were very innocent, at least in one sense of the word," Eve said.

"Yes, yes we were," Adam said, again with a chuckle in his voice.

The two of them recalled the events of a year ago, with the fondness of heart that memories often afford us all.

"We were only moments outside the entrance to the Garden of Eden before we were arguing about our curses, remember?" asked Eve.

"Yes, it didn't take long, did it?" Adam said.

"Our first fight ended with you proposing marriage. Now that was a good way to end that argument," said Eve.

So, the first fight had ended with the first marriage proposal. This first marriage would be an example for men and women going forward, as Adam and Eve would deal with their individual curses in very different manners.

Adam and Eve's fight began just moments after they left the garden, as the two of them tried to figure out who they were, where they were and where they would go.

Adam's memory of a year ago, God says to Eve: *"Your desire shall be for your husband, and he shall rule over you,"* and I thought, *it does seem as though Eve is looking to me for guidance. This should be easy.*

"Life is not going to be easy, is it?" These were Adam's first words to Eve as soon as they found themselves outside the garden.

"No, it appears not——not anytime soon."

The two were a little uncomfortable together but were starting to warm up to each other a bit.

Then Eve recalled what God had said to Adam: *"The ground will be cursed because of you, and you will struggle to provide for you and your family."* Remembering this, said Eve to Adam, "It seems I received the worst of the two curses."

Adam thought for a moment and asked, "You mean the pain of bearing children?"

"No, not really." Eve had no concept about having children or about pain. She was thinking about the fact that she would have to look to Adam for leadership and the fact that she would have to be ruled over by him, a duty she was willing to accept, though she was not thrilled about it.

Adam had been deluding himself into thinking that Eve would want to be ruled, but now he thought differently. Standing to emphasize his words, he asked her, "Are you saying that it will be less painful to have children than it will be to follow me? Or are you saying that I am not capable of leading us?"

"Adam, it was your lack of leadership that got us exiled from the garden. You should have protected me! Then when God spoke, before and after we ate, you heard what you wanted to hear, but you didn't listen to what He said."

"I listened; I heard exactly what He said. Exactly," Adam exclaimed.

"Oh yeah?" Eve glared at him.

"Exactly," Adam repeated, confident in his memory.

"First of all, I am not your wife——not yet——and the way things are headed, that may never happen," said Eve.

"Is that a threat?" asked Adam.

"No, it is not. It's just reality. Deal with it," she said.

As he looked at her, Adam realized that Eve was right. He had heard what he wanted to hear when God had spoken to him. Now Adam knew this was all going to be much more difficult than he had originally thought. Only moments before this, he had been thinking, *This is actually going to work out very nicely. I will lead and she will follow.* Now Adam shook his head in bewilderment. *How quickly things change.*

"So are you saying you will not marry me?" he asked.

"First, you haven't asked me. Second, don't ask me, not the way you are acting now," Eve shouted. "You won't like the answer."

Now, responding quickly and without thought to Eve's well-thought-out comments, Adam retorted, "This is not going to work.

It just isn't. I'm leaving." With that, he stormed off and marched away along the river bank. Eve shook her head in silent agreement as she watched him leave, thinking, *He is right about one thing. This is not going to work.*

The two of them hadn't been together outside of the garden for more than a few thousand beats of their hearts before their hearts began to beat farther and further apart as Adam rashly deserted the only other human on earth. Thanks to a wise Father, Adam knew deep inside that no other creature on earth interested him. How long would his pride continue to interfere with his needs, which would surely turn to desire? Maybe only time would tell.

Adam left the area of Eden's garden gate and headed west, while Eve remained near the entrance to the garden. The flames held by the guardians at the entrance provided her with light and would also keep away any animals that might appear. The garden area was safe, but she was not too sure about the world beyond it, so it made sense to stay close to what she knew. Even here, just outside the garden, it was quite nice, and she had no idea what the rest of earth was like. Earth seemed rather large and untamed, and when God had told them to tame the earth, Eve had assumed that this would be the man's job. So, she decided to wait for Adam to take care of all that before venturing farther out into such a strange place.

Eve rested comfortably that night. She assumed that Adam would be back soon. Yes, they'd had an argument, but she didn't take it personally. What she had said was reasonable, and she was comfortable in the belief that Adam would return to her, so she waited for him.

Eve had a lot of general knowledge, but she didn't know where it had come from. Her context was very different from Adam's: she was a woman, made from Adam. Her memory went back only a few days, during which life had taken some dramatic turns, and she figured that many more twists and turns were sure to follow. She was alone, but she didn't have enough experience to understand or know anything about fear, so she wasn't afraid. The only thing she would fear would be Lucifer if he were to show himself again, and she felt assured that Father had taken care of him for now. But as Eve lingered at the entrance, she did start to miss Adam.

The next day——and she was yet only eight days old——Eve awoke with feelings of loneliness. Then a new feeling began to emerge. As Eve considered all of the unknowns, she began to worry, and she didn't like worrying. It was an even worse feeling than the loneliness, so she wondered if it might be a part of the curse that God had spoken of. Now she was worried that Adam might not return. Just yesterday she had assumed that he would return. This was the beginning of self-doubt for Eve and she didn't like it. *This must be the major part of my curse,* Eve thought.

As Eve negotiated all these new feelings, she realized that Adam had been gone for only one day, but now she was missing the man she had just fought with. These new conflicting feelings confused her. She was as confused as she had been after she had gotten what she wanted at the tree of knowledge.

While she was lost in the midst of these thoughts, yet another new feeling emerged. It dwarfed all of the others. Perhaps it had been brought on by her self-doubt. What she now wanted more than anything was to see herself——to see who she was and what she looked like. Well, anyway, it seemed that who she was could be linked to what she looked like. This was quickly becoming an obsession. So she tried to figure out how she might be able to see herself. Though she could feel her face with her hands, she could not see it. What she felt with her hands was not enough to satisfy her curiosity. She wondered if she could better deal with all of her new feelings if she could see herself.

How does one see oneself? Eve was experiencing vanity for the very first time. It was the kind of vanity that eventually would largely control the lives of each and every one of her daughters. While Eve thought about her new obsession, she also realized that these desires were closely aligned to her feelings of loneliness for Adam and her desire for him to return. Then her thoughts took another turn, as she pondered man's desire for a wife. *If I am obsessed with how I look, will not the man also be obsessed with my appearance?*

As Eve daydreamed about her future, trying to see where it might lead her, that vision was no clearer than the elusive reflection of her own face. One thing she clearly understood was that how she looked would play an important role in her life. *Perhaps a woman's appearance will be a powerful force, a force that needs to be wielded cautiously?*

Eve was as smart as Adam was, but she had very different priorities, so she soon discovered ways to catch glimpses of her reflection. At first, she tried to see herself in a shadow, and this kept her occupied until it got dark. The next day, she caught a dim but somewhat satisfying reflection of herself in a small pool of water near the garden.

Eve spent some time looking into the shimmering pool while reflecting on thoughts inspired by this first real view of her image——thoughts far deeper than the depth of the shallow waters——and for the first time, gained some idea of who she was. She also experimented with her appearance by combing her hair in various ways. This kept her occupied, body and mind, for a while that day.

The next day, Eve had to deal with death for the first time. She caught a whiff of a very unpleasant odor coming from the carcasses of the lambs that God had slain to make their clothing. The rotting corpses were becoming a major problem due to their stench that grew by the day. The corpses were also attracting all sorts of unpleasant creatures, buzzing around, crawling to and from the putrid mess. Eve was surprised when she noticed that various rodents were eating the remains, *Animals eating animals?*

This was her first encounter with what happens after death. *Is this what will assuredly happen to me someday?* Eve wondered. She also had a more immediate concern——what to do about the smell and the mess? Either she would have to leave, or she would need to move the dead animals from where they were lying.

Eve really didn't want to touch the horrible, stinking, dead creatures, but Adam was still nowhere to be found. *This is something that a man should do,* she thought. But the smell was becoming unbearable, and since the man had left her for who knows how long, she was forced to take the matter into her own hands. Not knowing what to do with the stinking rotting corpses, she decided that the easiest way to get them far away from herself would be to dump them into the fast-moving river that was nearby. One at a time, she grabbed each ewe by a leg and dragged it to the river. There they floated away westward. She was more than happy when this ordeal was over and the smell was gone.

Despite all the new feelings she was feeling and the challenges she continued to face at the outskirts of the garden, Eve was becoming comfortable in her new situation. She found things to keep her occupied while she awaited the return of Adam or her Father. Food, shelter, the reflection pool, a place to sleep, hygiene——all of these things she now understood or was figuring out——but it was clear to her that life would continue to be complicated and that she had much more to learn.

Several days had now passed since Adam's departure. With each new day came new experiences; with each new experience came a fresh and new perspective. Now she began to prepare for a longer stay than she had originally anticipated as she awaited the return of either the man or her Father.

Meanwhile, a few days' walk away from the garden, Adam was not faring as comfortably as Eve. He had been gone for six days now and had no idea what he was doing or where he was going. *Should I go back?* God had given Adam life, but now it was apparently going to be his decision where to live and more importantly, how to live *his* life.

Adam had two major problems——his feet were starting to hurt, and his mind was totally preoccupied with thoughts of Eve. *I wonder if Eve is still at the entrance to the garden? I wonder if she expects me to return?* Adam missed Eve, in spite of the things that they had said to each other, and he disliked being alone as much as she did.

His thoughts turned to their respective curses. First he thought of the curse that was supposed to make Eve desire him. *But where is she? She isn't following me. She didn't even try to stop me from leaving.* From Adam's perspective, that particular curse didn't seem to be at all effective.

Adam continued to suffer the guilt from the tree, and now he suffered from loneliness, too. *This is not going well, and my feet are killing me*, he thought. *I am going to have to fashion something for my feet. How did I even get here?* He grew frustrated as he tried to make something to wear on his feet. He was confused and tired, and the many blisters on his feet were causing him great pain. In his frustration and pain, he cried out and even began to weep.

Adam was learning his first lesson in life, one that would stick with him for the rest of his days and that he would pass on to anyone who would listen——life is not easy outside the garden.

God had given Adam and Eve much general knowledge, but it had not been possible for God nor the tree of knowledge to impart wisdom to them, as it was yet to exist. Wisdom concerning the creation was something that could only be discovered over time and only by looking back——something that only spiritual beings such as man and God could do.

The future and the past do not exist.

Life is only lived in the present but to spiritual beings the things in life that don't exist (the past and the future), can be far more pleasant and or far more painful than life itself.

God had thoughtfully and knowingly chosen to create man with such a nature that not even He could know for sure just what choices each man would make——that nature is free will and free will can only exist in an eternal being.

The option to love is only available to those with free will. The inherent risks involved were well known and discussed among the Godhead before They created the first free will being. In the end, They, with the Son's blessings, decided to risk it all for love. A choice that They freely made in unison.

God Himself could not change the nature of love. Love, like life, is freely given; neither can be coerced, purchased or annihilated. Only eternal beings can make such a choice. That choice, freely made, has many an eternal consequence. After all, said and professed, love is nothing more than an "I do" spoken by a free man to a free woman.

While Adam didn't have much wisdom, he and his children would possess pride and guilt because of his rebellion at the tree of knowledge. Pride and guilt kept Adam from calling out to God for help. As a result, he would never know if God would have answered him.

Adam thought back to the argument that had led him to abandon Eve. *I thought that leaving her was the right thing to do, but now I am not so sure. I didn't think about the decision at all. It was a bad reaction and I will have to learn to control such bad behavior, especially on such important matters.* Adam wondered if Eve was angry with him. *I wonder just how upset Eve is because I abandoned her. I just wanted what was best for her, as I knew it to be. Why didn't she understand?* Adam was confused, but he did believe that he was learning.

Adam had traveled west from Eden as God had wanted them to do. His sore feet were slowing him down, but he continued walking for another day. He walked aimlessly as he wondered about the woman, the woman he had deserted. He was lost, literally and mentally.

After another long day of walking, Adam was hungry, thirsty, lonely, tired——and it was getting dark. *What should I do? I need some direction.* Somewhere in the distance, he could hear running water. He thought, *the sound of that river beckons me; I can reach it by nightfall.* So he set off, hoping to find something to eat along the way and to reach the river before it quieted for the night. The River Tigris——and all of the rivers that flowed from the Garden of Eden——slowed as the moon rose in the evening. By night, the pull of the moon lifted the land and replenished the fountains of the deep. Then the rivers ran swiftly again as the day arrived and the moon fell.

So Adam found some food, found his way to the Tigris, found a place to lay his head for the night and hoped to find a good night's sleep there.

Adam felt better. He was now experiencing some of the same feelings that Eve was but to different degrees. Like Eve, he had never seen himself, though this did not bother him as it bothered her. Also, like Eve, he was detecting a really bad smell. He quickly realized that he was the source of the odor——body odor——something had to be done.

He removed his clothing, which also stank, and jumped into the river, sinking like a stone. Adam was astonished to find that he didn't float. He struggled back to the bank of the river and clawed his way onto dry land. He was breathing heavily and was quite relieved to have survived. *That was a close one. I couldn't breathe; I am lucky to be alive.* This was a new feeling for Adam. Only a few days old now, he wondered, *Is this desire to live innate? Why and for whom do I wish to live? Does Eve have these same feelings?*

As he went ashore to retrieve his clothes he realized, *I am naked but not ashamed.* This confused him, as he had been so ashamed of his nakedness in the garden after his fall. Then he realized that he was only ashamed of his nakedness when he was in the presence of Eve. This was yet another strange notion for him to comprehend as he continued to gain insight into the earthly creature that he was.

Adam still needed to clean up, but he would have to find a place where the water was not moving so fast. He came to a spot where the river had formed little pools and wasn't too deep. It also was a good place to learn to swim, which he did the next day. Adam was very strong and agile, a perfect specimen of a man, just as God had intended and designed him to be. Man was designed to negotiate many a terrain, survive many a trail and trial during their lifetimes. Largely self-repairing and self-healing. God was pleased with the physical aspects of His design and at this time no changes were in order as part of His strategic curse of man.

After just a few moments of learning, he was swimming like a fish. He enjoyed swimming very much. Other than eating and sleeping, this was the first activity he had found that he really enjoyed. As he marveled at the fun he was having, he wondered what, if anything, could be as much fun as swimming. *Swimming has to be the most exciting thing there is to do*, he thought.

Adam's mind turned again to Eve. He missed her even more than he had before, and he wondered how he would ever find her again. He thought to call out to his Father for help, but his shame stopped him. *Now what am I to do?* At that moment, he saw something in the water that looked familiar. *Is that one of the carcasses from the garden? Could it be one of the lambs that God had slaughtered?*

He swam out to it and found that, sure enough, it was one of the lambs that God had slain to make their clothes. Excited, Adam realized that he now knew how to find Eve. She must have put the carcass in the water for him to find. *She must still be at the entrance to the garden.*

The following day, Adam began a course back to the garden entrance by following the river back to its source. His hope was that Eve would still be there, just where he had left her. He didn't know how far he had traveled, but it was about eight days since he had left, so it shouldn't take any longer than that to return.

As he traveled, Adam was also on another course, one of thought. He wondered, *What were the chances of me seeing that ewe's carcass? Was Eve sending me a message? Was God sending me a sign? Is Eve in trouble? Was that just a coincidence? How am I supposed to know? Wouldn't Father want me to know?* These many questions had no obvious answers, but he was glad that his finding the ewe was going to lead him back to Eve——if she was still waiting outside the garden.

It took a few days of slow walking on his very sore and severely blistered feet until Adam knew that he was close to the garden. The terrain was beginning to look familiar to him, and he began to feel fearful, as he knew he was coming close to the place where he had left Eve. He had been ashamed, angry, tired, hungry, sad, sore, hurt, confused, and lonely——and now he was afraid to see Eve. Adam didn't know how to handle all of these emotions, so he stopped walking to think: *I don't understand why I am so afraid to see Eve. What will I say to her?*

Then, suddenly, there was Eve, greeting him from a few arm lengths away. "Adam. Adam. I was concerned. Is everything okay?"

Adam slowly turned towards her and smiled. He was now happy for the first time, and he liked this feeling. He felt even better as she smiled too, and he suddenly realized how beautiful she was.

"Yes, Eve. I am fine. Well, except for my feet. We are going to have to learn how to protect our feet. They can be very sensitive," he said. His tone then changed to one of regret. "I was wrong to desert you. I am sorry, and I won't ever do that to you again." Adam could not have come up with words more pleasing to Eve's ears. She smiled again, and then her smile turned to an expression of desire.

Adam could tell that Eve was glad to see him, and he was thrilled to see her, too. He didn't know why, but he was seeing her in a new way. During his two week journey, something had changed in him. He had experienced a lot of new emotions. Eve seemed to have changed as well. Their short time apart had worked wonders for the two of them. Though it hadn't been a long period of time, it was long enough for both of them to understand that life and their lives were all too real.

Above all else was the two of them realizing that all they had was each other. That was it——just the two of them——together yet alone. They did not look up nor did they bend a knee in an effort to seek wisdom from their Father. This gained the Father's interest, as He decided to peek in for a moment.

Neither one of them felt as if their Father would or should intervene between the two of them and they were right. They would have to work out their differences, themselves.

The Father was pleased and looked away to give them the privacy that He trusted they would soon need. He was a proud Parent. At least for now, Adam nor Eve looked down for their consul, giving Him the confidence that when the time was right, they would indeed look up for their guidance.

Adam tentatively reached out his hand and touched Eve in a new way. As they touched, he felt a new stirring within him. It was the strongest feeling he had ever felt. Now he felt no pain, no hunger, no distractions of any kind; all he felt was his desire for Eve. A new and very strong urge was developing deep within them both; this was a feeling that God had purposely and carefully designed to ensure procreation.

As Adam gently touched her shoulder, Eve slowly closed her eyes and savored the moment. They both knew that this was something special, something that would bring them together in a way that neither had experienced before. This was something they both very much wanted.

These stirring new feelings from deep inside of both of them were arising slowly and beautifully. They took each other by the hand and walked for a moment as Eve led Adam back to where she had made a place to lie.

"Adam, I have been sleeping here at night. It is quite comfortable. Please sit, relax for a moment," Eve insisted. Adam sat but he did not feel relaxed.

"Eve, please join me," he said as he struggled to maintain his outward appearance of calm.

From where they sat, they could see the cherubim with the swords and the flames that kept them from the two trees and the garden and beyond that, the beauty of the garden, which was a sight to behold. But Adam was oblivious to that beauty. He was preoccupied with Eve's beauty. Eve sat close beside him, not yet touching him, and Adam turned to her.

"Eve, will you take me to be your husband?" he asked as he took her hand in his.

"Adam, thank you for returning to me. I was made from you and for you, and I am yours forevermore," Eve said, gently touching the face of Adam.

"May I kiss you?" Adam asked.

With a smile from Eve and a kiss from Adam, they became husband and wife.

Time seemed to stand still as the two, now one, explored all these new feelings and new thoughts, making themselves comfortable in the bed that Eve had made. Not another word needed to be said as they became closer and closer to each other in thought and deed. They were intimate in every sense of the word. They were now husband and wife, and it was good.

As they became one flesh in matrimony, they became a bit more comfortable with the idea of stepping away from the Father and contemplated leaving the area of the garden. While God would always be their Father, they now had each other. These newly discovered inner feelings of love and desire for each other became pillars of strength. They would now depend on those feelings as a new foundation to get them through the hard times that surely lay ahead.

They now had each other and that would have to suffice for the foreseeable future–the next time that they felt the need for their Father, they would appeal to Him as one.

Exhausted from the exertions and the emotions of becoming husband and wife, they slept. When they awoke, their outlook on life was very different than it had been when Adam deserted Eve twenty days before.

Perhaps these curses were not such bad things after all, thought Eve, while Adam thought, *I can already see that my curse is going to be a blessing. I will provide for my wife; I want to provide for her and build our family.*

Eve had been finding food to eat on a few trees and plants close by, and she brought her husband a nice meal as he rose. They honeymooned in that spot for a few days, and then Eve experienced a new feeling. Adam's wife began a new process of life as she started her first monthly cycle. When God had instructed them to fill the earth, He had also given them some of the general knowledge they needed to produce children. (KJV Gen. 1:28)

"Adam, we can bear a child soon. I will begin a new cycle in a few days," Eve told Adam, although she did not want, at least not yet, to experience the curse God had spoken of concerning childbirth.

"Eve, we need to wait. I want a son and I am sure you want a daughter, but, until we know just what life is going to be like outside the garden, we would be smart to wait," Adam said.

Eve was thrilled with this answer; it was the answer she had wanted. *This is a man I can follow*, she said to herself. "Yes, Adam, you are right," she agreed, allowing Adam to feel as though he had convinced her.

That went well, Adam thought. *She is going to listen to me after all. This is going to be easy.*

So it went.

Adam and Eve. Theirs was a marriage not made in Heaven, not made in a garden, but made only of one man and one woman designed for and from each other——broken and now stitched back together as best as could be in a fallen world. Each one, by and with the nature of love, would have to sacrifice many of their individual desires for the sake of the other, one day at a time.

Adam was once again feeling the pangs of guilt that were not so easily dealt with. "Eve, we need to leave here. The sight of the garden is not healthy for us; it will only bring us remorse and sorrow. We need to leave this place——not to forget it but so that we won't dwell on what happened here." Eve looked to Adam, and nodded in agreement.

God had told them to go west, so they walked towards the setting sun, never to return to the Garden in Eden again. As they walked away from the garden for the last time, Adam asked, "Eve, are you going to miss this place?"

"Yes, I am. Father had wanted us to live in the garden and we threw away that opportunity. Now we will have to make our own opportunities, make our own garden," she said. Then she asked Adam, "How about you?"

"Well, no, I don't think so. Every time I think of the garden, I see that damning fig tree . . . If I never see Lucifer's tree again, I will be a happy man," Adam said. "Eve, you know, while I was gone I learned how to swim. Have you tried it yet?"

Other than bathing, Eve had not really done any swimming. "No, I haven't. Not yet. You will have to teach me."

"I will. It's a lot of fun," Adam told her.

As Adam thought about fun things to do, his marital bed with Eve came to mind, so he added, "Swimming used to be my favorite thing to do." If God was listening, He would have heard, as did Eve, the very first time that a man laughed out loud. Eve gave him a strange look and shook her head as if to say, "*just what was that?*"

A DIFFERENT TYPE OF SACRIFICE

Adam and Eve soon discovered that marriage, like life, was not going to be easy. Within a couple nights of their departure from the entrance to the garden, another of life's struggles began with the first matrimony.

Disagreements ensued on just how to live and where to live their lives, at times they became heated. Fortunately, they also discovered an opposing force to those difficult times; it quickly became obvious to them that the challenges life on earth placed in their way were navigated significantly easier together in marriage. So, the two of them worked together and their relationship grew strong watered with their interdependence on each other.

In the months that followed, Eve could see——and Adam freely admitted——that the guilt he suffered because of his actions at the tree were having a cumulative effect on him. He had his work and he had his wife, and both greatly helped him get through the days when he was busy. But at night, Adam struggled. Even his marital pleasures did not exhaust him enough to give him a full night's sleep. Though their life experiences were limited, they had faith that a loving Father would provide a way for them to discover peace, so Adam and Eve continued to reason together as they looked for a remedy for Adam's burden of guilt.

Adam's guilt was compounded by his understanding that all men who would ever be born were in his loins, so he knew that his fall would be the foundation for all men to come.

Though Eve would likewise be the mother of all——and she is given credit for that in her name——she would not bear the blame for the fall of man. (KJV Gen. 3:20) It was Adam, not Eve, whom God had instructed not to eat from the tree of knowledge. Adam had failed his first test of leadership. Now, for all of eternity it would be Adam's actions at the tree that cursed man, not Eve's.

One afternoon, after a hard day's work and in utter exhaustion, Adam lay down in a field to rest and closed his eyes. As his head hit the ground, a new thought struck him as well. He recalled Eve's description of what had happened after their fall——there had been a breeze, and they had sensed fear from that breeze. *God was afraid!*

It had been God's fear that had driven them from the garden. This was a new possibility and it caused Adam to rethink things. *What if, after having seen what we had done, eating from the tree of knowledge, God had been afraid that we might also eat from the tree of life? Why would the possibility of us eating from the tree that gives life cause God to be fearful?* As Adam searched his mind for a reason why a loving Father would withhold such a clear blessing from His children, he could come to only one conclusion: *It is not a blessing to cure guilt. A cure without a payment would have been an irrevocable curse. Irrevocable in that, without guilt, the idea of a payment would never come to mind again.*

Wow, thought Adam, *this is big.*

Adam knew not from where this realization had come, but when it did, his countenance lit up. *Father did not remove us from the tree as a punishment,* he said to himself. *He did it to save and protect us so that we might learn and grow to understand the price of rebellion.*

Adam brought this revelation to Eve.

"Eve, I have had the most amazing discovery. I think I have figured it out. I think I know why God exiled us from the garden. It was to protect us, not to punish us. It was a blessing." Eve looked at him in surprise, and Adam continued. "If God had allowed me to eat from the tree of life, my guilt would have disappeared, and then I would never have felt the need to repent." Adam was experiencing an epiphany. "This guilt I feel is a blessing in a way, as it is directing me to look towards the tree of life. What I have to do now is seek that tree——not to eat of it——it's too late for that remedy. I need to discover a way to symbolically eat from the tree of life."

"So are you cured now?" Eve wanted to know.

"Well, not exactly, but this will lead to a cure. I can feel it. I feel better. I feel that I have direction. I will need to reason this out more, and Father will provide a way," Adam said.

"So, how exactly will you pay for that rebellion of ours at the tree?" Eve asked.

"Eve, you've got it. You're right. I do need to pay. I don't know how one pays our Father, but I have to figure out a way, and that will be my cure," Adam said, as he embraced and thanked his loving wife. That night, Adam slept almost the whole night through, and the next morning he awoke eager to discover the best way to pay God for his rebellion.

Adam began to reason.

I went against my Father by eating the fig, but if we hadn't rebelled, we would have still felt the effects of our flesh from time to time. Headaches, stress, and perhaps even guilt of another kind, one not due but perceived. Or guilt against each other and not against the Father.

Not knowing evil would have little effect on some of these everyday concerns. I have lived long enough to understand clearly that the earth is pulling us downwards and no garden setting will limit that pull. Man would absolutely need a tree of life, a way to rid the stress, freely giving it up to the Father. But what I did was not a freebie. My rebellion has a price now, and I must figure out a way to pay my debt. A personal debt and then others could follow the process to pay their personal debt.

Adam could not be sure of every remedy the tree of life might hold, and never even considered any age limiting effects the tree may provide, it wasn't important to him, his only concern was getting right with his Father.

Adam now fully realized that he had falsely accused his Father. God's actions in exiling them from Eden were in no way a form of punishment, only a form of protection. That realization changed his view of the Father from a false one of condemnation to the true One of love.

And Adam prayed.

Father, I am so sorry . . . Father thank you for protecting us from what would have surely been an eternal separation of fellowship with You. Please Father help me find the way to pay my debt. Amen.

The relief and newfound eagerness was life-changing for Adam——it would be the most significant emotional experience Adam would ever know.

The heavy burden of guilt, the dark curtain that had obscured life itself from Adam, was lifting. The curse was subsiding, and the remedy was the result of being thankful. Adam now understood that guilt was the primary fuel that had kept Lucifer's rebellion burning. Guilt is a powerful, fleshly emotion. Adam's chronic obsession with guilt had brought upon him all manner of debilitation, and he could see that this is how it would be for all his sons, because he would raise them. He had rebelled, and he could not act as if it hadn't happened, or make it go away, so his sons and daughters would be rebellious too––an inheritance, but not a good one. The best he could hope for was a temporary, personal cure that would work on an individual level for him and his progeny.

God and Lucifer understood the opposing foundational principles symbolized by the two trees. So, after the fall of man, God, who had planted the trees with full knowledge of each tree's symbol, gave the tree of knowledge——the tree of guilt——to Lucifer. The forbidden fruit on that tree was symbolic of the law. The fruit on the tree of life was symbolic of a freely given love relation with the Father.

Adam had finally discovered that the fruit of the tree of knowledge only brings condemnation. That condemnation sired the guilt within Adam. The two trees, the two concepts, the two symbols love and law; are direct opposites, as are their leaders, as are their followers.

Neither of the trees' foundations had changed since creation, and the tree of life lived on as the Father's love assured its survival.

Going forward, countless men would find themselves clinging to the tree of knowledge, hoping to find comfort in its knowledge, in its direction, in its promise, in its religion of rules and regulations. This tree was the perfect symbol for Lucifer's dominion of guilt.

In Heaven, God, the Father, now eternally limited by the actions of His son Adam, would make the best out of a fallen world. So the wise Father contemplated ways of using Lucifer's tree to direct men to the other tree, the tree in the center of the garden.

On earth, Adam still needed to find a way to remove the fuel of guilt from himself and quench the flames that tormented him. One day he had a vision of the moment when God had clothed him and Eve with the skins of slain ewes. He saw the entrance to the Garden of Eden in his mind's eye.

After God had clothed us we no longer felt naked, he recalled. Adam had forgotten about that feeling, but it had been such a relief. He closed his eyes, vividly remembering the scene at the garden's exit. Adam understood intuitively that God never reasoned or acted arbitrarily; everything that God did, He did for a well-thought-out reason.

Adam now believed that there was no way God had chosen His means of protecting the ingress to the garden without very specific reasoning. He further believed that discovering that reasoning was going to lead him to his remedy. All the information he needed to rid himself of his guilt would be discoverable there. God had provided the symbols that would solve the puzzle. Adam only needed to look back in his mind, back to the garden's entrance.

At the entrance to the garden he envisioned the fire, the swords, and the slain ewes.

After the ewes had been slain, Adam thought, *Eve and I were no longer ashamed. God was not merely clothing us; He was teaching us.*

The clothing was not the main point. The lesson was far more important——there is a price for rebellion——death——a lesson that anyone who would choose to look back could learn.

Furthermore, God could have protected the entrance to the garden in a thousand ways, but He chose fire. Why? The swords alone would have kept us far away from that entrance, so why were the swords also on fire? There was also smoke in the air and the air had a burnt smell. Maybe it was the blood on the swords that I smelled burning?

Then he wondered, *What if I were to slay a lamb with a sword, taking no part of the lamb for Eve and myself, and burn it with fire just as the swords at the gate burned the flesh of the ewes? I would be sending the ewe up to God in the smoke as a symbolic gesture of thanks.* He felt better just thinking about this and he was now on a mission to make an offering to his Father.

Adam didn't rush into this. He wanted to honor God by making a special place to set up this first sacrifice. There was a high place in the Garden in Eden that blocked access to the tree of life, so Adam built a similar high place of stone where he could perform his sacrifice. Here, he would have to look up towards God as he thanked his Father for blessing them by expelling them from the garden.

"It was a tenth . . . what I need is a tenth," Adam said to Eve. Sensing that Eve was not yet getting the picture, he said, "A tenth, a ewe, don't you remember? That was the tenth animal that God had me name." In his excitement, Adam forgot that Eve had not yet been created when he had named the animals. "Come, let's find a ewe," he said, "just like the ones that God used to make our clothes for us." (CEV Gen. 2:19-20)

"So your solution is to make more clothes?" asked Eve.

"No, it is not. Look, remember how we no longer felt naked after God clothed us?"

"Yes, I do. We have talked about it many times," Eve recalled.

"But Eve, there was more to it. We felt relief, not because we were clothed, although that was one aspect of it. We felt less ashamed for a moment because the ewes were a form of payment for what we had done."

"What is a payment?" Eve asked.

"Payment erases what I think of as a debt," Adam told her.

"Okay, what is a debt?" Eve continued.

"Remember when I deserted you just outside the garden and then, when I returned, I apologized to you?" Adam asked.

"Yes, I remember," said Eve.

"My apology made you smile and made me feel better. My desertion of you was wrong, so I owed you a debt; I paid that debt by apologizing," Adam said.

"I see your point, Adam. But now, moving forward, I fail to see why the blood of a lamb will pay for our rebellion," Eve wondered.

"I don't know why. I just know that the blood of the innocent will cover our rebellion. I just somehow know that this will work, and we are going to try it. I don't think it is an actual payment. I think the payment is our action in attempting to pay. Or, said another way, what really matters is our faith that the blood of the ewe will pay for our debt."

"Okay . . ." Eve sort of understood this reasoning and believed that Adam was making progress towards an answer.

As the two of them looked for a ewe, Eve asked Adam, "Why is it that when we are naked now, we are not ashamed?" But Adam had already figured this one out.

"We were ashamed in the garden because we were not yet husband and wife."

"You're right." Eve nodded her head in agreement, beginning to believe in her husband's ability to find the answer he needed.

The two of them climbed a small tree that was near a trail that led to a pasture. When a ewe passed below the tree, Adam pounced on it, causing it to squeal, and then he slew it with a sharp stick. The blood poured from the open wound, the ewe stopped bleating, and the earth accepted the ewe's blood.

Adam and Eve carried the ewe to the altar and placed it upon the fire they had built. They did not use the coat for clothing, the meat for food, or the fat for soap. Rather, they let the entire animal go up in smoke to God, to thank God for His blessings, without expecting anything in return.

Adam felt good. For the first time since he had eaten from the tree of knowledge, Adam felt free from guilt. He gave thanks to his Father as, for the first time in the year they had been wed, he enjoyed a guilt-free night with his wife.

Adam knew he was still guilty. But the heavy burden that the guilt had piled on him had been lifted by the blood of the lamb——by a sacrifice given completely and freely to God in worship and in appreciation for the blessing He had given them by blocking the entrance to the garden.

On the following day, Eve asked, "Adam, now that your guilt has passed away, what else has changed?" Eve intuitively knew there was more——she could see it in Adam's countenance that next morning.

"You're right, there is more, much more. In fact, it only gets better. Being guilt free, when we pass away we can pass directly into our Father's house, into His Kingdom, as our debt is now paid in full by the blood of the lamb that was slain."

"So there is no death?" questioned Eve.

"Our bodies shall return to dust, but it will be a bittersweet moment, as we depart our flesh we will enter into the presence of our Father, the eternal God of the universe, where we will care for each other forever more."

Adam's reasoning pleased Eve, as she could see that it pleased her husband.

Guilt was a complicated human emotion. It could be used as Adam had used it, to take responsibility for one's own actions, but it could also be used as an excuse to blame God for one's plight. Adam had come close to doing this. But instead he had used sacrifice as a way to deal with the terrible guilt he had lived with since his actions at the tree of knowledge. Adam vowed to pass this practice on to all of his children, so they would continue to sacrifice to God for the debt man owed Him.

— 3 —
THE FIRST BORN

Procreation was at the heart of creation——to fill the earth with beings who the Godhead could fellowship with. These procreated spiritual beings would be capable of love and those who would make the choice to love the Creator and each other would eventually populate the Heavens filling the galaxies with fellowship for eternity. (KJV Gen. 1:28)

Adam and Eve had been living outside the garden for six years now. The seventh year was upon them, and they would bear their first child in the eighth year of their lives. Many sons and daughters would be needed to begin populating the earth, and only Adam and Eve could provide them. The time and the place was as good as it seemed it was going to get, so the two decided to conceive their first child. Eve was a perfect woman. She would have no problem whatsoever with conception. So on the eighth day of her next cycle, the two conceived their first child on their first attempt.

As part of her curse——though it would be a blessing to the newborn——Eve's pregnancy would be forty days longer; her child would come to term in forty of the curse lengthened seven-day weeks, instead of forty six-day weeks. Her pregnancy went well, and she was fully active until the day her water broke——an event that surprised the first couple.

"This must be a sign that our baby is ready to be born," Eve confidently told Adam.

"Well, let us help our baby into our world," Adam responded and led her to a bed they prepared close to a stream with clear warm water and she laid down for Adam to help her in birthing their first child.

Her pain started quickly and Adam was fumbling around not really knowing what to do or how to help. Eve's sounds of discomfort were unnerving to him which was not helping either of them. After she labored for a time, Adam could see the child's head. Finally, there was something he could do, "Eve, I can see his head, I can help him out now." With that, he was able to provide more assistance to her, and soon the child was born.

Adam was taken aback as he held and gazed at the newborn. He looked closely at the baby and saw that something was wrong. The child had five fingers on each hand, five toes on each foot, perfect arms and legs, and seemed to be a healthy baby——but she was a girl.

Adam used a sharp stone to cut through the cord that attached the baby girl to Eve. Then he knotted it and again looked at the newborn.

For some reason, Adam had been convinced that their firstborn would be a son, but it was a daughter. Neither Adam nor Eve had ever given any serious thought about just how to have a boy or a girl.

"It is a girl. You have given birth to a girl," Adam said to Eve. Eve didn't notice the perplexed look on Adam's face. Eve took the child and held her close, not giving any thought to her gender.

As Adam attended to both Eve and to the newborn, he acted as though he knew what he was doing. It did seem obvious what both the baby and Eve needed, but he wasn't really sure. He cleaned the newborn as best he could and handed her to Eve. Then he began attending to Eve.

Eve was thrilled with her first child. The joy of holding her baby rendered the pain that she had just experienced irrelevant in the moment. The little blessing instinctively suckled on Eve's bountiful breast for her first meal.

As the baby suckled, Eve relaxed and her afterbirth emerged. This pleased Adam, who had been fumbling around trying to figure out just how to remove it. There was very little blood, and once Adam had both of them cleaned up, he picked the both of them up in his arms. He carried them to the marital bed and carefully laid them on it.

Content, Eve closed her eyes and reached for Adam's hand. As she held it firmly, she felt very happy, and a tear rolled out of her eye. Adam returned her reassuring touch, while he looked at the baby girl and wondered when he would have a son.

That day unto the night, Adam continued to care for the mother and child, who were fine. The proud parents knew that their first duty was to name the child.

"Adam, we need to name our first born. What will we call her?" Eve inquired.

Adam had done all the naming to date, with the naming of the animals and even the naming of Eve; so, without putting much thought into the matter, he said, "Well, we are going to have many children. Let's give the girls names in sequence of their birth and our language——after Eve comes Eva. The name Eva comes to mind, so Eva is to be her name. We can do the same with the boys——after Adam, the name Abel comes to mind, so he shall be called Abel."

The two held hands again and admired their child. But this time Eve's eyes were open, and she could see in Adam's eyes that he was not of the same frame of mind that he was expressing through his embrace.

"Adam, why do you have that puzzled look in your eyes? Are you worried about Eva?" Eve said.

"No, she seems perfect. She is beautiful and this is truly an amazing thing——birth. I don't think I have fully grasped it yet, how we have created a new being," Adam said, evading her question. He didn't want to tell her that the real reason for his confusion was his disappointment that Eve had not borne him a son.

Adam had quietly convinced himself that the first child would be a son. A son was what was needed, at least as he saw it, and he had been convinced that God would indeed give him a son first. Adam was concerned that what he had been given was not what he had wanted. This was shallow thinking, when deep thought was what was called for.

"Our first grandchild is born," announced the Holy Spirit in Heaven. "Procreation has begun. As designed, Eve's first child of water is a female. Looking forward I can see that there will be more daughters to come before a son of water is conceived, this is good development, very good."

"The Spirit is wise," said the Son.

"Indeed," acknowledged the Father. "Indeed."

Adam, so focused on his own desires that he failed to ponder the deeper meanings of life, would never understand that procreation would have a much better chance of success if it started out with females. If sons had been born first, the needs of men and power struggles between men might have endangered Eve, the only woman. Now the reverse would be tested, as the only man would be Adam.

Eve nursed Eva for close to five years. When Eva had been weaned, Eve started her cycles again, and the couple looked forward to having their second child.

Adam and Eve wanted the next child to be a son and so did Eva. "Mother, can I have a brother next?" asked Eva.

"Well, dear, we shall see. I sure hope so. We will have to wait and see," Eve told her. That was indeed her hope as well——to birth a son. By this time, Adam and Eve had discussed just how one goes about choosing the sex of a child and had come to the conclusion that God determined the sex of a child, and that they had no control over this.

God had instructed them to procreate without adding any details of the exact process within the womb. They knew that they were made by God, so they assumed that God played some role in the procreation process of bringing into being a new being.

Eva, even at her young age, was a big help with birthing the next child——but the child was another daughter, they would name her Elva.

Eva, Eve and Adam all felt some disappointment that the child was not a son; but they said little about it, as they believed this was all up to God.

When Eve was with child once again, Eva was ten years old. She was becoming a unique individual, an individual who lived up to her name and her status as the first born of water. Eva was eleven years old when Eve's water broke with her third child. This time, Adam took his place behind the young girl, Eva, as she helped her mother deliver a sibling who turned out——no surprise——to be another sister.

Eva was growing into a young woman who was in many ways indistinguishable from her mother but only in appearance. Eva had not been born an adult; she didn't know of the trees in the Garden in Eden, and she didn't know the ways of adults. Eva would be the first to mature in what would forever after be the normal course of events for every boy and girl. The road to adulthood would be navigated for the very first time by Eva, with guidance from parents who had never traveled that road themselves.

The first born Eva's similarity to Eve was uncanny. Adam, more than Eve, observed Eva carefully as she began to blossom. He had no idea just how and when Eva would become a woman, and he was very cautious in his contact with her at that point, because she looked just like Eve.

Before Eva's birth, there had been no need for modesty between Adam and Eve. But now, unlike Eve, Adam felt it was necessary to be careful and modest around their girls, even at their young ages, and he was determined that none of the girls would ever see him as Eve knew him.

"Mother, why does father hide himself from me?" Eva would often ask her mother. "Eva, privacy is something that your father and I learned in the garden. We learned it quickly, but you will learn about privacy in a very different way," Eve would say.

"I feel that Father is distancing himself from me. He doesn't hold me the way he holds you. I feel that he is afraid of me for some reason," Eva, not yet a woman, told her mother.

"Eva, your father loves you as I do. Please understand that this is all very new to your father and me. Raising you, our first born, is a delicate balancing act, and we are doing our best." That was the best explanation that Eve could offer to Eva, and it was the truth.

Eva was not yet a woman, and Eve was pregnant with her fourth child. This was the final time that Adam would assist with the birth of a child. This child was yet another sister for Eva. Eva wasn't surprised, but she was concerned and talked about her concerns with her mother.

"Mother, when will you bear me a brother and a husband?" Eva would ask frequently.

"Eva, I wish I knew. I really do. We must trust in God to provide a husband for you," Eve would say on these occasions.

As Eva was now becoming a woman, her only adult female role model was Eve from whom Eva would learn at least one bad habit. Eve didn't feel the same need as did Adam to show modesty, as he was the only man and also her husband. Eva, following the example of her mother, was not as modest as she should have been in front of her father.

"Eva, cover yourself, now." Adam would scold his eldest as she walked past him in loosely fitting garments.

Why is Dad so concerned with the way my clothes fit? Eva wondered. Eva had little insight into the desires of men, as the only man on earth was her father. Her father's actions, far more than his words, would be her only guide to just how a man desires a woman. At this moment, she clearly saw that her father was angry with her, which didn't please her. Eva's journey to adulthood would be fraught with challenges by being the first born.

"Eve, you have to be more modest in your dress. Your daughters take after you, and it will lead to no good end," Adam told Eve. "Also, we must no longer show affection for each other in front of Eva. Eva looks at us with eyes that show me she is far deeper in thought than I want to even know," Adam said.

"Adam, don't be silly. Eva is just curious, nothing more," said Eve, hoping that it really was only curiosity that Adam was seeing, rather than lust. "But yes, we must be more careful around the girls," she said. "The girls take after you and they will do as you do, not as you say," added Adam.

He is right, she realized, and said, "Husband, you are right. It may be too late to teach Eva modesty, but from now on I will be more modest in my ways and hopefully the girls will follow suit."

When their fifth child——another daughter——was born, Adam and Eve could see and sense each other's concern, but they did not speak about it. Eva was of the same mind, and she wondered, *when will a son be born?*

With the birth of the sixth daughter, Adam and Eve again said not a word to each other about their mutual concern over their lack of a son. Eva, however, was no longer silent, and she shared her concerns with both her Mom and her Dad, though separately.

"Father, I need a husband. You need a son. What can I do to help?" Eva asked her father.

"I don't know. God will provide you with a husband. I am sure. I just don't know when." Adam would deliver these words without much enthusiasm though, as his disappointment grew along with Eva's.

Then Eva would move on to her mom, "Mother, I need a husband. You need a son. There must be something I can do. Please don't tell me it is up to God. I have heard that enough. There must be something I can do."

Eve shook her head, not knowing what to say, and changed the subject.

"Eva, we need to talk about men," Eve said.

"Mother, we are talking about men," Eva said in frustration.

"My dear, I am talking about men and their needs and their desires for women," Eve said. She continued, "I have been a bad example to you, I have. My husband is the only man and this has caused me to recklessly lose my modesty in a large way. You have witnessed that lack of modesty far too often. That is not how a woman is to behave. You will have to learn to be modest."

"Mother, I have never seen father, you know, in that way. I don't know what a man even looks like."

Eve was smiling, and with a slight shake of her head and a single exhale that turned into a small laugh, she said with a slight grin, "I don't know when your brothers will come, but they will come. God has far too much invested in creation and procreation not to follow through with sons. When your brothers do arrive, you will have to be modest around them until one of them commits you to marriage, just as your father has been modest in your presence. Otherwise, your marriage will not be special as it is with your father and me."

Eva pondered her mother's words and said, "Mom, I will try. I will be as you ask me to be. I will prepare myself to be a good wife. Perhaps that will be the key to God providing me with a husband."

Eve felt good about Eva's goal to prepare for marriage but felt bad about having perpetuated the idea that God would provide a husband for her, because Eve now believed that having a son was not up to God alone. She reasoned, *I don't believe that the child's sex is random. I can't believe that God does anything in a random or arbitrary way. So, just as Adam discovered sacrifice, I shall discover the answer to this mystery.*

Eva also worried that the first male child might be claimed by one of her sisters, so she tried even harder to ensure that she would deserve that first male child, whenever and however he would be born. She made it no secret that the firstborn male child was to be her husband, and her sisters seemed to acquiesce.

The lack of a son continued to be a major point of discussion between Adam and Eve.

"Husband, why do you think we have not yet had a son?" Eve asked again.

"As always, I don't know, but I am not going to worry about it. In time, there will be sons," said Adam predictably, though he no longer believed his own words.

This was a typical answer from Adam, who had never been insightful on this particular issue. So, as usual, Eve changed the subject. "How many more children do you think I will need to bear?" Eve asked one day, while nursing her seventh daughter. "To make a good start at filling the earth, we will need perhaps a dozen families. So that is twelve boys and twelve girls. It seems to me that you should be through with having children in a hundred years or so," said Adam.

"That sounds about right. And if we don't have a son?" Eve asked.

"We will have many sons. Perhaps your female seeds will run out and then it will be all boys the rest of the way," Adam suggested to Eve.

That's an idea I haven't thought of before, Eve realized.

As the first born, Eva played an increasingly larger role in raising her sisters. She helped birth them, always in anticipation of the birth of her future husband and was again and again disappointed. The adult girls in the family had discovered sympathetic lactation, and they enjoyed helping their mom feed the newborn girls. Adam and Eve discovered that this shortened the time between Eve's cycles, so the kids started coming faster.

Eva's desire to have a husband of her own was becoming unbearable. Each time another child was born, her hopes were dashed once again as she helped to deliver yet another sister. Eva thought about this, and then she prayed. *When will I get to raise my husband? I want to have my own children. The first male will be mine; I have worked for this, and I will fight for him. Father God, I will be a good wife. I will be a modest and proper wife. I will provide him with a good family and as many sons as possible. Father, please provide for my needs. Thank You, and I love You. Amen.*

Eva was now close to 30 years old. She was a woman whose beauty was only surpassed by that of Eve, her mother. Eve was well aware of Eva's beauty and felt that she was not the only one aware of it. *Adam must see her beauty. How could he not?* Eve asked herself.

Eva's sisters, especially the ones who were now women, were less willing than before to let Eva have the firstborn son automatically. They began to compete in their preparations to be ready to deserve the firstborn male. Sibling rivalry was there and then born with their struggle for a husband. This competition was serious, real, and heated. Eva, as the eldest, had some standing to claim the firstborn male, but it was no longer a fait accompli that she would succeed.

EVE'S CURSE

Eve was aware of the competition among her daughters, and she didn't feel as secure in her own position as she once had. Eve had yet to fully know her own beauty, as the reflection of her face in a pool of water or a shiny stone was only a vague representation of her image.

Adam and Eve were close to their daughters and cared for them directly. Eve watched as her husband worked with their adult daughters very closely, every day, and she was concerned. These close relationships——and the lack of other men——made Eve more conscious of her desire for her own husband. As she watched her daughters looking at her husband, she read into those looks far more than she knew to be true.

Presently, Eve was with child again. The eighth, then the ninth, and then the tenth born were all once again daughters.

Now her curse of pain during childbirth did not seem at all important to Eve. The true nature of her curse was becoming clear, front and center in her mind. Her desire for her husband was getting stronger while her beauty diminished with childbirth and age; all the while the beauty of her daughters were on the increase. Eve's desire for her husband was now far more of a factor in her life than was any pain caused by childbirth. She succumbed to it every day and was soon with child yet again. There was no surprise when the eleventh child born, Elez, was again a daughter.

Two long years later, Eve was once again able to conceive, but she was not in the mood to have any more children. As Adam approached his wife that night, a wife rebuffed her husband's advances for the first time in history. Adam was not pleased. But Eve could not tolerate any more competition; Elez would be her last child.

"No. No more children," said Eve.

Adam sat on the side of their marital bed, mentally and physically frustrated, and said, "Look, I understand that it is painful to give birth to a child, but——"

Before he could get the rest of his thought out, Eve stopped him and said, "What are you talking about?"

"Well, you said no more children and that must be because of the pain of childbirth, correct?" Now Eve was the frustrated one as she reminded Adam, "We need a son."

"We do," Adam agreed.

"Yes we do!" she shouted, frustrated.

"Eve, I understand. We have been over this again and again. It will happen when God wants it to happen," Adam reasoned.

"So you're saying it is up to God when we have a son?" Eve asked. Unbeknownst to Adam, Eve had come to change her mind on just exactly what role God played, if any, in the act of procreation, and she blurted out her new mindset.

"That makes no sense. We are the ones who are procreating. God told us to go and procreate. That is what we are doing, and we are not having a son. So, no more kids," insisted Eve. She went further. "Have you not seen our daughters? I know you have seen them, and they see you as well."

"Do you think that one of our daughters will give us a son?" Adam inquired.

"Wrong answer, Adam! You idiot. You want to try that again?"

"Not really," Adam said. "Eve, I don't know what is going on here. I just want to go to bed with my wife."

"It is not going to happen. We are through with having children." Eve was adamant.

So she rebuffed her husband, and that is how it would stay until she could find a way out of her now stronger-than-ever desire for her husband——another daughter, which is all she was capable of having, would not help at this moment. Her desire was coalescing into jealousy of her own daughters. Jealousy, completely unfounded, wholly created in Eve's troubled mind.

The perceived pressure she felt was the weight of all procreation, alone she would try to withstand that enormous burden. With this burden pushing her down, she believed that it was only a matter of time before Adam would turn to one of his daughters to give the world what she was apparently incapable of providing——a son. Eve had no other reason to believe that Adam would take this action; it was her desire for her husband that once again wholly created this idea in her mind.

Adam and Eve lay alongside each other, both frustrated, as they considered just how to procreate a son. What hung in Adam's mind was the idea that perhaps having a son would require that he procreate with one of his daughters, something he had never considered and was not at all inclined to do. This would never have occurred to him at all if Eve had not brought up the subject of their daughters, but now he did consider the idea.

The tensions grew between the two of them as they struggled to deal with this very real problem. As Adam's frustration grew, Eve quickly realized that her decision to rebuff his marital desires was definitely not the solution. She grew even more fearful of what she believed would be his inevitable response to the situation. Something had to give, and soon. Desperate, Eve ran far enough away to find some privacy, and there she cried out to God.

"This curse is more than I can bear. We need a son, and I can't bear one——but I can't allow my husband to procreate with my daughters." Crying out gave Eve some relief, and her frustration was replaced by contemplation. Being alone, away from her husband, was a new experience for her, and she took advantage of this new opportunity to think deeply. As she calmed, so did everything around her. Then she felt a gentle breeze and that seemed to come out of nowhere. She closed her eyes, and for the first time in a long time, Eve asked God to help her in her moment of need. This calmed her further. Again, she closed her eyes. She kept herself very still so she could hear any small voice that might bring her knowledge or a message. She heard nothing, but the feeling of calm persisted. *Was that, perhaps, the message?*

As she sat, she contemplated her next move. Then, she spoke aloud to God, but not with any expectation of an answer from Him. She was really looking for an answer from within.

"Should I just leave? I can't have a son. Adam can take one of our daughters, and she will surely give him a son. I will just wander alone, as I can't return to see my husband with one of our daughters. I won't." She started to cry. She was broken, and she was right. This curse——her desire for her husband——was more than she could bear, and she continued to weep. She wept hard and long and finally fell asleep, just as it was getting dark. Eve had felt pain in childbirth, physical pain, but this mental and emotional pain was far worse than any pain she had felt before.

Eve had been gone now since midday, and Adam grew increasingly more worried. Adam didn't know where to look or in which direction Eve may have gone. He called out to her but to no avail, so he gathered the older daughters and they all fanned out to look for Eve. Eve never went off alone——never——and that worried all of them. They looked everywhere they could think of, but she was not to be found.

Her absence focused Adam's attention far more than her words had ever done, and he began to take Eve's concerns much more seriously. This current struggle——now a few weeks in the making——was coming to a head, and Adam needed to find his beloved wife.

He soon realized that he was not going to find Eve the way he was going about it. He needed more help than his daughters could possibly give him, so he reached out to God. Adam went to the altar he had built for sacrificing, and he spoke to God.

"Father, I need Your help. I need You to help me find my wife. I can't do it without You," Adam prayed again and again, but there was no sign or wisdom given to him in response. It was close to dark when Adam, in fear——real fear that he may have lost his wife——prayed, "Father, protect Eve; Father, my wife is in pain. It is not physical pain, but it is pain all the same, as real as it can be. She suffers. Please help her so that she will return to me." Again, Adam could feel no response. It would soon be dark, and this would be the very first night since becoming man and wife that they would spend apart.

As the sun set and the moon rose to light the earth, Eve began to stir. She had been asleep for a while and she had dreamt. Now, as she rose from her rest, she remembered how she had cried in desperation. Now she fully understood her curse——what would be the curse for all women——that they would desire their husbands. After rising, instead of heading out into the wilderness to wander alone, she headed back to claim her husband. She had been given a new determination to love her husband and to make sure that he remained hers and hers alone. She would confront her daughters and make it very clear that they would have to wait for God to supply them with husbands of their own.

She felt sure that Adam would be at the altar, so she headed in that direction. After walking a short distance, she could see the small fire that Adam had built as he was praying for her return. She was nervous as she drew near to Adam, and she realized how he must have felt some fifty years ago as he approached her after having been away for some two weeks. Adam sensed her presence and turned with a huge smile. He ran towards his Eve and lifted her high in the air and then embraced her with an intensity that nearly took her breath away.

"Eve, where have you been, I was so worried," Adam said.

"I went to find some answers, answers to deal with my curse," Eve said.

"Eve, don't ever leave me again!" Adam said, as he looked deep into her eyes.

"I will not ever do that again," Eve told her husband, and Adam believed her. As they held each other, they knew that their commitment to each other was strong, and they knew that they would have to address their problem together——together would be the best and only way forward.

They were near the altar where the fire still burned. As they looked into each other's eyes, they knew that they needed God's help.

"Adam, I prayed to God to give me an answer and a son for you, for us, and for our daughters. I need to have a son more than you can understand, as I am jealous for you and do not wish to share you with anyone."

With those words from her, Adam began to understand. "Eve why didn't you tell me before of your concerns?"

Eve only shook her head, not sure of the answer herself. As Adam took his wife's hand, they knelt at the altar and Adam prayed aloud.

"Father, give us wisdom. Father, give us the knowledge we need to provide You with a son."

Then Eve surprised Adam by also asking God for help, something that she had never done before in his recollection. With fear, anger, and tears, Eve cried out to God. (CEV Gen. 4:1)

"Father, I will not share my husband with anyone. Father, I need a son; my daughters need husbands. I now fully understand my curse, and I can't bear it any longer. I won't deny my husband his needs——nor myself mine. Father, I will do as You ask me, but I will await Your asking. Thank You, Father, and I love You."

Still holding hands, they walked back to their home, where they would share their marital bed. Eve realized that she could possibly conceive again, but she was not going to withhold herself without her husband's agreement ever again. They retired together and quickly fell asleep in each other's arms after a mentally and physically exhausting day. But in the deep calm of the night, Eve stirred and sensed a presence outside. She went out to investigate.

She could see a small light close to the altar. "What could that light be?" She wondered aloud. The light was illuminating the pathway to the altar. She carefully walked the short distance and discovered that the light was coming from a fire. It was the fire that Adam had built earlier that day, the wood was not being consumed. As she gazed into the fire, she was amazed to realize that there was a presence within it. She didn't know what or who this was, but it was surely not of this world, and she bowed her head to acknowledge the Spirit that was in the fire.

"Eve, We have heard your prayers, and you will not have to share your husband with your daughters," said the voice in the fire.

"Thank you, Father. Thanks for taking this burden from me."

The voice in the fire continued, "The Father is in Heaven. You are in the presence of the Son. I will now inform you, and all daughters to come, how to bear a son. (CEV Gen. 4:1)

When your body cleansing is complete, count out fourteen complete days before having relations. That is sixteen days before your cleansing begins anew. If you count the days correctly you will cain a son. Each time you wish to have a son, you must wait, *sixteen* (cain) days before your new cycle to conceive." Eve acknowledged the Son. As she rose the wood was fully consumed, and now there was only the reflection of the sun from the moon to light her path back to her husband's bed.

She kept her new knowledge to herself as she fell asleep, sure that this had not been a dream and that in the morning she must tell Adam what had transpired.

When Eve awoke early the next morning, she knew that she had indeed been in the presence of the Son, and with great enthusiasm, she sought Adam out and told him happily of the events of the night before.

"Adam, sit with me," Eve said. "The most wonderful thing happened to me last night." Adam began to interrupt her, but she quieted him. "No, listen to me. As you slept last night, I awoke and walked outside. I could see a light by the altar, and the light guided me to where you had built the fire as you waited for me to return. In the calm of the night, the small fire that you had tended was still burning unattended." Adam shook his head in disbelief, but Eve placed her hand on her husband's cheek and assured him that what she was telling him was true. "It was the Son, our Lord. He came to me in the fire, and it was the most amazing thing that I have ever experienced." Adam was silent while he reflected on his wife's words, and she continued, "Dear Adam, our Lord came to me, came to *us* in our desperation, to help us. He gave me the wisdom we need, the wisdom to have a son, the wisdom that will ensure that you will remain my husband alone."

"Okay, Eve. Wisdom——our Lord told you how to have a son? Okay, how? How do we do it?" Adam inquired.

Eve took a breath and said, "We are to cain a son."

"Cain a son? How do we do that?" Adam waited anxiously for her answer.

"The Son told me that your seed must rest for fourteen days as my cycle will begin anew. After fourteen days, when my body is *fully* ready to conceive, we are to have relations, at which time your seed will *quickly* provide us with a son. Those were the Son's instructions," said Eve misquoting the Son but getting the essential details correct.

"Are you sure it was the Son?" Adam asked.

"Yes, I am sure," Eve retorted. "I am very sure. Do you remember the garden? God came to you and told you not to eat of the tree of knowledge. You didn't do as He asked, and well, that didn't work out so well. Now the Son has come to me with guidance, and this will work. I know it will. We must do as He said. He said that if we faithfully do as He told me, we will have a son," said Eve.

Adam was as skeptical as Eve must have been when he had told her not to go near the tree of knowledge, but he agreed to go along with the plan to cain a son.

"What shall we name him? Let's use Abel, since he will be born from our faith in our Lord," Eve suggested, and Adam agreed. Before long, Eve was weaning her youngest daughter and she soon began her cycle. Her first thought was to tell her husband immediately, but then she thought of Eva. *First I will tell Eva about her soon-to-be cained husband.*

"Eva, I know you have been waiting, so I have come to you before I even go to my husband with this news——in a few days, I will conceive your husband," she told Eva with great excitement.

Eva was thrilled, and she embraced her mother with great love and gratitude. "Mother, thank you, I just hope you are correct. With all my heart, I hope you are correct."

Eve said, "I am sure. I must go now and tell your father that he will have to wait for two weeks so his seed and my seed can rest in preparation to cain a male child." She went off to tell her husband.

"Adam, my last cycle is ending. The fourteen days will begin in four or five days." Adam listened to Eve. "Let's begin the waiting now. If we start now as my last cycle finishes, an extra five days, that will ensure that it works." Adam was a bit skeptical of Eve's plan to stray from the Son's strict admonition to wait fourteen days. As Eve herself had pointed out, questioning God hadn't worked out so well in the garden, but Adam willingly agreed that they would wait until her new cycle had started and then fourteen days to cain the boy.

For Adam, the days passed slowly, but at least he was busy providing for his wife and the girls. Eve, however, grew impatient as she watched her husband working closely with his elder daughters. She became increasingly impatient in her desire for her husband. The days seemed to last forever. Eve couldn't understand how just two weeks could seem like an eternity. As she looked at her beautiful, fully grown daughters, she desired her husband's full attention.

Adam's seed had now rested eighteen days, and she was thirteen days into her body's new cycle. With one day to go, Eve went to the private place where she knew Adam would be bathing. Eve saw no harm in warming up to her husband for the following night's big event. Sure enough, Adam was there, bathing in the cool waters. Eve secretly watched from afar as he lay there relaxing on his elbows, head back, toes in the sand, with the water rolling softly over his legs. Again, the calm in the air was palpable. With no concern for the possible cost, she continued to allow herself to be tempted. Her desire for her husband was overwhelming, and she ignored the wisdom of the Son as she allowed the lust of her flesh to control her. Her desire for Adam was unrestrained when he discovered the now fully unclothed Eve watching him. And he was, above all else, a man. So, in that moment of lust they took each other, and another child was conceived one day before the waiting period was to end. Elew, their twelfth daughter, would be born forty weeks later.

No one was more disappointed than Eva.

"Eva, I am so sorry. I am. I want you to listen to me. What I am going to tell you is very painful for me to admit, but the only way you will believe me is if I tell you the whole truth." With that, Eva reluctantly sat and looked at her mother. "I once told you that I was a bad role model because I was not as modest as I should have been. Well, I have failed you again. I did not wait the full fourteen days that our Lord instructed me to wait before conceiving. In a moment of lust, I considered not what you needed, but what your father and I wanted. I was driven by my lust, and that is why you now have to wait yet another year or two for your husband to be born."

It would indeed be another two years before Adam and Eve would have another opportunity to conceive a son, at this point they had totally forgotten their desires to name the firstborn Abel. The name Abel had now become a synonym for faith and they weren't feeling all that faithful as their firstborn son was actually being conceived.

This time they strictly adhered to the exact caining method. They painfully waited the full fourteen days after Eve's cycle. A full sixteen days before her new cleansing would begin to have relations.

The male child was born Cain. He was borne of the knowledge they received from the Son. After many trials and tribulations, they had finally learned how to conceive a male child. Now they would have a series of male children who could be husbands for their daughters. (CEV Gen. 4:1)

Because the firstborn was conceived by trials, tribulation and the spiritually painful works of Adam and Eve the name Abel was not even contemplated as a name for the first baby boy.

Three years later, Adam and Eve with a very different demeanor filled with faith and love of God, cained another male child. Cain's younger brother, the second-born male, made his entrance into the world. Cain and Abel, one whose birth had been guided by knowledge and one whose birth had been guided by faith——their story would forevermore be key to all those who would seek out wisdom from the beginning of creation. (CEV Gen. 4:1)

Eva, a grown woman, was thrilled with Cain's birth and with Abel's birth after that, and she personally nursed each of them many times. She thanked God for her blessings. *Father thank You for supplying me with a husband; I will be a good wife to Cain.*

Eve went on to cain a series of sons for her daughters and the competition between the sisters subsided. Clearly, there would be husbands for all of them. Eva, for her part, was so content with the idea that she would soon have a husband forgot her desires for the firstborn——as she had come to know the very different characters of Cain and Abel.

―― 4 ――
THE BROTHERS' JOURNEY

dam took the lead in raising the boys, as did Eve with the girls. These two created beings had no experience whatsoever in being children or rearing them. They would have to use what little they knew about their Father as their sole role model of parenting.

"Adam, just how do we raise our children to be good like our Father?" Eve wondered aloud to Adam shortly after their first child's birth. Adam paused for a moment as he considered what he had not yet pondered, *just how am I going to father my children?*

"Father did tell us that we were made in His image. Let us try to imagine that image and we shall use that as a starting point." Adam proposed to Eve and closed his eyes to see what he could intuit. In Adam's mind, what appeared and then reappeared again and again, was his failure in the garden and he quickly concluded; "To be good, one will have to be Godly." Eve with a nod of her head showed her approval so he continued. "The most important thing that we will teach our children――is our failures, so they will hopefully not make the same mistakes that we've made." Eve listened with more nods of approval. "If we would have loved, honored, and respected our Father, we would have never rebelled. If our children learn that lesson, everything else, in the course of time, will fall naturally into place via that love. Perhaps some of our children will rebel but if we raise them correctly, they will, in time, return to their upbringing."

Now it was Adam who was nodding his head, as he lamented the irony of his intuition; that only in the face of being a father did he come to contemplate the difficulties that his Father faced.

Teaching the children to honor their mother and father laid a solid foundation for the children and society. Adam had a few other practical lessons he felt should be taught on an individual level to each child, as each child was different.

Adam wisely understood that God's act of cursing the land meant that every man would need a skill, a skill that worked the land in a way that would limit the effects of the curse. Adam further reasoned that God would be pleased if man also turned out to be happy and productive, so he tried to direct the boys into areas of work that suited their talents and their desires. Looking forward, Adam also kept in mind what would be good for his family and also someday for society. Though He never told Adam, God was pleased with Adam's actions and reasoning.

From the womb, Abel was a pleasant child. He learned quickly and was a great aid to his father in all of his endeavors. He gladly obeyed his father, who rarely felt the need to discipline him. He was a mild-mannered child whose interest in animals revealed itself at an early age.

Abel was the first human to truly befriend dogs. As a boy, he raised them from pups and trained them to be great companions and trusted aides. He had many dogs——he was faithful to them, and they were faithful to him. Looking at them together, it was difficult to know if their loyalty was a natural instinct of the dogs or if it was a reflection of Abel, their master.

So it was a very natural fit that Abel became a herdsman, training his dogs to help him guard and herd his flocks. His dogs were very beautiful, and he loved tending his flocks with these beautiful dogs. (KJV Gen. 4:2)

"Abel, can you help me?" his sister Eva asked him one day. "I want a puppy. This one is so cute." Eva was holding the little pup as if it were a precious little baby, close to her face as the little guy licked her cheek, the now giggling Eva, said. "Please can I have it?"

"Of course, my sister, it is yours. What will you name it?" Abel asked.

"I shall name her——oh, excuse me, I shall name him Gent," she said.

"Gent he shall be. I will help you train him. The more you love Gent, the more Gent will love you back," Abel told her. "I have found that these particular animals seem to take on the personality of their owner, so I believe that Gent is destined to be a kind, caring animal as he grows, with you as his master."

This young man, Abel, born of faith, was a very loving and kind soul, slow to anger and endowed with a peaceful spirit. He was a person who always listened carefully, and his responses were always wise and thoughtful.

Eva, as she walked away holding on tightly to her Gent, glanced back at her brother Abel, in what was clearly more than appreciation for a puppy. A glance that Abel returned in kind. Abel was no longer a boy and as their eyes parted ways, Eva sensed that fact and held it as close as her newfound love, Gent.

Of the firstborn male Cain on the other hand, Adam would often say to Eve, "That boy has been rebellious from the womb." Countless times Adam attempted to discipline his eldest son——mostly with words and warnings——but improvements in Cain's demeanor were few and far between. Cain's rebellion came in various forms, some of which he hid well from others, but not Adam.

Adam knew Cain's shortcomings but never took the steps needed to stop his firstborn's opposition to order. On several occasions while still a young boy, Adam and Cain knocked heads and while Adam considered corporal punishment to break the rebellious spirit of Cain, he always rejected it. Adam loved Cain, just not enough to do what was needed in the form of corporal punishment.

As small boys, Cain and Abel suffered no shortage of affection. They had twelve sisters raising them, who took turns caring for them. But Cain, unlike Abel, never really bonded with any of the girls, not even the first born, Eva. For about two years he had been the only baby boy, and all the girls wanted to take part in the boy's upbringing. They would often giggle while attending to Cain; they had never seen male anatomy before.

By the time Abel was born, much of the mystery and newness of baby boys had worn off for the girls, so Abel was handled differently than Cain had been. Eve was still spending her time raising Cain, so it fell to Eva to spend a lot of her time raising Abel. Eva and Abel developed a strong bond. Eva never thought back to her promise to God that she would make Cain a good wife. Slowly, she became enamored with Abel and forgot the whole idea of Cain becoming her husband.

Cain and Abel were only two years apart in age and were often in competition with each other; Cain seldom lost to the younger Abel. Other brothers came along, but none of them would ever come between these two; in the full sense of the word, they were brothers. Cain excelled at many things but perhaps his greatest skill was as a runner. No one on earth could out run or jump Cain.

Cain was fit, muscular, and tall; he was a hunter, a woodsman, and a builder. Some of the lessons that Abel learned without effort were just incomprehensible to Cain, whose rebellious nature caused him strife every day. Cain was far more interested in his own thoughts, desires, and goals than he was in those of his family. He was certainly not interested in his father's plans for him.

As a young man, Cain was industrious, and Adam kept him busy with a number of important projects——mostly building shelters but also making the tools they needed for everyday life. Adam had succeeded in teaching Cain many skills, even more skills than Abel, but his strongest skill was laying stones. He could lay stone upon stone to make structures that were absolutely beautiful, and it was clear that he enjoyed building. He was just as skillful in making the tools that were needed to do his work.

While Adam succeeded in teaching Cain many practical lessons in life, the spiritual lessons remained aloof. Adam would never succeed in getting Cain to respect his mother, father or God. Adam loved Cain just as he loved Abel. It was a love borne by a father wanting the best for his children but his love was largely unrequited.

Cain, as he grew older, grew more distant from the rest of the family, though he continued to be close to his brother Abel.

Being the firstborn male had given Cain standing within his family that he had only earned by birth. The girls wanted and needed husbands, and Cain would, of course, be the first to wed. This concept of superior honor and status being conferred upon the firstborn male at birth would be forever ingrained in their culture, though this particular firstborn male wanted nothing to do with it. Cain showed little interest in his sisters as they raised their eldest brother, and the feeling was mutual.

"Mother?" asked Eva.

"Yes, dear?"

"Mother, I don't think Cain is at all interested in marriage. He is becoming a man——maybe he is already a man——but I don't see him taking an interest in any of my sisters."

"Yes, dear, I see what you see. Cain is a very complicated young man. Your father and I are aware of a conflict deep inside of him. It appears that Abel is also aware of this."

"Abel?" Eva said, looking coyly at Eve.

"Abel, is it?" said Eve.

"Mother, I just adore Abel. His heart is so much like mine," Eva said with the sigh of an enamored woman.

"You have been a good sister to them both; I am sure that you will choose wisely," said Eve, and Eva replied, "Mother, I have chosen, and Abel has chosen as well. We have kept it a secret, but we will marry soon. Please don't tell Cain. Or Father."

"Dear, I suspected as much, and your secret is safe with me. I am very happy for you," exclaimed Eve, as mother and daughter embraced.

Eva truly wanted nothing to do with the man Cain had become. There were several other brothers already born and surely more to come. All of the sisters would soon enough have husbands, and it seemed that all of them were willing to wait for a better man than the man Cain was likely to become.

Cain's cold and distant demeanor to his sisters was exactly the opposite of what they all saw in Abel. That fact was obvious to all.

"Cain, come sit with me," Adam asked of his firstborn son.

"Yes, Father, I am here," said Cain, as he sat down at his father's table.

"Son, your sisters need husbands, and you are now a man. Why not take a wife?" Adam inquired of Cain.

"Father, every week, I am always at the sacrifice. Every day I work at building structures that benefit the family. Adam, generally I do what you ask of me even though you know I don't want to do

most of those things. Are you now demanding that I take a wife?"
Cain asked defensively.

"Son, no I am not. Son, I love you, and I want the best for you,
but I fear that I have waited too long to talk to you about this, and
your tone confirms my suspicion," Adam lamented.

"Father, yes, you have waited far too long. I am a man now, and I
have no need for a father's advice," retorted Cain.

Adam, lowered his head closed his eyes, and lamented his failure
. . . *Father what can I do to help my son?* Adam prayed. When
Adam's head rose and his eyes opened, Cain was looking at his
father, clearly seeing his emotion but he was unaffected by his
father's sorrow.

"Son, you, too, will someday be a father. I only hope you will do
a better job as a father than I have done," said the glossy-eyed Adam,
staring at the firm-eyed Cain.

Adam had only one hope left for a way to influence
Cain——his brother Abel. Abel and Cain were very close; Abel was
Cain's only friend. *Maybe Cain can learn from Abel. Or maybe I
could plant a few seeds with Abel that would spring up through him to
also grow in Cain?*

Cain's foundation was the root of his inner conflict. The whole
family knew the circumstances of the birth of Cain: he was the
thirteenth born, borne of knowledge. Then Abel, the fourteenth
child, had been conceived through faith. That everybody knew of
the circumstances of Cain's birth was not helping him. In reality,
Cain's birth had been no different from any other birth. But in the
minds of men, the fact that he had been the thirteenth born made it
different. Thirteen was a number that had come to mean
rebellion——as it had been on Friday, the thirteenth day of

creation, that Adam had eaten from the tree——and this day would be remembered forevermore as unlucky.

Adam had told his wife on many occasions, "We should have kept the circumstances of Elew's and Cain's births a secret. If we had it to do over again, we would keep that spectacular failure of ours from the children."

Eve asked Adam, "Did we name Cain or did God have us name him 'Cain?'" Eve could not recall, nor could Adam.

"Perhaps we would have been wise to ask God what to name our firstborn son," Adam said. They agreed on this, but it was a moot point now. Cain was not a good choice of names. Cain's first idea of who he was had come from his name——it was not a good start.

Growing up . . . Cain and Abel were very close as brothers and as friends, yet they always seemed to be locked in conflict. Their goals were different. They had different trades and different positions as leaders, but the greatest difference between the brothers was in their attitudes towards Adam.

"Father, why won't God talk to us the way He talked with you?" Cain would ask Adam frequently.

Adam didn't know the answer to this for sure, but he always responded to the best of his ability. "Son, my Father works in mysterious ways that I don't yet fully understand."

"But Father, Lucifer talked with you more freely than did God. Why was that?" Cain persisted.

"I don't know, but I am sure God thought it to be the wisest course," Adam explained. "The relationship between my Father and Lucifer is a mystery to me; perhaps it will always be that way. But I am in no way blaming my Father for my rebellion. The blame for that is all mine. Cain, please always take responsibility for your own actions, and don't ever blame God."

On one occasion, Adam went further: "Don't ever give God credit for something unless you're absolutely certain He had a hand in it, as credit can turn to blame very quickly. God is never to blame for our circumstances. He just isn't."

"Even if God were to become a man someday, and you believed that that man had become a stumbling stone to you, only a child or a fool would blame that good man rather than himself for his own stumbling into a fall. In the end, it is not the stone that caused the stumble but rather our failure to see what can be clearly seen, the rock itself," Adam said.

"Cain, you have heard the story many times about how I blamed God for barring me from the tree of life. Look how long it took for me to realize that it was a blessing and not a curse to be exiled from the Garden in Eden."

Adam had become a wise man.

God, like any good Parent, was learning, and He chose to have a very different relationship with the sons of Adam than the one He had had with their father. God did not directly interfere with Adam's parenting, and God's presence in the boys' lives was based far more on intuition than it had been in their parents' lives. For one thing, God's actual presence was terrifying to most now that rebellion had become a reality in the world. Even Adam and Eve felt shame and hid themselves from God, though they knew that God would find them if and when He wanted to. In the meantime, God was evaluating exactly how, when, and where He should interact with His offspring. God's only goal is to do what is best for His children.

Cain and Abel were close but were heading down different paths. One was heading in the direction of faith, hope, and love——a narrow road and difficult to navigate. The other was on a wider and seemingly easier path, very similar to Adam's early path.

Adam's greatest fear for his own children, and God's biggest fear for mankind, was that they would follow a leader who would lead them down the wide and easy path towards the tree of knowledge. Adam, hoping that he was wrong, worried that a struggle between good and evil was brewing——especially between the two brothers——and that far too many of his children would get caught up in that battle.

Often, Adam regaled the family with stories of the few days that he and Eve had lived in the Garden of Eden. All of their children marveled at what their parents had experienced during their first days on earth. Although those six days of innocence had passed very quickly, Adam remembered them well. God and Lucifer had kept him very busy during that first week.

The first task that God had given Adam was to name the animals. Adam left out some of the finer details of that story in the retelling of it. "It was on the sixth day of creation, and at that point I wasn't really sure who or where I was, but I knew I was safe, as I could feel the love of my Creator. That morning, God had told me to name the groups of creatures that populated the earth. He seemed very interested to find out what I would call them. I categorized each of them into one of three groups: birds, tame animals, and untamed animals. Then God brought me nine of the tame animals and said to me, 'Adam, you are to give each of these creatures a specific kind of name.' I could also tell that God had chosen these nine animals Himself." Each time Adam told the story, the children were quiet, hoping for new details. One of the details that Adam would always fail to mention was that he had been naked, while naming the creatures. (CEV Gen. 2:18–20)

"So, I did as God had asked. I took a close look at each animal and gave each one a name. Looking back on it, it was fun," he would tell the children. "God seemed to be happy with the job that I had done and the names that I had given those nine animals.

'Then, after a short period of time, God brought me a tenth animal, a female animal. After taking a close look, I named its kind a "ewe." God was watching closely and seemed relieved after that event. It didn't take long to name the ten animals, and the next thing I remember is waking up from a deep sleep with this scar on my side, of which you all know," Adam said. "Then, for the first time, I saw your mother. Wow, she was very different from the ewes. She was obviously made just for me." At this point in his recounting of the story, he always looked at Eve with a smile. "She was awake when I woke up. The expression she had on her face reminded me of how I had felt when I first realized that I was alive——it was a very strange feeling. God and I made her comfortable, and she was not afraid," said Adam.

In time, Adam had come to understand the deep sleep he had experienced and why he had a scar on his side. In asking him to name the animals, God had been evaluating what He had created in His image. God watched as the naked Adam named the animals, none of which aroused the man——this was one detail that Adam had never elaborated on with his children——God then made the final decision to go ahead with procreation, a risky move but one made with the due diligence of a loving Father.

Adam, as he remembered back to that day alone in the garden with God, could remember no temptation whatsoever to mate with the ewe. *It never entered my mind.*

Having his own rebellious son helped Adam understand some of God's prior actions. God was in no way provoking or tempting him. God was simply observing the dynamic animated beings that He made in His image.

Procreation was at the center of the plan for creation, so it was critical that Adam and Adam's mate be well-tuned to ensure a close harmony between the two of them; otherwise the plan would fail. Physical life is information-based, and the information in Adam was absolutely critical to procreation. Rather than risk starting from scratch, God would use the now proven design of man as the foundation for creating the man's mate.

God had taken a flower pod from the garden that was capable of causing a deep slumber, condensed and refined it, and then administered it to Adam. He had then made an incision in Adam's flesh and removed a large portion of one of Adam's ribs, closing the wound and leaving the scar. God had personally modified the information that made Adam a man in such a way as to provide Adam with a mate. Using the newly formatted information sequence, Adam's rib, and some additional clay from the ground, the Son fashioned a fully mature mate for Adam. (KJV Gen. 2:21–22)

Since she came from Adam, she would be called a woman. God had instructed Adam that, unlike the animals, every person was to have an individual name, as each man and woman would be a spiritually unique individual. Because he had named the tenth animal a "ewe," with a double V, that coincided with that animals' anatomy, Adam named the woman Eve, with a single V anatomy, and she would be the single mother of all mankind. (CEV Gen. 2:20, 22, 3:20)

The children always pressed for more when Adam told them these histories.

"Father, what about the other days before the fall? Please tell us more!"

"Lucifer kept us busy for the next few days, teaching us the ways of the garden. We had many questions about sleeping, eating, drinking, and other bodily functions," said Adam.

Whenever Cain was with the children listening, and Adam reached the part about Lucifer, Cain would always exclaim, "Tell us more about the tree. Please."

Cain was always most curious about the tree, a fact that did not go unnoticed by anyone, especially Adam. Adam was never thrilled talking about the subject, which was embarrassing to him; but sometimes he would start out talking about Lucifer and attempt to put the blame solely on him.

"Looking back to those six days in the garden, I think I now understand why Lucifer was there, but I was never comfortable in his presence," Adam would tell the kids. "He was very vain. I never saw him as a snake, but from what your mother has told me the snake talking didn't seem impossible to her at the time. It was odd, though, that he didn't bother to also disguise his voice. He was a very strange being. He was definitely male but with very feminine characteristics."

On one occasion, Adam elaborated a bit more, and this only fueled Cain's curiosity about the tree.

"At the time, it seemed that Lucifer was far more interested in man than God was," Adam said. Adam knew that Lucifer had been created before him. He didn't know how long before, but Adam had a sure feeling that God had known Lucifer far better than He knew man.

Adam wondered out loud, "Perhaps it was the angel's idea to create man. Or perhaps Lucifer's free will was different from ours and he was unable to love, and that shortcoming inspired God to create man. Perhaps creating man was the only way to inhabit creation with eternal beings capable of fellowship, capable of love. If that was the case, God would have wanted to find out as quickly as possible if man had the ability to love. That would explain a lot. But to this day I don't understand the nature of the relationship between God and Lucifer..."

After a long pause, Adam continued, "At the time, I did think that God wanted Lucifer in the garden with us to guide us and to give us some instruction and protection. But, looking back, I realize that God knew Lucifer better than He knew me. That knowledge of Lucifer must have influenced God's choices for the two of us. Perhaps God thought it was better to lay out our choices before both man and angels sooner rather than later.

"Time may have been of the essence; procreation could have started within a few days and that would have added an additional layer of complexity. Perhaps God literally had only a few days to observe us before making His next move."

Adam glanced at his eldest son, who always hung on every detail when a story turned to Lucifer and the tree. "It seems to me, as I look back on the dynamics between the three of us at the tree, that God was more interested in knowing me than I was in knowing Him. I guess He knew that I would come to know Him, but He also knew that there wasn't much time for Him to get to know me, if that makes sense."

"Was God surprised when you ate from the forbidden tree, the tree of knowledge?" Cain would ask.

"It seemed to me at the time that God was very disappointed," Adam said. "I didn't think God was surprised about Lucifer's betrayal. At least He did not seem as concerned about Lucifer's fall. Man's fall seemed far more important to God than did the angel's. When I went against God and ate from the tree, I caused the condemnation of all men because all men were in my loins.

"My failure, my fall, allowed Lucifer to gain a stronghold on earth through the tree of knowledge, and every man will have a choice of which tree to live under. I have often prayed to God that

He would someday, in some future generation, give man another chance.

"Perhaps then He will choose a man who is older and wiser than I was and allow Lucifer to tempt him; maybe that man will do a much better job of resisting than I did." That became Adam's frequent prayer, "Father please give another man a chance to do a better *job*."

No matter how much of this story Adam shared with his children, Cain always wanted more information, more details, and more knowledge. More, perhaps, than Adam was willing or able to give him. Cain soon realized that there was only one way to acquire the knowledge he wanted——he must go to the Garden in Eden and see this tree for himself. He didn't know how or when he would manage it, but he knew he had to go to the garden. He would have to think long and hard about how to achieve this, and he would need help——he didn't think he could accomplish the difficult feat alone.

One evening, as Adam was concluding his storytelling, Cain spoke up.

"Father, we want to go find the garden," he said, motioning to include Abel. Though surprised, Abel didn't say a word, but Adam was not nearly as surprised as was Abel. Adam had guessed that this would eventually come up, and he quickly told Cain, "your mother and I will talk it over and then let you know our decision."

When they were alone, Abel asked Cain, "why did you say that I wanted to go to the garden? I never said that."

"Brother, it will be fun. We'll have a great time, and I can't do it without you. I need your help in this, so please go with me?"

Assuming that Adam would never allow it anyway, Abel agreed. "Okay. If Dad says it is okay, I will go with you."

With that, Cain was on a mission. He had a new purpose, one that could bring him both the answers he craved and a meaning to his life.

While Cain was making plans to make his way to the garden, Adam was making very different plans. Adam's plan was to try to rescue Cain from his obvious obsession with the tree and the garden.

"Eve, I think it is a good idea for the boys to take the journey to look for the tree," Adam told his wife.

"Why is that?" Eve asked.

"Cain is obsessed with the tree. You know how difficult travel is in the dense undergrowth. They will never get there. For the first time, Cain will have a challenge that he will surely fall short of achieving. The hard work he will pour into this effort will sap his strength to a degree that the pull of the tree will not be able to match, and then something will give.

"Plus, spending some time away from us will surely be good for him, just as being away from our Father has been good for us——it is a good thing. You know as do I, that we love our Father more today than we ever loved Him before. He has been very wise as a Father. We need to be likewise. The boys will have to depend on each other on this journey, and that will help Cain understand the meaning of being a brother," Adam said.

"Perhaps you're right," said Eve. Then she added, "But what if he does find it?"

Adam felt sure that the task Cain had set himself was too difficult to end in success. But to address Eve's concerns he added, "How about we make Cain a map that leads to nowhere?"

"That might work," said Eve. So, as the two conspired to rid their eldest son of his obsession with the tree of knowledge, Eve prepared a map that would lead up a river to nowhere. When it was ready, they would *reluctantly* allow the two boys to journey to the garden.

"When the time is right, I will slip the map to Cain, telling him not to tell you," Eve told Adam. He agreed with this plan. Adam was not surprised when he later saw that Cain was already beginning his preparations for the journey to the garden. Adam would be ready when Cain again requested permission to go.

The boys knew through their parents' stories that the rivers that supplied water to the earth all sprang from the garden. More than once, they had made halfhearted attempts to venture upriver in hopes of catching a glimpse of it but had never gotten very far. It was clear to both of them that a trip to the garden would be a very difficult endeavor——the earth was overgrown with vegetation, making the way very difficult, if not impossible, to traverse.

The odds against success were high, and they both knew it. The only way through the jungle of plants would be by using narrow pathways found here and there that allowed both man and beast to pass. Some of the larger trees shielded the sun enough to create areas where there were fewer plants. Those were the only places in the jungle where one could move freely, but those places held other dangers. They were home to every form of beast, bird, and crawling creature on earth——and many of the interesting creatures wandering around did not look friendly to man.

Their challenge would be to stay close enough to the trees so they could pass through the jungle but at the same time avoid being noticed by the dangerous animals of all sizes that were lurking in the shadows. They would have to watch out for lions, tigers, alligators, and bears——while trying to stay within earshot of the Tigris River so they wouldn't get lost. It would be dangerous, but that would make it exciting as well.

The more immediate challenge for Cain was to convince Abel to go with him. To entice his brother to go, Cain used the promise of excitement and adventure.

"Brother, are you not tired of tending your flocks?" Cain said. "Let's bring some excitement into our lives. Come on, brother. It will be so much fun to get away——the adventure, the unknown. Come with me, please." Unlike Cain, Abel always thoughtfully considered things, and he now thoughtfully considered his brother's request. Eventually, without any explicit demands, he acquiesced to his older brother's desires, simply saying, "Cain, you are my brother and I will help you in any way I can." With that they began to prepare together for the journey to where their parents had been created, to the Garden in Eden.

Even though Abel was now on board, he still insisted that they once again ask Adam to give them his blessing on their plan to find the garden. Cain, seeing he had no choice, agreed with his brother's decision.

"Abel, you be the one to ask Father," Cain told his younger brother.

Abel agreed, and together they approached Adam.

"Father, Cain and I have been planning our journey to the Garden in Eden. We will be gone for perhaps a year. We are going to journey back to Eden along the Tigris, but we understand that we cannot be guided by the Tigris alone, as it has many tributaries. We can only hope that it will bring us close enough so that, given enough time, we can discover the way to Eden. We now ask for your permission and your blessing to go."

"Boys, you need not go on this long and dangerous adventure. It is just not that important," was Adam's halfhearted attempt to dissuade them. Abel looked to Cain. Everyone there——Adam, Abel, and Eve——knew that Cain was the motivating force behind this proposed journey. So everyone waited for Cain to speak.

"Father, I need to go. I have to go. You and Mother both know that this is very important to me. Father, I know of your past obsession with finding a cure for guilt. Now I have an obsession that, in a way, is much the same," said Cain.

Adam allowed them a moment to think. As Eve and Adam had planned, he was going to allow them to go, but at the last moment he added a caveat. "You can go, but I ask of you one thing before you leave. Both of you come to the altar and give a sacrifice in case you should perish on your journey." In this, Adam was correct. Both boys were old enough to have knowingly done things that would cause a separation between them and God, so a sacrifice was indeed needed.

"That's a good idea," agreed Abel. After a nod from Cain, Adam agreed to the journey adding, "There are some truths that you will have to discover for yourselves on your journey. We will ask God to help you to discover them."

"Perhaps this journey will be good for both of you. You will learn to depend on one another in ways you have never had to before." Of course, he hid from them his belief that they would never actually find the garden. Abel was pleased with the idea of making a sacrifice before departing; Cain, typically, was not. Cain was religious unto attending the weekly sacrifice but was never enthusiastic about it. His feeling that the ritual was an obligation caused him to resent the practice more and more. Cain, a very practical man, believed that there was more to life than making silly sacrifices in return for undefined blessings. Adam would destroy much of the offering in a fire, and this made no sense at all to Cain, who was always pragmatic.

At the altar the next day, Adam conducted a private sacrifice for his sons, taking grain from Cain and a lamb from Abel. "Son, it is time," Adam said and looked to Cain to slay the lamb.

Cain, who was known for passing this duty on to others, as he found it offensive to kill an innocent lamb, looked to Abel, and Abel willingly stepped in to help his brother. Adam was not pleased but said nothing, further enabling Cain to shirk his duty. Regardless, the sacrifice was made, and Adam was now comfortable with letting the boys depart for their long and possibly deadly journey. Adam took a moment, as he often did, to talk to his boys about life, about becoming men, and someday, fathers. Abel listened to the wisdom of his father, but, as usual, Cain paid little attention to anything that didn't involve the tree of knowledge in the garden.

"Father thank you. The sacrifice was a very special moment. I will not forget it," Abel told his father.

"Son, why did you step in to perform the duty I had asked your brother to perform?" Adam inquired.

"Am I not my brother's keeper?" Abel responded, trying to deflect the obvious answer.

"Son, you protect your brother to what end?" asked Adam as he shook his head, thinking this would lead to no good result.

"Father, I know what you speak of, and my brother means well. He just doesn't feel the love of the Father as I do. He feels the obligation to sacrifice, but he does not feel a need or a desire to do it."

"Abel, you are a good brother. I only hope that Cain doesn't continue to use that quality against you."

"Father, I clearly have a weakness when it comes to standing up to my older brother. I will work on it, I promise," said Abel.

"Well, my son, go and get a good night's sleep. In the morning, you will set out on a journey that will, without fail, be quite the experience for both of you."

That said, father and son embraced.

Adam would never worry about Abel, as Abel's foundation was even firmer than his own. Adam did worry for Cain though, who seemed only to have an obsession with a tree as his only foundation to guide him. Adam could only look to himself when he thought about Cain's lack of a good foundation upon which to base his life. *I wonder if God sees me in the same way that I now see Cain. Perhaps the first son is the most difficult for a father? Perhaps being the first son is more difficult for the son as well?*

The next day, Cain and Abel said goodbye to their parents, brothers, and sisters and set off on their journey. They had packed their satchels with only the absolute necessities, as they knew their journey would be a struggle through difficult terrain. As they left their home, Eve slipped Cain the map she had made to show the way to the garden, just as she and Adam had planned.

"Cain, take this. Take it. It is a map of the way to the garden. It will guide you through the many tributaries and help you find what you are looking for," said Eve. She hugged both of the boys and said goodbye. Cain tucked the map away in his backpack, intending to look at it later that night.

Eve had a secret that Adam would never know——she had made the map as accurately as her recollection would allow, hoping that the boys would find the garden. For Eve disagreed with her husband's judgment on this point. Cain would never stop looking for the garden until he found it, so she had provided him with as much help as she could.

The landscape did not disappoint the brothers. They traversed long, narrow canyons with steep walls and used vines to struggle up and down the many obstacles. They crossed many rivers as they branched out from the main river, the Tigris, which had been named by Adam.

As the moon rose and the rivers slowed, they would rest and talk and forage for food and drink. One evening, Abel said to Cain out of the blue, "When we return, I am going to ask Eva to marry me."

After a long pause, Cain said, "This doesn't surprise me," and he sat down.

"Brother, I wanted to tell you first, and in a way, to get your approval," Abel said.

"Brother, you need not my approval. You know that."

"Yes, I know that. I guess that is why I seek it though. You are the firstborn son, and Eva is the first born daughter. Our sisters may expect that you would marry the first born of them," Abel said.

Cain, with a laugh, said, "You know that is not true. You show me far more respect than I am due, brother, far more. Please, marry Eva. She deserves better than I could ever offer her. You know that. She knows that as well. I . . . well, I am just not interested in marriage."

That night, a dream had Cain stirring restlessly.

"I am here. I made it. There it is . . . the tree, the tree of knowledge. It is so beautiful and so big . . . Brother, look, we made it. Brother, where are you? Brother, where did you go? Come enjoy its beauty with me. Is it me who made you leave my side? Why would I do that? Brother, brother, brother."

"Yes Cain, I am here," Abel said, as he shook his dreaming brother awake. "Cain, you were having some kind of dream and you kept saying, 'Brother.'"

"Yeah, I dreamt that we made it to the tree but you weren't there, so I was looking for you," said Cain, clearly rattled.

"Well, don't take it to heart. If you make it, I will make it," Abel assured Cain, who was still half asleep, and they prepared for another day of trekking through the dense foliage. The journey wore them both down physically. But as Cain grew ever more impatient, it also wore on him mentally.

"Abel, would you hurry up? You are slowing us down way too much," Cain yelled at his brother.

"I'm not slowing us down at all. If we're going slowly, it's because of you. The path you're taking is not well thought out. Take your time, brother, and we will go faster in the long run," said Abel.

"Maybe you're right," Cain said. "Why don't you lead for a while?"

Abel agreed to this.

Cain was not coping with the challenges of the wilderness as calmly as he needed to in order to quickly advance. It seemed that the farther they walked, the more frustrated and irritable he became. He wasn't a patient man to begin with, and as they hiked through the jungle this became ever more apparent.

Abel wanted to see the garden, of course, but Cain *needed* to see it. Abel's interest in seeking the garden was that of an explorer. He had been pulled into the quest for the sake of adventure. Cain, on the other hand, had been drawn to it by some spiritual force or yearning deep inside of him that needed answers. It was as if the tree of knowledge was reeling him in like a fish on a line. The line that drew Cain was the same line that his father had crossed when he ate from the tree, and the pull on Cain seemed to become stronger as they got closer to the tree.

Cain had not even consulted the map that Eve had given him; he believed he would know the way instinctively. But after a few more days of slow and painstaking progress along what they believed to be the Tigris, Cain's temper was growing short. The vegetation was so thick it was almost impassable.

In many areas, the river was the only clear and open space available for traveling, but it flowed too fast in the wrong direction for them to get anywhere by rafting or swimming.

"Cain, do you know why the tree has such a pull on you?" Abel asked his brother. The timing for the question was fortunate. It seemed to focus Cain as he stopped to rest; he pondered with his brother, for the first time, just what effect the tree was having on his spirit.

Once he had caught his breath, Cain looked into Abel's eyes intently and said, "I feel connected to the tree in some way. Dad's rebellion at the tree is at my foundation——it is at our foundation. The tree will give us structure to live by and I can't live without the foundation it will provide. I think that if I can see it and touch it, it will answer so many questions . . . I don't know. I just know that I need to go to it, as if it calls to me."

Typical of Abel, he considered his brother's words carefully, desiring to respond to him as best he could. It was time to tell his brother something that he had never told anyone else, it was a secret, one that he had held close for years now. To break this news to his brother, he would have to set the context out well or this revelation that he had withheld might be devastating to Cain.

"Cain remember a year or so ago when Dad decided to abstain from eating meat on Saturdays?" "Yes," said Cain. "Do you remember why Dad stopped?" "Well yes, I also stopped eating meat as did a couple of our sisters." Cain responded but didn't answer the question as to why.

Abel continued, "Yes I know brother. Please take a moment, close your eyes, and don't rush to find an answer that you think will please me, close your eyes–dig deep and tell me why you stopped eating meat?"

Cain did as his brother had asked him. After a moment of silence while Abel eagerly awaited Cain's response, Cain opened his eyes and said. "It was easy for me to stop eating meat; I never really liked the idea to begin with."

Although Cain remained unresponsive to the actual question, Abel saw an opening and ran with it. "Brother, from your words, can you now see how easy it is to do something you want to do?"

Cain heard his brother's words but didn't understand his message. Abel continued.

"Dad loves meat as do I, it is truly a sacrifice for father to not eat meat on Saturday . . . With the altar ablaze, with the smoke billowing up filling the air with the aroma of burning fat–trust me Dad wants to eat! His abstaining is a very small personal sacrifice to show his love to his Father." Cain acknowledged Abel but found no deeper meaning in the story.

"Brother, you and a couple of our sisters have also picked up on Dad's practice, but with you and them, it is clearly a ritual nothing more. It is not done out of any love for God–your ritualistic practice is a product of the tree of knowledge. While father's acts are a product of love and the tree of life."

Cain was on the verge of understanding and asked, "Brother, why does one's motivation make a difference, when our actions are the same?" Abel was so pleased that his brother had caught on to the powerful force behind the two trees–it was now time to reveal his secret.

"Cain, it makes all the difference in the world. It was God's desire for our love that motivated Him to ask us to not eat from the tree of knowledge, not because the food was no good . . . indeed *figs* are perhaps the most delicious fruit there is. He asked us not to eat the figs as a simple act of love and respect for Him, nothing more." Cain caught on the word figs.

"Abel, are you saying that the tree of knowledge is nothing more than a fig tree? How do you know this?" At this moment, Abel realized, it was a mistake to tell Cain his secret. It had sidetracked Cain's thought process . . . but it was too late now.

"Brother a couple years ago, I heard Mom and Dad talking about the tree of knowledge as they were eating at the fig tree north of the altar back home, they never saw me and they don't know that I heard them reminiscing. They were eating freely of the ripe figs and laughing about their foolish behavior in the garden. I understood the concept immediately and so I never saw the need to ask Father about it and I never felt the need to tell anyone until now." Abel confessed.

"It was just a fig tree?" Said Cain shaking his head in disbelief. *I don't believe it and I don't believe Abel!*

"Brother, if we get to the garden, if the tree of knowledge is still there, I can eat from it because it has no standing in my life. Or I can abstain; it literally makes no difference, because it is the love of my fathers that will guide my actions, not some silly ritual and certainly not some stupid fig tree." Abel told his bewildered brother.

By this point Cain was not hearing his brother–he was still reeling from the idea that the tree he was obsessed with might be nothing more than a fig tree. It was unlikely that Cain would ever believe that fact unless he was to see it with his own eyes.

Abel meant well by sharing his secret with his brother, but it would end up only encouraging Cain's obsession with the tree of knowledge.

Outwardly Cain laughed in disbelief, "A fig tree, really you would have me believe that the tree of knowledge is nothing more than a fig tree?" It was now Abel who was listening.

"Brother, you have a different way of thinking, perhaps it is our very different foundations that produced our ways. You are Abel, and I am Cain, we can't change who we are." Abel knew Cain was speaking about the circumstance of their births.

Cain continued, "You're the child of faith, I am not. I was cained, you were not." Cain had taken his name to heart, and though the manner of his birth had been no different than the births of his brothers, his name and the circumstances of his birth were indeed different. Then, wanting to change the subject, he added, "Who knows, if God still has the entrance to Eden guarded, we will only get to look at the tree, no more. But if the guards are no longer there, well, that must mean that God is no longer concerned about us eating from the tree."

"Cain, you know as well as I do that the tree God was really guarding was the tree of life, not the tree of knowledge. My guess is that, now that we have sacrifice, God has removed the tree of life, that is where the danger lies, that really is a tree we dare not eat of!" Abel said.

The brothers talked a bit more to release some of the tension——mostly about Adam, whom the two boys saw with very different eyes.

"I know that Father is not perfect, but to me he is," Abel told his brother.

"I don't expect him to be perfect. I just don't understand his ways. Sacrifice is so important to him, and it simply isn't important to me," said Cain.

"Don't look to what Dad does or did; look to the love he has for you as his son, nothing more. You know, all fathers want the best for their children. They really do." Abel said this with all the deep love and passion that he felt for his brother, yet he could see that Cain was still not convinced.

As they rested that night, both were deep in thought. If Adam could have seen them, he would have been proud. They fell asleep thinking well of each other, and feeling pleased with their journey. But, once asleep, Abel dreamt of the tree's pull on Cain.

In his dream, Abel was tending his flocks with his best dog, Nine. It was a beautiful day, sunny and full of promise, as man and dog watched over their flocks. Suddenly, Nine vomited near Abel, who was relaxing under a tree. The sight and smell of it were horrible, and with that, the dream became a nightmare. Nine gave him a strange look and even snarled at him. Nine had never done this before. Abel stood and watched as Nine returned to his vomit, as dogs will do. Then Abel suddenly awoke. He was sweating and disturbed by the dream. From that moment on, Abel felt uneasy about their journey.

They had been traveling for a few weeks now, and Abel was no longer enjoying the adventure. The disturbing dream continued to haunt him. He believed that Nine's returning to his vomit in the dream was a representation of Cain's desire to return to the tree. It would probably only enrage Cain if he discussed this with him, so he kept his dream to himself.

"Let's rest here for the night, brother," Abel said, dropping his leather satchel to the ground and sitting down on a large rock.

"Rest? Did you say rest? That's why we can't find our way to the garden. Every time we seem to be getting close, you want to rest. Then we lose our bearings and get lost. No! There's at least another hour of daylight left, and we're going to walk until it gets dark."

"We don't lose our bearings because we rest——we don't have a bearing. Face it, brother. We've been traveling along this river for weeks now, and though we may think we're making progress, we both know we're not." Abel was thinking that the garden could be sixty, ninety, or even more days away if they continued at their current pace, and he was beginning to wonder whether the journey was worth the effort. "I'm thinking we should head back home tomorrow," Abel said.

Anger welled up in Cain's heart, and he couldn't stand the fact that deep down he knew his brother was right. But that didn't matter anymore. He'd come this far and he wasn't turning back now.

"Then I will go on alone," Cain screamed at his brother. "You're just being a coward, Abel. You're afraid we might actually find it. You're afraid that you might eat from the tree."

"You're the coward, Cain. You're afraid we won't find it. I'm staying here for the night, and in the morning I'm heading back," Abel responded angrily, immediately regretting his uncharacteristically angry outburst. He should never have yelled at his brother, but his dream still haunted him.

Cain was furious. He watched as Abel got to his feet and began gathering branches and leaves for his bed.

"Fine!" Cain shouted. "I'll go it alone."

Not allowing himself time to think, Cain turned and plunged deeper into the undergrowth. Abel waited, hoping his brother would return once it got dark——the animals they had seen in the daytime looked frightening enough; what creatures might be roaming around at night?

Abel realized that, until he had his nightmare, he had been enjoying the journey despite Cain's impatient and childish behavior and his obsession with the garden. Perhaps he was reading too much into the strange dream. To a large extent, he was glad his brother had talked him into going along on the trip. It had turned out to be a nice break from work and even from their parents. It had also been an exciting and invigorating experience so far. After all, there wasn't much excitement in the day-to-day chores of tending sheep and goats. Plus, he was getting to know his brother better than he had ever known him before. But it had been a long journey, and he had a strong feeling that it was time to go home. Abel's mind wandered as he tended a small fire at their camp, waiting for Cain to return. As he was falling asleep, he hoped that he would not have another nightmare.

Adam, as Abel had justly said, was not a perfect father, but he was a loving father who wanted the best for his children. Unfortunately, Adam could not undo what had been done, and it was affecting Cain's life profoundly. It was Adam's rebellion at the tree that enticed Cain. That rebellion, that had taken place long before Cain's birth was proving to have more influence on Cain than any of Adam's love, words, or attempts to impart wisdom as he raised the firstborn son. Cain would not have been so drawn to the garden because of the tree alone; he was drawn because of what Adam had done there so long ago. Cain felt that he was connected to that tree——or even, somehow, related to it.

As the sun rose the next morning, Abel awoke after a restful night's sleep and was disappointed——but not surprised——that his brother was nowhere to be found. *Cain could never find his way back——if he was even trying to,* thought Abel.

Abel walked away from his camp to think and reason what he should do now. *Why does the tree of knowledge have such a pull on my brother? Don't eat from the tree . . . Wait a full fortnight to cain a son . . . Father's failure at the tree . . . Father's failure to cain a son of faith? And as Father learned . . . They named me the child of faith. That was surely a crushing blow to Cain in his frustration over how he was conceived and who he was meant to be. My brother's foundation is deeply flawed, and I must help him. But how?*

"Cain!" Abel yelled, but there was no response. "Cain! Where are you, brother?" Still, there was no answer. Abel continued to call out his brother's name but to no avail. At this point, Abel felt he had no choice but to try to follow his impetuous brother, so he set out to track Cain to make sure that he was all right.

Cain was stronger. Cain was more courageous. Cain was an almost perfect physical specimen of a human, his musculature and brawn second only to Adam's. But his poor judgment had exposed both brothers to great peril, as they were now separated and probably needed each other to survive. Abel would now have to risk his life to find his brother. Cain's foolishness had committed them both to an outcome that was far more uncertain than what they had been faced with just a day earlier.

As Abel focused on the task of searching for his brother, he became greatly aware of his surroundings. He could sense the slightest movement; he could hear the quietest sound, and he was making clearer judgments than he had ever made before. He somehow felt safer than he had felt just hours ago. *Faith gives me the strength I need now, and it will be all that I need going forward; faith that my loving Father will not forsake me.*

As he tracked Cain, time seemed to move swiftly for Abel, and he felt no pain or fatigue. But could he find his brother? His inner faith was providing him with almost everything he needed, but it was not giving him a bead on his brother's location.

Abel was confident that his brother's actions were anything but well thought out, and that would work to Abel's advantage as he searched for Cain. Abel took each step methodically and was hopeful that those deliberate steps were bringing him closer to Cain. *Cain must be tiring; his frustration must be hindering his movements,* Abel reasoned.

Abel was right. Not far ahead of him, Cain was moving erratically and had no idea where he was going. He was trying to force his way through the jungle relying on his strength and endurance alone. As it became clear to Cain that his efforts were to no avail, his frustration grew. He was very strong——many times in his life he had proven himself capable of great feats of strength——but even he had his limitations. He was pushing himself to the edge of those limits when he suddenly came upon a deep ravine.

Cain looked across the crevasse where water had once run, not paying any attention to the danger that it presented. Blinded by his obsession with the tree of knowledge, Cain foolishly felt certain that he could jump over the ravine. After all, he could do almost anything that he put his mind to.

He lobbed his bag over to the other side of the ravine and then backed up to get a running start. He began at a slow jog and was sprinting at top speed by the time he reached the cliff, pushed off, and took his leap. He stretched out as far as he could, confident that he would make it to the other side——but he was wrong about that. The pull of the tree in the garden was not one that could help him to bridge this physical gap, and his misjudgment now might claim his life. Cain realized while he was in midair that he was going to fall short.

Desperately, he clawed at the air, hoping to grab something that could halt his descent. To his astonishment, his leap had taken him far enough across to reach the sheer wall of the crevasse. Cain now found himself clinging to a wall of dirt and rock with some bits of vegetation protruding out from it. There was no way for him to climb up. His feet could only find one small branch, and it would surely break if he were to rely on it any more than he already was.

The impact of hitting the cliff hit him in other ways as well, it impacted his single train of thought away from the tree and onto more internal matters. *All of this is for what exactly? How did I get into this mess?* he wondered, *and how am I going to get out of it?*

He quickly assessed his predicament, and he decided not to try to climb upward. His position was too precarious. Going downwards was his only possible course of action, even going down he might fall. That's when he heard it. From below came the sound of a large, powerful beast chewing on something.

Overwhelmed with panic and dread, he realized that a downward course was not an option. With each tiny movement he made, more of the earth gave way. If he didn't remain perfectly still, he would surely fall into the pit and be devoured.

Strangely though, for the first time in several days, Cain began to think clearly. As he dangled there, heartbeats away from plunging to his death, he realized how foolish he had been to let his emotions take over and to strike out on his own, away from Abel.

Cain thought while he rested his head against the straining muscles and bulging veins of his tired arms, his vain attempt to find answers from the garden now seemed unimportant. *I deserted my brother because of my obsession with a tree.* This was as close as Cain would come to repenting.

Cain hung above the pit in silent thought for what seemed an eternity until he suddenly sensed his brother's presence nearby, and this completely reinvigorated him. "Help!" he screamed at the top of his lungs. "Abel."

Abel had been drawing closer to his brother's location, and he now heard his brother's cries for help. He dropped his bag and sprinted towards the ravine, where he was shocked to find his brother hanging from the cliff, holding on for dear life. This was a sight he'd never seen before——Cain needing assistance, wanting help.

"Cain, I'm here," Abel quickly reassured his brother.

"Oh, thank God," Cain shouted. "Throw me a vine or something. Tie it off on a tree." Cain's grip was slipping as Abel scrambled to find some vines to tie together.

"Hurry, brother," Cain cried out.

Abel flung the end of his vine rope to the other side of the crevasse, and Cain frantically wrapped them around his hands. In a swift motion, he grabbed his bag from above his head and dropped down into the ravine.

Cain's initial reaction was that the rope was just a little too long, as he continued to fall into the darkness. Cain hoping not to feel the long arms of the monsters that awaited him in the pit, hoping that the slack in the vine would soon run out as he feared he was getting far too close to whatever was lurking at the bottom. At the last moment, Cain felt the slack finally run out as it jerked to stop his descent. He then swung upward toward the other side hitting it as well, but this time the impact tightened his grip and his resolve to survive.

"Okay, now pull" he yelled at his brother, "Pull!"

Abel began pulling Cain up the face of the crevasse with strength he hadn't known he possessed. Cain struggled to hold onto the vines as the creatures below snarled, grunted, and snorted, hoping the human would plunge to the bottom and provide them with a meal. But he did not fall and he never looked down, he didn't want to see his would be carnivores. Cain managed to climb the sheer wall with the help of Abel's lifeline, and after a few hundred heartbeats of teamwork, Cain and Abel were reunited at the top of the cliff. They dropped to the ground in exhaustion.

"Thank you, brother. I owe you my life," Cain said, with unseen before emotion. The battered and bruised older brother was, perhaps for the first time, keenly aware of his mortality——and momentarily humbled by that awareness.

"Can we go home now?" Abel asked him and then grinned, certain that the answer would be yes.

As Cain nodded yes, the brothers turned and looked across the crevasse towards their unfulfilled promise of the garden. Silently, each in his own way, they lamented the fact that their efforts had been for naught. They would have to abandon their journey here on the edge of a crevasse that was not so terribly wide but that would leave a chasm in Cain's life which would not be easily filled.

Cain's emotionally draining encounter with near death had eclipsed his obsession with the tree of knowledge——long enough, anyway, for Abel to convince his brother that they should go back home. Abel, for the moment, had bridged the gap between them.

Abel was disappointed that their journey had been a failure, but he was more disappointed for his brother. As he looked at Cain, he knew that his brother was in no way free from his obsession with the tree of knowledge.

As Abel patted him on the back, Cain looked at his brother and thought sadly, *perhaps some other men would feel the pull that I feel, but men of faith like my brother will never know the power that tree holds over me.*

Adam was not risk averse; not for himself and not in guiding his sons. *Better they grow up sooner rather than later; and in many ways, their journey was far less risky than the one my Father allowed me to traverse.* Adam had shown wisdom in allowing two of his sons to risk everything in their pursuit of answers and adventure. It had been a difficult choice to make, as a parent always fears the worst. But it had also been a dutiful one, as no particular outcome is ever guaranteed in life.

They had not discovered the garden, but they had made some difficult discoveries about themselves. Even Cain, so grateful that Abel had appeared during his moment of need, had found himself thanking God. Only time would tell if, when Cain had called on God in his moment of need, he had in fact discovered a new sense of faith in his timely rescue.

On the first part of their journey, it had been Cain who was leading his brother towards the garden. But it was Abel who took the lead as they returned to their home and to their father. So it would ever be between these brothers, one would lead in one direction and one would pull in the other.

Adam and Eve were thrilled and proud of their sons when they arrived safely home. The entire family gathered to hear of their experiences and adventures. But, as Abel told his version of the tale, Cain looked out into the distance, obviously still haunted——probably forevermore to be haunted——by the pull of the tree. Then, suddenly, Cain remembered the map that Eve had given him. He had no need for it now, but he decided, *I am going to hold onto this anyway; I just might find it useful someday.*

— 5 —
A New World Order

The man ran faster than he would have ever thought possible as he jumped over boulders and other obstacles that were in the way of his escape. His world had transformed in a moment's time, and he felt himself transforming with it. Faster and faster he pushed himself. His lungs felt as though they would explode as he gasped and struggled for every precious breath. He marveled at his own strength and endurance. He wondered where it came from as he continued at a frenzied pace. He sensed a change within himself that might be both a burden and a gift. He didn't know what was happening to him or what it meant, but it was energizing him right now, so he kept on running.

Running for so long calmed him and drained his emotions so that he was able to focus on his current situation. This single focus was necessary, as his purpose was escape. He did not seek to escape from others who might be chasing him but rather from the crime that he had committed. He was not aware of this, but it was going to be much harder to escape from his reality than from his pursuers. But as long as his energy held out, his mind could and would avoid the painful truth that would overtake him soon enough. His agility was deserting him though, and he attempted to hurdle a fallen tree only to land hard upon one of its branches that was concealed by brush. As he fell to the ground, he finally tried to grasp what he had done, but he wanted no part of that. So, with what little stamina he had left, he pulled himself up and ran again with as much speed as he could muster.

Inescapable guilt over what had transpired earlier that day began to sink deep into the man's spirit. Unbeknownst to him, this was the beginning of a very long process that would bring much pain upon him and upon the world.

Walking slowly now, though his mind was racing, he stepped into a small pool of water where a reflection caught his attention. There was a flicker of light in the still water, and this was a welcome distraction. The shade of a giant tree had created a dark reflection in the pool, and there Cain caught a brief glimpse of himself which was encompassed by a strange shimmering glow. This was new to him and inexplicable. He had never seen an aura like this around himself or anyone else before, and it filled him with awe and wonderment. His thoughts of guilt were abruptly replaced with a feeling of uncertainty.

Have I died and become some sort of angelic being? Is this the mark of a murderer? Does this strange light have something to do with my newfound strength? Could this be my punishment for murdering my brother?

Cain had no idea what was going on, or whether anyone had actually been pursuing him, but he did know that he felt a strange sensation of something breathing down his neck. Cain was learning what it meant to be guilty of murder——yet somehow he was stronger than ever.

Weeks earlier, Cain had been busy working on his latest tool. In his maturity, he had become a worker of the land. He tended trees and plants in order to harvest their grains and fruits. He was very skillful at fashioning tools with which to work the ground. He was a man of many abilities and some ambition as well. He felt confident that he would not always be a farmer. (KJV Gen. 4:2)

One day, he had taken a tree branch, roughly the size of his forearm, that had a fork in it where he could attach a sharpened stone using vines and other vegetation. Once he had finished making this newest tool, an ax, he held it in his left hand as would a mighty conqueror, brandishing it as though it were a weapon. In that moment he felt invincible, and he couldn't wait to put this new tool to use.

Cain could provide for himself. He didn't need anyone else. He was going to do things his way, not his father's way. Not the ways taught to him, especially the concept of sacrifice.

When it came to the weekly sacrifice, he rarely put more than a token effort into the ritual. He was getting by just fine with the façade and figured he could continue it for a long time. More often than not, he would wait until the last possible moment and then manipulate his brother, Abel, into providing a worthy sacrifice on his behalf.

The real problem for Cain, where sacrifices were concerned, was that his heart simply wasn't in it. Cain reasoned that there would be plenty of time for making sacrifices after he amassed his fortune and his power. Then he would be giving the best sacrifices. After all, Cain was mighty and cunning; soon he would be in a position to do good things for others——just not yet.

Cain was a very skilled craftsman, and had a special knack for devising and building ingenious items that were useful in everyday life. His skills in design, assembly, and construction soon led him to discover what his real ambition was. He wanted to become a builder. Whenever he wasn't going through the motions to appease his father Adam or God, Cain pieced together structures using trees, rocks, and mud. He had already built many structures in and around the Square, but his family members did not make a habit of living on the ground. The Square of Adam was just that, a simple four equal sided place where people gathered for commerce and worship.

Almost everyone in the Square lived in the giant trees that surrounded the area, but that didn't suit Cain. For some reason, Cain preferred to be on the ground, and there continued to be only one tree in Cain's life——the tree of knowledge. Cain was drawn to the earth just as he was still drawn to that one tree, and that led him to a new, albeit temporary, obsession.

Cain's greatest ambition——was to build a great city someday, with giant structures made of stone. He would build the ground up in his own image, and nothing would get in the way of that dream——especially not silly sacrifices that wasted precious resources.

Cain, in addition to being talented in many other areas, was a successful farmer. He would always have plenty of grains, beautiful fruits and vegetables to trade for a sacrificial animal, if and when he chose to. His brother Abel, as a successful herdsman, always had a plentiful supply of V hoofed, or two toed animals. These animals had the highest value in trade and as such they were also considered not to be the best sacrifice.

Each family, usually in line with the desires of their patriarch, tended to branch out with items needed in the Square. As brothers and sisters saw the need for either goods or services the gaps became obvious and they were filled with the desire to trade one good for another. As was the custom, only clean animals were burned on the altar. However, grains, fruits, vegetables, and many other goods were needed at the sacrifice and were freely traded in the Square.

Cain, on the day of sacrifice, could always manipulate Abel into accepting poor produce in exchange for a clean sacrificial animal, while Cain kept his best fruits and grains for himself to trade for items he desired.

Abel, having the finest herds, had an advantage over his brothers. But he always traded evenly, and Adam was pleased with Abel. But Adam could clearly see trouble brewing, and he advised Abel to show better judgment when helping his brothers, especially Cain.

"Son, I know you mean well when you help others, but you must be careful. Helping is good, but if you contribute to your brother's self-indulgence, that is not good," Adam said, hoping to plant a seed in Abel's mind.

Abel got the message. "Father, how does one tell if helping someone indeed helps them?"

Adam didn't know the answer, and he struggled to find one. "Well, my son, we may just have to figure this one out together through trial and error," he said finally.

"I guess I will have to be on guard going forward, and I will only know whether I have done a good thing by the results of my previous efforts," said Abel. Both of them knew they were speaking of Cain, but they didn't name him.

The seed I plant must be subtle. I really shouldn't name Cain as the one we need to teach. It could come back to me or to Abel looking like some kind of parental preference, reasoned Adam.

"It would do us both good to pray for more wisdom," said Adam. "Perhaps help can only be understood through the distance of time, as we reflect upon it through the spirit that God has given each of us."

Abel listened, and mulled over the meaning of his father's words, because Abel truly desired to help others, especially Cain.

Abel loved his brother very much, but he could also clearly see that Cain was always finding ways to avoid his responsibilities at the weekly sacrifices, and if he truly loved his brother he would have to stop enabling him.

Time and again, every Saturday, Abel ended up doing for Cain what Cain should have been doing for their fathers. Abel didn't mind helping his brother——after all, he was his brother's keeper——but when he carefully thought over Adam's words he was confronted with the realization that helping Cain to shirk his duties was in no way loving his brother. As he thought about it, he became convinced that his attempts to help Cain had in fact been a detriment to Cain, and he prayed, "Father, I am sorry. What I intended to be an act of love has hurt my brother. I am sorry for my lack of wisdom and my cowardice towards Cain. I repent. As I gain strength and wisdom from You, I will truly love my brother."

FRATRICIDE

Some weeks later, Abel was resting under a giant poplar tree in a field when he saw Cain gathering supplies to use for building his latest structure. Adam's recent words came to Abel's mind, and he reaffirmed his decision to repent: *I will act wisely; I will do the right thing; I will risk the consequence to loving my brother.* The repentance of just a single faithful man would change things for all and forever.

That Saturday, as was often the case, Cain bartered with his brother to secure an offering for the Saturday sacrifice. After some heated arguments they did not agree on the terms for a lamb. (KJV Gen. 4:4) They had not spoken since then, and there was an obvious tension between them. Abel knew that something had to be said, understanding that the issue would only get worse if it was allowed to fester.

To Abel's relief, Cain spoke first. "Brother, come with me into this field so that we can talk." (KJV Gen. 4:8)

"Did you see Father's reaction to your offering today?" Abel asked with a tone of condemnation.

"Yes, I did. Why did you not help me?" replied Cain in his usual angry tone. He hated it when Abel challenged him and spoke to him as though he were a child in need of discipline. Ever since Abel had saved Cain at the ravine, Cain had felt that his brother was trying to lead him where he did not want to go——away from the tree. He wondered if he might have to teach his weaker brother a lesson, show him who the real leader was.

Then Abel explained with sorrow and sincerity, "Brother, I have helped you many, many times at the sacrifice, and my help has led to dependence on your part. My foolish attempt to help you, which I intended for good, is now destroying you. I am so sorry for my lack of judgment and the pain that I have caused us both. Though I meant to help you, I fear I have harmed you far more than I have helped you."

"Are you not your brother's keeper?" Cain retorted, hoping to force his brother to return to his subservient ways. Cain had gotten by for a long while by manipulating his brother, and he believed beyond any doubt that he would be able to continue in the same way.

Abel gently shook his head in disbelief, realizing that his brother didn't get it. "It is because your heart is not right, Cain. God enjoys a cheerful giver and only accepts our best. You bring Him spoiled and soiled figs from the ground and expect His approval? (KJV Gen. 4:3) I have helped you to become lazy. Brother, by accepting your pitiful produce in exchange for a clean animal, I have harmed you. Please believe me——I had the best intentions in my actions towards you, but now I know I acted foolishly, and I am sorry. I will no longer help you destroy your life, because doing so could destroy mine as well. Father warned me about this, and at first I did not see his wisdom, but I do now. I will no longer put up with it and nor will father. We expect you to offer a worthy sacrifice. I am my brother's keeper, but no longer will I be my brother's enabler."

"Father," said Cain. "I knew it. Dad put you up to this. This is not fair."

Again, Abel was shaking his head, not understanding what he was hearing. *Fair? I don't know the meaning of this word. What is he talking about?*

Anger welled up inside Cain like some unholy beast, and his thoughts became random and misguided. *My brother is nothing more than an agent of my father. Okay, my sacrifices are not always what they should be, but at least I make them. I follow the rules. Father loves Abel and he resents me. It's my independence that makes him jealous of me. Why do all the sisters look to Abel? Why does Eva choose Abel over me? I am the better man, the better craftsman, the better builder, the better farmer. I am stronger and more powerful. They will all see.*

For a moment, Abel was encouraged by Cain's silence. But this moment was dashed when Cain shook his head and said quietly, "No. Our parents' rebellion caused this mess, and now they try to blame me. I am the innocent one here, and they are the guilty ones."

Abel had little clue to the inner workings of Cain's mind, but he realized that Cain was contemplating what he should do next, so Abel made a suggestion that he hoped would take them together in the right direction.

"Brother, come with me tonight and together we will make a special evening sacrifice. Bring your best fruits and your best grains, and I will provide a tenth, a ewe. We shall please our fathers together," he said, trying to guide his brother.

With that, Cain's random thoughts became clear. He knew who he was and what he needed to do.

"Why? So you can take credit for my changed attitude and my new compliance? So you can show once again to everyone how good you are and how bad I am? You understand that everybody knows I don't want to perform sacrifices, don't you, brother? I haven't changed, and I don't want to. You should have just helped me today when you had the chance," Cain said.

"What do you mean, 'had the chance?'" asked Abel.

Cain approached his brother, enraged. He felt more hatred brewing inside him than he knew what to do with. Then he realized that maybe there was something he could do with it after all.

"Yes, when you had the chance," Cain repeated.

Abel saw the anger in his brother's eyes, and for a moment he felt fearful. He decided it would be best to defuse this situation before it turned into something more serious, so he turned to go back to his work. After all, he knew he was no match for Cain physically, and he wanted to make things better for Cain, not worse——though his brother obviously didn't believe that.

Cain shook violently as his anger took complete control of him and obliterated every last remnant of love and respect he felt for his brother. He lunged at Abel, pushing him to the ground. Abel bleated like a sheep being led to the altar. Cain's rage was now uncontrollable and growing.

With a new sense of urgency, Abel sprang to his feet and attacked his brother with every ounce of strength he had, but he wasn't strong enough. He thought that if he showed some strength his brother might stop the madness, but he was wrong. Abel tried again and rushed towards Cain.

Cain sidestepped Abel and landed a crushing blow to his face. He could feel his brother's cheekbone fracture and give way against his closed fist.

With a badly split lip and shattered face, Abel stood and took up a fighting stance, but what he really wanted to do was run. Abel wondered why God was allowing this to happen, and he silently prayed that He would intervene and save him from this beating. *God, please save me.*

"Father will hear of this," he wheezed at Cain. He hoped desperately that his enraged brother would come to his senses and end the fight.

Cain's only response was silence and a sinister grin. Abel turned his back on Cain. But this sent Cain into another frenzied rage. He grabbed Abel, turned him around, and pummeled him in the face again.

Abel could barely stand on his feet now, and he looked around for something he could use as a weapon to aid him in his defense. He grabbed a rock and managed to strike Cain on the arm with it, but that made Cain even angrier. Then, in an uncontrollable yet deliberate move, Cain gripped his new ax, which had been hanging at his left side, and with a strange, malevolent smile, he whispered, "Are you not your brother's keeper?"

Abel——now frozen in place with his hands limp by his sides, his eyes partially closed, his head drooping——realized that his life was at its end.

Cain, still wearing his wicked grin, tilted his head to meet his brother's eyes in one final attempt to show Abel that he was the better man. With one smashing blow of his ax, Cain split open Abel's skull, ending his brother's life.

Then all was silent. Everything in nature, from the birds in the air to the insects on the ground, ceased making any sound at all, as if to inform all of creation what had just transpired. Abel slumped to the ground, falling slowly backwards. As his head hit the ground, his eyes were wide open but unresponsive. Cain's manic grin slowly faded as he stood silently over his bleeding brother and realized what he had done. Now he was a frightened man. Yes, he had wanted to hurt his brother, but he wondered, *did I go too far?* He dropped his ax. As he watched the blood pour from his brother's open skull, it reminded him of the juice from one of the oozing, rotten fruits that he would pick up on his way to the sacrifice.

Cain continued to watch in silence as the crimson fluid flowed from his brother's broken head, pooling around him but not entering the earth beneath him. (KJV Gen. 4:10) Slowly, Cain regained his senses as he picked up his ax. He stared at it as though it could explain to him why all of this had just happened. But, the cold and lifeless ax was silent, just as it had been when it whizzed through the cool afternoon breeze and split Abel's skull open. It offered no answers.

In the continuing silence, Cain thought to reach out to God. He certainly needed help. He had just murdered the only person who had ever, in his mind, sincerely tried to help him.

With his eyes tightly closed, he mustered all of his resources to try to bend his knee and speak to God. The thoughts and questions were ready, the cry for help was poised on his lips; but he could not make his knee bend, and he could not make his lips move. He would not humble himself; Cain was unable to reach out to God for answers. He would have to find his answers elsewhere.

—— 6 ——
THE MERCY AND WISDOM OF GOD

Abel's life, spirit, and consciousness were in his blood——blood that oozed slowly out of his skull as he lay motionless on the ground. As his spirit flowed out of his dead body, Abel's spirit cried out in despair for vengeance. (KJV Gen. 4:10) With deep anguish, the Godhead heard Abel's cries and in unison uttered a whisper of regret for going forward with procreation. Time——the Present——the Past with the Future were now, for the moment, sorry that They had made man.

Now Abel's blood was at odds with the ground underneath his body. His blood pooled just above the surface, like oil on water. Abel's wandering spirit, having left his lifeless body, now had no place to dwell. So the ground, with no concern for the Present or for the Past, tried fiercely to draw Abel's spirit down into itself. But because of the sacrifices that Abel had made, the Son of God intervened and dwelled with him. Abel would not be doomed to the depths of the earth after all, thanks to his sacrificial offerings.

Each week, while he lived, Abel had honored his father and God by bringing his best sacrifice to the Square of Adam. Abel would choose from his flocks what he thought would please Adam the most——usually a tenth, a ewe. The blood of those lambs, which had been spilled on the altar, would now stand in for Abel's blood, and he would be spared the darkness, the despair, the torment, and the eternal company of Lucifer inside the earth. Adam's temporary solution for guilt, in its first eternal test, had worked, and Abel became its first eternal beneficiary. Adam had been wise to seek out a cure for his guilt, wiser still to wait for that cure before having children, and wiser again to teach his children to sacrifice. The combined love of the fathers had saved Abel from a separate eternity away from his Creator.

As Abel's blood pooled above the ground, Lucifer's demonic hands were just below it, he coveted the spirit of Abel more than his own as he desperately tried to bore a hole up to it, wanting to drain it unto himself. But it wasn't to be.

The Son held Abel's spirit in a special place far away from Lucifer. Since the Son denied Lucifer this first wandering spirit, the anguish inside the earth intensified dramatically. Lucifer, who had won the first battle at the tree, now lost the second battle because a man of faith——a man who felt no need to eat from his tree——had been withheld from his eternal spirit in darkness.

Because the pull from the depths of the earth was so strong, God proclaimed that it was indeed a fitting home for rebellious spirits akin to Lucifer's.

At that moment, Abel was the only created fleshy being who was now devoid of flesh. Though he was no longer in the flesh, he still desired vengeance against his brother for his murder.

The Son in Heaven spoke; "Father We can all sense Abel's desire for vengeance, even absent of his flesh, he senses a great imbalance." God responded, "When the scales are balanced, We shall all rejoice that justice has been achieved."

Flesh or no flesh, the Trinity could now clearly see that justice was an innate character within man, as They had hoped it would be.

The Holy Spirit said, "Man has an eternal balance that yearns to be level, Our image is intact within the heart of man. All that remains is for each and every person to discern the separate and different principals; vengeance, justice and mercy and for all man's created earthly institutions to properly reflect those yearnings." God added, "Justice is the end, mercy is the beginning and vengeance will be the last resort should mercy fail to bring repentance."

Abel would wait in comfort for things to play out on earth. There would be a final judgment for all; but as the first man of faith to die, the outcome of his judgment was assured. The outcome of Cain's judgment was by no means assured——but where there is life there would always be hope.

"Cain feels some remorse for what he has done. This is evident in his struggles to escape his guilt," God thought out loud. "Is mercy justified here? Should Cain not have some time and some opportunity to repent before his eternal judgment?"

The Godhead knew that earth and man were not ready or even capable of delivering justice to Cain at this point. Any judgment for him at this moment would have to be an eternal judgment, one administered directly by Them. That would require ending his life on earth and having him face the Son to answer for his actions, once and for always.

The Father continued, "A swift and painful judgment would be best for creation and perhaps best for Cain. If the Son were to confront Cain now, giving him a brief period of time to repent, it would be favorable in the short term. But in the long term, that would keep Our children dependent on Us to judge them in their dominion, and We can All see that that scenario is untenable. The children must learn how to judge themselves, and the sooner they learn to do this the better it will be for all of creation."

The Son added, "If I inform Cain directly of Our decision, My standing at the right hand of my Father, will assure Cain and others that it is indeed just and wise that We have delayed his judgment."

God replied, "The duration of Cain's mercy will largely depend on Cain himself; Our end goal is, as always, for man to repent. Cain is a very healthy man, and it will take a long time for him to feel the physical consequences of his actions, if he ever does. A painful and slow death is the blessing Cain will probably need in order to repent, but that could take nine hundred years or even double that."

No matter what decision was made about Cain, there would be many more equally consequential decisions for a good Father to agonize over in the years to come. The decision to go ahead with procreation was irreversible, and because of that the Trinity's choices in connection to God's creation would be limited for all eternity. Procreation gave fleshly beings an eternal nature, and the decisions made by these eternal beings would now limit the Trinity's capacity in countless ways.

The Holy Spirit, looking ahead to what would now be a bloody future, was more mindful than the Others of just how consequential this decision would be and was hesitant to agree with allowing mercy for Cain.

"This decision before Us will severely limit how far into the future We can see. While I can see no more effective way for Our children to learn these lessons, this dispensation of mercy will be very painful for Us to watch." Then the Holy Spirit warned the Others, "This is not a long-term solution."

"Yes, mercy is only temporary," the Son added. "There will have to be a more permanent solution for Cain and all others who choose to live in the way of Cain. A solution for those who are faithful——such as Abel, the firstborn of faith——will also be needed."

"Yes, my Son, I agree. You are more than able to provide the way for those who choose the path of Abel if You are willing to do so," the Father said.

"I am," responded the Son. "We knew what the risks were after Adam ate from the tree, and yet We chose to go forward with procreation," He added.

"Cain has set in motion a series of events that will be very painful for all of Us to watch, should We choose to watch. Our wisdom will be seen in Our children."

"The Son is wise. He truly loves Our children in a truly selfless way," the Holy Spirit proclaimed.

"My story is yet to be written," the Son pointed out.

The Father looked on with love and compassion while the Son was making the case for mankind. "You do not have to suffer, My Son. If it comes to that, then it will be by Your choice that You accept the bruising."

"Yes, Father, I know. Flesh is a burden that I may well someday know. It is worth My sacrifice."

"But mercy alone will not safeguard Cain's life. We have written the concepts of right and wrong in the hearts of man. Vengeance will rise in the land," said the Holy Spirit.

"Vengeance is Mine alone," proclaimed the Son. "Vengeance can only be administered in the Present." (KJV Deut. 32:35)

"Then it is settled. We will bestow mercy upon Cain, affording him a long life in the hope that he will repent," God announced.

The Spirit added, "Cain's future will be a painful one and that is the best We can hope for, as his pain may lead him to repent."

Once this decision had been made, an angel appeared on earth from the heavens and proclaimed, "All who know Cain will know his mark——a mark of protection, an angel. (WYC Gen. 4:15) The angel will protect Cain from vengeance. If anyone attempts to take the Son's vengeance from Him, vengeance will come down upon them sevenfold that of Cain's."

The mark, an angelic being sent to reside within the murderer ensuring his survival and another blood line on earth——the new blood line bringing a significant new dynamic on the one contiguous land mass created for man.

"The line of Cain will produce new challenges for Us." The Holy Spirit informed the Others. "And new opportunities as well." Noted the Son. "A Separation is good, it opens up choices for all men, and choice is the only child of the freedom that all men yearn for," said God. The Spirit viewing the possible outcomes added, "If the dynamics of two blood lines is good then, three and perhaps far more will be better yet." On this, the Three agreed.

The mark of Cain would come to mean different things to different people, but every man, woman, and child would know that killing Cain was forbidden and that to succeed in such an attempt would be eternally risky.

God understood that the decision to show Cain mercy was going to have complicated ramifications. All actions of God or man are perpetuated for all eternity, but this particular decision carried more significance and was of a magnitude of complexity beyond any that had ever come before. It would assuredly produce very mixed results.

This is how it would be with free beings——as they would be capable of love, so would they be capable of rebellion. The choice had been difficult to make but would have been even more difficult to avoid. It was inevitable that God would have to show the world mercy at some time and in some place. Mercy would be a fact of life, and as God withheld judgment upon earth each and every day, the effects of mercy would become known.

In this matter, God's choices had been limited by God's Son. God had been compelled to protect Cain in order to preserve the rights of His only eternal Son, and this would inevitably create confusion among men. The added dimension to protect Cain would likely prove to be just as confusing to man. This mark of protection would assuredly be misinterpreted as a pardon. But it would in no way be mercy if Cain were to be killed by someone who lacked the proper standing to judge Cain.

Adam and his Square were in part designed to judge civil matters, such as disputes over trade or contractual obligations. But no criminal matter had ever been brought before him, let alone a capital crime such as murder. Without a criminal justice system to put forward someone of standing to judge Cain, there was the real possibility that Cain's life might be ended by yet another act of murder. This would escalate the present problem, as God would then be faced with determining consequences for Cain's murderer. So, the correct decision had indeed been made——preserve the rights of the Son as One with proper standing.

While the mark of Cain would protect him from a vigilante seeking justice for the murder of his brother, it certainly would not prohibit any other earthly judgments short of death that may befall him. Furthermore, it would not help him as he roamed the wilderness in an attempt to escape his past. The mark of Cain would be the instrument of mercy that would prevent Cain's murder, nothing else.

God, through the wisdom of His Spirit, spoke to His Son: "I hope that every father going forward will look to the consequences of Our decision——the intended good results and the unavoidable bad results, the extent of which are not yet known——when making their assuredly similar decisions regarding their children. Our actions will have been deemed worthy if many gain wisdom from Our efforts."

"Yes Father," the Son agreed.

As Adam mourned the loss of his faithful son, Abel, the cries for vengeance increased daily among the sons and daughters of Eve. Adam struggled to understand the wishes of the Son that vengeance was to be His and His alone. *Why does the Son want vengeance withheld for Himself? Is this personal to Him?* Adam came to the conclusion that the Son had some special personal plan that he, Adam, knew nothing about. He decided that he would just trust that the Son had a good reason for reserving vengeance unto Himself.

Adam was the judge among the people in the Square, and they looked to him for justice in all matters. Now, with this first capital crime, Adam was looked to by all in the Square for a remedy.

Adam was torn by his love for his sons, but he knew that justice for his faithful son Abel had to come first. In his grieving mind, justice delayed was justice denied, as he struggled to understand why Cain had been afforded mercy by God.

After a few days, the people in the Square began pressuring Adam with inquiries as to what would be done.

"Father, what will happen if another brother or sister takes a life?" Elez asked.

"I'm working on it, Elez. I'm working on it," Adam said, trying to avoid committing to anything just yet.

Another daughter asked him, "Father, is Cain ever coming back?"

"I don't think so," Adam replied.

"Father, why not?" she continued.

"Well, I don't know for sure, but I would guess he is afraid to come back," Adam said.

"Does he have reason to fear returning?"

Adam was not prepared to confront these issues and questions, and the worst part of his dilemma was that his indecision was obvious to all of his children.

The questions from his children quickly devolved into grumbling, and this caused him to reconsider his impulse to judge Cain. Now he was glad that Cain could not be found, as this would give him more time to consider what must be done.

Adam's children could see that he was working on a solution or process for dealing with Abel's murder. His efforts would afford him some time in the Square with his children, where he could think about God's motivations in both cursing yet protecting Cain.

Possibly Cain had been given mercy in order to give Adam time to devise and build a criminal justice system. Because, with no criminal justice system in place, if Cain had been dragged into the Square with blood on his hands chaos would have ensued——brother against brother——in a vain attempt to get some kind of justice for Abel.

So Adam had yet another blessing to thank God for. Trying to figure out what God wanted him to do was becoming second nature to Adam. That exhilarated him, as he knew that only the wisest of men could seek out and discover God's intentions.

Adam reasoned that Abel's murder would not be the only murder ever. Even if it turned out that it was, he intended to be prepared for the next capital crime just in case. Being prepared, and far more importantly being seen to be prepared would be a deterrent far beyond any proclamation Adam could ever make.

For this to work out, Adam would need to know and understand the reasoning behind God's actions in showing mercy to Cain. He needed answers for his children in the Square. He needed to devise a forum or system that could handle these matters. Adam loved the Square and was dedicated to keeping it as peaceful as possible for his children. Wisdom was the only possible means to that end.

Adam might never know all of the reasons why God had decided to show Cain mercy, but he was depending on God's reasons being good reasons. Adam had long understood that God was in no way arbitrary. But discovering His reasoning might take some time.

As he thought more about God's decision, Adam could come up with only one theory: God wanted man to deal with the capital crimes of man. Adam had judged many civil disputes, but crime would be a much more difficult issue to tackle and capital crime the most difficult of all. It was going to require a significant amount of work and reflection to get this started, let alone to get it right.

That God had exiled Cain certainly helped. This would give Adam a window of time and the right atmosphere within the Square to work on a new branch of justice that would be equipped to hear capital crimes. If Adam did well, either there would be no more capital crimes, as the people would sense there was no escaping justice; or God would feel comfortable enough with Adam's justice system to let man deal with the crime.

Adam didn't know how much time he would need for this. Some people talked openly about how they wanted Cain to be punished for what he had done, and Adam tried to calm those concerns by assuring people that he was indeed working on it. He cautioned everyone: without a formal process in place, any vengeance will likely lead to yet further chaos and we will likely end up far worse off.

As Adam pondered the task of creating a criminal justice system, he thought of another possible reason why God had shown Cain mercy. Although God had decided to spare Cain's life——an earthly judgment, short of death——meant that Adam could still punish Cain in countless other ways.

The mark would protect Cain's life on earth but could not protect his freedom or his resources. Restitution was the only recourse Adam had available in civil proceedings, so he began planning an adaptation of that for use in criminal proceedings. Adam had much work to do, as restitution for crime would be a very different and far more complicated matter than restitution for civil disputes.

Adam felt he was making progress in convincing his children in the Square to buy in to some of his plans, but then there was Abel's grieving widow, Eva, to deal with. Eva was irate about Adam's apparently forgiving stance towards Cain. Eva and Abel had been married for only a short time before Cain struck down his brother. Distraught, she was becoming increasingly passionate in her pursuit of justice for Abel. Eva was normally quite restrained when talking with her father, but she was becoming much less so, as it appeared to her that Adam had little interest in making Cain pay for his crime.

"Father, my brothers and sisters are spreading rumors of how you plan to deal with the murder of my husband. I, more than any other, need to know what your plans are. The loss of my husband has brought me much sadness and grief." Eva felt that Cain's life should be taken in accordance with the rule of "an ox for an ox" that was common in civil proceedings. But, as God had forbidden vengeance unto death for Cain, Adam had the unenviable task of explaining to Eva why no one could seek to take Cain's life.

Adam tried to calm his daughter. "Eva, I have a few ideas on how to proceed. Please keep in mind that killing Cain is not an option. But there are other things that can be done to seek out justice to quench the vengeance that we all feel the need for. I will need only another week to sort out the ideas I have, and then we can go over them together," Adam promised.

Adam had so much more to deal with than Eva's issues: a dead son, a son turned murderer, his duties as a father, and now his duties

as a criminal judge. But, as promised, a week later he met with Eva
again to discuss the issue.

"Eva, I need to develop a system to deal with crime. As you
know, we don't have one now. Over the next few weeks, I will make
a decision on a just way to proceed. The system will be designed to
discover the facts and to judge the accused based on those facts. You
will be the first to know the details as they emerge, and perhaps Cain
will someday stand as the accused. But I need more time," Adam
told his first born child.

Eva acquiesced, but she was thinking, *Accused? But Cain is
guilty.* She held her tongue though. Eva was not pleased, but she
could see that Adam was working on the matter, so she decided to
wait and see.

Adam had many ideas about criminal justice–one of his first
ideas was recusal——because he didn't believe that fathers could
impartially judge their own sons. But in this particular case he was
the only judge available, yet another reason——perhaps——why
God had given Cain mercy. Adam thought that one brother judging
another would be acceptable, maybe even a good thing. But the idea
of a father judging his own son was problematic to him. He thought
that God might find it so as well. A son is largely the product of the
wisdom and work of his father, and when he is older he is a
reflection of that wisdom, or lack thereof. So a father judging his son
would really be a father judging himself.

Men of standing would have to be found to serve as judges.
Those men would be providing a service to the Square and to society
and would be rewarded with even greater standing. After a few days,
he went to discuss things with Eva once again.

"Eva, my plan for future situations such as this is to sit in
judgment of the matter, but this one is very difficult for me. Cain is
my son. As a judge I would inevitably be biased, which limits my

standing on the issue. I think it wise for us to just wait and let things sit for some time while I contemplate all that is at hand."

Eva waited while Adam finished putting his thoughts together. "Eva," Adam continued, "trying Cain and judging Cain are simple matters that one of your brothers or sisters could easily do. But as for how to make a guilty man pay, at this moment I have no answer for that. I do not know of a way for a guilty man to pay for the crime of murder. I don't believe it is even possible."

Eva could see his point. *Even taking Cain's life would in no way pay for Abel's life, but it would make me feel better and perhaps deter others from doing what he did. Maybe this issue is much more profound than my own need for vengeance? But, then again, whose needs right now are above mine as the aggrieved?* Eva was now thinking for herself.

Adam laid out his arguments for Eva: "Justice on earth, to the extent that it is possible, will be an elusive and difficult thing to achieve. Yet that is my goal," Adam told her. "Whatever system we devise must have, as its goal, not only restitution and punishment to comfort the aggrieved but a sentiment among the people that justice exists. I must be very careful that nobody, especially the Square itself, benefits from any crimes that are committed.

"Punishment must be designed to be painful in order to discourage perpetrators from repeating their actions but also to prevent others in the community from committing any infractions at all. So, what types of pain would yield repentance? If it is unjust in any way, it might encourage retribution and further harden the heart of the criminal.

"I don't think that long-term discomfort, such as confinement, would be an effective or even just method of exacting vengeance. I have concluded that intense pain of short duration would be the most effective way to bring about repentance. But who should administer the vengeance, and where on the body should that punishment be carried out?

"Should we bruise the fat of their posterior unto repentance as if they were a five-year-old child? If the punishment is not seen as just by most, it will have failed in its purpose," he concluded.

"Whipping Cain as if he had done nothing more significant than bearing false witness would hardly constitute justice in this matter," Eva cried.

"Eva, please, let's reason together. God felt so strongly about His prohibition against taking Cain's life that He took measures to make it extremely difficult for anybody to do so. Don't you think He must have had a very good reason for doing that? Let us take the time to figure out what God wants us to do," Adam pleaded, "and we will be in a better position to rightfully avenge the death of Abel that would result in a just outcome."

"What if God's reason for showing Cain mercy was that He is not yet sure what man is capable of? What if He is waiting to see just how evil man might become before He is ready to give us further direction on handling these issues? If that is the case, then the more successful we are in handling this situation, the better we will know how to restrict future crimes. Eva, I am the one who discovered sacrifice by looking back at what God did in the garden. Given enough time to analyze how God handled Cain's exile and protection, I believe that I can determine how God would have us handle crime." Adam could only hope that his words had won Eva over for now.

"Father, now it is my turn to speak. You have clearly given this a lot of thought. In my grief I have not been capable of thinking so clearly about these matters. So, thank you for your effort and for sharing your thoughts and ideas with me."

Adam smiled, relieved that his reasoning may have won the day.

"I understand that this is not easy for you, but I also sense that this is not as important to you as it should be," Eva went on. "When the pain of guilt was plaguing you, you worked on it day and night until you found a cure, but I don't see you working day and night for a cure for my pain. Father, this is plaguing me, and if you don't act, I will."

"Then help me figure this out so we can cure your pain as I cured mine," Adam replied.

"I am trying, Father. That is why I am here today," Eva went on. "What if God exiled Cain because that is what was best for society? What if his exile is meant to be a type of confinement, keeping him away from others?"

"I don't believe God would ever approve of long-term captivity for man," Adam said. "No, I will not make a cage for man; cages are for animals. Caging an animal in no way takes away its rage. I can't imagine a cage taking the rage from man either. Even if the cage were as beautiful as the Garden of Eden itself, it would still be a cage," Adam told Eva.

"What if God didn't exile Cain? What if the words we heard from God were just an acknowledgement of what He knew Cain would do———run?" Eva asked, as she wondered aloud.

"That is a thought. That very well could be. Exile is very different from being a captive. I don't believe that the size of the world is arbitrary in comparison to the size of man. So it must be large enough that no man could ever feel like a captive, much less one imprisoned by God," Adam said.

As Eva left him that afternoon, Adam, though pleased with how things had gone with her, realized that her desire for vengeance was still with her and that she would not be letting go of it any time soon. So he would need to put more effort into this, immediately.

Eva understood Adam's concerns, but this did not temper her desire to avenge Abel's murder. The only thing holding her at bay now was that she needed time to process the matter. She thought over Adam's concerns, but her thoughts were not taking her in the direction in which Adam had hoped to lead her. In fact, she felt increasingly alone in what she now considered to be her own personal fight for justice. Eva was the persistent type, but the combination of the murder of her husband and the lack of justice for him was transforming her persistence, a normal and good human trait, into obsession.

Cain's brothers and sisters tended to see Cain's exile as part of a curse, being separated from them and the benefits they all enjoyed from their interactions. But Eva saw it as a blessing to Cain. In a way she was correct. As Adam and Eve's exile from the garden had been both a curse and a blessing, so it was with Cain's exile. The difference now was that, while actual guards had been put in place to prevent Adam and Eve from re-entering the garden, it was his family's desire for vengeance that kept Cain from being able to re-enter society. Eva did not want Cain to have the benefit of this blessing of exile. She wanted him back so that Adam, and perhaps even God, would be motivated to act.

Her resolve simmered for a few days. When she could no longer restrain herself, she sought Adam out to confront him, formally and publicly, about his duties as the judge of the Square. She bided her time until she found Adam among her siblings in the Square, and then she called out to him with authority.

"Adam, I have more standing in the murder of my husband than does God. My rights are paramount here and will remain so as long as Cain lives."

Clearly caught off guard, Adam turned slowly to face his daughter, who was standing a few arm-lengths from him, as Eva's brothers and sisters formed a circle around them.

As they looked on with great interest, Eva repeated even louder, "I, Eva, widow of Abel, have more standing than God in this matter!"

All stood in stunned silence. She did not have to explain herself, and the crowd did not question her; they all knew her very well, and they knew how she had suffered because of the loss of her husband.

"Your son——my brother——has murdered my husband. I am the one who has been wronged in this, not only God. I am the one who should decide Cain's earthly fate for as long as he lives." said Eva.

Adam fumbled for some words he could use to calm her. "Eva, I understand your pain and I share your concerns, but at this point there is nothing I can do, we have been over this in private, making a guilty man pay is an extremely difficult task, even for God."

What else could he say in the face of such an argument? He could hear his sons and daughters muttering to each other and reaching the conclusion that Eva was right. She had won her brothers and sisters to her side; they were nodding their heads in agreement with Eva's argument.

The support of her siblings gave her strength, and she clung to that strength. "Let us seek out Cain together as a family and return him to the Square to face me," she demanded. "Then we will see how he answers for his crime." Once again, she received great encouragement from her brothers and sisters in the crowd. She added, "Please, Adam, don't offend me again by calling the murderer Cain, the 'accused.'"

The crowd anxiously awaited Adam's response, but there was nowhere he could go with this. His argument was not going to win the day or the crowd. With a deep sigh, he spoke.

"God has shown Cain mercy, and God's word will be final here today."

Adam turned to walk away, but Eva was not finished.

"That will not be the final word," Eva lamented. "God has not spoken here. We have only heard the voice of Adam. God has been silent. I will defer to God in His decision to spare Cain's life, but beyond that Cain must pay for his evildoing, to the extent that a man can pay."

This stopped Adam in his tracks, and he turned to face his daughter. He had run out of words. He had run out of arguments. He was overwhelmed with grief because he felt like a failed father and a failed son as well. Abel was dead; Cain was a murderer; and his love for his sons was undermining his relationship with his beloved Eva. Adam cherished his Eva as much as he did his boys——after all, she was literally the first born child.

Adam took Eva lovingly by the hand and said, "Eva, I am so sorry for your loss. I truly wish there was something I could do." Very few could hear or see what Adam had said to Eva, but silence fell upon his children as Eva showed signs of relenting.

Feeling defeated, with her head slowly falling forward and her eyes closed, Eva felt a tear beginning to form. She furrowed her brow tightly, trying to hold back that tear, but this only caused the tear to grow in size.

Then she could feel that single tear as it rolled slowly down her cheek. Eva opened her eyes and watched that tear fall ever so slowly from her face. The moment was so intensely emotional that, to Eva, it seemed the tear was falling in slow motion. It seemed to take forever to drop from her chin to the ground.

Her heart was pounding as that single tear made a tiny splash in the dust in front of her feet. For Eva, time stood still. She could hear no sounds, and all she could see was the tiny puff of dust that her tear sent into the air.

The beating of her heart was all she felt and all she heard. It was loud and it was slow. After several more beats . . . she regained her sense of hearing and her awareness of her surroundings. That single tear that she had focused on so intensely had focused her thoughts and her purpose in a bold new way, and she had more to say indeed.

Looking across the Square, she saw Adam walking away and pronounced, "Mercy, you say? You quote God's decision while you ignore His intent." Her voice grew bolder with every word, and it was clear that she was not going to relent.

Eva continued, "Your back may be turned, but I don't need to see your face to know that you are as sad as I am determined. This will not change unless and until we act."

Adam, still with his back to her, mumbled, "Eva, do what you think is right. I can't and won't stop you. Eva, with my broken heart, I wish you well."

Eva, now looking into the heavens, said to Adam, "Father, I love you." There was no sound from the other children as they looked on to see Adam weakening against his daughter's words. Adam's head fell, and his eyes glistened with emotion. Eva, sensing a change in her father, decided to continue. "Your reluctance to stand in judgment of your son is clear, and it is seen by all. Your standing, not mine, has been greatly diminished before all who watch and listen here on this day."

Astutely sensing that Adam had said all that he would say, Eva turned to face her siblings and said, "With your words, along with your failure to act, Father, you have ceased to be the leader of the Square that bears your name." She looked back and saw her father walking slowly away with his head down. Eva walked away too, but her head was held high. There was nothing left to be said.

Adam, still downcast, was shocked by the things that his daughter had said to him. But her bold words were causing him to question his decisions. More than ever, he was beginning to grasp just how crucial all his decisions about the Cain situation would be. Eva's determination had helped him to confront his duties as her father. Adam was now starting to understand that what God had proclaimed in this matter would have little practical effect on what he was obligated to do, to properly father his children.

STANDING OF A FATHER

Adam had long understood that a son's actions can limit his father's actions, but now he had a new understanding of something akin to that. He saw that a father can't always be limited by another father. Fathers have duties regardless of the actions of others. So, when a son becomes a father and his duties turn to his own son, he feels less like a son and more like a father. Furthermore, a father's duties to his younger ones will always take precedence over his duty to his older children, to his father, and even to society.

Finally, and of great importance, there was the issue of hypocrisy. The father's prior actions should never be a consideration in limiting the actions of the wiser and stronger man he has hopefully become. Even if the current actions of a father fall short, as they surely will from time to time, he should never use that as an excuse not to teach his children what is good, decent, and just. When the children become aware of their father's hypocrisy, their father should not deny it——he should teach them the tricky lesson: remind them that they also will be parents someday and will be faced with similar challenges when their own children's paths go astray. Teach your children to "do what I say and not what I do," though this is a very narrow trail to pass, to be sure.

The paths to wisdom are narrow, as far too few choose to navigate them. One can only travel these narrow roads on one's knees in prayer.

If the children witness the humility of their father, they will observe the sincerity that guides him. The strength of that guidance can only be limited by his flesh, his character, and his foundation upon past wisdom.

Wisdom can only mature in man when its origin is acknowledged before each new step is taken; wisdom cannot grow otherwise. It is step by step that man discerns the truth, and his foundation will be strong if each step is taken knowing that the previous one was wise.

Adam contemplated all the decisions that being a father required him to make, and then he thought about his Father's duties in Heaven and on earth.

The Father's duties are great and complicated, and they have the potential to put Him in conflict with His obligations to His many children. Adam was confronted with the realization that his current dilemma was a consequence of God's duty to His Son. Adam had no doubt that God had been just in allowing vengeance to be reserved unto the Son, but Adam also had a duty to his daughter. Should his ability to fulfill his own obligations be so significantly affected by the obligations of his Father? Adam had stepped back far enough in his mind to gain wisdom, but he was unsure of just what steps to take going forward.

Adam began to feel doubtful about how he had handled Abel's murder, and now he considered taking a physical step back to seek out Cain. Should he have sought out his son and judged him? Maybe he should have enslaved Cain to Eva to take the place of the slain Abel. Would that have pleased God? What was of primary importance? That Adam listen to his Father, or that he be a father to Eva and to Cain? Or was there some middle ground that he should be treading?

Adam was confronted with the need to understand God's desires, his own duties as a father to Eva and Cain, and his obligations as an earthly judge. Adam's standing in his Square was great, therefore he had the power to judge should he decide to. The constraints placed on man by another Father looking out for His Son were diminishing in Adam's consideration, as his duty to father his children came first. *I can, if I decide to, give Eva the justice due to her as the aggrieved. But I may need to step back, if it is not too late?*

Whatever action Adam decided to take would affect literally everyone. He concentrated first on the problem of the justice due Eva. *Perhaps Eva, and only Eva, could justly demand a punishment that might be in conflict with the rights that the Father had reserved for His Son. Thus, the onus would be on my Father to Judge on this matter——whether to deny me my standing, or to deny Eva her standing?* This line of thought took Adam to one conclusion, but he feared that he had delayed too long to be able to act on it. As Eva's father, he should have given her the standing she was due regardless of the desires of any other Father. Adam would have to learn, discern, and decide how to proceed with his fatherly obligations——and the sooner the better. If he acted wisely, perhaps he could prevent further crime from occurring in the Square and on the rest of the earth.

I believe that vengeance in the hearts of men cannot be satisfied unless a life can be taken to compensate for the loss of a life. But I will need to teach my children that, at least for now, the afterlife is where justice will be eternally administered, and whatever earthly system we devise to avenge crime will merely be temporary and will offer only a partially just resolution for all involved.

While Adam contemplated these complex issues on behalf of his children there was grumbling in the Square, but his children could see that he was struggling to find a solution to the inequities that Eva had brought to light. But, for now, the fratricide had not impaired the fraternity among the brothers in the Square.

Adam addressed the Square: "I do not believe that my Father ever intended——nor wants or imagines——sparing Cain an eternal judgment. I tell you now, and it is true, that upon Cain's death, Cain will face the Son. Then he will receive a judgment based on what transpires during the remaining days of his life on earth. The mercy that has been shown Cain is temporal and temporary; his past, his future, his choices and his sacrifices will be judged rightly upon his death."

While Adam struggled with the dilemma of how to justly handle criminal behavior, Eva suffered no such struggle; she received no indication from God or from her father that her stance was wrong. In her mind, justice delayed truly was justice denied. It was clear now to everyone watching that Abel's death had taken a far worse toll on Eva than it had on Adam. After all, it was she whose husband and brother——the love of her life——had been taken from her without cause. That night, Eva returned alone to the now empty Square to pray. Though it seemed that her brothers and sisters supported her cause, she was there alone at that moment, and she felt alone.

"Father, I love you. You know this to be true." Tears flowed from her eyes. When she regained her composure, she continued, "Father, there are no men here to do what needs to be done. Must I, alone, do what justice demands? Can anyone help me?"

At that moment, she felt a warm and calming presence by her side, and she opened her eyes to discover that it was Abel's favorite tracking dog, Nine. The beautiful animal began to nudge her in an odd way. As she petted the dog, she felt as though Nine was trying to communicate something to her. After a few moments, she understood that the dog wanted her to follow him.

"Did God send you?" Eva asked him, as if Nine could answer her, and she slowly followed him as he walked. Eva was encouraged and puzzled as to what was going on. *Could this be a coincidence?* As they walked, the dog frequently looked back to be sure that she was still following him. Then Eva asked, "Nine, can you lead me to

Cain?" Nine slowly turned and returned to her side. It was obvious that Eva was now Nine's master and that he would lead her if she would follow him, perhaps to Cain.

Thus encouraged, she vowed that this was not over. She would seek out the justice due to her; she would risk the consequences, regardless of the pain that might cause her.

She was again following Nine when she took a moment to look back to Adam's Square as if she would never see it again. She trusted that it was no coincidence that Nine had come to her aid, nor did she believe it to be a coincidence that she was suddenly recalling these words of her father's: *Don't ever give God credit for something unless you're absolutely certain He had a hand in it, as credit can turn to blame very quickly. God is never to blame for our decisions.* Eva, torn between these two "coincidences," made *her* decision as she headed off to hunt for Cain by Nine.

When Adam discovered that Eva had gone missing, it was no mystery to him what had happened. She had no attachments to hold her to the Square. Having been married only a short time, she had no children, and she was alienated from her father due to his inaction. She really had only one course to take . . . she would follow her *good* obsession——seeking justice.

— 7 —

MERCY AND A MARRIAGE

Cain was still on the move, still on the run, still pursuing an escape, and his emotions were still running high. Time seemed to pass quickly as he pushed on through his fatigue and pain. He ran aimlessly for long periods of time, not knowing if the sounds of pursuers behind him were real or imagined.

He felt a presence close to him. He did not know if this was real or imagined either, but the feeling became more pronounced and mystifying with each passing day. *What is this strange feeling that follows me, that aids me, yet mystifies me at the same time? Am I marked in some way?*

As Cain's body became more distressed, as his endurance dwindled, his emotions broke through to the surface. In his weakened state he cried out, "Father. This is more than I can bear. (KJV Gen. 4:13) They will catch me, and they will kill me! I am marked as a murderer. I know because I have seen the mark."

Then, for the very first time, Cain heard the voice of God. "Cain, where is your brother? His blood cries out to Me." (KJV Gen. 4:10)

Dead silence was Cain's response. Then the arrogant and foolish Cain retorted, "Am I my brother's keeper?" (KJV Gen. 4:9) With his rhetoric, Cain was knowingly mocking God, and this added insult to the injured in Heaven.

"Cain shall be marked so that no man shall slay him," said the Son. (WYC Gen. 4:15)

The mark was for protection and not for condemnation? As Cain finally realized this, he was astonished by the meaning. *Could this possibly be true?* Then he heard another voice.

"Vengeance is Mine," the Son proclaimed. "Cain's life shall be spared, and anyone who attempts to take his life will suffer that vengeance sevenfold." (KJV Romans 12:19, Gen. 4:15)

Cain could hear this pronouncement as clear as day. He did not know if this message was being heard by everybody on earth, but he was sure that it was real and not imagined. Cain could sense that the Son was standing at the right hand of the Father, which denoted His great standing within the Godhead, and Cain believed.

Cain continued to listen carefully, not wanting to miss a single word. For the first time in Cain's life, what God had to say was of great interest to him. He listened carefully but heard nothing more. For a moment, his spirit felt a semblance of the peace it had always longed for. He waited a few more moments in silence, hoping that God wouldn't attach new conditions to the protection He had granted him. When he heard no more, Cain felt an enormous burden lift from his shoulders; he would live.

Why exactly God had granted him a reprieve, Cain was not sure and his selfish mind put little thought into it. One thing he did put a lot of thought into was where he was going to live——in Nod, otherwise known as the wilderness. (KJV Gen. 4:16) Cain never felt that returning to the Square was an option, so he never really considered it. While the news from God was in one sense very good, the truth was that not much had changed. Cain was still guilty of murder. He was still on the run from his community, and he was not fully convinced that his brothers and sisters of the Square would obey God's orders to spare his life. (KJV Gen. 4:14–16) One thing he was sure of, though: he was alone. Now, survival itself would be a daily challenge, even for the mighty Cain. He would have no one else to depend on for some time to come, perhaps even forever. Cain was a marked man; he was just not marked for death.

MERCY ON EARTH

Over the next millennium or two, the impact of the decision to grant Cain mercy would be fully realized. The better men understood why God had done this, the better it would be, at some point, for earth's inhabitants.

Adam's desperate efforts to develop a judicial system quickly seemed to be too little and perhaps too late. God's perceived pardon of Cain confused the many men and women who were inclined to react first and think later——they had difficulty understanding that the concepts of justice, vengeance, and mercy, though related, are significantly different.

The children of Adam and Eve had a very powerful sense of justice that they were born with and further borne out of their respect for their parents, and for the most part this had kept the peace in the early days of life on earth. Now the murderer Cain, who had been rebellious from the womb who was somewhat void of those innate restricting elements would seek out a new life apart from the others. This dynamic was yet to be seen, but chances were not good for any progeny he may sire.

MERCY'S SONG

With all the unknown that would become known,
Man would now learn what he needed to know.

For God to know man and man to know God,
From the tree in the garden to the Circle of Nod,
The time had come for God to know man and man to know God.
For mercy was essential at some point in His story,
For God to know man and man to know God.

His story would be written on the fallout of mercy,
For God to know man and man to know God,
Mercy was given from the garden of God to the Circle of Nod.
From the tree in the garden to the Circle of Nod,
For God to know man and man to know God.
In Cain was first seen the mercy that God would give to the world,
For God to know man and man to know God.
Many would know while many would not that mercy was given,
For God to know man and man to know God.

Was it enough for a man to concede that mercy he need,
For God to know man and man to know God?

For far too many the lesson was unclear, that mercy was given,
For God to know man and man to love God.

THE HUNTRESS AND THE FUGITIVE

The marriage of Eva and Abel had been cut dreadfully short by
Abel's murder. Eva's next marriage would be as tragic albeit in a very

different way. The traumatic bonding of the huntress and the fugitive would be the cause of much more suffering, as Eva would mistake Cain's lack of abuse for kindness and repentance.

Cain was still on the run, but after a few more days of travel he became paranoid and his actions irrational. He was utterly exhausted, and he needed a few days to recover. He had discovered a cave in a secluded area behind some large trees and vines and decided that this was a spot where he could rest his weary body and soul for a while.

After a couple of days spent close to his hideaway, Cain was gathering food and drink when the unthinkable caught him totally by surprise. He felt a sharp, stinging pain in the back of his skull that was unlike anything he had ever felt before. He was being attacked. He dropped to the ground and as the attack continued, he heard a woman's voice that was screaming obscenities at him, each one followed by his name. As he struggled to get up, he saw a familiar sight. It looked like one of Abel's tracking dogs, Nine. How could that be possible? Then he recognized the voice, and when he was able to regain his senses, turned to face his adversary. It was Eva, his sister and the wife of the brother he had murdered. She continued to strike at Cain repeatedly with the sharpened stick, her fists, and her feet. She was getting her due vengeance, and even though God had shown Cain mercy, she adamantly disagreed with that decision.

"You killed my husband! You will pay. I promise you will pay," Eva screamed over and over to a stunned and now, a badly bleeding Cain.

"But I've been marked by an angel. You cannot attack me," Cain cried, astonished that the angel wasn't doing his job.

"Apparently *I can* attack you, you fool," Eva hurled at him as she continued her barrage of blows with every ounce of her strength.

"But, for disobeying God you will be punished sevenfold of my punishment," Cain shouted, hoping this would discourage his enraged sister from continuing her onslaught. Though Eva was a woman, she was the first born of Eve and therefore very strong and powerful. She and Cain had nearly perfect human physiques and were near equals as they clashed.

"Hah. Just the way that you were punished for disobeying God?" she cried. She had a valid point. Eva, having caused Cain a considerable amount of blood loss, felt a satisfying moment of justice. Blood was pouring from Cain's worst wound. Eva looked at her weapon and it also was blood soaked and it started to cover her hands as well. This satisfied her craving for vengeance, at least momentarily, and she slowed her attack.

Cain, now able to stand again, kept a watchful eye on Eva and put some distance between them as he began tending to his injuries. Both of them were panting heavily, and neither knew how this might end.

As Eva caught her breath, her thirst for vengeance welled up again. She circled around the wounded murderer planning her next move, one that would finish him off.

"Eva, please stop your attack. Please. I am sorry for what I did to our brother. I was wrong!" Cain shouted.

Eva was surprised by Cain's apology and slowed her pacing as she contemplated this turn of events. Cain also thought about what he had just said. It had been a truthful admission, and this surprised him. *I do feel sorry. I was wrong. Am I sincere in my apology?* Cain wondered.

Eva, after some consideration, discounted his contrition as insincere and resumed her circling as she sought an opening to strike him a killing blow.

He pleaded with her again as she got closer to him. "Please, Eva, I am sorry for what I have taken from you. Truly, I am." This time

Eva thought he sounded more sincere. Then she noticed something that she found far more puzzling than his professed sorrow.

Cain could not see his most severe wound because it was on the back of his neck, but Eva could see it. When he took his hand away from it, she could see that the bleeding had all but stopped. *How can that be?* she wondered.

She was positive that this particular injury had been deep and serious, but now it looked almost superficial. While she was distracted by this confusing state of affairs, Cain seized her sharpened stick and shoved her away from him.

He grasped the weapon with both hands and seemed to be about to strike her with it. Unafraid, Eva raised her head and put her arms up in defense. But, to her surprise, he smashed the stick against the outside wall of his cave and handed the pieces back to her saying, "Eva, I really am sorry for what I did. I was wrong to kill your husband. Our brother was a good man."

Eva shook her head in confusion. It seemed to her that his remorse was genuine, but she could not reconcile his remorse with the fact that he had killed his brother.

Eva looked at the remains of her weapon. Her thirst for vengeance could not be as easily shattered as her fighting staff had been.

The sense of relief that the blood of Cain had brought her was fading rapidly, and Eva now had to face the fact that her mission to seek justice for Abel had failed. As Cain was stronger and able to take control of her and the situation, the consequences of this failure could be drastic for her.

Cain could easily see that his sister was now lost and confused. Though he was a murderer, he was fully aware of the right and proper way to treat a family member who was in distress, even when he was the cause of that stress. He could see how much his actions had hurt his sister, and after a few moments of silence he reached out to Eva in an attempt to comfort her.

"Eva, where will you go now?" Cain asked her quietly.

"I don't know," Eva said. "I don't know."

"Eva, I really meant what I said. I am sorry for taking my brother's life. When I apologized, the words came out in the reactionary manner that is typical of me. But, seeing your grief plainly now, I must say it again and make you believe that I truly mean it. I am sorry," Cain said, but he showed little sign of actual emotion as he said these words.

He looks and sounds like the Cain I know, the Cain I raised . . . detached, fighting some internal battle, not letting anybody else in, and perhaps struggling against Dad? Eva thought.

Cain had been as sincere as he was capable of being. But an apology, no matter how sincere, could not change the past. And it paid an insignificant portion of the debt that was owed to Eva.

Cain was struggling to reconcile the injuries he was nursing now with what he had been told by the Son about being protected. Then he thought, *I almost wish Eva had succeeded.*

But, inevitably, his thoughts soon returned to his own needs. Eva's presence was an opportunity to have a companion and to minimize the effects of his curse.

He could try to manipulate her as he had often manipulated his brother to get what he wanted or needed. This would be more challenging than it would be to force her to stay, but the situation would be far less difficult to manage in the long run if he succeeded. He would wait for the right moment to make his first overture.

Eva looked again at Cain and was amazed. *The wound on his neck has already stopped bleeding and seems to be almost healed.* Eva then looked at his blood on her hands. *I don't ever want to wash these hands; the sight of Cain's blood soothes my soul.* She closed her eyes and savored the moment, knowing that the memory would fade quickly.

Her dog, Nine, gave her a nudge of comfort, and she opened her eyes. As she petted her loving companion, the blood disappeared from her hands into the fur of her only friend.

Eva looked at Nine, hoping for another sign from him like the one he had given before, but saw nothing. He didn't appear to be intent on leading her back to the Square of Adam, anyway. *My sisters, my father, are not here for me,* she realized. *My only friend in the world is Abel's dog.* With a tentative smile, eyes glistening with tears, Eva shook her head slowly in disbelief and confusion, feeling lost and alone. Nine's fur had wiped the blood from her hands, but nothing could erase the pain from her heart. Her separation from her family was not just one of physical distance; it was also of the heart.

Eva had done everything she could to win Abel's love and desire, but her victory had also brought her the animosity of some of her sisters. Now, as she planned her return home, she thought about those fractured relationships. She was not exactly pleased with her father, either. But, without a doubt, as she contemplated a return to her home, her most distressing concern was, *there are no available men for me.* Her sisters had taken and would take the next available brothers, so it would be at least fifty years or more before she could possibly have another husband. She would then be over one hundred years old. *A young man would not want me,* she thought.

So she came to the conclusion that the only man on earth available for her was the murderer, Cain. Her partial smile had faded, her tears of disbelief had turned to tears of sorrow, and her desire for a husband was clouding her judgment.

Cain sensed her inner struggle, and he decided that the time was right to further insinuate himself into her calculations. "I can offer you protection for the night, along with food and drink. It will give us a chance to talk," said Cain.

What options do I have? If I wasn't living this moment, I wouldn't believe it. Eva thought this, but she said nothing and pretended not to hear what Cain was saying as Nine continued to console her.

Cain saw her silence as an even greater opportunity to manipulate her and the chance that he had hoped for to partially end his curse. Now he anticipated that maybe he could have Eva as a wife, not just as a companion. Back home, the idea of a wife had held no appeal for him, but he realized that a wife would be absolutely necessary now.

He knew that he could force her into submission, but he did not want to resort to that. Even the murderous Cain had his ethical limits, though he would not let her become aware of that. He waited for Eva to accept or decline his offer of shelter for the night. That is when she made her first big mistake——in the trauma of the moment she misinterpreted his lack of overt abuse as kindness.

"No, I must leave; I need to leave." Then she paused, remembering a prayer she had made some thirty years earlier. *Father, I need a husband. I want to have my own family; please provide me with a husband.* She wasn't sure why this memory had come upon her at this moment. *That was the prayer I made as I assisted in the birth of Cain.*

"Eva, Eva . . . is everything alright?" Cain asked her, as she seemed to be in a daze.

"Yes, I——I am fine. I am just exhausted," said Eva, as she avoided sharing her inner dialogue. Again, she remembered what her thoughts had been on the day she had helped to deliver Cain.

God has fulfilled my prayer and I now have a husband, she had thought at the time. *I saw him as my future husband,* she remembered. Eva was now confronted with her memory, her worldview, and her circumstances. *Did I make a mistake by marrying Abel? Did God intend for me to marry Cain? How am I supposed to know? It can't be possible that all of these things are coincidental. Nine coming to find me and leading me here, the memories of those long forgotten past events . . . these things can't just be coincidence.* Eva had just made her second big mistake——wrongly assuming that the situation in which she now found herself might be God's plan.

Cain sensed that Eva's confusion would improve his chances of getting what he wanted. "Eva, surely there must be something I can do to help you?" the master manipulator asked her solicitously.

Eva then made a final mistake in her early dealings with Cain——in her despair, she allowed back into her life the man she had helped to birth, and she lost sight of the man she hated. "Broken" would be the best description of her mental state as she allowed herself to listen to and reason with her husband's murderer. Her foundation was not solid, and that was why she was making some critical errors that could only exacerbate her tragedy.

"Yes, Cain, what should I do now?" she asked him sarcastically.

"Sister, you have achieved much of what you set out to do," he said and then paused. "I watched as you wiped my blood from your hands. You have done far more to punish me than Father or any of the others in the Square have done. Be proud of your actions, sister." Eva nodded her head in affirmation.

"You know me as well as anyone does, so you know that I respected all of my sisters. I never improperly touched any of them. With your actions today, I hold you above all of them." Cain could see he was gaining ground with Eva, as she again nodded her head in silent agreement. Cain was amazed at the progress he was making. It had been almost effortless, and it even seemed that he had been truthful, which was unlike him. *Perhaps intermixing truth with lies will prove to be the way to get what I want?*

In Eva's mind, the way that these events were lining up meant that they could not be mere coincidence. This led her to yet another dangerous and false premise: *Is this what God wants me to do?*

So Cain continued to work on Eva, to soften the blow of the circumstances in which they found themselves. Always he avoided the subject of the blow to Abel's skull that had caused them both such pain. Cain knew that there was no other good option for Eva, so he methodically reasoned away her deep negative feelings about him.

And it was working.

"Cain, why did you kill Abel? Why?" Eva asked. She needed to know. Cain was thrilled that she was starting to speak to him again. But now he was the one at a loss for words.

He searched his memory for the words that he had rehearsed, but then he simply told Eva the truth: "Father and Abel had talked about me. They conspired to try to change me. I don't want to change. I just don't. They were trying to manipulate me into wanting to offer sacrifices." *I am the manipulator, how dare they.* For a moment, Cain's internal struggle was revealed by the grimace on his face.

Eva understood exactly what he was saying. She knew of the many struggles between her father and her brother Cain. The truth was, Eva knew Cain better than probably anyone. Eva was once again silent as she looked on towards her clearly troubled brother.

Cain continued, "Abel was a good man, and I am not. I lashed out at my brother because of his goodness. I could never have been the man that he was, never. In a moment of anger, I found a way to remove the goodness so that I would not have to be reminded day after day what a good man Abel was and that I am not good. From the time that we were young boys, I have always known that Abel should have been the firstborn son rather than me."

Cain is right. Abel should have been the firstborn son; I would have been delivering Abel as my husband. This made sense to Eva. The way that Cain described the situation made sense and fit with what she remembered of her father and her brothers, so she believed what he was saying.

Looking back on all that transpired, it had been a fatal calamity for Abel, a personal tragedy for Eva, and was a catastrophe in the making for all mankind.

Eva continued to listen to Cain as they calmly discussed the situation. She was not yet of any mind to forgive Cain, but she was coming to terms with her situation and what she might have to do to survive.

Eva felt little reason to return to her home and she also realized, *Cain, as evil as he is, has been far more open with me than Father was.*

"Father didn't even want to come after me, did he?" Cain asked Eva.

"No," she said.

That is a relief, Cain thought.

"Your murder of Abel was very hard on him, perhaps even harder than it was on me. Father was just not up to seeking you out, and anyway, he is confused about what God would have him do," Eva said. *As confused as I am right now,* she thought.

Eva's thoughts turned to her immediate safety, where she would go, and how she would survive. Without a husband or a family, she would be alone. Eva was a strong woman, but even the strongest are not able to survive on their own. *Even if your companion is far from good or desirable,* she thought, *isn't that better than being alone?* Cain was the real exile here, due to his flight from vengeance. But at this moment it was as though she was an exile too, because of her lack of desire to return to her family.

The faithful dog, Nine, was still by her side, but he could not provide her with any further guidance, and guidance was what she needed. So she had to rely on guidance from within herself, guidance from her own foundation. Unfortunately, that foundation was blighted because of the curse and the decisions of Adam and Eve. Cain sensed that Eva was weakening further, so he pressed on.

"Eva, I took everything from you, and I am sorry. Let me repay you as best I can.

"I will take care of you. I can't take Abel's place in your heart. But I can stand in for him by providing for you, at least until your circumstances are much better than they are now," Cain said with determination.

I can't believe I am even considering his proposal, Eva thought. *Is there any way I can justify even considering this?* Then she wondered, *if I do stay with Cain, might I in time have another chance at getting my vengeance?*

Eva recalled how angry she had been in Adam's Square just before her departure. She knew that she had been right in her desire to seek justice at the time. Her challenge now though, whether or not to forgive Cain, was an equally difficult one. She had the right and the standing to forgive him, but she had no obligation to do so short of Cain's full repentance and payment for his actions. Only time would tell just what her decision might be.

In light of her dilemma, she made a reluctant but practical decision. "Okay, Cain, I will stay with you and, I guess, go with you. Where do your escape plans take us next?" Eva asked him.

So Cain got what he wanted and was surprised at how easy it had been. His curse had been diminished with Eva's decision. But Cain would never get an "I do" from Eva; she would only give him an "I will." Now, Cain would lead them to Nod.

God had shown mercy to Cain, but Cain had not been forgiven by neither God nor man. Eva was not likely to break rank with them.

I now see perhaps what Adam saw; I will grant Cain limited immunity from my due vengeance. Perhaps this is what God wanted me to do in the first place. I can revoke this mercy at any time that I choose, as long as Cain and I live.

Unless and until she believed that Cain had fully repented for murdering Abel, the mercy she was showing him now could end soon enough.

So Cain and Eva, the hunted and the huntress, would be fellow travelers on their way to a new land——the land of Nod. Nod was not a known place. It was an idea that had been placed in Cain's mind by God, and it was a wilderness far away from what had once been his home. Cain believed that he would know the place when he finally found it, so they headed on their way, not sure of where they were going but knowing that they would end up even farther away from the Square of Adam.

It was slow going. Cain and Abel had travelled this same type of terrain when they tried to get to the garden. But this trip was different in one way——because they were heading in the opposite direction, away from the garden instead of towards it, they could use a river for transportation and not just as a guide.

"Eva, we need to make our way to either the Tigris River or the Gihon River and navigate down one of them. It would be much faster and easier," Cain said.

"Which one is closest to where we are now?" Eva asked.

"I am not sure. I think the Gihon is to our right, maybe eight or ten days' walk, and the Tigris is to our left, one or two days' walk," Cain said, as he pointed in each of those directions.

"I know the Tigris is more dangerous to navigate, but it also has the capacity to get us out of here faster, so I say the Tigris," Eva said.

"The Tigris it is," replied Cain.

They made slow progress to the Tigris, but they could hear it after two days of walking and were pleased to know that they would reach it soon.

This would now be their fourth night together in close quarters. Cain continued to give Eva all the respect she was due.

"Cain, now that we can hear the river, we should make camp here for the night. I will prepare some places to sleep, and you can gather water and food," Eva said.

"Okay. There is a small clearing just ahead. That would be a good place to stay the night," Cain agreed.

Four days previously, they had only shared one goal: escape. Now they had another shared goal: survival. They didn't know what to expect in the coming days. Despite their growing mutual interests and the fact that food was plentiful on trees and in the ground, this struggle would take a mental and physical toll on both of them. The obstacles they faced forced them to rely on each other, and they developed a closeness borne of this dependence. But this was not either ones first choice, and there was no love yet found between the two.

Cain was used to being alone, but was now forced into a relationship with his sister. Surprisingly to Cain he was learning to enjoy these male-female interactions with Eva.

For Eva's part in this team effort to live apart from Adam, was a hope for a good future, at least as good as possible considering her predicament. Eva was a lot like her mother Eve, she was capable of just about anything, and above all else she was a survivor.

At each day's end they were exhausted by their travels and by their efforts to stay alive. Their exhaustion was a blessing, as it kept them too tired to argue about anything, ever.

Once they reached the Tigris, they stuck to the river bank as they continued their trek and watched for an opportune spot to enter its fast-moving waters. At last they found what they had been looking for.

"This is a good spot. The river opens up just ahead, see?" Cain said, pointing downriver. "We can navigate these waters."

"That is good news," Eva said, coming over to look. "We need the rest, and floating down stream will allow us that rest." Eva was glad to finally see a solid plan coming together.

Less than a month into their journey, they began making long-term plans. As they had seen the widening of the Tigris, they could see their future opening up as well.

"Could this be the land of Nod of which God has spoken?" Cain asked himself aloud.

"Let's hope so," Eva replied.

Wanting to see more before the end of the day, Cain climbed a tree on the bank of the river. "This body of water is as wide and as long as the eye can see," he shouted down to Eva. With this, they both gave some more thought to their futures.

Eva had to come to terms with the notion of becoming Cain's wife, and she was thinking about the bad choices, foundational cracks, and mistakes in judgment that had brought her to this crossroads.

Cain was thinking too. *I need a son and helper. I need to build a city in his honor——I will be a different kind of father than Adam was——I will be my son's friend. I will see that he does what he wants to do, and I will not limit his choices as my father tried to limit mine.*

"Eva," Cain called out as he made his way back down the tree. "Eva, tomorrow I will start building a raft for our journey to Nod."

"How can I help?" Any observer could have seen that Eva was a good woman, a far better woman than Cain was a man.

"Let's make camp here for a few days. Seven or eight days should do it. I will begin construction at morning light," Cain said.

"I will find us some bedding and food for tonight, and tomorrow I will begin gathering provisions for our stay and for the raft," Eva told Cain.

Cain arose the next day at first light. After a quick bath out of the sight of Eva, he returned to find that Eva was also up and attending to the needs of their camp. She watched as Cain eyed a straight and narrow tree to use in building their raft. As he reached for his ax, the same one he had used to murder Eva's husband, a heavy sadness filled her heart. When she heard the first blow of the ax striking the tree, she sobbed for the life she had once had. For the first time in many days, her past slammed up against her present, and she once again felt devastated by the loss of her husband, her family, and her home.

The pairing of Eva and Cain was a match made in haste, not in heaven. But it was more evident with each passing day that they needed each other now. Their mutual needs were even forcing them to bond to some extent.

When Cain's pile of lumber for building the raft had become quite substantial, Eva went over to check out the progress. "Eva, you are a good woman. Your goodness makes me so very pleased to have your company, and it makes me so very sad for what I have taken from you," Cain said to her.

Goodness, isn't that one of the reasons Cain killed my husband, and now he sees that in me? Not a good sign. Eva thought.

"Eva," Cain said again. "Eva, I have taken everything from you, but I tell you now, and you can believe it to be true, that I will never take you for a wife without your consent."

They had never actually discussed becoming man and wife. But by this time they both figured that it was inevitable, and Cain was remorseful enough about what he had done to Eva to give her the space she needed to come to terms with her decision. While Eva appreciated Cain's honorable behavior in this matter, it merely made him more tolerable in her eyes, not more desirable.

This trip to Nod was an adventure for Cain, but it was becoming a dilemma for Eva. She feared that her decision to go with Cain had been another mistake, and she was coming to regret that decision. But it was too late now. So she decided to make the best of this bad situation. She had no choice anyway.

While scavenging for supplies one day, she discovered a small clearing next to a pool of water——a very nice place to build and launch a raft. She helped Cain carry the wood that he had chopped for the raft over to the clearing.

"Thank you, Eva. This is a good place to build the raft," Cain said with approval.

"How can I be of further help?" asked Eva.

Cain looked at the food she had collected. "We will need more food. It would be nice to load some fish or fowl aboard the raft, so please continue with that, and tomorrow you can help me start the assembly process," Cain told her.

Both Cain and Eva had learned how to catch fish in the bodies of water close to their home, but now they had none of the nets or spears that had been available back there. Nonetheless, Eva scared a number of little fish into a small pool of water and then managed to catch quite a few of them. Cain was pleased when he discovered what she had accomplished and flashed her a smile.

"Eva, I am so hungry. You are amazing. Thank you so much," Cain said. She hadn't gone to the effort of catching the fish for Cain's benefit——she had caught them as food for herself to eat——but Cain chose to see it as a reward for himself. This is how things went between the two of them.

Cain had kept to a schedule while building the raft. After seven days, it was sturdy and safe and almost ready to board. Cain could tell that Eva was impressed, and rightly so. It was large enough for both of them and the dog, Nine, who would surely make himself useful in their new home in the land of Nod.

The travelers had few possessions to bring with them on the trip. Cain had a few items of clothing, his shoes, a belt, a couple of pieces of rope, a couple of animal skin bags used to carry fruit juice, a small knife made of wood and stone, and his ax.

Eva had not provisioned herself much better; she hadn't realized that she was leaving home for good when she had begun to follow Nine. Her backpack had always contained some essentials though: a hair comb, some tools for sewing, toothpicks, stones for making fire, an extra pair of shoes, and some soap. She had also added some clothing and food before leaving.

They loaded Nine and their meager possessions onto the raft. As Cain pushed off with one of the oars that he had made, they said goodbye to their temporary home.

They had now spent several nights together in close quarters, but their quarters would become even closer on the raft. "Eva, I know it makes you uncomfortable being so close to me so much of the time. I will not force you to become my wife," Cain reiterated what he had said a few days before.

He was right. Eva was not comfortable with the situation, and every time Cain brought up the subject she was forced to think about her decision. She knew that it was time to reply.

"Cain, I trust that you will not violate me, but I also know that we will need children to provide us with a future. So I have little choice, and I am dealing with that choice in my own way," Eva said, not looking at him. "Look, both of us know that this is not a good time or place to become husband and wife," she added.

"As always, you are correct. Thank you for telling me how you feel. That really helps me a lot," said Cain.

Eva sat uneasily, with her chin in her hand, very serious, and looked directly into Cain's eyes for the first time. She felt as if she were looking into his soul——with words she had already rehearsed, she said, "Cain, if you want to take me as a wife, if we are to have a family, you must first provide us with a home——a good home——where we can be assured that the children we conceive will thrive."

As she finished her statement, she saw Cain as she had never seen him before——it was his mark that she was seeing. Her eyes widened in surprise. The aura that she had occasionally perceived at night was now strong enough to be visible in the bright light of day. She found this glow somewhat disturbing. She had just effectively agreed to become Cain's wife at some point. Now she was forced to consider again what and who she would be marrying. Eva sensed that the mark had some self-interest in the situation.

"Cain, do you . . . do you know what is happening?" Eva asked anxiously. Whatever this mark thing actually was, she did not like the look of it. But then it vanished from her view.

Cain was unaware that his mark had made itself visible to Eva while she talked about becoming his wife, so he did not understand her words. And Eva only wanted to forget the strange incident.

Cain sensed Eva's doubt and said, "I will provide for you. You will see, Eva. I can never give you back what I took from you, but I will be good to you from this day forward."

And so they drifted on towards Nod.

Eva was a good woman and would strive to get the best out of her soon-to-be husband. But she was right in thinking that that would be no easy task.

As they moved on the water, they spotted a few pleasant places where they could have settled, but they had hopes of finding an even better place. At the end of another day on the water, they went ashore for the night as usual. With an hour or so of daylight left, Eva prepared separate beds for them to sleep in while Cain went off to hunt fowl for them to eat.

When Cain was returning, Eva heard him exclaim, "Eva, I have found Nod."

"Okay, sounds good to me," Eva said when he got back.

"I climbed a small hill just to the east of here. I saw all the fields of the earth. It must be Nod, as a man could wander forever in those fields," Cain told her excitedly.

"Wander forever? That is what we seem to be doing now. How will these fields change that?" Eva inquired.

"Fire. I will build a fire in the east and let the winds take it west until it burns no more, and then those fields will be for building and not for wandering. We can build a city," Cain said.

City? What is a city? Eva wondered. Right now, she was tired of floating aimlessly down the giant body of water, so she agreed to Cain's plan. They agreed to call this place Nod, and then they went to sleep.

The next day, Cain began collecting some wood that he would use to start the fields ablaze in a few places. After two days' work, he used Eva's flint stone to set the fields alight. When he started the fire, the wind was but a gentle breeze. As the wind grew stronger so did the fire, and it grew into an enormous blaze, which they watched from a distance. While the fire pleased Cain, it horrified Eva.

This fire raged for forty days and cleared a massive area of land before burning itself out. The smoke covered the entire earth. Eva viewed the area from a high place, and as far as she could see there was now only death and destruction. It looked ugly to her, but Cain was proud and pleased with his accomplishment.

As he surveyed the area, he observed a low place that looked as if it would be easy to irrigate. He also spotted a higher place where they could build a home for the two of them. There would be no square as per the society that Adam had designed——Cain would add a fifth side. The fifth side was to be his government, which would take a fifth of everything for its own needs, his needs. This pentagon would be at the center of his city. As he looked out over the destruction the fire had wrought upon the once golden fields, Cain knew that this would be the foundation for his city, the city that would be his home for the next millennium.

Cain had an ulterior motive in creating such a large blaze. He hoped the smoke from the fire would bring curiosity, and attract some of his brothers and sisters to join him in his new city. All would be welcomed as he would need many people to help him build it. But he also knew that this strategy might not work, so he would also need to have at least one son and one daughter. Fortunately for him, Eva agreed that it was now time to begin a family.

That night, in a small clearing, Cain laid out his plans to build.

"Eva, come and see." Cain took her hand, something he had never done before, and led her to a bluff. "You see down below there, that clearing just above the edge of the stream?"

"Yes, I see it," Eva said, as she withdrew her hand.

"What do you think? It would be perfect for a home. I'll start construction in the morning. It should take no more than six cycles to complete," said Cain.

Cycles, Eva thought cynically. *I know what he wants.*

Cain could see Eva wrestling internally with the idea of Cain becoming her husband. Though they had become dependent on each other and learned to rely on each other, it was clear that Eva did not love Cain, and Cain didn't know if he was even capable of loving at all.

"We should talk," Eva said. "Cain, it would be *wise* to have a son first." Cain listened anxiously. Then Eva was amazed and concerned to see that Cain's mark was once again becoming more visible. The strange glow distorted her perception of Cain's presence. *This is going to be far more difficult than I had imagined*, she realized, and she looked away to avoid seeing the mark.

"Cain, when my next cycle is complete, you will stay away from me, and I from you, for fourteen days and nights, and then we shall cain you a son," she stated, as a tear welled up in her eye.

"Eva, I will. I will do as you ask. I will also provide a good home for you and our son," Cain promised her, as he began to walk away to give her some privacy.

"Cain," Eva called to him. "Cain, do you understand the concept of 'until death do we part?'" She understood that the bond they would soon undertake would be one that could only be undone by death, as her bond with Abel had been undone by his death. "Do you understand this, Cain?"

Cain's silence told her that he did not understand this. He would be a good provider, but he would certainly never be a good husband. Her obvious frustration prompted him to come up with a response.

"Eva, I will try to do the best I can. I will really try to be a good husband," he said. She knew he was only saying what she wanted to hear. Cain would never be capable of being good; the best he would be able to manage would be to *try* to be good, as being good for Cain was always a result of work, never desire.

Eva started a new cycle.

After thirteen days and nights had passed, Cain asked her, "Eva, do you know what night this is?"

"Of course I do——it is the thirteenth night," Eva said, without giving it much thought.

"Yes, but do you remember what happened on the thirteenth night, long ago, with Mom and Dad?" Cain asked her.

"Yes I do," she said and laughed. It was one of the first lighthearted moments that Cain and Eva had ever shared. "Yes, I heard the story many times. Mom actually confessed to me how the whole thing happened. The only one that benefited from that muddle was our sister, Elew. You aren't considering repeating that same error, are you Cain?"

"Eva, of course I am not. I find comfort in the law, and it is the only thing that guides me," Cain said.

"Cain, where did you get this notion of law? I never heard Father speak of law, only of love," said Eva, baffled. Cain wasn't sure what he had meant either, and he pondered the profound question that his soon-to-be wife had just asked him. *Abel and now his wife torment me with this idea of love of our fathers. More talk about the tree of life is coming I know it. I am not interested in the tree of life; my desires are only for the tree of knowledge.*

Eva thought, *Is Cain talking about the tree of knowledge? He must mean that is the law ... don't eat from the tree?*

Eva had to wait a few minutes for Cain's response as Cain was letting his demeanor calm. This was unusual for him. He normally reacted impulsively to everything that confronted him. It made Eva feel optimistic to see this new, thoughtful Cain, though she realized that this thoughtfulness might not last.

Finally, he said, "You know, Eva, I don't know. I do not know where I got the idea of the law, but it is very deep inside me, perhaps it goes back to my birth. And you know of my obsession with the tree of knowledge. It consumes me and my life. I guess it is the law in my life. The law forbids me to eat of the tree, and that is why I am obsessed with the tree."

Eva didn't understand his obsession with the tree, but she could certainly understand wanting to do something that is forbidden. *These trees, in the garden, they truly are opposing forces, one that is guided by love and one that is guided by law. Love is only by choice and law is never by choice, truly opposites.*

Eva had been brought up to love and respect her mother and father——that was her foundation. She didn't see the need for any other law in her life. Her love and respect for her parents had guided her life and her actions. After marriage that love and respect had then largely been given a priority towards her husband, Abel.

But that relationship had been torn asunder by his murder, and now Eva was confused. She wanted vengeance for Abel, but she had previously always followed the guidance of her mother and father. So Eva had no understanding of law, only the guidance of love and now–vengeance.

Neither Cain nor Eva slept much that night. They talked as they tossed and turned in their beds, trying to resolve decisions that had been based on a foundation of a myriad of bad decisions and tough choices. Eva knew Cain's feelings about Adam and Eve and said to him, "Perhaps law is needed for those who don't feel love for their mother and father. Perhaps without the restraining power of love, there is need for other restraints, like this law you speak of?" Cain didn't say so, but he appreciated Eva's thoughtful words and would probably think about them again in the future. *Eva might be right about that,* he thought to himself.

Once the fortnight had passed, Cain approached Eva that evening. "Eva, my actions have brought us to this point. I, far more than you, should be paying the price that you will now pay as you lie with me. I was overcome with anger when I murdered my brother. That anger is long gone, but now I am controlled by self-interest as I take you, his wife. This is more painful to me than I could have imagined," Cain said to Eva.

Eva lay down for Cain. She did not tell him that she was only in this for self-interest as well. She wanted children and desired to know a man again. A few bad decisions based on a false worldview had undermined, fractured, and weakened her foundation.

As the fractures of her foundation split open, so would her womb to birth a future for her and Cain. As Cain lost his virginity that night, Eva let go of her memories of her husband, Abel. She and Cain had one goal now, to conceive children to assist them in navigating the long nine hundred years or more of life ahead of them. Procreation became all that their marriage was about.

Eva believed that she would lose herself to this man in matrimony, but their intimacy was not what she had expected. When she had become one flesh with Abel, it had been very different. The idea of becoming one flesh now took on a whole different meaning for her. Eva understood now that becoming one flesh does not only mean the actual physical relations; it means that you have decided to unite as husband and wife, with Cain the 'I do' was missing.

Eva would never have the feel of one flesh with Cain as she had with Abel. Furthermore, she was uneasy about Cain's mark. When she lay down for Cain, she could tell that the mark was outside of Cain but close to him. It seemed to grow in strength, yet move farther away, during their relations.

It was as if Cain was not alone with her, as if the mark was slowly taking some sort of control over Cain. She needed to know more about the powers of this angel that protected him. *Maybe I will be able to use its powers to my advantage someday?*

There had been no love involved in Eva's relations with Cain, and this left her feeling unfulfilled. The outcome that she had foolishly wished for was just not possible with Cain. She had desperately wanted a husband, but the marriage had not turned out the way she hoped it would. She wondered what to do now. And the involvement of this third entity, the mark, made the situation even worse.

— 8 —
A Son Is Cained

Cain and Eva were expecting their first child. (KJV Gen. 4:17) Assuredly, it would be a son as they had followed the caining rules to the letter. What to name the firstborn became a subject of great importance to Cain. Cain fully understood how his name had affected his life and he never wanted his children to be anything but proud of their names. Cain understood how important a child's name can be, as it would be their first sense of who they were and who they might become.

"Eva, I know that my brother and you had talked about having children, did Abel ever disclose the names he wanted to start with?" Without much thought Eva answered him truthfully, "Yes, we had talked about it, Abel agreed with Father's choices and of course Enoch was going to be our firstborn's name." and so it went as they discussed the names that Abel and Eva had wanted to use to please their father Adam.

Cain, there and then, decided to usurp the names that Adam and Abel had conceived for the offspring for the firstborn of faith, Abel. Starting with the name Enoch. Which meant "the dedicated son" but Enoch would take on a new meaning through the line of Cain to mean "the disciplined son."

Cain's twofold motive was first; to give good names to his children and second; to supplant the bloodline of Abel with his own. It was a misguided and self-serving effort to demonstrate, to Adam and others, some honor towards the brother he had murdered. Eva went along with this idea and even supplied the list of names; she genuinely wanted to commemorate Abel. Nobody would ever come to believe that Cain's motives were pure in this——and they would be right.

Enoch was born forty weeks later. (KJV Gen. 4:17) Enoch would need a wife, so as soon as he was weaned, Eva conceived again. Five years after Enoch's birth, Eva bore a daughter who would grow up to become Enoch's wife. They would be the founders of the City of Enoch.

Eva knew that Cain could carry on without her, now that he had a son and a daughter, so she was beginning to feel very insecure about her future. Sometimes when she cried out to God, in whom she strongly believed, she was reminded of the sacrifices that both Adam and Abel had offered on her behalf. She prayed that those sacrifices would hold her in good stead with God until she could yet again be protected by the sacrifices of a godly spouse.

Even after Enoch and his sister had been born, Cain had wanted to conceive more children. Eva modestly resisted, but now she had a new plan. She would have several more children with Cain until he truly no longer needed her. At that point, she would work to convince two of her children to leave with her. Maybe they could find their way back to the Square or find another place, any other place. Traveling back to the square would be very difficult and she would need help if she ever hoped to make it. In a new place they could start over, and she could find some semblance of happiness. And more children were born.

Eva had listened to Cain talk about his plans for a city many times. Now that Enoch was old enough to understand these concepts, she prompted Cain to talk about his plans again so that she could see Enoch's reactions as she held the young boy. "Cain, explain to me again why you wish to build a city?" Eva asked.

"A city. Well, it is a place where you can dwell among many others," Cain said.

"What was wrong with the Square back home?" Eva asked.

"A city is different——and better for me. It requires structure and rules. It needs law, and it needs a ruler. In a city, you can become famous or anonymous. That is what a city is," Cain explained to Eva.

"Why would anybody want to be anonymous?" Eva wondered out loud. But before Cain could even answer, she realized that anonymity would be a criminal's best friend——a criminal such as Cain. Adam had taught his children to be accountable to their brothers and sisters, but in a city that would be difficult to do.

Cain responded, "Eva in the city, everyone will know us. We will be famous! If our fame becomes an issue, we can disappear into the city to avoid those who seek to take advantage." Eva just shook her head, not understanding Cain's opposing desires for fame and anonymity.

Cain's vision for city life were based on two-opposing pillar's; fame–anonymity. Those principles struck Eva as evil. But the city's namesake, Enoch seemed to be very interested in Cain's ideas——like father, like son. She now knew that no good would come of a city built by Cain and his offspring. (KJV Gen. 4:17)

And in addition, there was still the mystery of Cain's mark. What dynamic would Cain's occupying angel bring to the city of Enoch? She had no way to know for sure and was in no way encouraged with the added unknown mark of Cain.

After many years, Enoch had grown up to be a cold-hearted and tough young man. He was even bigger and stronger than Cain and even more detached from any concerns about right and wrong. Eva became fearful of her son. The boy soon to become a man Enoch was now looking at his mother, in a way that was overtly lustful in the mind of Eva. *So much for the wisdom of having a son first,* she thought. Cain could also see what Eva saw, and was also concerned about just how uncontrollable Enoch was becoming as he grew ever stronger.

Cain had never told Enoch of the tree of knowledge, as he didn't want Enoch to be limited by its law. Nor did he want Enoch to become obsessed with the tree as he was himself. Of course he would not teach Enoch about sacrifice or about honoring one's mother and father. Cain would never perceive the great benefits that he would have garnered from honoring Adam, Eve, and God. His lack of perception became his reality.

To Cain, hypocrisy was the only evil. *I will not be a hypocrite; I won't teach my kids to do something that I refuse to do.* Cain in rejecting any type of corporate morality left only one evil action available to him, and to all, hypocrisy.

Cain did instruct Enoch in many trades, though, and Enoch became as good a stone mason as Cain was, maybe better. They worked side by side every day.

One day, when Enoch was almost a man, Cain saw him looking at his sister with lust. "Enoch, we must talk about your sister," Cain said, taking him aside. "I see how you look at your sister, but she is not yet of age. You will have to wait."

"Father, at what age can I marry her?"

"Son, with my sisters, it was always different. You will have to wait. It could be three, four, five years or more, but you will have to wait. If you even try to take her before she is a woman, you will forever poison your marriage with her, and I will punish you," Cain cautioned Enoch. Enoch had never been limited or subjected to restrictions of any kind before, and he found it very disconcerting.

Enoch snickered and said, "Okay, Father, I will wait for my sister to become a woman but not a day longer," he sternly cautioned his father.

Cain shook his head despondently as he came to the conclusion that his son, Enoch would someday challenge him physically. Cain would have to do whatever he could to postpone that inevitable clash and to minimize the impact it would have on both of them. Cain wanted nothing to get in the way of the building of his city, including a misguided son. A son who he all of a sudden was losing control of.

Cain began to realize that he had not done a good job of raising his first son. His approach, which had been deliberately the opposite of Adam's approach, to date, had yielded poor results. The consequences of his own flawed worldview were coming to fruition. Yet Cain could not raise his children in any other manner, it was just not in him to look back. It was just not in him to learn from his father. He could not and would not humble himself to anyone for any reason. His philosophy was far more important than was reality.

Some months later, on a Saturday, the day of rest, Cain encountered the young Enoch relaxing under a poplar tree in a field. Cain thought it a good time to talk with his son. As he approached him, he found the similarity of this place and this situation to be very familiar . . . and his thoughts turned to Abel.

The memory, long suppressed, of the blood flowing out of Abel's head and pooling above the ground came flooding back to him as though he was living it again. Enoch sensed his father's disorientation and chose this moment to become aggressive with him.

"What is it that you want of me?" asked Enoch harshly.

Cain, lost in memories of old, woke to Enoch's question. Cain looked towards his son but said nothing. Again, Cain was lost in thought, *I will never be able to escape, this guilt for killing Abel.*

"Cain, do you want something from me?" Enoch asked again, firmly.

Cain hearing his son's tone confirmed what he already knew, it was too late to father Enoch any further. He had squandered his opportunity to lead this boy, his son, who was now a man. Suddenly, Cain's feelings of guilt were overshadowed by fear.

He knew that Enoch would no more show him mercy than he had shown Abel mercy that day long ago in an eerily similar field. The only advantage available to him now was his mark.

Cain approached his son cautiously as he noticed Enoch was in possession of an ax. Cain believed that, because of his mark his son could not defeat him, but he hoped that this encounter would not come to blows.

Memories of Abel's blood again raced through Cain's mind, and he realized that if he or his son were to perish this day, in this pasture, the ground was not likely to show either of them the mercy that it had assuredly shown Abel. There had been no sacrifices to take their places. If their blood was shed, the earth would not be restrained from pulling them down into its darkness.

"Cain, I am a man," Enoch asserted. "Yes, Cain. I am a man now. I don't need a father."

"So you are, my son. So you are," said Cain, turning and walking away, leaving behind his hopes and dreams of raising a good son. Cain, to the extent that he could be, was saddened. He was through for now with his son, but his son was not finished with him.

Enoch again sensing weakness in his father called out to him. "Cain, are you afraid?"

Cain stopped walking and turned to face his son. Enoch was surprised, as he could see Cain's mark in daylight for the first time.

Enoch had seen the glow around Cain before as Cain slept and he had asked his mother about the strange power that God had given his father. Eva had explained that the mark had been given to him by God as protection against vengeance and that God had given a warning that anyone who killed Cain would be cursed sevenfold.

Enoch, now confronted with this new view of Cain's mark, would have to do some thinking about it before attempting to test its limits. He was by no means convinced that he could not defeat his father, but this was not the time to test his beliefs.

"Cain, you have raised me to be strong and independent, and I am as you wanted me to be. Do you now want me to change? Do you want me to bow to you or to anyone? That is not who you raised me to be," Enoch said.

Cain could not argue with anything his son had said.

Cain, for the first time in his life, looked back and recalled the teachings of his father in the Square; that children should love and respect their parents. A teaching had he taught his children, would have been hypocritical of him.

The opaqueness of his dedicated hypocritical-free life-style suddenly opened to the point where he could see, where he could hear . . . as his now closed eyes echoed back to a time long ago where Adam had spoken to him. "Wisdom is seen in her children."

In the cold eyes of Enoch, Cain now saw his lack of wisdom grown to fruition. And it was far too late to help Enoch. Cain had set no limits for his children, so all of them would grow up to be wicked. A wise father was always limited by his children's errors. But Cain never had been and the wickedness of his son Enoch was a direct result of his own lack of wisdom in raising his son.

"Enoch, you know of my mark. You know you cannot defeat me, because of it. You also know that God will curse anyone who tries, sevenfold," Cain warned Enoch.

"Words of God?" Enoch said. "They have no meaning whatsoever to me." Enoch didn't know God and was not interested in meeting Him, or in knowing anything about Him. He was going to be a better builder than his father, and he was going to live for a thousand years. "You received a mark for killing your brother," Enoch said. "Perhaps someday I will be given a mark of my own." Directing a disparaging glance at Cain, Enoch lay back down under the poplar tree.

Now, more than ever, Cain understood the tragedy that would result from all that was transpiring. No good would ever come of this. This was the beginning of the rebellious line of Cain: brothers would kill brothers to gain standing among the remaining.

A short distance away the two of them saw Eva and her daughter walking. Enoch took notice of the two of them, especially his mother. Eva did not like the way that Enoch was looking at her, or at her daughter. Cain saw Eva's reaction and quickly he looked towards Enoch to only confirm Eva's concerned look. Cain was not at all happy.

"Enoch," Cain said, as he walked over to where Enoch was lying at rest. "Enoch, this day I have resisted the urge to use my mark against you." Cain went to the feet of Enoch and towered above him so Enoch could not easily move.

"While you rest, rest assured that if you touch your mother——if you ever touch her in any way that displeases her or displeases me——you will suffer the same demise as did my brother." At that moment, Cain's mark appeared very brightly to Enoch; it was as the sun itself. Cain and the mark were jealous of Eva, and now Enoch knew this. For now, when it came to Eva, the powerful Enoch was limited by Cain——and even more so by his mark.

When she was a young girl of nineteen years, Eva's first daughter had no choice but to marry Enoch——he was the only man *available*. Eva cried for her daughter, for fear of the life she would lead with Enoch. In large part, for her own safety, the girl had been kept away from Enoch, but that distance would soon be closed by matrimony. Life as the wife of the son of a marked murderer didn't hold much promise, but that was her only prospect.

And so she awaited her wedding night.

She knew that she had been conceived for one reason only, and she could see that reason in the eyes of Enoch as he waited. These were not the eyes of a loving man. They were the eyes of a lustful man who was hungry for the pleasures that the flesh of his young wife would soon bring to him.

Like the serpent of old, Enoch understood that there is power in numbers, and he wanted to have a large number of children. Those two beings were very like-minded. They had yet to meet each other– but Enoch certainly seemed on a course to soon enough meet with the evil one of old.

"The time for us to wed has arrived. The sun is low in the sky. The night comes, and you will come with me," said Enoch to his sister. Her hand slipped from her mother's grasp.

The young bride-to-be spoke to her mother one last time before being wed. "Eva, you were a good mother. I will try to be a good daughter and make you proud." Her words were intended to console her mother, but Eva was devastated and cried uncontrollably for her daughter. She knew that she bore the responsibility for her daughter's coming pain. Eva took responsibility for her plight, after all it did no good to blame Enoch–Eva wisely concluded that it was never a good idea to blame others over which she had no control over.

After taking his wife, whom he ruled with a firm hand, Enoch became bolder. His boldness kept his wife in fear, and he was just fine with that.

Enoch and Cain were in a state of détente while they made long-term plans to build their city. Their City Enoch would need people, lots of people. Their vision would be the basis for the two of them getting along to achieve their desires for fame and anonymity. All the girls, as soon as they became women had very little choice and they were married quickly and began having babies just as quickly.

While Cain and Enoch were in front of their children they seemed to be as one, but in private with their wives it was very different for one of them. Both of their wives knew that more children were necessary to build the city.

Enoch gave his wife no choice in the matter, and she was sufficiently defeated that she would not resist. But not Cain, he was finally a hypocrite. Cain had never taught Enoch to respect his wife but he would for now and for always show Eva respect. Something that Enoch could plainly see and just as plainly reject as hypocritical.

Cain may never know or realize it, but he actually loved his Eva, and in return she usually complied with his wishes in this regard, and many children were born.

Cain saw Enoch growing stronger as time went on and realized that sooner rather than later he would need the assistance of his mark.

Cain had yet to discover how to control his mark or its powers, but now he realized he would have to harness its power somehow. He started by trying to talk with it, call on it, but he never got a response. He was aware of its presence at times; at other times he was largely unaware of it. Cain had noticed that he felt the presence of the angel when his emotions were at their peak, more than at any other time.

He had spent many days and nights trying to interact with his mark. The angel had never given him any indication of its mission, its abilities or its capabilities. The mark remained largely a mystery to him. Cain would not concede defeat in this matter, he would just have to try harder to conquer it or take control of it, and so he could use it to his bidding.

One approach that he had not yet tried was to command the mark as he would a child. He decided to investigate this possibility by instigating a confrontation with someone. This confrontation could certainly not be with his Eva; it would have to be with someone else. But Enoch was the only other man in their land, as Enoch's brothers were still just boys. Confronting Enoch would be problematic, though. *If I confront Enoch, I might even regain my standing. No, I mustn't try; the risk is just too high. I will have to find another way to test my mark. A stranger is what I need for this purpose. A nephew or cousin from the Square would do nicely. So I will just have to wait until one shows up.*

Cain's plan was to initiate a confrontation and command the mark to strike out at them. But in the thirty years they had been in Nod they had not seen another soul, so this would have to be a long-term plan. He would have to wait for the right moment to test the powers that resided within him and hope he wouldn't need the use of those powers before then.

While Cain was making his plans to test the mark, Eva was making other plans. They didn't know it, but their plans were on a collision course. Cain would get a chance to test his mark sooner than expected but not in the manner that he had envisioned.

Eva, after all these years of being unhappy, found herself feeling alone, and alone she was as she fell to her knees and cried out loud to God.

"Father help me, I am in such despair." Her cry for help brought forward tears, tears that cleansed her eyes as those same tears released emotions that also cleansed her soul.

Eva was never the one that believed in coincidences–she found it hard to reconcile some things that had happened in her life to be just happenstance. And it was happening again–as she recalled that she had almost killed Cain. She looked down at her hands and closed her eyes causing one last tear to roll down her cheek. The drop hit her hand as if it were the blood of Cain.

I can see Cain's blood; I can feel the warmth of it as it soothes my pain. I want to feel that again. I want, I need to rid my need for vengeance, and I will not know peace until I know vengeance. Once again, her thirst for the vengeance due her was becoming an obsession.

I must try again to avenge Abel. My hands drenched in Cain's blood worked to ease my pain. Now that my pain has returned–I must try again to find that sense of relief. But I want it to be permanent this time.

Eva didn't care what consequences she might suffer if she made another attempt on Cain's life. The promised relief that only vengeance would deliver was her only concern. *Abel, I will avenge you.* Eva didn't have much reason to believe that she would succeed on her next attempt either, but she had a theory about how she could improve her chances. So, once again, she plotted to end Cain's life.

To undertake her new scheme of vengeance and then escape from Enoch, Eva would need an accomplice, a son. She would need at least one child anyway, preferably two or even three, to help her make a new start. At least one of them would have to be a son to side with her against Cain. Convincing a son to side with her while Cain was alive would be very difficult, because Cain's influence would carry the day with any sons older than four or five. So, for her plan to work, she would need a very young son.

Eva considered her theory. *Cain is vulnerable when we are intimate, and I can clearly perceive the presence of his mark outside of him when we are having relations. That is the time to strike him, when his mark cannot stop me. Then he will die before his mark can save him.*

Eva would wait until her current three-year-old son was weaned. Then, while engaged in intimacy with Cain, she would once again use a sharpened stick to try to kill him. This time she would have to get him right in the heart to ensure a fatal injury. She reasoned that she could then escape with her young son from the wicked city that Enoch would continue to build, albeit without his father's help.

In due time, the youngest son was weaned. "Cain, let's cain another child," said Eva. Cain was caught off guard by her willingness to bear another child so soon after the last one.

"Eva, we need a daughter now for the weaned boy. It would be best to have a daughter next," Cain said. He was right. There was no good reason to cain another son until a daughter had been born for the latest boy. But Eva wanted two sons that she could raise to side with her and help her to get away from Enoch if she managed to kill Cain. She also planned to bring one of her older daughters to be a wife for one of the boys. So, in order to cain a son instead of a girl, Eva would deceive Cain as to the schedule of her cycle. With this in mind, she approached Cain.

"Cain, I have just finished my cycle. We can conceive a female in seven days," said Eva. Of course, Cain was all for this, and so he brushed away any slight suspicions he felt about her willingness to conceive so soon after the birth of the previous child.

So she now had seven days to prepare a weapon and to stoke her courage to use the weapon on Cain. She made a staff of hardwood, sharpened the tip, and carved out a handle that she could grasp firmly. It was obvious that it was a weapon, so she kept it hidden. By night she kept it under their marital bed. During the days, when Cain was working, she practiced removing it from under the bed and using it. She would have only one chance at this. Seven days later, feeling determined and confident that the time was right, she called for Cain.

"It is time," Eva said to Cain. Eva was prepared; the sharpened weapon was in place under the bed. She lay down for Cain and sensed the mark departing him, so she reached under the bed with her right hand to grasp her freedom tightly. She was as anxious for the moment to arrive as she had been the last time, but this time she would be more careful and get it right. Slowly she slid the weapon out from underneath the bed.

As Cain was experiencing his release, Eva sought her permanent release by thrusting the sharpened stake deep into Cain's chest. His screams were deafening. He grasped the handle with both hands as he fell away from the bed.

Success! She had done it. The stake was protruding from Cain's chest and he was bleeding out; he was not moving and he made not a sound. Having finally achieved vengeance for the murder of Abel, she felt free. Relieved, she wept as the pent up emotions of the past fifty years drained from her. Then she seized her sleeping five-year-old son and held him close, closing her eyes and dreaming of a new life. She would raise him on her own, very far away from Nod, and she would teach him to sacrifice so that the two of them could live a godly existence.

As she was leading her son away from the bloody scene, Cain rose. Eva gasped when she saw him. The hardwood stake was still embedded in his chest and blood was still oozing from the wound; he was being assisted by his mark, which she could now clearly see. It appeared that Cain was going to survive, as his mark had rescued him from certain death, and was attending his wound.

The angelic being was not a fleshly creature, yet somehow with some unexplained power of its own, removed the wooden dagger from the heart of Cain. Then he embraced Cain's back and held him up in a way that seem to mold the flesh of Cain's wound back to his chest. The angel was moving Cain's chest back and forth to keep his heart beating. Within moments Cain was no longer bleeding and was regaining his self-awareness.

The angel, out of self-interest, would not easily let go of the flesh that it had been protecting for all this time, as it lusted for Cain's knowledge of Eva. Unbeknownst to Cain, his mark had no right to stop true vengeance, of which only the wife of Abel had. The mark had been corrupted and was now acting in full autonomy. The blood that bled from Cain's body had gladly been accepted by the earth, but it was far from enough blood to bring Cain's spirit along with it.

So, once again, Eva had been denied her vengeance, and she was heartbroken. Her only hope of escape had failed, and it was very unlikely that she would ever get another chance to try this again. Now she would, without doubt, receive a severe punishment from her husband for her attempt to take his life. In her troubled state, she considered that her own death might be a good thing. Crying tears of exasperation, she held her five-year-old son to herself and waited for what must come.

Cain, assisted by the strange angelic being, sat down next to Eva, who was still clinging to the boy, protecting him as best she could. The mark was now supernaturally tending to Cain's wound, that was all but healed.

To her surprise, Cain said, "Do not be afraid." Cain was indeed very angry, but his anger was not directed at Eva. He was furious with his mark. "Why did you *save* me?" Cain muttered to his mark, surprising Eva again and she shook her head in disbelief.

Cain is not mad at me? He is angry at his mark, for saving him?

Cain's injury was healing quickly as he looked at Eva. "Eva, I have known of your disdain for me for a long time now, and as always, your feelings are not misguided. You are right in seeking justice for Abel. I can never take that right from you, and I wouldn't even try," Cain said. Somehow even Cain understood that Eva was due this vengeance and that this had a powerful hold on her. What did surprise him was that it had taken her so long to seek her revenge a second time.

Cain's focus then quickly turned back to his mark. He had long wanted to test his mark, and though this was not the test that he had envisioned the test had been successful, and now Cain had a few things to say to his mark.

"Why did you not protect me from this attack?" Cain yelled at his mark.

Cain was confused as to why the mark had failed to protect him from Eva's attack but had then brought him back to life afterwards. Eva was confused about this also.

Cain pondered this for a moment and then remembered that he had experienced a feeling of justice right before the mark had brought him back to life. Hence his initial anger with the mark, as he had wanted that *feeling* to continue. In that brief moment, Cain felt grateful to Eva for what she had just done by almost killing him. He had never before experienced the feeling of being dead——if that was indeed what it had been——and he would long remember the feeling. *What was it that soothed my soul during those moments? Was it death? Or was it justice being fulfilled?*

Then he heard a voice: "I was doing what I was sent to do," said his mark. Eva could not hear this, but, nonetheless, she could tell that Cain was communicating with his mark. It was the first time the mark had ever interacted with Cain. It was indeed an angel——a spirit——and though it was male, it was definitely not a man. Eva could see the strange being and it was intermittently visible to Cain as well. The mark clearly had no flesh yet it was capable of fleshly actions, a spiritual life form very different than her own.

"I was slain and perhaps even dead!" Cain yelled at his mark. "You were sent here to protect me, and you didn't."

"The Archangel Michael himself prohibited me," replied Cain's mark. "He said, 'You are to withdraw from Cain during acts of procreation.'"

Cain was confused. "What are you talking about?" he asked.

The mark continued, "When you have relations with your wife, I depart from you. And there is more."

Cain had not yet processed what he had just heard but he demanded, "What else is there?"

"I am empowered only to protect you from vengeance, not to fend off justice."

Now Cain was even more confused; *on one hand I now understand that only Eva can successfully attack me——as she is seeking justice, not vengeance. So why did the angel save me? Whatever the case may be, I need to know before Eva knows. Or I will be at her mercy.*

"Eva, do you see the mark?" Cain asked her.

"Yes, I do. I see a being that comes and goes from your body. It is strange. I think it is an angel."

"Can you hear the angel speak?" Cain was worried that she could.

"I only hear you talking to it. If the angel is responding, I can't hear it," said Eva. So Cain would have to be cautious when speaking with the mark in Eva's presence. He excused himself and walked away from her so he could question the mark further. At least he now understood why the mark had behaved the way it did when Eva had attacked him.

Eva was distraught as she realized that she would probably never have another chance to get away from Cain——not with a son anyway. With this new turn of events, Cain's mark was taking on a new role in their lives, and she was sure this would not be good for her.

"How exactly is this going to work?" Cain asked his mark when he was sure of their privacy.

"I told you. I am to prevent vengeance against you, nothing more."

"Eva will kill me if she figures this out. Come to think of it, why, then, did you save me from certain death?" Cain responded.

"I have been with you for many years now, and being so close to your flesh has weakened me. Your flesh has weakened my spirit. I now want the knowledge of the flesh, the knowledge of Eva, but I dare not acquire it. It was those desires that prevented me from allowing you to die," said the mark.

"Look, I don't care about what any of this has done to you, or about any instructions you were given beyond the orders that you were given to keep me alive," Cain insisted.

"I understand," said the mark.

The mark would need to keep its lust for Eva a secret from Cain and from Michael the Archangel. This would ensure him a continued degree of latitude and autonomy in marking Cain. All the hosts of Heaven knew of the fate of Lucifer and his followers who at one time had enjoyed the same latitude and autonomy. The pull of Cain's flesh on the spirit of the mark was a powerful force. Well aware of the possible consequences, the mark was gladly taking the risk, because of its desire for the knowledge of Eva.

Cain looking around to find his mark said, "You are never to leave me again. Is that understood?"

"Yes," the mark gladly agreed as it anticipated knowing the flesh of Eva. *If this works, perhaps I will become increasingly independent; as Cain's flesh allows me dominion over him, perhaps I will have offspring?* thought the mark. So the mark set out to encourage Cain to have relations with his wife again as soon as possible so that it could acquire the knowledge it lusted for.

After this, the separate identities of Cain and his mark became less distinct. Cain was becoming the mark and the mark was becoming Cain. Pretty soon, the mark was having relations with Cain's wife while Cain was in something like a trance, and Cain's seed became co-opted with the spirit of the mark.

With this dire development, God apologized to His Son. "Son, every thought and deed of man is corrupt, and now his seed also is being corrupted with the spirit of another realm of beings. In Your Name I repent that I have made man. Son, I am sorry." (CEV Gen. 6:6, 6:11–12)

God, in His sorrow, looking through the Holy Spirit, could see that many changes would have to be made to take man in a different and far better direction. God could see that mercy without a justice system was wreaking havoc on earth. Every thought, act, and deed of man was becoming evil. (KJV Gen. 6:5) What had been intended as a lesson for both God and man had instead come to be license for man and sorrow for God.

"Now that God knows man, it will soon be time for man to meet God," said the Father. The type of meeting that God had in mind would not be pleasant for the vast majority of those who would be greeted. "Through Our mercy, We have learned that beings of the flesh are capable of great depths of depravity——depravities that never occurred to Me as even being possible," God told the Son.

The Son responded to God's sorrowful words, "The risk was known, Father, and I understand your concern for Me, but I pray that We continue on with man. It will be worth My sacrifice, a sacrifice that will guide many to love Us," said the Son. "The Spirit informs Us that a new dispensation is the best course to follow, a dispensation of law, as only law tends to restrain those who know not love," added the Son. "Now, We only need to select the right men to take the lessons learned into a new world, and a new era governed by man, with principles that We shall give them," said the Son.

"For Our children now on earth, We shall warn them; hopefully some of them will repent," God continued.

"A prophet who is known to be from Us should be effective in making that happen," the Son added.

"Good, my Son. For the wise among men, We shall give them a prophet. We shall afford to this prophet great standing, eternal standing. His prophecy will not be of his own words but Ours," said God.

This left the Son with a question: "The majority of men neither listen nor think. How will a loving Father change the hearts and minds of the many?"

"My Son, I share your valid concern, but with man there can be no prediction of outcomes. I suspect that a period of suffering and a swift final death will be the least painful and most appropriate road to repentance," said God.

"Pain . . . I, too, may learn of pain," added the Son.

"My Son, each man and woman shall be judged individually and rightly, and the eternal destination of each child will be decided in the days that follow his or her swift earthly death," God assured the Son. He added, "The children are innocent and will suffer less than they suffer now on earth. Let Us now look to the Holy Spirit, Who will guide Us with the wisdom of the Past and with hope for the

Future, so that together We may choose a good and faithful man who will bring Our message to earth."

GOD LOOKED FOR THREE MEN

God said, "Through the Spirit I can see the need for three men of faith: a prophet, a wise helper, and a comforter."

"It is a good plan that You have conceived," said the Son.

"Yes, I can see into the future far enough to know that it is a plan with a good chance of success," agreed the Holy Spirit. The Holy Spirit then added, "Adam and Eve have born another son of faith whose descendants will include men who can do this work. This birth brings Us hope."

More than eight hundred years before this, in Adam's one hundred and thirtieth year, Adam said to Eve, "We have many sons and daughters, but we have never named a son to take the place of our slain son Abel, our first son born of faith." Eve nodded in agreement. "I believe it is time to do so. We should cain one last son and bless him in name, honor, and guidance so he can stand in the stead of our first son of faith, Abel."

She added, "Indeed, Abel, if he is watching, would be proud of this gesture to honor his memory. We shall name the boy Seth, and his sons and daughters of faith will be a tribute to the memory of Abel." She realized something else. "Further, I believe that from Seth will come the men of faith that God needs to work with and through."

Seth was born and was so named. He would live nine hundred and twelve years and sire many sons and daughters of faith. (KJV Gen. 5:8) From these children, God would choose three good men.

The Godhead now held the promise of two good men and the hope of a third who would spring from those two.

First, They would need a prophet. Second, They would need an older, wiser man who would mentor and assist the third man who would be carefully prepared from childhood for his mission as the comforter. The comforter would grant a new start to all mankind, to all of creation, and all men would be descendants of Seth.

First God looked to Enoch, the Sethite. Unlike Enoch of Nod, this Enoch was a good man who looked to Abel as a model of a man of faith. The matter was of such importance that God Himself decided to approach Enoch.

Enoch was a lion of a man who, from a young age, was a master of all forms of defense. Though a lion in battle, he was a lamb in the house of his fathers. He was dedicated more than any other man to the defense of God. He often tried to identify others who were like himself in their defense of God, but he never found any such people. He viewed himself as a divine warrior. Maybe someday he would encounter another such man, another ally in God's defense.

"Enoch," whispered God one day as Enoch was walking alone in a pasture. "Enoch," He whispered more firmly, and He was satisfied that He had not frightened Enoch.

"Father, maybe I am dreaming, but I sense that this is indeed You," Enoch answered.

"No, Enoch, you are not dreaming. My Son has a task for you," God said. Then a cloud materialized in the sky. Neither Enoch nor any other man had ever seen a cloud, the closest thing they knew of was an occasional morning mist that was close to the ground. This cloud slowly descended from the sky and floated about Enoch's head. He bent his knee and humbled himself, as he sensed that the presence of the Son was actually within the cloud.

"Enoch, the Spirit is with you, and you are with the Spirit. God always has need of men like you. Your name will long be remembered," spoke the Son from the cloud.

Enoch acknowledged His presence. "Lord, I am at your service. I will serve You and only You, my Lord."

With that, the Son told Enoch, "Plans have been made in Heaven, and you will bring Our plans to the world."

"Yes, my Lord," said Enoch. (KJV Gen. 5:22)

The cloud moved closer to Enoch. "Listen carefully, for you are now a prophet for God. You are to warn man that judgment is coming. It will begin in six hundred and sixty-six years with a drought that will plague the entire earth. This drought will last for three years. At the end of that drought, in six hundred and sixty-nine years, every man and every woman will be judged. For those who survive the drought, a comforter will ensure that their misery ends with a swift and certain death and then their judgment," said the Son.

Enoch remained on bended knee in silence and thought about this honor. The prophecy he was to give became part of him, deeply embedded in his spirit. He remained on bended knee, with his head bowed, sensing that his Lord had more to say. "Enoch, only men and women who follow the example of Abel shall be spared the agony of their eternal judgment in darkness."

"Yes, my Lord," said Enoch. He understood clearly the way of Abel, the first man of faith. The way of Abel was sacrifice.

"Enoch, preach it far and wide. When the time is right, I will come for you, and you will depart from the earth, witnessed by many," said the Son.

"I will faithfully do as you ask, my Lord." As Enoch said these words, he raised his head and stood, watching the cloud float back into the heavens. Enoch was three hundred and sixty-two years old when the Son came to him in the cloud.

Knowing that he had been chosen by God greatly encouraged Enoch to be bold as he went forward to preach. The Lord God, through the Spirit, had made a wise choice in choosing Enoch. For three years, Enoch would preach that man should repent and sacrifice because the day of judgment was coming.

He preached to all who would listen and to many who didn't want to listen. In his wisdom, Enoch knew that his words would have much more standing once God took him than they did now. "Remember what I have said. When you see me depart with my Lord, you will believe that I have spoken the Word of the Son."

Enoch didn't know how long it would be before the Son returned for him, but with the urgency that he preached the prophecy, he must have believed it would not be long. He wasted no time warning men over and over again about the coming judgment.

Enoch preached the prophecy to many thousands. Among these was his son Methuselah, who was to be the second of the three good men that God would choose for His work.

Methuselah had been a good boy and was growing into a fine young man. He loved his father, Enoch, and accompanied him everywhere. Enoch taught Methuselah about many things, such as how and why to sacrifice, how to defend himself, and of course, his prophecy. Enoch was preparing his son well for his future, a future that was largely unknown to Enoch. But Methuselah, like his father, wanted to serve his Lord, and the Lord was pleased with Methuselah's progress.

Methuselah was big, and he was as strong as an ox. Yet, true to his name——which means "man of the dart" and "man of the mission"——he had the ability to be seen yet unseen like a dart in the whispering wind. This ability would serve him well in the future.

His size and his skills would make him a perfect fit for the mission God had in mind for him——just what God had needed, had been hoping for, and would be able to depend on.

Methuselah never tired of hearing about the meeting between his father and the Son, and many times Enoch retold the story of the prophecy. Methuselah also listened to Enoch speak of it countless times more while speaking privately with others or preaching to groups of people.

Methuselah believed in the prophecy as unconditionally as his father did. It was as much a part of him as it was a part of Enoch. Then, one day, Enoch recalled a detail of the prophecy that he realized he had never repeated to anybody. Maybe this important detail was intended for his son and only for his son. On this day Methuselah asked, as he often did, "Father, tell me again about your meeting with the Son of God."

"It was so exhilarating when the Father whispered to me," Enoch told him. "It was so pleasing to feel His love. Then, suddenly, I found myself in the presence of the Son. I was humbled; I couldn't look up. I felt unworthy to look upon my Lord." Enoch had never hesitated at this point in the story before, but he did this time. His jaw dropped in surprise and he exclaimed, "Son, I just remembered something else He said to me. I can't believe I haven't recalled this until now."

Methuselah was on the edge of his seat, eager to hear the rest. "What, Father? What? What else did the Son say?"

Enoch paused again as he wondered why he had not remembered what the Son had said until this moment. Then he said, "My Lord said there would be a 'comforter' to end the misery of the drought on earth."

"Father, what does that mean?" asked Methuselah anxiously. Enoch was slow to answer and then said that he wasn't sure. But then he added, "Son, I think I remembered this detail for your benefit. I have always believed that your role in history would be more important than mine. Now I believe that even more strongly. I believe that this part of the Lord's prophecy will be very important to your mission after my Lord takes me."

Methuselah thanked his father and asked him, "Father, could I please be present when the Son comes for you? It would be a great honor to witness this."

"Son, that will be up to my Lord, but I hope so. I would love to be able to wave to you as I ascend into Heaven. I will miss you more than any other part of my earthly existence, but we will be together again in Heaven after you have served the Lord as I now serve Him." The good father and the good son embraced.

As Enoch continued to preach, many of the Sethites became believers. In time, word spread to the rest of the earth but, other than some of the Sethites, few believed. After three years had passed it was time for Enoch to be given the standing among men, the standing that would convince many more people that he was indeed a prophet of the Lord and that his words were from the Son of God.

So God walked again with Enoch, and God was pleased that man had been given sufficient warning of what was to come, so He took Enoch from the earth——alive——and held him close. (KJV Gen. 5:24) This gave Enoch the standing that God wanted him to have, which was more than enough proof for those who chose to look.

God had seen that Enoch's son Methuselah had heard and believed that his father was a prophet; so in God's eyes, Methuselah was qualified to carry out the tasks that God had in store for him, as God had hoped he would be. Enoch had completed the work that God had required of him. Now His attention turned to Methuselah and would soon turn to another: the comforter.

Methuselah had been two hundred and ninety-seven years old when his father, Enoch, had told him of the coming drought. Three years later, Methuselah had been a witness as his father ascended into the heavens. (KJV Gen. 5:23) Neither of them felt sadness; they were happy for each other because they could feel the Father's love for them. As Enoch rested in the cloud that had wrested him from an earth that never rested in its attempts to pull this worthy man of God unto itself, Enoch shouted out a final word from the cloud to his loving son:

"Methuselah, after the judgment, the days of the year will forever bear my current age as further witness to my standing with our Lord." Enoch was three moons past the age of three hundred and sixty-five years.

Methuselah would never understand the last words his father Enoch had said as he was taken by the Lord, but he believed them to be true, and he would pass that final prophecy on to others whenever his spirit urged him to do so.

A group of perhaps five hundred watched as did Methuselah as a sparkling white cloudy vapor, formed around the feet of Enoch. Then Enoch very slowly moved up into the air a few arm lengths above the ground, supported by only the mysterious vapor. Now looking down on the crowd he smiled and once more repeated the prophecy.

The crowd grew silent and then afraid as the cloud moved further and farther away. Seeing is not always believing, and some of the fearful shouted out their unbelief. Methuselah shook his head also in unbelief, unbelief in those who now discounted their own eyes. The objectors were the clear minority, mostly men who were there to laugh at Enoch while he awaited "the lord," they didn't get what they had hoped for and now in their unbelief they were so afraid.

The tales of that day spread far and wide, every man confessing to others about the amazing event they had witnessed. Many who heard believed; many who heard did not believe.

Despite the fact that many had witnessed Enoch's ascension into the heavens, the prophecy dealt with a time so far in the future that most considered it unimportant. It would be centuries yet until the arrival of the drought, and most people were concerned only with living their lives and couldn't care less——at least for now. Many would promise to pass on the word of the Lord, but beyond that the prophecy had little impact. Methuselah was one of the very few that would never ever forget the prophecy his father had been given.

Methuselah had a son, Lamech, a Sethite. In the days before the birth of Lamech's own son, Methuselah dreamt that this child was destined to comfort many, and this dream reminded him of what Enoch had prophesied to him about a "comforter." He discussed this with his son Lamech, and they concluded that this child should be called Noah——one who will bring comfort to the many. (KJV Gen. 5:29)

Methuselah now believed that God had been waiting patiently and confidently for a good man to be born and that this child of Lamech, Methuselah's own grandson, was the one. Methuselah believed that his own role in this was not by chance and that God was depending on him——perhaps as much as He would depend on the comforter——to go forward with Enoch's prophecy.

Methuselah was three hundred and eighty-seven years old when he began to mentor his grandson Noah, who would soon be a man. After all these years, Methuselah still clearly remembered the day the Lord had taken his father, and he taught the boy to understand the meaning of his name and the duties that would be upon him someday.

"Noah, I need you to trust me. It was I who asked your father to name you 'the one who brings comfort,' and this was because of a dream I had." Noah listened attentively. "I saw my father ascend into the heavens some eighty-seven years ago. Son, I was not dreaming then. As sure as I sit here, what I tell you is the truth." Noah continued to listen eagerly. "I don't know how I know this, but, as with my father Enoch, your name will be known by all men. You will be known as the comforter who served our Lord."

As Methuselah paused to let this sink in, the boy said, "I do believe you. I, too, have had a dream." Now Methuselah was eager to hear more.

"It is as you say. I am to bring comfort first to those who will suffer in the coming drought and then to those who will suffer in all droughts to come after it. In my dream my family and I are saved, with the help of the Lord, from the drought which will end in judgment," the young boy said. Methuselah was thrilled, but he wanted to hear more.

"How? How will you be saved? In a cloud, like the one that took my father to Heaven?"

Noah paused for a moment and said, "I did see clouds, many clouds, but neither I nor anybody else was in these clouds. The clouds I saw were weeping. Those weeping clouds will bring comfort to those who work the ground." He continued, "God made it clear to me in the dream that it is my faith and not the clouds that will save me and my family."

Faith was certainly not unknown to Methuselah—after all, his role model was Abel.

Methuselah was very pleased with the young man. He would help Noah's father, Lamech the Sethite, raise the boy and teach him to honor his fathers, including God, the most important Father of all. They would encourage Noah's many interests, including his fascination with water and with making things that could float on water.

Noah grew up to be a man of few words; he was more prone to listening, studying, and learning. His interests were diverse, and he wanted to understand how things were made and how things were done. Once he mastered one process, he immediately moved on to the next challenge. He had been a fascinating child and had become a fascinating man who knew that he would need expertise in many areas to be able to provide comfort to others in the future. Noah's vision, knowledge, and faith would eventually take him to places that neither he nor any other man on earth had any notion of.

—— 9 ——
AWAITING THE COMFORTER

Six hundred and sixty-six years and three moons would pass between the departure of the prophet Enoch and the arrival of the foretold drought.

This was a long period of time, yet less than the life span of a single man in those days. With the judgment date set according to the prophecy, man and God had several hundred years to wait, time that was needed for the earth to mature. A sun matured earth would be pivotal in providing the energy needed for the post judgment inhabitants.

As the earth matured so did God's wisdom. God knew that this would be the one and only opportunity for a corporate earthly judgment of the innocent and of the guilty. Fully knowing the heart of man, under these circumstances, was critically important to the Godhead. They would use this wisdom to formulate the changes They would initiate in the post judgment earth.

Never again would God and all men to come have the benefit of this type of insight into both the heart of man and the mercy of God. God would record the events——the what, the where, the who, the when, the how——and then decide what to disclose to man to most benefit His children.

This was a lengthy and painful ordeal for man and for God. Man had reached new lows of depravity that God had not foreseen as being possible, but the depths of man's depravity was still not known, as they continued their downward spiral.

God's goal with any new dispensation would be that self-correction must be a larger part of its dynamics, and the Godhead were still optimistic that at some point the heart of man might become self-correcting. All of God's creations had mechanisms for feedback. Looking beyond the coming judgment, God, with His newly formed wisdom, would introduce and incorporate much more personal and societal feedback into the dynamics of man's environment. God had found the wisdom He had coveted but man had not, and God the Father grieved for His children's futures. God would reveal to man at a date yet to be determined the history man would need to learn for themselves.

THE TWO SOCIETIES, THE TWO BLOODLINES

The population of the earth, that was one single land mass, rapidly increased in two regions, each with its own bloodline and each with its own way of life. The earth was very large, but there was only one land mass, Pangea, and there was only one language spoken. Thus, these separate populations, with their very different cultures of life, could not possibly remain isolated from each other forever.

The Cainites lived in the land of Nod. Their city had a pentagon at its center, which had five pinnacles and five points that delineated a circle, the Circle of Man.

The Sethites lived in the Square of Adam. With its four corners, it was Adam's admirable attempt at a godly form of society. While adding one extra side might seem a superficial matter of geometry, in reality the differences between the two systems were exponential.

In the Circle of Man, in Nod, God had been replaced by government, while God was central to the inception and design of the Square of Adam. The government of Nod consisted of tax collectors, regulators, and judges——known collectively as "the watchers." These men had great power and used it to enrich themselves at every opportunity. If you were involved in trade in the Circle of Man, the men of power received a cut, and the amount of their cut was always increasing. Goods that were discovered to have been traded untaxed were confiscated.

The only worship in the Circle was worship of the government; not in so many words, but those who profited from the large corporate government would support it at all costs. Those of the government cult always paid in full, with all they had——first their reputations and then their souls——never at any cost forsaking their devotion to their *tree* of control, the government.

In the Circle of Man, people would gather in groups to try to exert power and influence over the government, but the biggest and most powerful group was the government itself. It dwarfed all other corporate entities combined.

As the Circle grew, its influence grew. Soon, every locale on earth would be pierced by the points of the Circle's pentacles. Dense jungles and fast-moving rivers were minor obstacles, as the corporate self-interest of the pentagon advanced closer to the Square of Adam.

The population of the Square of Adam had expanded quickly, as the many sons and daughters of Adam and Eve had themselves many sons and daughters. By the time Adam was an old man, he had hundreds of thousands of descendants, and long after Adam's death, hundreds of millions of people would populate the earth.

Early on, as the population of the Square had grown into the hundreds, a place had been needed to gather, to resolve disputes, and to trade. A natural site for these activities was near the altar where the weekly sacrifice was offered.

The Square of Adam had been envisioned and created by its namesake. On one side of the Square was the altar for sacrificing to God. The opposite side of the Square was where Adam would stand whenever a judge was needed. To the left of Adam's podium was the marketplace where all men could freely trade. To the right sat the elders as they shared their wisdom and advised the young; those in need of work or charity gathered there as well. In the center of the public Square was a beautiful park where the children played. The children brought a sense of innocence to the Square that helped to temper the ways of merchants.

Cain's murder of Abel had corrupted the Square to some extent. Adam had done a reasonably good job creating a criminal justice system, but it lacked the death penalty, so there would always be some sense of injustice in the square.

Despite that major flaw, the people of the Square fared much better than did the inhabitants of the rest of the earth. The Square, with the dynamics from its design and its conception, was resistant to the infiltration of crime and largely immune to the small amount of corruption feeding back to it.

In Nod especially, the land was badly blighted by crime. The villainy would, in time, spread and eventually plague the entire earth, and the two populations of the earth were not far enough apart for the Square of Adam to be forever immune from that infection.

In the public Square administered by Adam, he received a portion of each sacrifice brought by his grown children and managed and maintained the Square with those offerings, thus allowing for free trade.

Each Saturday, the final day of each week, most of the people flocked to the altar that Adam had built so long ago, and each would deliver an offering to Adam. Adam would faithfully select the very best from these to burn on the altar as offerings to God.

To encourage people to rest on Saturday and participate in the sacrifice, Adam used a figure of speech. "Anything made on Saturday would be lost on Sunday," he would say.

The Square was about three hundred and sixty arm-lengths across, and the altar was directly across from the judgment seat. This was because Adam felt more at ease if he was facing the altar and could look up at it when he had to pass judgment on any of his children. He believed that this is what the Son would do if He chose to be the One to administer justice in the Square. Further, he believed that all men would eventually be judged before the altar of God.

Adam's seat of judgment was always clean. People respected it, just as they respected Adam when he sat there on the occasional Saturday to adjudicate matters, something he had done for centuries now. Adam always realized that his rulings only held whatever standing that he himself was seen to hold. His standing as being the first man was long gone, the only standing he had now was what he had earned being a just judge, and stood above all others.

Adam considered the seat of judgment a very important symbol to inspire self-restraint in all men, and he believed this to be of great benefit to the Square. He noticed over the centuries that the millions of people who had passed by his judgment seat displayed a different reaction than those same people did when they passed before the altar.

Adam imagined that the people walking past the judgment seat were being introspective——that they were self-evaluating, which is what he did himself. Adam believed strongly that the judgment seat should remain in the public eye, as this led people to be honest with themselves. People who kept themselves honest were a great asset to the Square and to the entire community. Adam knew that the Square would no longer function properly without this communal self-restraint, so he always kept the altar and the judgment seat in good repair and in good rapport.

In the Square of Adam, the only corporate entity was the family. As was the case in the squares elsewhere on earth, the primary component of preserving one's freedom being that of self-interest tempered with self-restraint.

Squaresville, as the teenagers called it, may have been boring, but it was safe——as the children matured they came to appreciate its sanctity. The Square was a model of how a good community could be run, and it was duplicated by many of Adam's children in various locations to the west.

Though the other squares that had been founded had their own unique characteristics, they had all followed the same basic pattern that had been set by Adam's Square. They were very clean and very cheerful for the children. No such squares could be found in the land of Nod.

Adam and Eve lived close to the Square, in a home built of stone. It was nicely adorned with cherished memorabilia of their many children. One beautiful adornment for their home was the clothing that God had made for them when they were being forced out of the Garden of Eden. These amazing wool garments never seemed to age. Sons and daughters would travel great distances to see and touch these amazing garments that had been made by God, and Eve used them time and again to demonstrate to her daughters how to sew and how to fashion beautiful garments.

This simple act of God, giving Adam and Eve clothing, had been a huge blessing in an incalculable number of ways. From the threads used to stitch the seams, from the linings of the hides, from the conditioning of the skins, there was much to learn from these God-given garments. A garment-making industry had sprung up in the early days of man on earth, and it had prompted man to conceive of many other trades. Many of the women in the Square took to making garments, and they made them in many styles and from many different materials and fabrics. Men and women always needed new clothing, so trade among individuals was brisk.

Despite the curse of Adam, that all men would have to work the ground as a consequence of his rebellion, life was not that difficult for most. Maybe things were not easy compared to life in the garden, but Adam had learned that "not so easy" is actually easier in the long run, as his labor kept him focused on what was truly important in his life. Providing for his family.

Sure, the ground had to be worked to produce food, but the food grew quickly, and there was plenty of good soil in which to plant the crops. There was plenty of fresh water available from springs that welled up from the ground and from the rivers that rushed by their homes. Generally, the people were healthy. Sickness was uncommon and fleeting; cuts and bruises healed quickly and left no marks. The effects of the curse were mild in the Square of Adam, as Adam learned——and taught men——how to deal with it.

It had been a long time since God had communicated with Adam, but Adam loved his Father more than ever. Though they had never discussed this, it did seem to both of them that the less God was involved with Adam, the stronger was Adam's love for Him. The love and respect Adam had for his Father did not come from his long past interactions with God, they came from his introspection of God. Introspection that unavoidably led Adam to his understanding that it was not necessary to see or hear God to love Him, all one had to do was look around at what had been created for man, in the creation every man can see God's love.

"Adam, let me see. Come on, please, just one more time?" Adam heard this question thousands of times from his children, young and old. Over and over he would lift his shirt and let them see that he had no navel. They would move their faces closer to him, and they would try to touch him with their hands, still skeptical. Adam grew weary of the constant repetition of this event.

"Why can't you just believe? Why must you see? Why must you touch? My son, it really isn't necessary to see to believe. It just isn't." Adam knew what their answers would be———and he did not know what he could possibly say to make them understand that you can only have faith by practicing faith.

Over time, Adam also became weary of explaining how, when, and where he had discovered that the ritual of sacrifice was a way to thank God and to eliminate the burden of guilt in one's life. Adam in his later years was losing interest in his Square and as a result, the quality of life in the Square declined.

In hindsight, Adam believed that he should have closed down the Square when he had begun to detect this decline. He considered turning its management over to someone else, but even under new management, it was Adam's square, that would never change fast enough to mitigate the obvious decline.

He would have been wise to have closed it down to allow the land to heal. Then as the land healed, another, younger man could have taken charge with a new sense of purpose that the elder Adam could no longer bring to it. Adam, after a long and full life, came to understand that you cannot un-corrupt the corrupted———you can only start anew.

ANOTHER SIDE TO LIFE IN A PENTAGON, IN NOD

The small change of adding a fifth side to a square brought about a big shift in ideology———from one of freedom to one of control. As it was with man, the foundation of society was fundamental to the direction in which it would grow. In Nod, the curse of Adam was far more obvious than it was in Adam's Square, because the residents of Nod were burdened not only with thorns and thistles from Adam's curse but also with taxes and regulations from the fifth side.

The watchers from the fifth side added new hurdles day by day. Regulations——when, where, and how business was done——changed daily, always increasing the watchers control and decreasing the people's standard of living. Thorns and thistles from the curse of man in no way hindered their pursuit of their objectives. The curse and the watchers were allies in a way, as they shared a common enemy——freedom.

Thorns and thistles restricted man in many ways, but by far the most destructive aspect of the curse was how other men usurped it to their own benefit. Out of a lust for power these men who coveted God's standing in the lives of others, would point to the curse as something that they and only they could fix.

Those men, these bureaucrats who pledged their allegiance to the largest corporate entity to ever exist, the government——day after day, pointed to the curse always saying they could make it better. Every day, every problem had the same solution——give them more power. A task made easy, as most men were incapable or unwilling to simply look back at what God had done and why. Or even look back to see if the bureaucratic solution worked, looking back was painful for man and men avoided pain at all cost.

MARRIAGE GREATLY OFFSET ADAM'S CURSE

Without doubt, from the time of Adam to the time of Enoch the Cainite, the effect of Adam's curse had diminished, and quality of life had been enhanced by fruitful marriages. This was the custom that had come down from Adam——one man and one woman becoming one flesh. By man and wife as one standing on the shoulders of those who came before them.

Adam was never *told* to take only one wife, and that is *why* he never took another.

On a few occasions, Adam would explain that concept to his grandchildren, "I think God tricked your grandmother and me into monogamy." That bit of satire always worked as Adam watched the kids gather around.

Then Adam would explain, "I learned, by looking back at the tree of knowledge, that forbidden fruits are far more enticing than those that are not——God by not forbidding either of us an additional spouse took away all the enticement to do so——so yes my Father tricked us into a wonderful and beautiful marriage." Adam would pause, "Life is full of ironies, that was the first one", and ending his tale with a good laugh, a very purposeful laugh.

The kids would not join in the laughter as they pondered the irony of forbidden fruits. Life seemed to be furnished with many of them, a decor that is only seen by looking back, and only truly understood by living and laughing at one's ironic adventures. Adam believed that laughter was the key to learning; comedy in life gave relief to its many tragedies and laughing emoted a path to understanding the why of the former.

But Adam's concept of marriage, in Nod anyway, had come under attack during the reign of Enoch, son of Cain, and the situation was exacerbated under the rule of Lamech the Cainite. This began in the pentagon of Nod when there were many more women than men. The women who were without husbands lusted for men in all ways imaginable. Occasionally, men and women committed adultery. Enoch the Cainite, when he ruled Nod and when confronted with this problem, made a law that would punish adultery with a fine. Of course, that fine was to be paid to Enoch.

So men began to believe that a fine could pay for——and absolve them of guilt from——their extramarital affairs. They soon came to see this as a license to do whatever they liked. Because of

Enoch's foolish law, men acted upon desires that otherwise may never have entered their minds. Adultery flourished at an alarming rate, and the situation grew worse with each passing day and year. Soon, men realized that they could avoid the fine by being very private with their affairs. It didn't take long for the fine to lose all of its deterrent powers but it stayed in place giving license to do as they were enticed to do by the law. Women realized that dressing provocatively could get them husbands. And then they came to give of themselves in the hopes of securing a husband, ending up used and used up instead.

Enoch, the son of Cain, recognized that it was wrong for the city to profit from this licentious behavior, but Enoch always wanted more money. Enoch didn't think this through enough to realize that, by charging a fine for this behavior, he was basically licensing adultery. He was taking the Circle of Man down an already treacherous path and even further into condemnation——not intentionally——but due to his lack of wisdom and greed for the fines collected by provoking his subjects.

AGE OF IRON

In the early days of building their city in Nod, Cain and Enoch had discovered some very special stones. These stones were dark gray in color and very heavy. In fact, they were far too heavy for building homes or other structures. But these stones were great for other uses, such as breaking softer and lighter stones into shapes that could be used for building. These unique gray stones were abundant in the land of Nod, and Cain often used them to make tools. Soon, many other uses for these dark gray stones, which came to be called ferro stones, came to light.

Men experimented with these heavy ferro stones for hundreds of years. Over time, they became known as iron. Then experimentation with a compound of iron and the carbon used to melt them resulted in steel, which was much stronger even than iron. Steel made its way into the life of every city dweller.

Soon men wanted and needed tools of steel in order to farm, to build, and to make powerful weapons. The demand for steel became great——anyone who could produce steel tools and weapons became wealthy and more powerful than the weapons themselves, and Lamech sought to achieve a monopoly over its production.

Intense heat was required to soften the heavy stones as part of the process of forming tools and other steel products. Thus arose the need for coal. Coal was not known to exist on the earth's surface; it could only be made from hardwood trees. Lamech realized that without coal there could be no iron, no steel, and no industry. So, as the creation of coal would be the basis for the manufacture of all other goods, Lamech ensured that he would be in control of all production and use of coal. As coal was foundational, it came to be the most regulated of all products on earth.

Thus, Lamech the Cainite, in Nod, made himself the king of coal and the king of steel. His steel rooms, the largest on earth, were in production all day, every day, as men worked nonstop making items of iron and steel. The output from these steel rooms increased exponentially as time went on. Steel items made life much easier in so many ways, and they were in great demand everywhere.

At night, steel production ceased, and most men went to sleep as the night shift went to work on coal production. Hardwoods would be partially burned and then the air that had fed the flames in the furnaces would be extinguished, allowing the partially burned wood to smolder. The next day, the smoldering hardwoods would be reignited and used as coal.

Some men would take advantage of the residual heat in the furnaces to glean the slag. They used the slag (left behind iron waste) to make small items of steel for themselves and for others.

THE FIRST DIES A NATURAL DEATH

Adam had been the most respected man in his land, and late in his life he had used his standing to teach. Teaching the children, as they were open to learning, was his greatest joy. Mostly, he would teach them about the things he had learned about God.

One of the many topics that Adam loved to ponder was the nature of God. Adam had always been able to see God in all of creation, and he often wondered if it had to be thus——if His creation must reflect Him.

"Can a master painter paint something worthless?" Adam would wonder aloud. "Can the Creator of the Heavens and the earth create in a way that doesn't reflect His glory? Can the Creator of the Heavens and the earth curse His own creation in a way that doesn't reflect His desires for His little ones?" Adam's conclusion: "God loves, and that love is a reflection that is unavoidable in all of creation. God's love is deep: layer upon layer it has no end, just as God has no end. His love for symbolism is evident in everything that He has made, because everything that He has made is a symbol of His love."

Then there were the two trees in the garden that God Himself had planted.

When Adam spoke of God planting the Garden in Eden he would say, "It was the nature of God to take the things that were of greatest risk to His children and let it be known that it was His decision to allow those risks. God carefully and mindfully planted two beautiful and special trees, thus creating two choices for me, two choices for man. He planted those two special trees precisely where He wanted them to be. One special tree was among the rest of the trees of the garden, and one was right at the center of the garden. He was hoping for the best outcome, while fully knowing the risk to His Son. God is not risk averse." Adam was very comfortable with the God that he had come to know through his sacrifices, a God that Himself would suffer for His choices.

After all this time, and after having been a judge in the Square for several hundred years, Adam had come to understand that the two trees in the garden were symbolic of Lucifer and God. Often, Adam would refer to the tree of knowledge as the "tree of guilt" because guilt is all he had ever experienced in connection with it. Sometimes he would call it "Lucifer's tree," because whenever he envisioned the tree, he envisioned Lucifer there as well.

He told generations of his progeny that they had a choice between God and Lucifer——between life and guilt. Long ago, Adam had assumed that the guilt he had taken on at Lucifer's tree was the serpent's greatest tool; but he had later come to realize that one could use Lucifer's tree to direct others to the altar and to offer a sacrifice as a means of counteracting the tree's effects. He urged them to follow God and to leave the guilt behind for those who wouldn't follow God. He would tell them, "While we can't return to the garden, the tree of life is still available to you at the altar with your sacrifice. If your brother has guilt, use Lucifer's tree, have your brother turn his back to it while you point him in the right direction——towards the tree of life, towards the altar."

Adam never guaranteed to them that an offering would achieve their ends. He simply told them that, if it did, they would know it. But he did assure them, "If your heart is humble in your offering, you will be rewarded with the peace and the love of the Father."

When pressed by those seeking deeper understanding, Adam would deliver more details about how he had discovered sacrifice as a temporary cure for guilt. Then he would encourage them with his belief that the altar would work the same way for everybody who came to it. "You never know what circumstances may bring you to the tree of life," he would say. "Just know that when you come to it, come to it humbly and with praise and thanks——you will be rewarded." Everyone who heard his words wanted to know about these rewards. Adam would say, "If it is reward you seek, then you're looking in the wrong place. Seek first the tree of life at the altar, and your reward will be everlasting life."

Adam realized that it was impossible for Lucifer's tree not to have a hold on all men in some way for some period during their lives, because he was the father of all and that this would be a factor in human life, on earth, forever. Understanding this, he cautioned all of his children: "Lucifer's tree has such a pull on the flesh that even if God Himself came down from Heaven, cut it down, bore its burden on His own shoulders, dragged it step by step to the top of a mountain, and hung it there for all to see as *it* slowly died, still some would rather cling to it than to God." Further, he would add, "I am not even sure if God Himself could silence Lucifer's tree——such is the strength of its pull."

"Is it God's plan for the tree to have such strength in so many people's lives?" the children would ask.

Adam would laugh and shake his head. "God wants no man to oppose Him, to do so is evil——He wishes of no man evil. I gave little thought to my actions at the tree, long ago. Men, perhaps, will never change. I was a child at the time, a child of six days old. My age made my offense worse. I was a misguided and rebellious child, with no reason whatsoever to do what I did that day," Adam would lament. "I would go on to struggle with the repercussions of that decision for quite some time. Of all the things I have done in my life, without any doubt . . ." Adam would pause and his eyes would fill with tears before he continued, "the turning point in my life came when I stopped blaming God for my guilt. Of all the things I have ever done in my life that was by far the wisest. It was the tree and my actions there, and Lucifer's actions there, that were the source of my guilt. When my Father kicked me out of the garden, that was but the action of a loving Father protecting His son from himself. There was no mystery involved, just love," Adam would say.

"When I humbled myself and thanked God, I could then clearly see, just as I am clearly seen. There are many reasons to bring a sacrifice to the altar. Sometimes they are brought in despair because of a significant loss. Sometimes they are brought by a guilty soul. Sometimes they are brought because of reasoning, and there are countless other motives. Everyone has their own reason to come to God's altar. Men and women who have gone against God, who now wish to go towards God. When they turn, they will sense the open arms of the Father welcoming them all. As long as they come with humility, knowing in their hearts that they are known to be guilty."

Adam was very old now, and he sensed that his departure from his earthly home was imminent. Adam's recollections of his encounters with his Father had evolved over his long life, but he had never forgotten those six days of innocence that he had experienced as a man-child with his Father in a garden, in a faraway place, long ago.

Eve had joined their Father a few years earlier, after nine centuries of marriage, and it was now time for Adam to join them too. So Adam closed his eyes on his first——earthly——stop in the eternal journey of life but then immediately reopened them on the next stop, exactly as it had been for Abel. Now he was looking at only one tree, the tree of life. This time, through humility, he had chosen wisely. (KJV Gen. 5:5)

Adam's earthly life had not been especially easy, nor had it been especially difficult. Perhaps that was the best sort of life that one could ever wish for. Perhaps a man's life would always be a combination of what he deserved and what was required for him to be able to see the two trees——the trees which represented two opposing ways of life: law and love.

Adam was God's first fleshly child, and while a loving father would have liked it to go very differently for him than it had, the only thing that mattered was that His little boy was coming home. On that day, God was so happy that He cried tears of joy.

—— 10 ——
THE COMFORTER

It had been well over a thousand years since the beginning of creation. Adam had been dead for some time now, and his Square was declining even faster in his absence. Many good men in the Square were painfully aware of the decline.

One man who was especially bothered by the prospect of the Cainite and Sethite bloodlines mixing was Noah. Noah didn't want his sons to be part of this blending of cultures.

Noah was closing in on his five-hundredth year of life, and according to the prophecy of his great-grandfather, Enoch the Sethite, the advent of the great earthly drought would occur in a little more than one hundred years.

Noah believed the prophecy, but exactly what role he was to play was not yet clear. His grandfather Methuselah had told Noah as a young man that Noah's role would be to provide comfort to those who would suffer due to the drought, but neither Methuselah nor Noah knew more than that. God only let man know that the drought would be severe and that many would perish before the coming judgment.

But at this moment, Noah was not thinking about a drought that was yet one hundred years in the future; he was far more concerned with raising his sons far away from the influence of the Cainite culture. Noah could see that the Cainite way of life was infiltrating everywhere that people lived. If their stories of the Nephilim were to be believed, if that corrupted seed were to make its way to the Square, the effect on the bloodline of man could be even more profound. The seed of man might become completely corrupted, and Noah believed that if that were to happen there would be no possible redemption for mankind.

Noah searched his mind and could find no good fruition from these mixed beings inhabiting the earth and was now willing to go to great efforts to *avoid* them.

God saw some things very different than did Noah. He also saw one thing that impressed Him–Noah's concern for his sons. God was not so concerned with the angelic seed; He was far more concerned with Noah's linear heritage from Adam, having no links to the rebellious Cain than anything to do with any mixed earthly beings.

Not only had the men from the Circle begun to breed with the Sethite women, but some Cainite women, who were of low moral character came from Nod to look for Sethite husbands. These men were far superior to the men of the Circle of Enoch, and the Cainite women would stop at nothing to seduce the mostly naïve men of the Square.

As the world became ever more corrupt, and every desire in the heart of man became progressively more evil, being in opposition to God, God looked down upon what was transpiring on earth and He felt deep sorrow. The mercy that had been given to Cain, because it had been misunderstood, had affected all of mankind. God in Heaven decided that it was time to once again walk with Enoch, whom He had brought to Heaven so long ago.

God enabled Enoch to see His servant Noah in real time, and Enoch was happy with Noah, as was God. God was pleased with Enoch's counsel and decided to go ahead as planned and carry out the prophecy that He had given to Enoch so long ago and that Enoch had then given to man. Noah was not yet aware of the faith that God and Enoch were placing in his ability to achieve what was needed. Nor did Noah even know yet of the plan for which he was now the cornerstone.

God watched as Noah, acting in his own self-interest and out of love for his children, made plans to leave the Square of Adam. Noah saw what was happening in his beloved home and knew that things were not going to get better. So, to protect himself and his family from the savagery that was spreading across the earth like a flood, Noah, in his five hundredth year of life, took his wife and three sons down the Pishon River in a boat that he had made, to seek out a land where they could start over. God was inspired by Noah's efforts. He took note of the means that Noah used and the extent that Noah went to protect his three young sons and was assured He had chosen Noah wisely. (KJV Gen. 5:32, 6:8)

Traveling down the Pishon River was now commonplace, and some maps of the route that Noah was planning to travel had even been created. Not sure exactly where he wanted to end up, he had grabbed the biggest map that he could find at the market for the cheapest price, figuring that it would be better than nothing. But as the five of them started their journey down the Pishon, the map proved to be of little use.

"Father, the river divides just up ahead. See here on the map? Which of these four routes shall we take?" asked his son Shem a few hours into their journey. But, before Noah could look at the map, a gust of wind snatched it from his hands.

"What was that?" yelled Shem, as everybody on the boat clung tightly to their belongings, even as the wind dissipated as quickly as it had arisen. "That wind seemed to have a spirit of its own," Noah said, wondering to himself what had just happened.

As the five of them looked at each other, Shem wondered, "Father, how shall we navigate without a map?"

"We shall steer to the right and then to the right again," said Noah. "It just seems like the right thing to do." So they kept a rightward course, and when the river opened up into three more branches, they maintained that rightward course. Again the river opened up into three branches, and again they chose the branch on the right. At times, the river moved swiftly. At other times, it moved slowly. Over and again, as their part of the river branched into smaller tributaries, they remained true to their rightward course, until Noah realized that they had been navigating a giant semicircle. When they determined that they had put enough distance between themselves and Adam's Square, they found a spot they liked and decided to settle there. Because their travels had taken them in a great half circle, Noah would create the name Havilah to take the meaning of a giant half circle.

Havilah was a beautiful place. The area was heavily populated with clean animals that tended and tamed the fields, and the earth gleamed with all manner of beautiful stones and shiny metals. (KJV Gen. 2:11–12)

While escaping the Square of Adam and its people had its benefits, it would also be very challenging on a number of levels. The land of Havilah was peaceful and abundant with food and animals. Both great blessings that would help them with their new lives. But, life without the benefit of trade with others would make life far more difficult. So, Noah and his sons——sons who were not even men yet——were all kept busy by just providing the basics. Noah's wife was the only woman, and the five of them were the only people that would exist in their land for the foreseeable future.

Noah was happy in this new place as he no longer worried about the Cainite culture corrupting his sons. God was also pleased and wasted no time in recruiting Noah.

God, once again, was being careful not to frighten Noah, just as He had done with Enoch. Noah and his family were man's best chance at making a good new start on earth. Over the next few days, the Father came to him in a dream, then as a comforting wind, and then as a small voice.

Just as God had wanted, Noah responded in prayer: "Father, if these signs are from you, I am ready to do Your will so that my sons might be saved."

That night, God approached Noah while Noah was praying. This was the first time that God had approached a man since He had approached Enoch, and Noah was not afraid——God had chosen wisely. So God walked with Noah. (KJV Gen. 6:9)

"Noah, you have isolated your family from the immediate threat posed by other men. Your actions have inspired Us to take your plan to the next level, so We are going to help you to make that separation permanent in a similar way." God went further and explained in some detail Their planned escalation . . .

Noah was humbled by this honor, which further confirmed to the Father that he had chosen the right man.

The next morning, Noah went to his wife and sons and told them matter-of-factly of the tasks ahead of them.

"God came to me last night. He told me that the judgment He is bringing upon the earth will be in the form of a severe, worldwide flood. He has asked that we build another boat, a much larger boat for Him——an ark that will ferry us and His animals, clean and unclean, from the coming worldwide deluge. (KJV Gen. 6:13–14, 17)

"Father, do you speak of the prophecy of Enoch?" asked one of his sons.

"Yes, Japheth, but we now know the drought will end in a flood."

"Just how large a boat will be needed to hold us and His animals?" asked Ham.

"God will soon give me the details as to the exact size of the boat and how and where to build it. It will take perhaps a hundred or more years to build the vessel. It is a very big project."

Noah's wife and sons became speechless as they tried to imagine the size and scope of this endeavor.

"My sons and my dear wife, I see the doubt on your faces," Noah said with a grin. "But if you could only have seen me last night walking with God . . ." As he talked of his experience the night before, the boys could see that something had changed in their father. "It was wonderful. The love, the pureness, the goodness that you feel when you are so close to the Father——I can't put it into words." Even Noah's wife was amazed at how Noah's face glowed when he talked about the love of the Father. "Oh, my dear family, my only wish is that you could have been there to experience what I did," said Noah.

He could see that their doubts, at least for now, were fading because they had never heard Noah speak this way before. So Noah added, "I will have much more to show and tell you in the days to come, as we begin our new adventure." Noah thought he was well on his way to convincing them, but then Ham spoke up.

"Father, we have heard all that you have said. We have all heard the prophecy of Enoch many times and we believe it. We believe that God took Enoch in a cloud. So, Father, why doesn't the God of the universe simply take us away from here in a cloud too, instead of asking us to build Him a boat that will take one hundred years to build? Isn't it far more risky to build a wooden boat?"

"Yes, you are absolutely right. It is far more risky to God, but it is far *less* risky to us," Noah replied, bringing the boys in close and looking at them intently. "Boys, listen to me. The love I felt from the Father is indescribable. It is captivating unto bliss itself. Do you believe me?"

As one, the boys replied, "Yes, Father."

"Now, if you felt that love for a long period of time, the time it will take to enter judgment unto this world, would you willingly return to this world?" There was silence. Noah's point was understood by the boys——God would need willing participants to re-inhabit the earth. If God were to save them all in a different way, in a much more comfortable way, would the boys be willing to endure the pain, the discomfort, and the misery of starting the world again from scratch? God cannot always make things easy. A king that is never limited by his children hates His children.

"Now that you can see the Father's dilemma from one point of view, I will add another," said Noah. "Risk to the children is always the major concern of all fathers, but I do not speak of physical pain or injury. I speak of spiritual risk. Do you understand that a child whose father is a king will confront the greatest obstacles to faith?" The boys were silent. "The power of a father is always seen quickly by his children. Our Father's power can easily be seen just by looking at what has been made . . . And the child's father is a fool who always gives them what they ask for. The more powerful the father the more difficult the fathers task will be, as he discerns what is in the best interest of his beloved children."

Still the boys remained silent, which was wise on their part. The things Noah was telling his sons merited thought rather than comments or questions. "Faith is what is required to give us the strength and the understanding to endure what is in store for us," said Noah. "Boys, I want the best for you, just as I know the Father wants the best for me. We have been given a great honor in the form of a great challenge. No man could ask for more than what we have been given. No man!"

Noah was getting through to them, so he continued. "Very soon, I will give you many more details. I will give you as much information as I can, as soon as I can, so that you fully understand each step before I burden you with the next one."

Noah paused looking at each son and then took the hand of his beloved wife, and returned to capture each eye of each boy, "Of all the tasks a man could be given, the God of the universe is trusting me and trusting you with this most honorable of gifts, a most honorable place in eternity. You need to be proud of this honor and eager to undertake this task that God has entrusted us with," Noah concluded. "We will walk into the new world together as a family." As Noah spoke, they were completely captivated and inspired by his passion, and they were filled with belief and faith in their father's.

WHY AN ARK?

Noah was going to help God and God was going to help Noah. This was the only way there could be a reasonable chance of success in the new world.

God had learned that giving help was a very personal and intimate gift that, when done correctly, was worth far more than any amount of riches that could be given or received. The gift of help must be given face to face, eye to eye, hand to hand, a gift that takes one's time. Time being the real gift——Time is the one and only true gift one can give.

True help is a very rewarding experience for all involved. It is not a flippant action or a mechanical reaction; it is a deed motivated by love and never by pity or guilt.

If the motivation for helping is based on alleviating some misguided or even perverted sense of guilt, rather than on actually helping someone, the result will be un helpful.

It had long been said, was widely believed, and was without a doubt true that "Wisdom is seen in her children." Now and forevermore, with guilt being so pervasive on earth, the same would be true about help. Only by looking back, will the helper discover the wisdom of their efforts.

All children learn at a very early age the power of their father and all men intuitively know the power of God by looking at what He has made. Powerful fathers have a very different set of burdens, while raising their children, than a powerless father has. All children and most men will take advantage of any help given them——always wanting, always demanding more help from their powerful father.

Man helping man is problematic, but for God to help the average individual is a far more difficult proposition. This would require great sacrifice on the part of the Godhead, and only through a true personal sacrifice could there be any chance of genuinely helping an individual.

So God had realized that helping His children was proving to be the most difficult endeavor in all of His creation. Only through the Holy Spirit's hindsight would the outcome of a well-intentioned Fatherly action be known. Unintended consequences were far more likely than the intended ones.

Man was a being who was mostly focused on his own instant gratification. He was generally unmindful of the end result of help received and so learned no lessons from it. Only time could temper man's reaction-based nature as age provided him a sense of his mortality——a sense of mortality that caused fear to progress to wisdom as men contemplated death, then meeting the Lord.

Man was generally unaware that the one and only thing they would take with them into death was–what they left behind–how they loved one another. Those who loved wisely, in the end, were the only ones who actually did love the other person. Acts of false altruism, guided by guilt, are the overwhelming majority of actions taken in the name of love on earth. Only true acts of love could survive a trip into eternity as treasures in heaven.

Altruism was something that God had considered, and for His part, He rejected the idea as cold, distant and disinterested to a point of uncaring——it was certainly not borne out of any wisdom He garnered from man thus far. Man's flesh is guided by the fall of man and the tree of guilt, guilt bearing a very different fruit than the tree of love.

Actions guided by love are not altruistic, they are loving. To love someone, you must take the time to know them. True love can only come with the investment of your time, an investment that promotes a self-interest——interest that develops into a close personal relationship——and will always yield an abundance of good will and good deeds that could never have come to fruition from disinterested persons.

Regardless of which way help flows, God to man, man to God or man to man, the outcome would only randomly be good if it flowed in only the one direction. God's conclusion was that help must be as nearly as possible a zero-sum game. In a zero-sum-game the outcome is known immediately, no wisdom is needed——a good fit for man, as man was generally unwilling to look back . . . and learn.

Looking back God could clearly see that when He or a man helped someone, expecting nothing in return, that *help* more often than not turns out to be a curse to the one who has been *helped*. But if help is an even exchange and both parties are satisfied with the outcome, then help is a benefit for all concerned, even unto the community.

Disinterested acts are as fleeting as the smiles of the disinterested parties being helped. A claim of altruism only muddies the water so that truth cannot be easily seen. Acts of love are extremely powerful and shall thrive for eternity, as eternity is changed by each and every act of love.

Looking back, the Holy Spirit informed the Others, "Men only have self-interest; Man's self-concern is ubiquitous so altruism will not be found."

God responded as He looked towards the Son: "A man that owes no one, cannot he act in a selfless manner? If a totally guiltless man were to perform a selfless act, would that not be altruistic?"

God's quizzing of the Son begged a response. "Perhaps a totally guiltless man would be capable of having no concern for Himself. No man such as this exists——if such a man did exist, that man would surely not be called a man for long." Said the Son, fully grasping the nature of His Father's point.

The Holy Spirit, looking forward, added, "If that person——should He be called a man——were to perform such an act, would He not be a help to all men?"

"No," God replied and looked towards the Son, "The altruistic act would only benefit those who requited His love by loving Him and loving His selfless act of sacrifice."

The Holy Spirit weighed in again: "What of the many who failed to love this *man* and ignored the sorrow and the pain of His altruism towards the guilty? This would likely break the heart of that *man*, break it unto His death."

"Yes, and only His death will confirm His act as selfless," the Son solemnly responded.

This was a somber moment for the Godhead, as the Three reflected on what must be done to provide a Savior for mankind as, to date, altruism was not found among men.

—— 11 ——
MAN HELPS GOD

The most difficult task in all of creation was now front and center——man needed God's "help."

"Helping man will not be easy. We have made the Heavens and the earth and all that is in them, but this task before Us is far more problematic," God said.

"Father, is it even possible for one man to help another, without giving of themselves in a very personal way?" inquired the Son.

"You are wise my Son," God answered.

"If this is the case for a man, how much more must it be the case for Us?" said the Son.

"Indeed, it is far more problematic for the powerful to help their children than is it for the weak. Children quickly discern how much power is held by their parents and they exploit that power in childish ways," God said. "It is the father's duty to limit his children so that the father is not further limited by them."

The Godhead continued to consider the matter. "Let Us consider two men: Our firstborn, Adam, and Our comforter, Noah," said the Father. "Adam was not burdened, as is Noah; Noah's hands are as leather, and his feet are as clay. His burden is the root of his desires, and his desires have inspired Our desires. Noah will have a much better chance of succeeding where Adam failed."

"Remember, Noah acted out of faith first to save his children," added the Holy Spirit.

"The Spirit is correct. We are of like mind with Noah. We can partner with him and take his idea to the next level–to a global scale," God said.

The Holy Spirit fixated on the word, "partner."

"Yes, partner with him," said the Father. "This partnership is now in the market for a large boat. Only a boat built by Noah will keep Noah invested into the outcome of Our joint venture." God added, "Man's efforts are crucial as it is men who must stay in this game until the end. They need to play a major role in their escaping what the earth has become."

God had given Adam and Noah very different obligations. Adam's was to not eat from a specific tree, whereas Noah's was to build a boat the size of a field and fill it with all of His animals. These responsibilities could not be further apart in size and scope, yet the first was perhaps far more difficult to achieve than the latter.

Perhaps if God were to start His creation from the beginning again, He would make sure that the garden was less of a paradise in order to keep Adam busy, tired, and humble. On the other hand, if God had not put the first man in a paradise, neither God nor man would have learned the lesson of the garden as quickly as they had, and the outcome may have been far worse.

The Godhead in the Spirit reflected on the Past, then on the Future. "Almighty . . . I am. Creator of the Heavens and the earth . . . I am. But those abilities are now severely hindered, all but useless, as We are now limited to depend on a manmade wooden boat to advance Our and man's sorrows unto a hopeful future."

The Others smiled in agreement. Then the Son asked the Spirit, "Will the men of the future ever contemplate Our current dilemma?" The Spirit considered this and replied, "Perhaps some of them will. But only a small number of those who choose to look back will be able to discern the truth, as the truth is naturally repugnant and frustrating to man. As men look back, the truth in their actions is unavoidably offensive, as it reflects accurately the offenses that have been made."

By uttering but a word, God could have created a giant ocean vessel capable of serving the purpose of the ark that Noah and his family had been contracted to build. But just what unintended consequences might befall Noah and his family, should God do all the work?

God could have assisted Noah, his family, and His animals in a myriad of other ways as well, but that may well have corrupted Noah and his family. Having Noah build the ark, a long, arduous and risky task, would result in a quid pro quo in which Noah will have a significant amount of time and sweet equity into the outcome, whatever that outcome may be. God would be risking all creation, and that risk would be well known and fully understood by the ark's passengers. Nothing risked nothing gained would be God's guiding principle for going forward.

Noah would be saving his family and himself, while at the same time saving the animals that they would need for survival in the post diluvian world. This would be an ideal situation for everyone——a zero-sum gain——if it worked out.

Except this would be a gamble on God's part, and this time, more was on the line than had ever been before. If Noah failed, man was a failure. There was no other way forward, and there would be no time extension. This was man's last chance. The time of the judgment was approaching, and it would not be stopped. Noah and his family were the only chance creation and procreation had of surviving. If they were not successful in this undertaking, all of creation would be wiped out, other than the fishes in the waters.

God was risking everything by relying so heavily on Noah in this way. God had been watching man for fifteen hundred years and had gained the wisdom He needed to make some strategic changes. The time was in sight for these changes to be implemented, and the risk was acceptable to Him. Noah had no way of knowing if God had a fourth plan awaiting his possible failure with the ark, but in light of Noah's actions and his dedication to the job of building the ark, it seemed pretty clear that Noah was taking no chances. At the very least, Noah believed that his family would only survive in the flesh because of the work they were now starting on the ark.

The biggest gamble eternity would ever behold was about to commence, and God was predicting success. There would be eight in an ark who would have one heck of a ride into yet another new world order. (KJV Gen. 6:7–8)

THE RICHES OF HAVILAH

Havilah, where Noah had settled his family, was a very peaceful and beautiful place. Noah came to believe that the clean animals who inhabited the area were the reason it was so calm and beautiful. The animals that grazed in the fields seemed to quiet the land and even to limit the downward pull of the earth. Noah's sons, who were becoming men, seemed to be at peace even though they had no wives. Noah was amazed to realize that his sons had complete faith that God would provide wives for them at some point.

Noah had just been getting settled in the land of Havilah when God approached him with this daunting enterprise of saving all of creation by building a giant ark.

The time frame that God outlined for Noah for completion of the ark coincided with the date that Noah had been given by Methuselah. God's projected date for the completion of this large vessel——the means of man surviving the flood——would be exactly ninety-six years from this day that God spoke of it to Noah.

The project would be more extensive, and the size of the boat much greater, than anything Noah had ever undertaken; but God promised to provide Noah with the means to acquire all the supplies and tools that he would need.

That same night, God sent Noah a dream that detailed everything he needed to know to build the boat: the types of wood, the quantities of timbers, the types and quantities of connectors and tools, the precise positioning of every iron peg, and precise instructions as to where the boat should be built.

He also gave Noah complete instructions about which shiny metals and stones of Havilah were of such value that they could be used to barter for materials in Nod.

Noah's first challenge would be to find others to assist him while still protecting his family and the land of Havilah from the corruption that was spreading throughout the earth. He did not know how he would accomplish all of this, but he had faith that God would provide him with the wisdom he would need when he needed it.

These people would have to be men he could trust and, of course, the first person that came to *mind* was his grandfather Methuselah. So he journeyed back to Adam's Square to request Methuselah's help. Methuselah was, without question, a very wise and moral man who could be trusted with any matter. He was both a man of God and the type of man who gave good advice. Involving him would please God and would be of help in ways that Noah could not imagine. In addition to all of Methuselah's great attributes, Noah believed that this was simply meant to be. He believed that it was Methuselah whom God wanted him to use as a helper, and Noah could not agree more with his Partner on this point.

A couple of months after he had walked and talked with God, Noah arrived back at the Square of Adam. Methuselah was thrilled to see his old friend——his grandson——back home, but he wasn't surprised. The night before, God had sent him a dream about Enoch and Enoch's prophecy.

Methuselah believed that God was with Noah, and after Noah explained everything to him, Methuselah felt privileged to be a part of this blessing. Noah informed his grandfather early in their talks that only Noah's immediate family would be saved and that there would be no room on the ark for anyone else, not even for Methuselah. But his beloved grandfather was neither surprised nor disappointed by this; it didn't matter to him that he would not be one of the occupants of the ark. Methuselah had always trusted in God, and he trusted in Noah equally.

While God had already given Noah the building plans, Noah didn't yet know where he was to acquire the materials and tools that he would need such as the iron pegs, saws, and drills. He didn't even know what iron pegs were, and this was one of the reasons that he had enlisted Methuselah's help. Methuselah had seen much more of the world than Noah had and would have knowledge of some of the materials and other requirements of the job, including iron.

Methuselah had also been born with an uncanny sense of direction that would serve him well. He would be on the road continually over the next hundred years as he traveled from the Square, to Havilah, to Nod, and back again, searching for the hardware required for constructing the ark. Noah and Methuselah spent a few days in the Square making initial logistical plans for the build, and they agreed that Meth, as his friends and family called him, should be the one to journey to the City of Enoch with precious stones and shiny metals from the land of Havilah to initiate trade with the Circle of Enoch.

God came to Methuselah in a vision, similar to the dream that He had given to Noah, detailing everything that would be needed to build the ark. With this knowledge, Meth planned his first trip for the project, which would be to the Circle of Enoch and its legendary steel rooms. Noah was concerned about secrecy, but Meth was confident in his skills as a navigator and in his gift for moving like a dart in the wind——visible, and then quickly invisible.

They decided on a supply route that would first take Methuselah down the Pishon River from the Square of Adam to the build site. Then, when traveling from Havilah to the City of Enoch, he would take a secret route, always alone. He would travel by river as much as possible, when returning to Havilah, to avoid establishing a land trail. Boats——provided by men from the Square of Adam——would carry the materials during this final leg of his journey to Havilah. Noah felt that it was necessary to keep their plans and preparations as secret as possible for as long as possible. Methuselah was to make the round trip journey from the City of Enoch in Nod and then back to Havilah via the Square of Adam two or three times each year.

They calculated that it would take a couple hundred such trips to gather all the tools, pegs, caulking, pitch, and other hardware that would be needed for building the giant vessel. Methuselah would contract with some Sethite boat builders south of the Square of Adam to build the smaller vessels that would bring the supplies, tools and hardware to the build site.

"Meth, other than my family, you are the only person on earth that knows of the coming flood. God wisely kept that hidden from Enoch. We must continue to keep the means of the coming judgment a secret, especially from the boat builders; we can't have them making any large vessels of their own that might survive the flood. If they question what we need all the supplies for, come up with something, but don't tell them it is a boat," Noah cautioned Meth.

Much of the burden of making this plan a success now fell on Meth and his ability to find, acquire, and transport the necessary supplies, and to find and hire trustworthy and capable workers to build the ark. Meth immediately made arrangements to go south with Noah, and he explained as much about his mission as he could to his wife, Edna. She was completely supportive of his plans, as she had great faith in her husband and in his favorite grandson.

As Meth and Noah traveled south to Havilah, they discussed old times and new adventures——they were thrilled to be together once again.

Meth's job would be the more challenging, at least in the initial phases, and he deliberated long and hard about how he would juggle the various demands that Noah would soon be making of him. For one thing, Noah had promised to send him off to Nod with items for barter that would be seen as very valuable by the people there.

"Noah, the items I am to use for trade——how do you know their value?" Meth inquired. The value of these items would be the key to his success.

"Meth, God has assured me that they will be of great value to the people of Nod, and I believe Him," Noah said.

"That is good enough for me," Meth replied, relieved.

Far away in the City of Enoch, Lamech the Cainite had come to power as its ruler. He was a great-great-grandson of Enoch the Cainite who was the firstborn son of Cain. Born in the Circle and raised in the Circle, Lamech was a lover of the sword. As a young man, he had witnessed the power that could be wielded by the master of a sword, and he coveted that power more than anything or anyone else did.

"The power this blade has is amazing!" the teenaged Lamech had said the first time he witnessed its slicing power.

"Yes, it is. You must wield it carefully, as you can do great damage with it," his tutor had replied.

The young man replied with a smile, "That is not the power of which I speak. Have you not seen the look in the eyes of men as I master this sword? They are fearful of me, even as young as I am."

His tutor quickly understood what Lamech meant, when he saw the look on the young man's face.

A man with control of this can control the many, the young Lamech had realized as he labored long and hard to master the blade, and he indeed desired to be the master of the many.

Lamech had been schooled at the foot of Enoch so that he could eventually take his place. Enoch had instructed his grandson in history and legends, and he had told him of some of his own misguided efforts and poor choices that had led to the Circle becoming so increasingly wicked.

Unfortunately, Lamech and his sword would only bring more wickedness upon all of Nod. Indeed, one of Lamech's first proclamations as he took over the duties of a ruler from Enoch did just that.

"Is there no way to get these whores out of my Circle? They're distracting good business men and attracting all kinds of human debris." Lamech demanded of the fawning sycophants who dared to draw near to his feasting table.

"Raise the fine for using whores," some of them shouted.

"Raise the fine? That is your solution?" Lamech sneered. "No one——not one man or woman——has paid that fine in weeks. They meet in the Circle and then they go outside the Circle to avoid the fine. You all know this. All of you here do this." After all, the men who were there were the worst offenders, and Lamech knew it. "Raising the fine is just not going to work." Lamech could clearly see this. "Every day, more and more business is driven outside the Circle, and we lose revenue from various sources not to mention the fines. I need a solution to this problem," Lamech said with resolve.

It didn't occur to Lamech or any of the crowd around him to look back to what his predecessor, Enoch, had tried to do about this problem. Had his policies and policy changes been effective? These people just didn't have it in them to look back and learn from the past.

"Make the Circle bigger; make it harder to escape doing business in the Circle," shouted one fool from the crowd.

"We could do that," said Lamech, "but that would be met with much opposition, and we would need more watchers to watch. What else? Anyone? What else can we do?" Lamech asked.

"Allow us to keep our whores as a second wife," came another voice from the crowd.

"Now that is an idea I can work with," said Lamech.

He put this plan into action quickly. (KJV Gen. 4:19) The next day he addressed the Circle and made a proclamation that quieted the crowd. "God has commanded me to take another wife," he said. "Since God commanded me to take a second wife, then I command all men of the City of Enoch to take a second wife as well." With that, Lamech had established polygamy. By having additionally given this practice the imprimatur of God, he made the practice evil. God never prohibited two wives or two husbands but he never endorsed it either.

Whether Lamech really believed that allowing men to take two wives would actually solve this particular problem for the Circle was irrelevant: it was a small matter in comparison to his use of God's name as an endorsement——he knew full well that God did not want this and had not commanded this. But Lamech was not through yet with using the name of God for his own ends. More of this would follow.

All of the City of Enoch and most of the earth knew of Cain and his mark, but few knew the truth about the mark and how and why it had been given to Cain. Many a legend was believed by the men of the City of Enoch, but one thing about Cain was clear to all——he was protected by some special power. The legend about Cain most widely circulated was that with his mark he could defend himself against any seven armed men. This came to be understood as the meaning behind the sevenfold curse. According to *a* legend, God had said that if seven men managed to kill Cain this would result in seven times the original curse. This led to the belief that it would require forty-nine men to kill any man who killed Cain.

The people also believed that any man who went the way of Cain would also be cursed. But God had spoken of this fifteen hundred years ago, and here and now, only the murderer knew for sure what He had said.

"Do you believe that Cain can be killed?" Lamech asked of a small cabal of his closest collaborators. "Have any of you ever seen his mark?" he added.

"Cain is a powerful man. I know this to be true. He has lived a long life already; he may live seven thousand years. The mark must be a sign from God. It must be a blessing," one man dared to answer Lamech's question. Actually, this man was partially correct. It was indeed a sign from God and an intended blessing——but a single look at Cain would reveal that a long painful life did not appear to be helping Cain abandon his obsession with the tree of knowledge in favor of the tree of life. What God had hoped for in blessing Cain with a long life was not evident, as Cain showed no signs of repentance.

"If that is true, then I deserve a sign from God as well," reasoned Lamech aloud.

"Cain received his mark because he killed his younger brother. You have no young brothers to kill, my liege," came a whisper from the group.

"If I can get a mark, fine. If I can't get a mark, then I will simply have to convince the mob that I do have one, and that will be as effective as having the real thing. The mob is composed of fools. Let us conspire now to deceive them into a willing compliance," Lamech proposed with a wicked smirk. "God has no standing here in the Circle of Man. Lamech and only Lamech will rule here in the City of Enoch," he proclaimed to all who could hear.

Then he embarked on a plot to match the circumstances in which Cain had received his mark: he would find two brothers of the same ages that Cain and Abel had been when Abel was killed, and then murder the younger of the two.

Lamech, like most men, did not understand what the curse of Cain was about and understood even less the purpose of Cain's mark. God was never going to protect the evil Lamech from the repercussions of this or any other crime. Lamech had taken God's words and misused them for his own evil purposes——just as many men would do so in the future.

One thing that Lamech would never know or fully understand is that he was partially correct when he claimed that God had no standing within his Circle. There were no offerings, no sacrifices, and no faith in the Circle, and God had no reason to look upon or attend to such an ungodly place.

Would a righteous man even enter into the Circle of Lamech, and if so, for what reason? If not even a single righteous man could be found in such a place, why would God want to look upon it? He surely wasn't wanted there, and even if He were by some, the wicked people of the Circle would surely try to sacrifice Him long before they thought about sacrificing *to* Him. However, Lamech——and indeed all of mankind——would soon learn the extent of God's standing over all of creation, including the Circle of Man.

So Lamech launched his wicked plan, killing the younger brother, as Cain had killed Abel and it worked as he had hoped, thus strengthened his power in the City of Enoch. The people of Nod fell for his claim of having a mark like the mark of Cain——they began to say that he bore the sevenfold curse of Cain, and they were afraid of him and afraid of his power. (KJV Gen. 4:23–24)

It had long been believed that, with his mark, God had given Cain the power to defend himself against any seven attackers. Now, Lamech was claiming that he had the power to defend himself against seven times seven plus seven men. Lamech didn't really care how many people truly believed his lies and manipulations. As long as they had enough fear not to come against him, he could rule for a thousand years.

12

THE SONS OF GOD AND THE DAUGHTERS OF MEN

Some years after Lamech came to rule, Eva had died while giving birth. It was rumored throughout the Circle that she had birthed a strange and very large child that her caretaker had named Tubal, a word that means "confusion", as it seem to describe the circumstances of his birth. Eva had been a very old woman at the time; she would be the oldest woman who had ever lived. She was far past the age of childbearing, and her contribution to procreation should have ended long ago. It was rumored that the infant had been so large that he had literally ripped Eva apart during his birth. Cain, who was assumed to be the child's father, was said to be distraught over Eva's death and he had not been seen since just before the child's birth.

The rumors about the child were true, and Eva had known well before the birth that something was very wrong with the child.

"Cain, this baby I am carrying is not a normal child!" Many times Eva had come to Cain to express her concerns. "I knew since the day of conception that this would come to no good. I don't know how I even conceived, as I am hundreds of years past the age of bearing children. This child is not of me." She believed that the seed from which she had conceived had been not of Cain alone but also of something inhuman.

Eva would not live to understand that her suspicions had been correct——the child she was ready to give birth to was not a fully human child. Because this child was obviously different from other children, the boy child would soon be thought of as a son of God from a daughter of men. Only Cain, Eva, Eva's midwife, and Cain's mark suspected what the origins of this child might be.

Cain was a bad husband and a worse father, but he did have feelings for Eva. Eva was now in great pain——pain that he knew was of his making. Cain could not bear his pain or hers——as he watched his wife giving birth to this low-bred being. This was a child of mixed seed——a child both angelic and of Cain——and in no way a son of God. This child had been co-created, not procreated.

Cain watched Eva's suffering and then broke down in tears for the first time in his life and could watch no more.

The confused and distraught Cain said, "Eva, I don't know what love is. I have been loved, but I have never felt love other than for myself. I will probably never know what love is, but I love you, and I am sorry for what I have done to you. I have been sorry for a very long time." Humility entered Cain's confused mixed spirit for the very first time as he said goodbye to his dying Eva. She was in too much pain to respond as Cain walked away from the only woman he was ever to know.

"Listen to me," Cain said, looking into the eyes of the midwife who had been caring for Eva. "If the child lives and is normal——boy or girl——you take over Eva's home and all of her possessions, and care for the child. If the child is not a normal child, flee to the wilderness with it. Do you understand?" The woman tried to focus on what Cain was saying to her, but Eva's screams of agony were unbearable for both of them to hear, and it was difficult for the midwife to concentrate on what he was saying to her. "You will never see me again," Cain told the midwife, and with that Cain was gone.

Eva had explained to the woman that the child inside her was probably the result of a mixed seed, from Cain and from the angel that marked him. "This child will not be a man. Perhaps he will be a giant, as he grows very quickly in my womb," she had told the midwife. Eva's screams in childbirth could be heard for a great distance, and the midwife did what she could to ease Eva's pain. The child of mixed seed tore apart the woman who bore him, and now Eva would sleep forevermore, but the male *child* would live.

The midwife recalled what Cain had asked of her, and she tried to comply, but the boy grew so rapidly that she lost control of him by the time he was five years old. Now he mostly took care of her, and she did her best to guide him.

Cain was in self-imposed exile from the Circle of Man when he heard that Eva had indeed been killed by the birth of her child, the birth that he had not been strong enough to stick around and witness. This news further broke Cain, a man who was already broken. Perhaps it was instinct, perhaps it was the pull of old, but his thoughts turned immediately to the garden, the only other thing that had ever mattered to him. Once again, it became his only focus.

Cain was now a very old man, and he found himself wandering once again. But this time it was not only in exile, it was in confusion. The madness within Cain was the result of having been possessed by the mark for centuries. He had felt great relief, a feeling of justice, long ago when Eva had killed him, before the mark had brought him back to the world. He longed to have that feeling again, even though he feared that the feeling of justice might be only temporal and therefore temporary. But the existence of his mark made it seem that death was impossible for him, which is perhaps why he coveted it.

His life of pain, for now, had convinced him that this long life was not a blessing. It was the worst part of his curse, and he wanted it to end.

Cain had not been seen in the Circle for some time and his whereabouts were unknown. While he was absent, rumors had been spreading about his large boy child. Lamech didn't know if the rumors about the child that Cain had sired were true. But he did know that if this child had some special powers he wanted those powers for himself.

"I have heard rumors of a large boy, an offspring of Cain's. Who can tell me of these rumors?" Lamech asked when he was in the Circle one day collecting taxes.

"Yes, I have heard the rumors as well, my liege. You know Cain has some very special powers," were the cautiously spoken words of a vendor who was paying his taxes.

"Where can I find the boy?" Lamech demanded. He threw the tax revenue he had just collected to the ground. This was a common practice: no one would dare to pick up the tender unless they were able to tender a correct answer in return.

Lamech waited, but no one in the crowd approached the bribe. They gathered closer to Lamech while he waited for the information that he wanted. In the Circle people knew about the child——he was somewhat of a local tourist attraction——but nobody wanted to be the one to tell Lamech anything about him.

"Such loyalty to a boy I have not seen in the Circle before," Lamech said, as he wondered why no one had yet come forward.

"The boy is from God," he heard from the crowd. (KJV Gen. 6:1–4)

"You protect him. Interesting," said Lamech. "I give you my word, the boy will not be harmed." While his word was not worthy of respect, it was enough to convince a few betrayers to split the bribe and give him the information he wanted.

When Lamech was told of the child's location, he demanded that the boy be brought before him. Lamech's men found him quickly. He was brought to Lamech along with his guardian, the woman who had been appointed by Cain. The childless Lamech was amazed by the size of the boy. He was said to be six years old, but he was four arm-lengths tall, the size of a large, full-grown man. Lamech immediately demanded to know who had been raising the boy.

"Woman, you have been raising the boy?"

She acknowledged this with a nod of her head.

"The boy's father——is he a god or is he Cain?" Lamech asked with a laugh. But he looked at the woman sternly, wanting a serious response.

"My lord, I was with his mother as she died during his birth. She told me that the seed of the child in her was not really known, but she thought it wasn't human."

"What more can you tell me?" Lamech asked her. Lamech's men grew silent as they listened to this.

"Eva had lost a lot of blood during the birth of the child. I tried to save her, but she was in such pain and had lost so much blood . . . I thought there might be some chance that she could survive, but when she looked at the child she had just given birth to, she quickly looked away, took a deep breath, and closed her eyes. To my amazement, it appeared to me to be a very peaceful and pleasant death. I felt relieved for her, as all of her pain had finally ended," she told Lamech.

"What else can you tell me? Continue," Lamech insisted.

"Cain was with us up until the final few hours, but then he could no longer watch the pain that he believed he had caused Eva. I saw him one more time after that, and that was when I gave him the news that Eva had passed. He broke down in sadness and then he flew into a rage at some invisible third person that he called his mark, and accused him of having done something to his seed. He was clearly out of his mind. Then Cain's rage fell away and he spoke as calmly as I am speaking to you right now. He gave me instructions on how I should raise the child." With this, Lamech had heard enough to decide that the boy would stay with him from now on.

The boy grew rapidly, and Lamech realized that due to his size and strength, he would be perfect for helping to produce steel. *How much bigger will the young man grow? Just how strong will he be? Will he remain controllable?* Of course no one knew the answers to any of these questions, but, for now, raising the boy was Lamech's number one goal.

He decided to rename the boy Tubal-Cain. He would be Lamech's adopted son and his first child, but he would not be in line to receive an inheritance. Lamech would not recognize Tubal-Cain for that honor. Tubal-Cain had his place in Nod, but Lamech would also need to have sons of his own blood, sons that would inherit his worldly kingdom.

Then and there, he conceived yet another deceptive plan. As Cain had tried to supplant the line of Seth when he had named his firstborn Enoch, Lamech would later sire a full human son and give him the name of Cain's giant son, Tubal-Cain. He would supplant the giant with his own son who would then live what would have been the legendary life of the real Tubal-Cain.

Lamech, in his attempt to make a pureblooded giant son, set out to look for the largest woman in all of Nod. He had taken the most beautiful woman in all of Nod, Adah, for his wife and was content to soothe his lust with her beauty. But now he needed a large woman to provide him with a large heir, and he wasn't disappointed when he found Zillah. She was a very tall and strong woman—she cast a big shadow wherever she went. She would now give Lamech a son. So he took her for his second wife. (KJV Gen. 4:19)

Lamech cained a son with Zillah, and to supplant the name of Tubal-Cain, they gave him the same name. After all, to their knowledge, the giant Tubal-Cain could not procreate. The two boys would be a few years apart in age, would grow up together, and would both become ironsmiths. In time, both would become men of renown, men of legendary strength and skills, and heroes to many. (KJV Gen. 4:22)

As the giant boy Tubal-Cain grew, Lamech spent a lot of time with him and realized that the boy's mind was not right.

"Why doesn't the boy speak more?" Lamech inquired of one of the maidservants. "He is big. I will give him that, but what good is a giant that I can't communicate with?" asked Lamech, frustrated.

"The boy is learning. He has learned much and will speak soon enough," assured his caretaker.

Lamech remembered a time many years ago when he had seen the mark of Cain. By that time, the rumors of Cain's growing insanity had become legendary. *The mark caused Cain great mental pain, as it seemed to infect and affect his brain... could it have corrupted his seed as well?* Lamech wondered.

He continued to reason, *If a man is more than flesh, if a man is also a spiritual being similar to a being such as an angel, (who is only spirit without flesh), then both of them are eternal. But God gives only fleshly beings the added spiritual dimension of procreation, a way to create a new being that is a combination not only of the flesh of the man and the woman but also of their spirits. If one of those spirits——and possibly even the flesh——were infected, how could it not affect their seed or any child that was conceived of it?*

With these thoughts, Lamech was coming to understand that the mark of Cain, the angelic being that had protected Cain for more than a millennium, had corrupted his seed, and the result was the man-child that he was now raising. A being that was half man and half angel had never been heard of before, and Lamech was excited by the thought of the opportunities that might come his way through this child. But he decided that he would forever keep this theory to himself and allow people to believe that the boy was a son of God from the daughter of man.

The boy continued to grow, and he grew to be larger than any man. He was nine arm-lengths tall——close to twice the height of Lamech——but Lamech was not afraid of him.

While he was being born, this child had caused his mother's death, and anyone who looked upon him could see that he was not fully human. Lamech decided to call him a Nephilim, which means "to cause one to sleep," as Tubal's birth had caused his mother to sleep forever.

Lamech quickly saw that, though his Nephilim was large and strong, he was not a problem to control. As Lamech became the master of Tubal-Cain, Tubal-Cain became the final arrow in Lamech's quiver. Now it would no longer be possible for anyone to challenge Lamech's rule over the Circle of Man. Lamech grew even more emboldened while he mentored and saw ever more potential in his new slave and monster, Tubal-Cain.

Lamech put the giant to work in his ironworks. (KJV Gen. 4:22) The giant was seven and one-half elbow to fingertips tall, a full two arm-lengths taller than the tallest men. Tubal-Cain was so strong that he could do things no one else could do. The hammers in the foundries were too small for Tubal and when a hammer was made to fit his strength, he could flatten a ferro stone in a quarter of the time that it would take an average worker to do the same. Tubal's weight was twice that of man. The only part of the giants' anatomy that was the same as a man was his head, which because of his enormous size made the giant look odd to say the least.

The other workers were amazed at what this Nephilim could do. All those men believed more than ever that God must be with Lamech, to have provided him with such a worker. Lamech strove to perpetuate their beliefs. Lamech had never been more satisfied than he was now, watching his power accumulate.

Very quickly, mostly due to his skill and strength with a hammer, the giant Tubal-Cain became a natural in the ironworks. Tubal-Cain was not a normal man in many ways, but he was nonetheless a skilled worker. But then, during Tubal-Cain's third month in Lamech's ironworks, there was an accident.

The ghastly screams could be heard from far beyond the ironworks, but these screams were different: louder and lower in pitch than those of a man. They had the intensity of the furnaces themselves, and they came from the giant, Tubal-Cain.

"Pain. Pain!" cried out the giant, as his hands gripped his leg near his loins. Injuries were common in the foundry, so there were balms on site to soothe burns, but this burn was very deep and severe. It was the type of wound that would be a death sentence if it became infected. The giant could not be calmed, so the workers sent for Lamech.

"My *God*, what has happened?" Lamech asked as he witnessed Tubal-Cain's pain. He was showing more concern than anybody had ever seen from him. "Get the best burn men, the best healers. Get them all. Money is no object. I want them all here, now." With that, Lamech went to Tubal-Cain, wrested his large hand away from the bloody burn on his leg, and held that hand as the healers cleaned, medicated, and dressed the deep wound.

The men of the foundry were amazed at the compassion that the compassionless Lamech was now showing Tubal-Cain. The touch of Lamech's hand seemed to be calming the giant. His screams faded to moans and groans, and he eventually fell silent. Tubal-Cain would never return to the furnace rooms as a full-time worker. "How could I be so stupid as to put your life in danger?" Lamech lamented to his giant.

Lamech could now see what needed to be done. Tubal-Cain was just one Nephilim. Cain was thought to be dead——or gone for good——so there might never be another. But Lamech needed many, many more. Lamech wondered if Tubal-Cain could breed. Tubal had the loins of a man, but was his seed that of men or that of giants? Lamech was determined to find out. If he could breed, Tubal-Cain could supply Lamech with an army of Nephilim, and Lamech would lead them and rule the entire earth——not just Nod——for a thousand years.

But Lamech first had to determine if his Nephilim was even interested in women. If the Nephilim could procreate at all then, as quickly as they grew, he could have an army of Nephilim in as little as ten years.

"How is Tubal doing? How are his wounds healing?" Lamech had found the woman who raised Tubal and brought her back to care for him. It had been over a month since Tubal's accident.

"He is doing better. He is up and walking around with very little pain."

"That is good news," said Lamech. "Let me ask you something. You have raised him and now you have been caring for the giant . . . has he shown any interest in women?"

"I know what you speak of. It is not a secret, and it is no longer a secret that his mother died giving birth to him," she said.

"Since you know the question I want an answer to, just tell me if you know——is the giant aware of women? Is he a man in that sense of the word?" Lamech asked her.

"I don't know. I have been caring for him since he was a child, and I can tell you that he is a man, at least physically. My guess is, if pushed to act, he will act as you want him to." With that, she excused herself and left. On the face of it, this was promising, but Lamech would have to test her theory.

"Tubal-Cain, come with me," Lamech asked the giant the next day. He treated Tubal-Cain better than he treated any other person on earth.

"Yes," responded Tubal-Cain. The vocabulary of the giant wasn't large, but he generally understood what was said to him when he was spoken to slowly and intently and would respond in kind.

"You will go with me to the Circle today. I want you to help me with some issues there," Lamech told him.

"Yes, I understand," Tubal-Cain said, and with that they were off to the Circle.

Lamech never traveled alone, so six of Lamech's men accompanied them.

"Find me a seductive woman," Lamech said to two of his guards. It didn't take long before the men had several whores accompanying them, but as soon as the women saw that Lamech was part of the group they ran away.

"This is clearly not going to work with me standing here," Lamech figured. "Tubal-Cain, I want you to go with these men, and they will take you to meet some interesting women." Then Lamech sent three of the six men to escort Tubal-Cain. "Guard him with your life. Do not let him out of your sight. You know what I want to find out. Discover the answer as quickly as possible and then bring him right back to me. Understand?" The men acknowledged their orders.

Lamech returned to his palace, and a few hours later the three guards and Tubal returned. "Tell me, what did you find out?" asked Lamech anxiously.

"Sire, he is a man in every sense of the word, though it took some doing. It took some convincing on both sides, but I believe that Tubal-Cain will have no problems having relations with a woman."

Lamech was relieved to hear this, but then one of the guards added, "However, it appears that the women will have to be at least willing and perhaps even be the initiating parties, because, as you know, Tubal is very shy." While this tempered his hopes somewhat, Lamech was still pleased. He began making plans to find a mate for Tubal-Cain in hopes that he would sire another giant like himself.

Lamech sent his men to find out what might entice women to breed with the giant man.

"You men know what is needed here. Find a way. Offer what you have to, lie as you need to, coerce as you are trained to, and find Tubal a willing mate," Lamech ordered, and the men went off as instructed.

"How exactly does Lamech think we are going to convince a woman to die for him?" asked one of his men. "I can't imagine anyone willing to die for another, so this is not going to be easy."

"I do know we had better at least put in a good effort," said another.

"I have an idea," said the third, as he approached a woman in the Circle.

"Miss. Oh, Miss. Can I have a moment with you please?"

"Yes?"

"How would you like to be the mother of a great and mighty king?"

The woman shook her head; she had heard that line before.

"What's the catch? What do you want? I am very busy, and my husband is right behind me."

Lamech's man continued, "Miss, Lamech seeks to give one——and only one——woman the honor of bearing a child king."

"Sir, Lamech has two wives; both are far superior to me. I don't know what you want, but I am not the one you seek," she said and was gone.

"How are we ever going to convince a woman to die for Lamech?" the men grumbled.

"We have tried using stature. Let's try using riches," one of them suggested.

"If we are going to try to seduce a woman with money, then let's look for a poor beggar. There are many beggars over there," one of the men said, pointing across the Circle. The men headed in that direction.

"Sir, I can see you are from the house of Lamech. Please, any charity will be met with the blessing of God," pleaded a very old and wretched woman.

The men did not answer her. The leader of the group turned to the others and said, "There is no way I would bring this human debris back to Lamech or Tubal. What does that leave us with as a strategy to find a woman for Tubal?"

The henchmen pondered what weapon they might try next and soon hit upon an idea.

"Pride and vanity are the strongest human emotions——how do we mold those weaknesses into bars strong enough to pry away a woman's life?"

They couldn't think of a practical way to use these weaknesses, and they eventually went back to Lamech to report that the women of the Circle were in no way interested in getting involved with any strange beings, giants or otherwise.

"Look, find a mate for Tubal, now. Go back and don't return until you do!" Lamech ordered them.

Lamech instructed them to offer whatever was necessary to entice a woman to be Tubal's mate, but again there were no takers.

This time, though, they hatched a scheme that would take the heat off themselves when they returned.

"Sire, we approached many women this day——they all knew what we wanted, but everyone also knows the fate of any woman who would bear a Nephilim. It seems the meaning of the name you gave Tubal's *race* (The Nephilim) prevents us from being able to deceive these women."

This plan worked. Blaming Lamech for their inability to find a mate for Tubal had gotten them off the hook, but this did not divert Lamech from his wicked plan. He would find a way to entice women to mother his army of giants, no matter what the cost.

At night, in the mostly empty iron furnaces in the City of Enoch, the gleaners would take the slag left over from the day shift and make products in exchange for keeping the furnaces clean and hot for the next morning's crew.

This night the gleaners were making pegs for God. The name given to the rather large nails by the customer. The gleaners were making them for a man they called Ox, as he was always accompanied by an ox that carried away the goods he bartered for. Ox bartered with some strange, shiny metals that had not been seen before in Nod. The gleaners took the shiny metals in trade for the iron pegs.

These shiny metals were very different from the iron they were accustomed to; they were soft and malleable, and they came in a variety of colors. Most of the shiny metals that Ox brought were silver, gold, and red in color. The gleaners quickly discovered that when these metals were melted down they could see their reflections in the pools of liquid metal. They quickly realized that their futures could be as bright as were their reflections in the molten metals. These reflections were far clearer than any reflections they had ever seen in water or a polished stone. "Can you believe how well you can see yourself?" asked one gleaner.

"This is truly a miracle," replied another.

Nod was rich in iron. But these shiny metals——silver, copper, gold——did not exist there at all. The gleaners were convinced that they were in possession of a commodity of immense value and that it would change the world. The desire of women to possess these *mirrors* as they called them would be incalculable. A man with a mirror would be able to get whatever he wanted in trade.

By the time the gleaners had made about ten of these oval metal mirrors, word of their existence had gotten out. This was such a massive innovation that it would have been impossible to keep it under wraps for long. Soon everyone in Nod was buzzing with the news.

"Lamech, look at this," one of his men said, handing him a mirror. Lamech was amazed, but he moved directly past that and on to what it could do for him.

"Where did you get this?" he demanded urgently. Lamech was more intensely serious than anyone had ever seen him. "Where?" he shouted.

"Sire, the gleaners on the night shift in the iron rooms are making them," someone said.

"Find them. Find every one of these men and bring them to me now. Let nothing——absolutely nothing——stop you."

It was not long before the gleaners of the night shift were standing in front of Lamech.

"Men, be not afraid, but be absolutely sure you tell me the truth. Understood?" said Lamech. "First, what do you call this?" he asked, as he held up the mirror that had been brought to him.

"It is a mirror. That one is made of what we call silver," the gleaner said.

"How many of these have you made?" Lamech asked.

"We have made ten of various sizes. The one you have is the largest size," said the gleaner.

"Very well. Thank you for speaking the truth. Now listen to me carefully. You will no longer be gleaners for the iron rooms. You will continue to work there but you will work directly for me. Tomorrow, you will begin making silver mirrors for me. You will keep none of the mirrors that you make. You will bring me the other nine mirrors that you have already made——I mean every one of them. Is that understood?" Lamech said.

"Yes, sire," they said sadly.

"Every mirror that you make will have my mark on it. If a mirror is found that does not have my mark on it, it will be confiscated. Is that understood?" Lamech said.

The gleaners had none of the shiny metals left to make mirrors with, but they were afraid to tell this to Lamech. The following day, Lamech visited the steel rooms to watch mirrors being made. He was not pleased with what he found.

"Where are my men and where are my mirrors?" Lamech demanded.

"Your men wait over there by the entrance to the main furnace room," said a worker.

His men cowered in fear of his anger as he approached them.

"Why are you not now making my mirrors?" he demanded.

"Sire, we have run out of the shiny metals. We have no more silver to make mirrors with," they answered him.

"When, exactly, were you planning to inform me of this?" Lamech was clearly angry and would have had the men punished, but he needed their expertise. He desperately needed those mirrors, more than anyone could imagine. When Lamech had first seen his own face in the mirror, the grotesque appearance that was reflected back to him made no impression on him whatsoever. He was completely blinded by his desire to see his vision of an army of giants come to fruition. He recalled the failed scheme his henchmen had cooked up. They had planned to exploit the pride and vanity of the women of the Circle to coerce them into bearing Lamech's army of giants.

Now, as clearly as he could see his reflection in his mirror, he could see that mirrors would be the very tool to use to pressure these women. These mirrors would appeal to their pride and vanity very nicely. "Well then, where did you get these shiny metals? Where did they come from?" Lamech asked, looking intently into the eyes of the gleaners.

Risking Lamech's anger, the men explained the source of the metals they had been using. "Sire, please, it is not our fault. We trade for the metal, and we have none of it left. Please, you must believe us. We have already used all that we had to make the ten mirrors," the men told him.

"Look, you're not telling me what I need to hear. Where did you get the silver?" Lamech thundered, his plans for the future dimming as quickly as they had brightened hours before.

"Sire, we trade the dross that we get from the floor of the furnaces at night for the metals."

"Okay. Okay. So get some more!" bellowed Lamech.

"Sire, the Ox won't be back here for about three months. It is he who brings the shiny metals."

These were the first words the men had spoken that hadn't further infuriated Lamech. "Who is the Ox?" he asked as he began to calm down.

"The Ox is a man——a big man and an old man-who comes with one or two oxen to trade for iron pegs. We are now making him five hundred iron pegs for his next visit."

"What are pegs?" asked Lamech.

"Sire, here——I have brought one with me," one of the men said and handing it to Lamech. "He wants them ready when he gets here; he doesn't like to stay in Nod any longer than he has to," the man explained.

"Do you know what he uses these pegs for?" questioned Lamech.

"No," they replied. "He says he uses them for God, but that is ridiculous."

"Now tell me, where can I find the man Ox?" Lamech asked, knowing now that this was not going to be as easy as he had expected. When no one answered him, he screamed once again in frustration, "Where can I find this Ox?"

"Sire, he is like a dart in the night. He appears and then he is gone. We have no idea where he goes. He just disappears into the night with the wind."

"What? You——all of you——you had better hope that he returns," Lamech warned them, clearly frustrated.

The peg that Lamech held in his hand looked like a common shellfish, a cone-shaped item with a sharp point on one end. In a mocking tone, Lamech asked, "A nail for God? No matter. I don't care if the man is mad. As long as he brings his shiny metals, he can have these nails for God."

Lamech then instructed the gleaners to continue making the pegs and to turn over all completed "nails for God" to him so when the man returned he would have to deal with Lamech. Lamech told them to take as much iron as they needed to make the pegs, which they did.

Lamech, the most powerful man in the world, was now forced to wait for a man he had never met, a man who was hard for him to envision as described, in the hope that the man would bring enough shiny metals for Lamech to achieve his goal.

He was not a happy man as he waited with his iron pegs stockpiled for Ox to return. Lamech had a simple plan. He would make high quality mirrors and use them to lure women to his palace where he would pressure them into accepting the seed of the giant, Tubal-Cain. It was not known whether the Nephilim's seed was of man or of angel, so he felt confident that he could convince the women that if they did this they wouldn't surely die. With his plan set, there was nothing left to do but wait for the man Ox and then for the mirrors.

Just as the sun and the moon are always on time, so was Meth. Six months to the day since his last visit, Ox arrived to trade with the gleaners. Lamech was summoned immediately. "What is your name, stranger?" Lamech asked him.

"Meth," he replied.

Lamech asked him, "Where do you go and where do you come from?"

"It is as they say," Meth replied. "I travel alone mostly, with my beast that carries my needs and my wares, to and from a land far from here."

"A salesman, are you?" Lamech questioned.

"I am a trader of steel and pitch," answered Meth.

"Very good. You barter with the shiny metals?" asked Lamech.

"It is as you say," replied Meth.

"Nails for God?" questioned Lamech, holding up an iron peg in his hand.

"If it comes to it, they may very well be," said Meth. Lamech thought the man was truly mad.

Lamech was pleased with how the meeting was going. He assured Meth that he could get the best possible deals in all of the land of Nod only from him. Then he warned him not to do business with any unlicensed dealers of iron. "Meth, do not buy steel that does not bear my mark. All untaxed goods will be confiscated. Also,

do not be caught transporting coal to your land." Meth readily
agreed to these conditions.

Meth used the opportunity to describe other items that must be
manufactured for him before his next visit to Nod six months later.
Lamech had brought in his best team of ironworkers to listen while
Meth described his requirements. Among those ironworkers was the
giant Tubal-Cain, who was now an instructor. As Meth was
outlining his needs, he was somewhat distracted by the sight of the
giant. He had only heard rumors of him; now he knew that the
rumors were true.

Some of the tools that Meth needed were large saws, drills, and
planes for woodworking. He would also need larger hammers than
the ones that were currently being made. Lamech assured Meth that
there would be no problem making the new items.

"Take a look at this," Meth said, handing a drawing to Lamech,
who then handed it to a foundry engineer.

"What is this?" asked the worker.

"Let's call this a saw," said Lamech.

"I see. This is the handle for the users?" the engineer asked as he
looked, clearly impressed with the detail of the drawing. "These
undercuts are for the cutting action?"

"Yes," Meth said.

Lamech interrupted them, "Look, we can make all your tools.
Don't worry. Just work with my men. If they can't make a thing, it
can't be made. Now, how about my silver? I will need sixty pieces of
silver for the tools and the pegs. I will give you the pitch as well, with
thirty pieces down and thirty pieces of silver on delivery," he offered.

He knew in his wicked heart that if he detained or killed Meth
he would never find the source of the shiny metals. Trying to follow
him would not be easy either. So, for now, his best bet was just to do
business with him. He considered these alternatives while he waited
for Meth's response to his offer.

"Lamech, we have a deal. Let's agree to another five hundred pegs," Meth told Lamech, "the same amount of pitch, along with the tools, and three firm oxen. When I return in six months, I will bring an additional thirty pieces of silver and thirty pieces of gold for you as the balance of payment."

"Gold? What is gold?" Lamech asked.

"It is good for many things," Meth told him. You will like it. If you don't, I will replace it with silver."

With that, their agreement was settled.

Once the deal had been struck, Meth seemed to disappear into thin air, much to Lamech's amazement. He was like a spirit in the wind——one could never tell where he came from or where he went. So he was gone now, but he was sure to return.

As Meth began his trek back to Noah in the land of Havilah, the source of the shiny metals, he thought about his encounter with the Nephilim. He had heard from his sources in Nod of Lamech's plans to breed these beings to be both servants and workers in the iron rooms. He realized that he too could use workers such as these. Giant men would be a great asset in building a giant boat. It was hard to ignore the possibilities. He would have to initiate a relationship with the large forger. If Tubal-Cain could breed, the Nephilim could be of great help in the future. After meeting Lamech, Meth knew he could get whatever he wanted or needed if he brought enough shiny metals to Lamech's table to trade with.

When Lamech had his new supply of metals, he didn't waste any time. He had his most skillful workers form the shiny metals into thin sheets. He had the thin sheets cut into oval shapes and then mounted on to hardwood frames and polished. He was amazed at just how clear the reflections in these mirrors were. Lamech knew that these mirrors would bring him a degree of power never before held on earth, and he would control the production and the terms of any sales.

Along with the mirrors, other products were devised that might entice women into the palace of Lamech. The high quality mirrors that were now available to a few were a catalyst for the inception and sudden expansion of many new industries dealing in jewelry, makeup, skin and hair care products for men and women. All of these small markets were about to explode, and Lamech would control them too.

With these products in development, Lamech would soon be able to launch his program of luring the unsuspecting women of the Circle into his trap.

It didn't take long. Interest in and desire for these new products was fanatical, and Lamech took full advantage of the women who desired them. He believed that there would only be a small window of time during which he could retain control of all these new products, so he would have to work quickly to implement the rest of his plan.

In order to test the power of the mirrors, Lamech personally set out to seduce a woman into becoming the mother of a Nephilim.

"We have found a woman whose vanity is beyond that of any other woman we have found," one of Lamech's men told him. "She is extremely beautiful and her husband is a very powerful man in the Circle."

"I don't care where or who she is. Is she willing?" demanded the clearly frustrated Lamech.

"Sire, I can get her here, and I can get you alone with her. She knows what you want. She knows what she wants. You will have to take it from there." The man told Lamech with great caution.

"Just bring her," Lamech roared, and soon the woman was standing before him.

"Where is your husband?" asked Lamech when he was alone with her in his chambers.

"Where is the mirror I was promised?" asked the woman.

"You will have what you desire. Just think, in only a few moments you——like everyone else——will know your beauty. You are a very beautiful woman. Such is your beauty that it is of an eternal nature. It truly is. Your reflection shall live on for eternity," Lamech told her.

Lamech was gaining ground——the woman seemed to be getting more comfortable as she eagerly awaited her chance to see her reflection.

"Ah, here comes your mirror now," Lamech murmured, as Tubal walked into the room carrying a large, beautifully crafted mirror with a handle made of fig wood. Her eyes were on the prize and not on the price as Tubal approached her with the mirror. She was so anxious to see her reflection that she grabbed the mirror from his very large hand. She was so distracted that she didn't even notice the giant.

"It's true. It's true! I am beautiful. You are right, Lamech. Thank you so much. How can I ever repay you?" Lamech believed that he already had her where he wanted her, but he continued setting the trap that he had prepared. Lamech watched as she continued to indulge in self-worship, prancing and posing. He also watched Tubal-Cain who was observing this woman with a level of interest that he had never demonstrated before. "You know, I can't let you keep the mirror though," Lamech said to her at last.

"What? What are you talking about? You can't take this back now," the woman cried.

"I am sorry. I only have a few of them. You can't keep it," repeated Lamech. So now the tables were turned on the woman——she had been deluded into believing that she was the one who was scheming to get something from Lamech.

"Surely there is something I can do for you in exchange for the mirror," she coaxed, and the negotiations began. In the end, having given up all that she normally negotiated with to obtain things that she wanted, the woman offered Lamech what he wanted——her life. Lamech sealed the deal with the words that he had learned from an ally: "You won't surely die."

A short time later it was confirmed that the woman was with child; she would not leave the palace of Lamech alive. Lamech was thrilled with the outcome of his experiment. He hastened to provide housing for concubines for the giant.

Lamech redirected all of his government resources to the project of building accommodations for more than one hundred women. He took whatever he needed from wherever he found it. He sent all of his men out to lure more and more women to his compound to spawn his low-breeds. This had to be done quickly, before the fate of the first woman could become common knowledge.

Within a few months, Lamech had achieved his first goal, as many women were now pregnant with potential giants. There was still one question left begging an answer though——would these indeed be Nephilim?

Soon the women realized that their pregnancies were not normal and that they might be facing the prospect of dying during childbirth. They could tell that the children were growing too quickly inside of them, and they were afraid. Lamech's palace, which had become a maternity ward, now had special quarters for the women who had become aware of the peril they were in——locked quarters. Some had become uncontrollable, and others had already escaped into the city and surrounding areas. So, from now on, any such woman would have to be imprisoned.

Smash!

One woman, who was five months into her pregnancy, hit one of the guards over the head with her mirror——her prize——distorting the fragile silver. and consequently, her own reflection.

"I never want to see myself again," she yelled hysterically. She had realized that her prize had become a debt that she would end up paying with her life.

Lamech had succeeded in conceiving an army, but he had stretched the limits of his power a bit too far, and he was losing control of his army before most of the giants had even seen the light of day. He would make every effort to maintain ownership of as many of the giants as possible, but he had been so distracted by the project of birthing his army that his control over Nod and the Circle had been slipping from his grasp. Since some of the pregnant women had managed to escape, Lamech would not end up being the only master of giants. Very soon the time would come when these giant newborns would begin to appear in and around the Circle and it would become increasingly difficult to get more women to fall into his trap to breed more of these monsters.

As that second generation of Nephilim grew and matured, many men wanted to own the giants. Like Lamech, these men would use any means available to them to coerce women into bearing more giants. Lamech had lost control of the enterprise. Although still very powerful, he no longer had a monopoly on either the mirrors or the giants.

Adding these giants to the population of the Circle only caused it to descend more rapidly into pure evil; even the ground below the Circle seemed to be sinking into the earth. (KJV Gen. 6:1–5) It was as if the dead in the earth were assembling below, eagerly anticipating each and every death for the small bit of relief it would afford them against the relentless agony they endured in their utter darkness.

As the second generation of Nephilim were coming of age, a significant difference between them and the first generation became obvious. Unlike Tubal-Cain, many of the second generation of low-bred beings had a lust for women. Women soon discovered the power that this lust afforded them and used it to their advantage. The giants were very easily manipulated, and as each day went by the women of Nod discovered new ways to control them. Like the power-hungry men, these power-hungry women lusted for more power, and they too were soon manipulating the unsuspecting among them into birthing yet more giants.

Nobody knew how many giants had been born. Lamech alone had bred at least a hundred of them. After a few years, it was generally believed that there were a couple hundred of them roaming the land of Nod. Their population continued to grow, though very slowly.

Eventually, travelers such as Meth would encounter Nephilim many times, and Meth continued to think about incorporating them into the building of the ark. He had yet to share this idea with Noah, and although God might have knowledge of his idea, he had not yet formally appealed to God for guidance in the matter.

The time came for Meth and Noah to discuss the details of construction. More men would soon be needed, and Noah looked to Meth for a solution.

"Noah, we should talk," Meth said. "I think I know of a good fit for the ark."

"You speak of the giants," Noah figured correctly.

"Yes, I speak of the giants. The giants are slow-witted, but they are extremely strong and skillful workers. It is as though they were tailor-made for this project," Meth told him. The two men agreed, and continued to think along these lines.

"Plus, using them would make it easier to keep our location and the nature of our project a secret, because the giants are slow and won't be curious about the project or chatter to others about it," Meth surmised.

"Meth, we should pray about it, and let us make sure we think this through all the way," Noah said.

"I could not agree more," Meth declared.

Meth still had about five years to decide who the needed help should be and to arrange how, where, and when to bring them to Havilah.

Much depended on the outcome of his efforts. He would have to evaluate the potential positives and negatives of employing the giants. If he determined that this would not be feasible or practical, or if God did not give His approval, then other men would have to be brought to Havilah as builders for the ark. Those men would surely discover the riches of Havilah; they would be curious as to why such a large boat . . . and thus would present a whole new set of challenges to overcome.

"Noah, if we can't use the giants to build the ark, what kind of men should we use? Do we look for those of the faith though we know that they will have to be left behind?" Meth asked Noah, "Or do we look for Cainites who just want the money but whose work will hardly be reliable? Of course, once those people learn of Havilah all could be lost."

Noah thought about this and said, "If we can't use the giants, we may have to do all of it ourselves. We can't risk bringing Cainites here, and I don't think it is just for a faithful man to labor for an escape and then be denied that escape. We will walk and work in faith that God will give us more time if we need it, or whatever other means we need to complete the job." Meth concurred with this. So they put together a five-year plan for enlisting the help of the giants. If this did not work out, then they would consider other options.

"If we figure out a way to secure the services of the Nephilim, we will still need to ask God if He approves," Meth reminded Noah.

"You are absolutely right. If we can make it work for us, then we will go to God in prayer and ask for His blessing," said Noah.

They could not help wondering——more than once——if God had contrived this good fit for them. A giant ark built by giants who were rumored to be sons of God——*could this be only a coincidence?*

The five years went by quickly, and a decision about the giants now had to be made. "Noah, I can get the giants we need from Lamech. He is as wicked as men get, and thus he is as malleable as the silver that I use to control his every action," Meth told Noah.

"The thing I like best about the idea of using the giants is that they are not capable of finding their way to Havilah on their own, so they cannot lead anybody else here. That is the most important aspect of this plan for me," Noah said.

Clearly, both men wanted the giants working on the project, but they still had to pray to God for His approval. Noah bowed while Meth, feeling some anxiety, prayed aloud. "God almighty, we need Your guidance."

The Father had long anticipated this request and calmed both of them with a gentle, cool breeze, and their anxiety faded rapidly as they awaited their answer.

God decided to walk with Noah once again. Meth could sense the presence of the Father while Noah was alone with Him. After a short time, Meth could feel that Noah had returned to his side. Noah was clearly moved by the experience. Slowly, he began to speak.

"God told me that we can use the giants, and only the giants, to labor on the ark and to load its contents," Noah said, still a bit foggy and fumbling his words a bit as he tried to describe his experience. God had instructed Noah that only Noah, his family, and the Nephilim would be permitted to build the ark and to contribute any other labor required. Meth desperately wanted to know if God had foreseen the need for the giants, to know if they had been a part of God's plan for the ark from the start.

"Noah, did God have anything else to say about the giants? Anything?" Meth asked, with anticipation. Noah's response was not what Meth had hoped for.

"God did not give me any indication as to any role He might have played in the creation of the giants," he said. Then he added, "But I am sure that He was pleased with us for looking to Him for direction and guidance, and that's all that really matters." Noah was still puzzling over the meaning of what God had said, just as Meth was. Noah continued, "If God had any role in the creation of the Nephilim, it is beside the point. The point is that we considered what God wanted more than we considered what we wanted," Noah said.

They looked at each other with amazement at the experience. They felt so humbled——and yet so amazed——about all that was happening in their lives. God was in their presence and giving them direction——direction that they wanted and needed. Meth told Noah, "I shall never forget this moment. I shall never forget the words that were spoken here today."

Meth was also extremely moved by the whole experience. Then Noah told him, "God also wanted me to tell you how proud He is of you and that you have been a great grandfather to me. Your guidance to me has been superior to any other guidance I have ever received. God is right. Your wisdom and input into this effort have been essential." Meth was incredibly honored that God had said these things to Noah about him. He bowed his head again in prayer, but mostly his bowed head was to hide his tears of humility.

Then they were quiet. After some time, they thought about the possible deeper meanings in what God had said to Noah. Noah thought again about Meth's question about whether God might have played a part in getting the giants involved. Then he recalled something else that God had said.

"God did say that our desires became His desires as He watched and listened to us justly desire them——that was His duty as a loving Father."

God's approval of their plan to use the Nephilim brought them great comfort. Noah and his sons were at ease with the idea of using the labor of the giants to build their escape vessel and then leaving them behind. Unlike the sons of Adam, the Nephilim were not considered eternal beings and were not believed to have free will. Noah and Meth felt confident that they would be able to secure the services of the giants from Nod. Now that they had little doubt that their source of labor was in place, they were ready to tackle the next of the many challenges they would surely face.

Five more years flew by, during which far more than twenty vessels loaded with steel, tools, and other supplies had come and gone. Then Methuselah returned from his fortieth trip to Nod with twelve giants ready to work on the ark.

Getting twelve giants from Lamech had been a job unto itself.

"Twelve giants? You want twelve giants to accompany you for six months? Meth, you ask for too much," said Lamech. "Twelve giants in the steel rooms over the course of six months will produce countless articles of steel, and coins for profit. I can't allow this," insisted Lamech.

Meth assured Lamech that he would return the giants, along with great amounts of shiny metals.

"Lamech, the metals are getting more difficult to find and remove from the ground," Meth told him. Lamech understood this, as the iron in Nod was also becoming difficult to extract. Most of the iron that was easy to access had already been taken; more and more often it had to be mined from pits. "No giants, no shiny metals," Meth insisted.

Lamech did not like being forced to let the old man Meth get away with the use of twelve giants for such a long period of time. So he devised a plan. "Okay. You can have your giants. But don't disappoint me, Meth. It would be very bad for your health," said Lamech. He added, "These giants are difficult to control. I insist that you bring one of my men with you to assist."

Knowing he would have plenty of opportunity to deal with what was obviously to be a spy, Meth agreed. "Sure, let your spy come along," he said with a laugh.

"Okay, forget that then, take the giants on your own," Lamech said. "Just know this, Meth. If I really wanted to find your land, I could and would," Lamech threatened.

Of course Lamech would still send a spy to try to find the source of the shiny metals——he had tried before. But this time, with the slow-witted giants involved, he felt he had a much better chance of discovering where Meth had come from. So Lamech's spy followed Meth's group. Meth knew what was going on, and he also knew that he would soon enough lose the spy when they went down the Pishon.

The last stop for Meth with his oxen and giants, on this part of the journey before the river Pishon, was a place south of the Square of Adam where Meth contracted the locals to build several vessels each year to navigate down the Pishon to Havilah. Meth did what he could to avoid allowing others to see the giants, but he could not keep the boat builders from seeing them.

Meth walked with the giants into the camp where the vessels were built. Upon seeing the giants, the men ran like scalded dogs. Meth had a good laugh at this and gestured to the giants, who were completely oblivious. "Did you see them run? They have never seen giants before. You are very new and different to them. Let us rest. Soon enough they will return to find out what they ran away from." With that, they made themselves at home, and began looking over the vessels they were to take south.

It wasn't long before the vessel builders were peeking around the trees and then walking towards the giants. When they did, Meth rose up and yelled to the giants, "Get them!" and then broke into the biggest laugh he had had in years. The giants didn't understand and didn't give chase, but they frightened the builders enough to make them run away again. Eventually, the men once again returned, not finding this funny at all. It was time for them to have their own little fun with Meth.

"Okay, Tubals, let's get these boats loaded," Meth told his giants.

"Wait–hang on there a moment, Meth," said one of the boat builders. "Only two of these boats are for you. I have had a better offer for the other two. I must take that offer," said the builder.

Meth was not pleased, and he started in on the man. But the builder added, "A guy came in the day before you did. I think he knows you. He was willing to pay more for the boats, so I had no choice but to sell them to him." Just when Meth was going to let the guy have it, the whole crew broke out in laughter. "Meth, do you think I would let my best customer down? That spy will not get a single one of my boats, rest assured." Meth joined in on the laughter and thanked the builder for being so loyal to him.

"My friend, I will need four vessels twice this year," he told them. "I know I can depend on you." With that, the men enjoyed a meal together. Then Meth said goodbye to the man he knew as Vessel and started down the Pishon.

Meth would need a minimum of twenty-four giants——two crews of twelve——for each six-month tour of work. Once they got back home, the giants would use the valuables that Meth had paid them with to buy their freedom and to try to seduce the women of the Circle——but, more often than not, the giants would be tricked out of what they had earned for their hard work.

The giants liked coming to the land of Havilah. They were treated much differently in Havilah than they were treated at home in the Circle of Man, and they became very loyal to Meth and to Noah. Meth was a good man. Everyone liked him and worked hard just to earn his respect. He always paid his workers on time and the pay was never short. The ways of the giants came to mirror the ways of Noah and Meth, which showed that being a good master results in molding good and faithful workers.

Each of Noah's sons worked with a team of four giants to cut and shape logs from cypress trees. They sawed them to precise lengths and widths according to the directions that Noah gave them. Five years into this work, the major pieces were finally cut and ready. With fifty-five years left until the deadline, Noah felt good about his progress. Again, he thanked God for this great honor that He had bestowed upon him.

From the perspective of an outsider looking in, one would have to say that Meth had taken on the more difficult task. Perhaps it was the wisdom of an older man such as Meth that had encouraged God to select him for the more difficult job——he was performing his responsibilities flawlessly. Though wisdom was important, he had faith working for him as well.

Meth continued to visit the Circle twice a year to trade. Always there seemed to be an invisible force between himself and other people, and he suspected that this originated from him. Maybe there was a spiritual shield around him. He was never sure if this phenomenon was a blessing from God meant to comfort him while he was doing His bidding, or if it sprang from the horde of the Circle because being in the presence of a righteous man made them uncomfortable. The origin and reason mattered little though. Meth was thankful that time and again he had been able to enter the Circle, obtain the steel, pitch and caulk that he needed, and escape without major incident.

Meth was not a very spiritual man. He was righteous, and he had felt the presence of God on more than one occasion, but he was primarily led by pragmatism rather than by spirituality. He was simply a man on a mission. Generally, Meth did not ask God for anything other than strength and wisdom. However, he had been in a few tough spots during which he had asked God for specific wisdom on how to handle a particular situation. Thankfully, it seemed that it had always been given, as Meth always made it through the tough spots relatively unscathed. He was always grateful, and he knew the Spirit was the source of his wise actions. Meth was in no way proud of his pragmatic side, but he figured it takes all kinds of people to do the work that God needs to be done, including some pragmatic types like him.

Meth, like Noah, had not made a sacrifice in Havilah as they worked on the ark. They were doing exactly what God wanted them to do, and they were both very satisfied with their lives and with the jobs that God had assigned to them. Even without having offered any sacrifices, it was understood that they loved God and God loved them. Their lives were their sacrifice, and for now no more was needed, as no guilt was found in their hearts or minds.

Noah had always known, though, that sacrifice would be their first action upon entry into the new world. They would have to thank God for the success of their joint venture.

Meth was largely responsible for trade between the Square and the Circle, and this trade had both good and bad aspects. On the negative side, it was going to bring the corruption and wickedness of the people of the City of Enoch to the Square of Adam. Meth had established a main trading route between the Square and the Circle of Man, and by the time the ark was nearing completion this route was well-traveled by many.

Over the years, people had traveled on the Pishon and other rivers in many directions, but none of them had discovered Havilah. Meth and Noah hoped to keep it that way, so they brought only Nephilim with them on their travels and never anyone else. The exact river route to Havilah was a very tricky one, and only Noah, his sons, and Meth would ever know of this very rich and wonderful land.

The route from Havilah to Nod was even more difficult, and it was even more important to keep this one secret. It was also the shortest route in time and distance of all their trade routes.

The Hiddekel River was a major obstacle for Meth on the route back to the Circle of Man in Nod. Eventually, with the help of the giants, Meth was able to make a bridge across the river. He knew of a narrow canyon through which the river flowed. He had the giants use tools of steel from Nod to fell a giant cedar over that canyon to make a bridge. They milled a flat surface on the top side of the fallen tree to make passage easier.

Upon exit from the bridge, one had to scale down a steep cliff of difficult terrain. This led down to another narrow canyon that swung back a few thousand arm-lengths to where it was possible to continue progressing towards Nod. The bridge could not be seen from the bottom of the canyon, and even if someone knew it was there, it was difficult to reach. Meth was very happy with this situation——it was effectively a hidden, one-way route from Havilah to Nod.

The route from Nod to the Square could be completed in thirty days by a strong man. The route back to Nod from the Square required ten days on foot and ten days heading east down the Hiddekel on a raft to the Circle of Nod.

As the trade routes developed, numerous outposts sprang up along the way and were especially common between resting stops. As the two cultures increasingly encountered each other on these routes and at these outposts, travel became much more dangerous.

Giants were sometimes used for protection by wealthy travelers, and that worked well. While giants would fight to protect their masters, the giants would not often fight each other. The giants of old were of a corrupt and perverse seed, but they had standards. It was very seldom that a giant would kill another giant or a human.

Every six months the free giants, (those without owners), who were building the ark were taken back to a location close to the trade route between the Square of Adam and the Circle of Enoch. There they would part ways with Methuselah, who would then journey back to Enoch with the giants who were owned by Lamech. Everyone would question the giants upon their return to Nod, but they could provide very little information about where Meth took them or how to return there other than by the river. Ironically, the giants would tell their inquisitors about how they were building a "big boat" for a man named Noah, but no one paid any attention to those details whatsoever.

Meanwhile, back in Havilah, Noah's boys were beginning to have doubts. God had given the measurements of the ark to Noah. But it was not until the timbers had been laid out on the ground and the boys got a good, real-life look at the dimensions that they began to understand how immense this boat was going to be and the outrageous scope and ambition of this project.

"Father, we walked the length of the project today. It is very large," Japheth said, broaching the subject with Noah one evening. The other boys listened closely. "It was more than two hundred and eight paces, end to end," Japheth added. "I personally don't think anything this size could possibly float." Japheth was neither an engineer nor a builder of boats, but he had now seen the size of it and thought it was too big to float.

"Dad, I remember hearing Grandpa, not long ago, talking about the first boat you ever built." Japheth reminded his father, giving the three boys and Noah a good laugh.

"Okay, Japheth," said Noah. "I was wondering when one of you would bring up my first attempt at building a boat. Though I had expected it would be Ham that would needle me about that first."

Noah's first ever attempt to build a boat had not gone well, and Meth had told the boys this story about their Dad several times. It went something like this: "When Noah was about sixteen years old, he started building rafts and boats. The first one, if my memory serves me correctly, sank rather quickly," Meth would say, and then he would add, "Perhaps God chose your father for this particular task because He has an irreverent sense of humor?" Then Meth, no matter how many times he told the story, would be laughing louder than the boys, and he had a very infectious laugh.

"Okay boys. Well at least you're paying attention, and I now see that the scope of this project is starting to "sink" in. Perhaps you are right to be concerned——no boat anywhere near this size has ever been proposed before and certainly has not been built," Noah told the boys. "Walk with me, and I shall try to convince you that it will work."

Noah and his sons went to the place where they would soon begin to assemble this giant boat. "Look down this way, then this way, then up along the bluffs on both sides, and then tell me what you think."

As Noah waited, the boys looked as directed. They didn't say much. "Do the dimensions that I received from God match up with the size of this location? They do. If you look closely, you will see that they match it perfectly, don't they?"

The boys were beginning to get their father's first point. They knew that their father had drawn up the plans God gave him before Noah knew of this place where God wanted the ark to be built. They also knew that Noah had never been to this place before, so a coincidence seemed unlikely at best.

"I didn't find this place, you know," Noah told them. "Do you think we just happened to stop here, and that the dimensions of this place just happen to perfectly match the dimensions I was given for the ark?"

Again, the boys acknowledged that it sure seemed like more than a coincidence. "Son," Noah continued as he took Shem over to one side. "See those cypress trees and those cedar trees over there?" He pointed to the left and to the right. "Would you agree that those trees are very straight and of very good quality?"

"Yes," replied Shem.

"You have been studying the plans God gave me for the ark for a while now. Looking at those trees, would you say they are the exact size we need to build this project?"

"Yes, Father," said Ham.

Noah wasn't even close to finished.

"Boys, look at the drawings of these tools we will use." Ham, who was very good at making and designing tools, now took the lead.

"This is a drawing of a drill," Ham said, as he looked at it. It was a cylindrical staff with a coil of hemp rope intended to be used by two men to spin it in order to bore a hole in wood. "It won't work," said Ham.

"It won't? Are you sure?" cautioned Noah.

"Yes. This would start the wood on fire way before it would bore a hole in it," Ham said with confidence.

"Ham, please take a closer look at the staff on the drawing and look at this marking——look at the notes in the details," Noah asked his boy.

Then Ham asked, "Ferro? What is ferro?"

Noah walked over to where he and Meth had been stockpiling the inventory of supplies, which was substantial. The most recent items that had come in were items made of iron and steel. From a pile of miscellaneous items, he pulled out a sharp object that had a hole in the center for the staff, exactly like the item he had been showing Ham on the drawing. "Ham, do you see this?" Ham took the ferro in his hands and was amazed by it; it was heavy and obviously far more durable than wood or stone.

Noah was making progress with the boys——they were convinced, at least for now, that their father was in possession of some very advanced and detailed knowledge to which they should pay close attention. But never having walked with God, they, like all men, still had their doubts.

As the project came together almost magically, Noah was winning the day. All the tools were made of iron, and they had never seen tools such as these before. Their father talked about these tools as if he had been playing with them all of his life, and this dumbfounded the boys.

Noah had built boats before, but they had been made with stone tools, pitch, and rope made of hemp. That had been nothing like this. The boys, for now, believed in their father and in this giant ark, especially as the evidence mounted that Noah was being directed by God. It seemed to be the only explanation for these wildly advanced engineering and construction methods. The size and shape of the timbers they had been cutting could not be a coincidence either.

"Father gave us these dimensions years ago. Then we cut all these huge trees to shape, not putting much thought into their sizes. But now while we are starting to assemble them they are fitting together perfectly. God must be with our father for this to happen," said Shem.

Ham was more creative than his brothers. He was more industrious as well, and perhaps even smarter. Of the three sons, he was considered to be the strongest, and he had amazing agility and speed. He excelled at everything he tried, from music to tests of strength and endurance.

He was also a woodcarver, and he frequently made adornments for his mother, with whom he was very close. Carving animals out of wood, along with images of his brothers and other family members, was how Ham passed most of his leisure time. He would also sculpt squares and blocks that could be used in various ways in the home and elsewhere. He carved spheres, squares, cubes, and triangles that served a variety of purposes in the construction of the ark. Some of his ideas and items were instrumental in keeping the ark plumb and square.

Ham also devised a three-dimensional geometric figure that fascinated him, a polyhedron, with a base inspired by the Square of Adam and sides based on the triangles that formed the pentagon he had heard of. He hoped to build giant structures of stone in this shape someday in the new world.

THE ARK TAKES SHAPE

By the time the ark neared completion, Meth had made around two hundred trips to Nod and back and was now a very old man. He was no longer walking the route that he had come to know so well. Now, he mostly rode atop a beast of one kind or another. The Nephilim also helped the old man as if they were his best friends, and in fact, some of them had become very close and extremely loyal to him over the years.

Ahead of their deadline, the ark was basically ready. The final crew of giants had been brought to Havilah. Noah instructed the leader of the giants, Anak, to gather and load their goods, provisions and food for Noah's family and the animals onto the boat. Harvesting and gathering the food had taken four months, and that task was nearly complete. There was a small mountain of grasses, hay and grains. Many extra fowl, for eggs and eating, thousands of pieces of dried meat and fruits, more than a thousand pieces of fire wood and a small amount of coal to purify water as needed. The crew's water supply was to be gathered from over the side and or from the roof of the ark. Noah knew that rain would supply much of the needed water, something that the others would take by faith in Noah. There were several places on board to incinerate waste and cook food as was needed.

It would take another week or so to load the goods on board. Since everything else was ready, Noah approached his grandfather with an idea.

"Grandfather, let us travel together to Nod, you and I, on one last adventure?" Noah wanted to go to Nod and preach repentance to the doomed. Maybe he could comfort a few about their unavoidable future.

Meth responded, "Noah I hear you and I understand your desire for men to repent. I even promised Lamech that I would bring him something more precious than gold on my final visit to Nod–a chance to repent. But I need to tell you one thing before you decide to do this: you will be risking everything if you go to the Circle. Are you sure it is worth that risk?" Noah paused to think about this, struggling to justify his desire to preach, and then he told Meth, "You know me. I am a man of very few words. I have always been that way, but I can't stay silent when I have an opportunity to save so many. I feel obligated to try at least one time to save at least one person. I do think that is worth the risk, and with you by my side I will be fine." With that, they began planning their last adventure together, to the Circle of Man in Nod.

The journey to Nod would take them about a month if things went smoothly, and a week later they were on their way. The landscape had changed, as the drought was now well into its third year. This made the path more direct and easier to pass than it had been before. The rivers were running slower and the trees and all other vegetation were parched. They arrived safely in Nod after about nineteen days of travel.

As they entered the City of Enoch, Meth held himself a few steps back from Noah to let Noah form his own impressions of just how wicked the rest of the world had become.

In the land of Nod, Eva had been dead for almost a hundred years now. Cain had resurfaced in the City of Enoch, but he was keeping a very low profile and no one bothered him. As the oldest man on earth, Cain had discovered that he had the freedom to do whatever he wanted to do regardless of what that was. He could do no wrong, even when he did the most evil of things.

Throughout the centuries, Cain had come to realize that unless he did something worse than murder, people would always overlook his misdeeds. After all, he was already guilty of murder, so what was to stop him from committing theft or practicing deceit? Technically, he could do no wrong, and this made him feel weaker than he had ever felt before. There were no rules for him, no guidelines and therein lay his dilemma: if nothing is wrong, then nothing is right either. There *literally* could be no bigger irony than this for a man who worshiped the tree of knowledge.

Just as Cain had envisioned, he was famous——and ironically, anonymous——in the city that he had founded with his son Enoch, who was now long dead. As the oldest man on earth, he was an attraction, and it was widely believed that he was cursed so that he could not die and could not be killed. But he didn't have the power that he had once held; he was alive, but he was a very old man.

—— 13 ——

NOAH IN NOD

When Noah and Meth arrived in the City of Enoch, Noah was shocked to discover just how far man had fallen. The effects of the drought were severe, and the suffering of the people was enormous, but Noah got to it and engaged the first man he saw as he entered the City of Enoch.

"Sir. Oh, sir," he called. The stranger turned towards him. "Sir," Noah said. "This drought will end badly. All will perish. It is time to offer a sacrifice and repent."

The man looked at him as though he was crazy. "Look, stranger. I am busy," he told Noah. "I am very busy. I don't have time for this, and I don't have any money to give you. Now, just leave me alone." With that, the stranger turned and walked away.

"Sir O sir," Noah called after him, but the man kept walking. "That man thought I was crazy," Noah said, looking back to Meth as his grandfather caught up with him.

"Repent, judgment, and sacrifice are terms that are not often spoken or heard here in the land of Nod," Meth explained to Noah.

Meth was right. The words that Noah had spoken had been completely foreign to that thirsty, decrepit man as he shook his head, mumbling, and marched onward to forage for food and water.

Noah soldiered on, and made another attempt. This time he stood on a tree stump and proclaimed, "Brothers, the prophecy of Enoch the Sethite is upon us." Noah was encouraged when a few of these people paid heed to his words, so he continued. "Brothers, there will be no surviving this drought, but you can survive in eternity. Brothers, it is time to repent and to offer a sacrifice to God."

Noah was delighted as the crowd around him grew, but he soon began to fear that it had grown too big when someone called out derisively, "Does Lamech approve of these sacrifices?" Noah tried to ignore the question, but it came again, and then the crowd started to mumble in chorus. Soon Noah's voice was drowned out by the ruckus of the mob. His earlier delight turned completely to fright when he noticed that two giants were rapidly leaving the area——maybe they were heading off to alert someone. Noah looked for Meth in the crowd but could not see him. He was on his own as he tried to get down off the stump to make a quick exit. But, before he was able to leave the scene, a hush fell over the crowd, and everyone turned their heads to stare at four giants with a man in their midst, all making their way towards Noah.

Suddenly Noah was face-to-face with the ruler, Lamech.

"Who are you to ask for a sacrifice?" Lamech demanded.

Noah bowed his head and answered him. "My liege, I am Noah, and I bring to you and to the people in Circle of Man the memory of God's prophet Enoch, the Sethite."

"The people of the Circle have no knowledge of your prophet, Sethite, but I do. I know of this prophecy. Do you believe it to be true?" Lamech asked him.

"Yes, sir, I do." The crowd remained silent. Noah now had the audience he had wanted. "God himself has told me it is true. There is no escape for any of you."

"God told you this? And is your fate the same, Sethite?" Lamech asked.

"Sir, the rivers and the lakes will soon dry up. The garden is refusing to allow the rivers to flow, and soon they will stop flowing completely," Noah told him.

"The Garden in Eden?" Lamech laughed, and the crowd laughed with him. "Noah, is it? Are you from a sect of the garden seekers?"

"I am not familiar with that sect. I am just a Sethite who seeks to warn all those who will listen," Noah said.

"Should I repent as well?" Lamech asked.

Noah understood the question and its possible ramifications, but he saw no other option but to respond. "Sir, I can see that you are powerful, and I can sense your resolve. It would be foolish of me to question your wisdom in my current position. I can say that you are an example to many, and whatever path you choose many will follow."

"You are careful with your words," Lamech said, "as you should be. But I don't think you shall escape me with clever and carefully chosen words. So, tell me Sethite why does the garden restrain the rivers?"

God had never actually told Noah that the garden would be stopping the flow of the water, but Noah knew intuitively that this was the case.

"Sir, the garden restrains the water unto judgment of the earth and the men on the earth. We are now in the last days; the time for judgment has arrived. God is sorry that He made man. The cost has been too painful for His Spirit to abide."

An old man wearing a cowl heard the people mumbling about the Garden in Eden, and his ears perked up. From where he was standing on the periphery of the crowd, he moved swiftly and with a sense of purpose, entering the gathering. The cowled old man parted the crowd and made his way towards Lamech. As he approached

Lamech, even the giants and Lamech himself allowed the decrepit old man to continue. Noah had no choice but to stand there and wait until the encounter between Lamech and this interloper was over. But then the old man removed his cloak . . . and pointed directly at Noah. Noah thought he was done for. *Why did I come here in the first place? How could I have been so careless as to bring this danger upon myself and endanger our mission?* He was sure that Lamech would now be coming for him. Indeed, Lamech motioned to four of his giants, and without a word he retreated to speak with some more of his giants who had gathered at the rear of the crowd. Noah had no idea what was happening.

Then the old man in the cowl advanced quickly to where Noah stood. Grabbing his arm, he tucked Noah under his cloak and led him away to a darkened passage. Noah was astonished to see how much standing the old man in the cowl had in this place, and he was grateful that the stranger had rescued him from certain peril. He caught a glimpse of the old man's face, and guessed from the size of his ears, the length of his nose, and the size of his jaw that he must have had lived through several sets of teeth. The man looked to be far older than Noah's grandfather Meth. Noah guessed him to be far beyond 1000 years old.

"Sir, I owe you my life. Thank you," Noah said, as the man hurried him along to an alleyway.

"Tell me, have you been to the garden?" the old man asked Noah briskly, indifferent to Noah's gratitude.

"The garden? No, I have never been there, but I know that what I say is true. I have known for a very long time that this was coming," Noah said.

The old man had been hoping to hear more than that from the preacher. "We have only a moment, as Lamech will be looking for you. I advise you to make your way quietly away from here. Stay in the shadows and do not preach again. I won't be there to save you the next time."

As the old man raised his cloak and began to walk away, Noah noticed something else about the old man. There was a faint glow about him as he stepped in and out of the shadows. Noah called out to the man, "What is your name?"

The elderly man stopped, he once again lowered his hood, turned, and flashed Noah a mysterious grin . . . And said.

"Well, I am Cain, of course." Noah could not believe it. Cain, the cursed man, the man who had brought chaos to the whole world, had just saved Noah's life, and had probably just snatched the mission of the ark from the brink of disaster.

Noah was speechless, and his mind raced as he considered what had just transpired. Events were moving quickly, so there wasn't much time for reflection, but Noah recognized the irony——God's greatest gamble had just been delivered from certain failure by perhaps the wickedest man who had ever lived. Now understanding that, even the wicked can do good-things even if they don't realize it. Noah knew that he would ponder this for a long time to come.

Cain had no idea who Noah was, nor did he know anything about the ark, and there was no time to explain any of that to him. Cain was in a hurry as he said goodbye to Noah and wished him good luck.

Noah had so many questions he wanted to ask Cain, but knowing he had time for only one, he asked, "What did you say to Lamech to get him to leave?"

Cain turned to Noah. "I told Lamech that we could turn the water back on if we went to the garden and, well . . ." Cain stopped short of revealing all that he had said to Lamech.

"Cain, have you been to the garden?" Noah asked.

"No, I have not been to the garden, but now it is possible that I will go. Your preaching has opened up that opportunity, so thank you——what is your name?"

"Noah. My name is Noah."

"Noah, you are a Sethite, aren't you?" Cain asked him.

"Yes, I am," Noah said.

"You risked everything by coming to the City of Enoch, didn't you?" Cain inquired.

"Everything——oh, yes, I did indeed," laughed Noah, shaking his head. "Everything!"

Cain turned to leave, but then he slowed and stopped. Cain knew the meaning of the name Noah, "the one who would bring comfort to those who work the land." He was also well aware of the prophecy that he had just heard Noah preaching. Cain murmured the name "Noah" and turned back to face Noah again. "Noah, I think we have time. I think we will make time." With that, Cain gathered Noah into his cloak once again and scurried him away to a nearby home.

It was an unguarded and beautiful stone dwelling. As they approached the entrance, Cain looked around to ensure that they had not been followed. Noah waited inside the entrance while Cain moved about the home lighting the lamps; as each lamp came to life, Cain revealed a little more of his life. His home appeared to be a shrine, honoring what one could only guess was the Garden in Eden. Every wall that Noah could see was adorned with paintings of a beautiful garden. As Cain continued to the last lamp, in the center of his home, Noah could see a painting of a fig tree. "This is your home, isn't it?" Noah asked.

"Yes. For a very long time, I have dwelled in and around these parts. Do you know what you are looking at?"

"Yes, I believe these are depictions of the Garden in Eden."

"You are correct. It is my vision of the place, the place of my obsession. Noah, please sit, and perhaps my lifelong obsession with that place will be of benefit to both of us." Noah was still reeling. So many amazing things had just happened, so fast. Now he was in Cain's house, and Cain was about to open up to him.

Well aware of the foolish risk he was taking——he could be discovered by Lamech at any moment——Noah sat down to listen, believing that he could trust Cain and thinking that meeting him *could not* be a coincidence.

Cain told him, "You see, for more than a thousand years of my life I have been waiting for a moment like this. For my whole life I have wanted to go to the Garden in Eden, and with your help, I have now figured out a way to make that happen." Noah listened carefully as Cain continued. "You're preaching of the drought and how all will perish in the drought unless they repent. The mob took that to be anti-Lamech rhetoric. This provided me with an opportunity to convince Lamech that we need to go to the source of the water——to the garden——and open the flow of the water once again, a journey that I am far too old to do on my own. The severity of the drought and the coincidence of your being here preaching have brought about what I never could have on my own——Lamech is now convinced that he must go to the garden."

As he spoke, Cain paced around his home revering the murals on his walls. When he reached the center of the room, he bowed to the fig tree as if in worship. At its base was a very beautiful box that looked very old and appeared to be made of fig wood. He lifted the box and presented it to Noah as an object of great value.

"Noah, take this. Take it and open it. You will be the only man ever to have looked inside this box other than myself." Noah took the box with the same measure of reverence and respect with which it had been presented to him. The beautiful box was indeed made of fig wood and was indeed very old. It might be as old as Cain himself.

Not able to even venture a guess as to what may be inside the box, Noah slowly and gently lifted the top. It was obvious that whatever he was now looking at inside the box was as old as the box itself. The item was dusty and it appeared to be a document. Noah said not a word as he looked to Cain for permission to continue.

"Noah, you are the only person to have seen this in more than a thousand years, and it is appropriate that you are here now and that you are looking at what I have," Cain said with a smile.

But the document began to crumble at Noah's touch. Fearing that he had destroyed it, he said, "Cain, I dare not move the document or even touch it again. It is so old and it is too fragile," said Noah.

"Yes, I know. I have known for some time now that it was all but unusable, but don't worry. I have made copies, many copies, over the years," said Cain.

"Copies of what?" asked Noah.

"What you see all around you is what you have in your hands," Cain said. Noah looked around the house and it suddenly dawned on him what the murals were. "Cain, your home, this shrine, all of these murals——am I looking at a map to the garden?" asked Noah.

"Yes, you are. The original is in the box you now hold in your hands. My mother gave it to me. It is now all but dust, but, as I told you, I have made many copies over the years, and I have dedicated much of my life to building this shrine unto the tree."

"You mean Eve made this map for you?"

"Yes, my dear departed mother made that map for me when Abel and I, as young men, ventured off in search of the garden," Cain said, remembering fondly.

Cain picked up another box, similar to the one that Noah had opened. "I told Lamech that I have a map to the garden and that I have kept it secret for sixteen hundred years. Noah, you have surely comforted me by giving me this opportunity to satisfy my lifelong obsession," said Cain as he opened the other box to reveal a copy of the original map Eve had made him, a map that he would now use to get Lamech to take him to the garden.

"I have comforted you?" Noah asked, as he looked at Cain in disbelief.

Then Cain asked, "What is your understanding of the meaning of your name? Does it not mean 'I am the one who will bring comfort to those who work the ground?'"

"Do you know what a cloud is?" Noah responded.

"No, I do not," said Cain.

"Soon there will be clouds high in the skies all over the earth, and water will fall from them. That will comfort those who work the land," Noah said. (KJV Gen. 2:5-6, 5:29)

Cain started to laugh. "Well, we could sure use the water!"

The two men smiled at each other and Cain said, "We must leave now. Lamech will be looking for me here very soon, and you must not be here when he comes."

"I am glad we met, so very glad," Noah said, as he embraced Cain. Noah felt strongly the need to comfort Cain but could think of no way, no answer, no course, no wisdom, no solution, no help that he could give——other than a hug and a smile of compassion for this assuredly lost spirit. Noah desperately wanted to save Cain. He had risked this visit to Nod in the hopes of saving even one man, and Cain was with him right now and needed saving.

As Cain turned to walk away, it was obvious that he was in a big hurry, eager to begin his final journey. Noah had to try something, so he called out, "Cain, if you make it to the garden, look inside——deep inside yourself——and see if you can repent." Cain turned his head, but Noah didn't get much of a response from him. Cain acknowledged the plea with a slight nod of his head, which seemed to say that he would at least try to do as Noah had asked.

Cain silently departed to prepare for his journey and Noah did the same——they had very different missions with very different goals, and their adventures would likely lead them to eternally different destinations.

When Noah and Meth reunited on the trail back to Havilah, Noah told Meth of his encounter with Cain, an encounter, that Noah could not reconcile as coincidental. As Meth heard the story unfold of how Cain had probably saved God's plan from complete catastrophe, he was astounded.

"Noah," said Meth, "do you think that when I am face-to-face with our Lord but a few days from now, I should ask him if your encounter with Cain was a coincidence?" Noah and Meth, wise fathers both, knew that a father doesn't always answer the questions of his children in the way that they would like them answered. After both men had given this considerable thought, Noah responded, "I think it is probably better not to know. Wonder pleases my spirit far more than knowledge ever could."

Noah had wanted to go to Nod and preach. He knew that preaching to the lost was always a worthy endeavor, and Noah was oh so glad that he had risked everything to save just one person——even if that one person was Cain himself, a man who had little chance of being saved. Noah was not the sort of man who believed that God was generally micromanaging the affairs of man but this one was one that he would find hard to not believe God had His hand in.

On the way back to Havilah, Noah and Meth were aghast to see that the water in the rivers and lakes was all but gone. Travel through this parched landscape was difficult, but they made it home safely, albeit with little time to spare.

God had told Noah exactly where to construct the ark, and He had kept two fresh water springs running there during the drought: one for the animals and one for Noah's family. Those two sweet water springs gave Noah great standing with his sons, as it was further confirmation that God was helping them. The animals for almost a month now had been gathering near their spring. Now the time was at hand, and the ark was ready for loading.

God had the animals gather and then caused them to form a line, and then they slowly and purposefully entered the ark two by two. Noah was the only person who was not amazed to see this behavior from the animals. (KJV Gen. 7:9)

In recent days, the Nephilim had not been as calm as they usually were. Maybe, like the animals, they sensed that something terrible was about to occur. But the animals seemed to know that they would survive this disaster, and maybe the giants sensed that they would not.

With the animals and food and other supplies on board the ark, the work of the giants was finished. The current group of Nephilim had been there for about nine months, and it was far past the time when they were due to return home to Nod, but they didn't know how to find their way to Nod on their own, and Methuselah didn't want to leave Noah at this point. The giants had received their full pay of gold and precious stones, but they were apprehensive——they seemed to know that this time something was different.

Meth brought the giants to the trail that led to the bridge across the now dry Hiddekel River, but he parted company with them there and returned to Noah's family and the ark. It seemed as though this might work out as they did not follow him back. But after a few hours——this was on the final day before the flood was to begin——the giants returned on their own. They had been lost, thirsty, confused, and looking for direction. They sat by the sweet water spring and watched, not understanding why everyone was now on the ark.

One thousand, six hundred, and fifty-six years had passed since God had first created man——time during which God had gained in wisdom day by day. This wisdom, gleaned from five hundred and ninety-six thousand days of history, would be all that the eight people on the ark would have to guide them into a new world.

The drought had already resulted in the deaths of millions, and still more were dying daily. But for the fittest and most resourceful who remained, continued survival would require of them one thing——get the waters flowing again.

Everyone knew of the legend that the garden was the source of all waters, and now all able men on the earth were making plans to go there. Nobody really knew why the waters had ceased flowing, but they all assumed it had something to do with the trees in the garden. After all, it was the tree of knowledge that had caused all problems since the beginning of creation, so it made sense to conclude that the trees were causing the drought. The only thing man knew to do with a troublesome tree was to cut it down. Every instrument of steel that could be found was rounded up to accomplish this goal, including the saws that Lamech's steel rooms had been producing since Meth had given them the design some sixty years ago.

Men believed that the trees in the garden were responsible for the drought, so they hated the trees and were determined to cut them down. But men also began to hate God. After all, He had planted the garden in the first place. (KJV Gen. 2:8) Many men openly cursed God and believed that God was deliberately withholding the water; they were not going to let that stand. These men were determined to get the water they believed that they deserved. The men didn't know it, but God had long ago decided that they should and would get the water that they "deserved." When the water of the rivers was all but dried up, Lamech himself, using the map provided by Cain, led a mob of Nephilim along the muddy river beds to get to the garden, to the source of water.

Once they reached the garden, his mighty men with their steel would open the waters back up to his lands, and he would gain accolades for this. During the journey, Lamech often cursed God openly. Cain stood beside Lamech, but he refrained from joining in with the chorus that was cursing God.

Cain was not looking for water; he was looking for the same old answers. He didn't want to cut down the tree. He wanted to meet it; he wanted to admire it in his own way. He wanted to understand it, and he wanted it to speak to him about his more than one-thousand-year-old obsession with it. If he could not find his answers there, at the foot of that tree, then there would be no answers for him anywhere.

In the Square of Adam, the Sethites were on the same page as the people of Nod but for different reasons. They knew that the waters arose from the garden, so off to the garden they would go to see for themselves just exactly why the waters had stopped. They marched along the dried up bed of the Tigris without knowing what they should expect upon arrival at the garden.

So the beds of the once fast-flowing rivers of the land were filling again——not with water but with men, giants, and every other kind of creature imaginable. Each day, as water became increasingly scarce, more giants and humans took to walking the riverbeds, thirsting for life itself.

As if they could smell the water they needed, they hunted alongside each other, past differences forgotten or ignored. Every man and woman who now made up the multitude traversing the dry beds of the rivers had only one goal——to drink of the water they so desperately needed which was being held back by the tree of knowledge.

Both groups traveled for many days via the dry beds of rivers that originated from the same source, taking what little water they could find along the way. Coming from one land was a pack of men and giants with tools of steel and beasts of burden. Coming from another land were the Sethites, who had very little steel and no giants but were just as thirsty.

As they all journeyed closer to the garden, they could see where the rivers converged into the one common source, and they could see the famous hills. The surroundings were beginning to look like the place from the old legends——the setting of the stories that had been taught to every generation since Adam over the past sixteen hundred years.

The two desperate groups of men traveling in different riverbeds would normally have been adversaries; but when they encountered each other now it was without much incident. The two bloodlines were now facing a common threat, attempting to reach a common goal, and going after a common adversary: the garden——or, specifically, the tree of knowledge. The tree was withholding their water, and to get the water flowing again they would cut it down.

The time was at hand. The day was turning to night as the front-runners of each group drew near their objective. The tree, of course, was still growing because it——and now it alone——had the benefit of the water that was forced up from below by the weight of the firmament of Pangea. "It can't be far now," they chanted. "It can't be far now."

This chant could probably be heard over the whole earth and into the Heavens. "It can't be far now!"

The chant grew louder and louder until it ended abruptly when the men and monsters made a final sprint to the base of the tree of knowledge. The garden entrance had not been obstructed, and the cherubim guards had long since departed. But as the thousands stood looking up at the tree——their adversary——their hopes were dashed.

A mob of tens of thousands was crowded around the immense base of the tree when a single large bird with a known wingspan of forty arm-lengths took flight from one of the tree's massive branches. The bird looked to be no more than the size of a fruit fly in comparison to the size of the tree, and that is when the throng of men realized just how enormous the tree really was. It would probably take a strong man a full day, perhaps two, to walk around the base of this very large tree. So, even with all their steel saws, and thousands of people willing to labor day and night unto death, it was preposterous to think that this tree could be cut down. An uncanny calm fell upon the camps of men as they accepted this new paradigm——there was nothing they could do.

A LAST CHANCE

Cain and Lamech, exhausted and at a loss for words as they gazed at this enormous tree, sat down together and pondered the meaning of it all. Cain sensed that his time was coming to an end, and wanting it all to be over, he said, "Lamech?"

"Yes, Cain?"

"You know my place in history. You know about my mark, and you know about my life in general . . . as it now comes to an end," Cain said as he pointed to a small ewe that was trying to drink from the base of the tree. "You see the innocent lamb?" Lamech looked at the sheep and he nodded affirmation. Cain continued, "Do you think that little lamb can pay for all of my evil deeds?"

"No, I don't. I don't. I don't see how that could be possible," laughed Lamech.

"I don't either. I just don't see how and I never have . . . But what if we are wrong about this?"

Cain was astonished that Lamech was listening to him as they sat in the garden watching the lamb struggle for a drink, just as they struggled for answers. But neither of them thought to look upward for their answers. If God was looking at these two men at that moment, He would have been pleased that they were at least acknowledging their problems and considering sacrifice as a solution. But in the end it would be their choice——a loving Father is always limited by the unwise decisions of his children.

Time went on as the hordes of people almost calmly waited near the tree, with little or no direction, and no place else to go. More and more people arrived each day, and each day the situation became more and more desperate. The small amount of water that was percolating from around the base of the tree was grossly inadequate for the thousands of people surrounding the tree——each one of them desperate for even one sip of water.

Eventually, the desperation reached a breaking point, and a chaotic onslaught of violence was directed against the tree as the thousands of people tried to get it to release more water. The flow of water didn't increase, but the flow of blood began. The tools of steel that had been brought to cut down the tree were now being used in every other way imaginable. The first to die were the animals——there was not enough water to allow any beast to drink, and the pools of blood from the slaughtered animals soon became larger than the meager pools of water that could be found. When those men and women who did not have steel attempted to take a drink, their blood too was spilled.

As human blood pooled at the base of the tree, it had a dramatic effect on the ground beneath it. The ground——or someone in the ground——wanted this blood and wanted more of it. Encouraged by the blood, the ground became increasingly harder and drier, until it seemed that it might crack open.

The thousands of people who had attacked, beaten, worshipped, and trusted in the tree took this as an indication that they were making progress in getting the water they deserved. Maybe the blood pooling on the ground was weakening the tree's grip on the ground, they reasoned. So they determined to provide it with still more blood. On that day, thousands upon thousands of swords were raised in random acts of bloodletting. The tree had stood in judgment long enough, and now it would receive the judgment that it wanted——with the blood of the guilty. Swords swung in every direction, never hitting an innocent man (as there were no innocent among them) while thousands were felled. Only the biggest and the strongest of men were left to stride atop the corpses.

Underneath it all, the demons in the abyss were at work. They were temporarily satiated with the blood that saturated the ground, and as they gathered to pull down more of the blood, the tree weakened even further.

Lucifer was leading the demons down below who, with their reckless lust for the blood of the men above, had now weakened their own tree. Now there was almost a joint effort——those still living above the ground and the demons and dead below the ground had become allies in the effort to get what they each deserved.

Blinded by their rage against this tree, the men didn't even notice when the large pools of blood began to swell quickly, as water found its way up from the fountains of the deep.

— 14 —
THE FLOOD

I t was early morning on judgment day. The last day of life for millions of men, women, children and the last day for a contiguous land mass.

Noah had not slept much that night, a night spent in deep thought, as he watched the sun come up as the perfectly smooth surface of the moon, that would never be the same again, went down.

He woke his family from their restful sleep on board the ark and they gathered for the family prayer. He knew that the awaited moment had arrived. It was time for the judgment of everybody on earth, with the exception of his family of eight. Though Noah's family's survival was secure, he was extremely somber, as millions had died and millions more would die. He even thought about what Cain's pending decision might turn out to be and hoped that he had touched Cain in a way that would humble him. Then he thought of his grandfather, Meth.

The night before, Methuselah had prayed: "Father, I love you. I always have. I hope you are pleased with the ark. It was a joy to accomplish such a feat. I am so incredibly blessed that you chose me to serve you, and I know that Noah feels the same way about your trusting him with this great honor. Father, looking back now on all that has transpired in my nine hundred and sixty-nine years of life, the love that I now feel from you completely obscures any memory of the pain or hardship that I have abided." (KJV Gen. 5:27)

Meth had been a faithful son, and on that last night God heard the prayer of His good servant and took him in the night as a sign to Noah. This sign was intended to comfort the comforter. Noah would be able to rest assured that Methuselah would not have to suffer a painful death by drowning. Those who had survived the drought would be in for a wild ride as the earth would violently break apart the very next day. Meth had not made a sacrifice for a hundred years. His life was his sacrifice: for him and Noah to have built a giant ark on dry land, far from water, was a demonstration of faith that equaled thousands of sacrifices. His final abode as a man of faith was secure.

Noah was very proud of his sons, as they had done all that he had asked of them with little complaint for one hundred years. But things would soon change in ways that he couldn't imagine. Noah's sons had taken no wives and were still virgins. Life and labor in Havilah——and the lack of women——had somehow protected them from their own flesh. Noah now hoped that his sons had learned from his example as a good father and a good husband. Noah was not likely to ever have another child, so Noah's three sons, once they had wives, would originate the three bloodlines of Noah that would populate the earth——if the three marriages held without adultery, of course.

Noah's sons had become strong men who were able to command the Nephilim. The three men were of good character and great intelligence and had mastered many skills. God's plan to save man would come to fruition over the next few thousand years. God's hope and Noah's prayer was that wisdom would be found in the way that he had fathered these three boys to men. Leadership and discipline would be required of them in this new world.

The dynamic of starting the new world with three bloodlines would be very different from the dynamic of populating the earth through the single line of Adam. In addition, the three boys were standing on the shoulders of millions of men, yet they would be starting out as Adam had——from a beginning. Part of God's plan was to create a new world where man would have far more opportunity to be free and thus to be more self-correcting. Men could learn from the trials and errors of their ancestors, should they choose to look back. The means to this end would start with the selection of wives for Noah's boys.

Methuselah, a short time before his final journey to Nod with Noah, had made one last trip to the Square of Adam on a very special mission. This mission had long been discussed among Noah and his sons. But the mission itself had been commissioned by God Himself directly to Meth. The mission. Meth was to go to the square of Adam and bring back wives for Noah's three boys, and this he had done. Before Meth left for this final trip to the square, Noah asked Meth to do him a service along those same lines, a private matter that, for now, would stay private.

Meth chose three young women from the Square of Adam, for Shem, Ham and Japheth. Methuselah worked very hard to find women, who would be good wives for his great-grandsons, as these three women would be the mothers of three new bloodlines.

Methuselah's job in choosing these three young women to take southwest to Havilah was more difficult than one might think.

His first requirement was that they be childless women who were well into adulthood.

He had some further instructions from God that were very important and very precise: he must find wives for Noah's sons who were diverse in skin color and hair color, and they must also be on their first set of teeth. One wife was to have fair hair and fair skin; one was to be of dark skin and dark hair; and one was to have medium complexion with red hair. Methuselah was to let Noah's sons choose from among them, and if there was disagreement they were to cast lots and let God decide.

But the sons had chosen without argument. The lighter of the sons chose the lighter of the women. The darker son chose the darker female. The son of mixed colors chose the woman of mixed colors. These three couples would create three bloodlines——three obviously different races——and this would bring the first new dynamic into the new world, a world atmosphere of self-correction for future men——three separate starts in the new beginning. Then more changes would be made as these new dynamics took hold on earth.

God had foreseen another key to building feedback into society——He would further encourage separation through different languages. Each son of Noah would have sons, who at some point would each speak a new tongue. If each of Noah's three sons had seven sons, and each of those sons had seven sons, there would be one hundred and forty seven languages given to man for the new world.

The next step would be to further separate men through the use of distance. This would be the last of the three new practical dynamics, and it would occur naturally as the continents and the land bridges settled below water.

Those who would choose to look back would prosper and reap great blessings as they acknowledged those who had come before them. Those who were prideful and refused to see the shoulders they stood upon would experience the curse of Adam, and the land would yield less gain to them.

It was God's hope that eventually the wise among men would look back and gain wisdom that would lead people to come together based on ideas and beliefs rather than on race and language. But these simple demarcations would have to do for now, with the end goal being *some* societies built on firm foundations of wisdom.

Noah was pleased with the boys and with their wives. "Father, I love You. It has been the blessing of a lifetime to serve you. My blessing can most be seen in my three sons, Shem——Ham——Japheth, as I bless them in their marriages. I ask, Father, that you do the same. May each one of them create great nations that will serve the Lord. Thank you Father, amen."

God did not rule over Noah, just as God didn't rule over anyone who didn't want to be ruled. Theirs was a paternal relationship between Father God and son Noah. God wanted Noah's love and respect, and He had it. God was pleased with Noah and walked with him on many occasions. Noah always saw God as a loving Father whom he loved, and God saw something in Noah that He had seen in very few other men: Noah had never feared God in the way that many others did.

Noah's sons never saw, heard or talked to God. Noah would often tell them that God was a loving Father and to know Him they should close their eyes and dream of a perfect father. "Don't dream of me," Noah would say. "Dream of a perfect father, which I am not. God has placed in all of our hearts the image of a perfect father——it is His image that you have in your hearts. Seek His image, and you will have the image of your Father in Heaven. Never be afraid of the first Father."

Shem, Ham, and Japheth, the sons of Noah, had just completed the building of the ark——a task designed to prepare them in many ways for the new world in which they would soon find themselves. They were proud of their achievement, and they were ready to embark on their new adventure.

Everything was set. Noah thought back and gave thanks to God for giving him the desire to leave the Square of Adam and for leading him to this most wonderful land of Havilah.

Noah and his sons would take many things with them to the postdiluvian world, but they could not take everything. They had previously depended on trade with others, but that would no longer be an option. Gold and silver would do them no good in the new world, as there would be no one to trade with. Clothing, bedding, tools, soap, food, and water were the kinds of supplies that would be essential for the foreseeable future. Also very important were Noah's birds. Noah had long kept doves, pigeons, and ravens as pets. They would be of great importance upon landing in the new world.

Noah would have no idea where he would land once the waters receded. Pigeons were known for their skill in sense of direction so his pigeons would be used to lead him. The ravens were scavengers and carnivores; he planned on using them to direct him away from the possible mountains of rotting flesh that may be awaiting their arrival in the new earth.

Noah and his sons had trained and prepared for this as much as they possibly could. They had learned as much as they could take in so that they could bring all of those skills and knowledge with them on the ark. They would no longer be able to rely on steel from Lamech or clothing from the Square of Adam. Simple things like pitch from the ground or figs from a tree were now going to be unavailable, and they were ready for this.

THE LARGEST WAGER EVER MADE

As for God, He was risking everything on Noah's ark. Noah and the boys had done a very good job of building it. It had been built in accordance to the plans that God had given them, so it was engineered to perfection. But having been built by humans and Nephilim it was not perfect, and Noah was not sure how watertight it would be.

Noah had been uneasy at times, knowing that there would be no opportunity to test the ark. Every boat that he had ever made before had undergone testing so adjustments could be made to make sure that it was watertight.

Noah believed that the ark had to be completely watertight from the beginning. He made some preparations for some minor leaks, as best he could, by supplying the ship with some ropes and containers to handle bilge water.

Noah trained a few beasts to aid the eight should they have to deal with a leak. The strength of the animals would also be used to help keep the ark sanitary during the year-long voyage. But Noah was really stuck on the sealing problem; he really desired that God would help him *insure* that the boat was well sealed.

Noah never told anyone about his concerns that the boat might leak too much water for the crew to handle. But God knew about these doubts, and Noah's boys suspected.

God and Noah were both risking everything on the success of this ark. God's whole idea behind having Noah build this giant boat was that God could help Noah in a way that would not lead to a tragic outcome in the new world. God in no way wanted Noah to become reliant on Him in an unhealthy way because of His help. Fortunately, Noah and his family remained humble and faithful, so no such thing happened.

Days before the flood was to begin, Noah faithfully prayed to God that He would personally close the door of the ark, and in doing so seal the door, its passengers, and its contents with His word.

The boys and the Nephilim had dressed the boat inside and out with thousands of buckets of pitch and caulking. (KJV Gen. 6:14) These materials were top quality, and the work had been top-notch. But even those thousands of days of work could not ensure that the boat would be seaworthy. In the end, it would be Noah's faith that would keep this vessel afloat.

God heard Noah's prayer, and the wise Father assented without acknowledgment.

The ark would be carrying an extremely valuable crew and cargo, and God Himself would make sure that all would survive the very rough seas that were on their way. Hence, with far less than a day to go before the great flood, when everything and everyone who should be aboard was aboard, God Himself closed the door (KJV Gen. 7:16), and He took the extra measure of sealing it to ensure that all would survive the rough voyage.

Unbeknownst to Noah, God would be doing something else at the same time that He was sealing the boat. He would also be demolishing the hopes and desires of the evil one, the serpent of old, the deceiver himself: Lucifer who had invented in his mind a future rebellion that he would lead roaming above the ground. A future he would be denied if Noah survived.

God spoke the word to ensure the ark, and so it was done. He had closed the ark to the world: to man and beast, and——most importantly——to water. Noah and the others on board would never know the extent to which God had assisted in sealing the ark against the coming waters and rough seas.

Ever the wise Father, God had waited until the last moment to seal the ark. Inside the ark, the eight passengers watched as the door closed on its own.

"Look, God is closing the door," said one of the boys.

This sight was very comforting to the crew of eight.

As it grew dark inside the ark, something else was happening outside. There was a flash from an intensely bright light, the heat of which could be felt by all inside the ark.

Even some of the animals were disturbed by it. This light encompassed the boat. The crew and animals could even feel heat emanating from below the ark. As it grew even darker inside the ark, the light from outside found every nook and cranny and cauterized every possible place where water might enter, thus sealing the ark.

Noah's family could not see the source of the light. But they could feel the source, and it was soothing, warm, and comforting. This was a living light, and it gave them a feeling that they would often long to feel again and that they would never forget.

The eight were greatly relieved by what had just transpired. In a moment of light, the fearful voyage they were about to embark upon had been transformed in their minds into a hopeful one, and it hadn't even begun yet.

Noah knew that his prayer had just been answered. So for, the last time, he closed his eyes to walk for a fleeting moment with God.

Noah could feel the presence of God, but neither of them spoke a word. At this moment, it was as if they were just two men, nothing more——two men who were pleased with the outcome of a risky and arduous joint endeavor. In the light of their achievements, both of them would enjoy a period of reflection as they pondered what was to come.

Noah felt gratified by God's appreciation of his accomplishments, and the love he felt from the Father filled his eyes with tears. The relationship between God the Father and Noah His son was forever solidified on this day, on the ark of eight.

Noah looked back on the promises each of them had made and kept and how they had secured a future for mankind unto a new world, beginning with Noah's family. Noah could see in a general way where his future would take him. However, he did not know what path the new world order would take for the Godhead, and as a good Father, God did not burden Noah with His problems.

God's reflections quickly turned to the desires of His Son. He knew that His only eternal Son had plans of His own, plans that might limit God's hand in many ways yet to be known.

The Son, being always in the present, was far more conscious of the consequences that mercy had produced on earth. His presence now confronted the past, as freely on His own accord, He would present man with a new way to live. He would increase His standing by someday paying the ultimate price. He did not owe this payment in any way, but He believed that His Father would accept it on behalf of those who truly owed the debt. Then anyone and everyone who would accept His payment would live.

The Father was very proud of His Son, yet very fearful of an event that might someday separate Them——Father from Son——for the first and only time. The Father did not actually assure His Son that He would accept His sacrifice in the stead of others, but the Son continued to make plans in faith that His Father would never forsake Him.

At that moment, far north of Havilah, the men and monsters who had been clawing at the base of the tree in the Garden of Eden finally received a response to their demands for water, a response that would comfort them in the depths.

The earth rumbled and shook as the fountains of the deep burst open and became giant geysers that sent huge plumes of water many thousands of man-lengths into the air——high enough to break free from the pull of the earth. (KJV Gen. 7:11)

The water catapulted with it countless numbers of boulders in all sizes. Some of the boulders weighed as much as the ark itself. The heaviest boulders comprised of heavy metals contained enough inertia to break free of the earths pull, entering into the heavens. Some of those pelted the surface of the moon, forever marring it for all to see each night——this gave unquestionable evidence proving Noah's account of the flood.

Water from the earth entered the heavens, to be deposited on the other bodies in the earth's solar system——some of this water would form comets.

Over the next forty days and nights, most of the trillions of cubic arm-lengths of water that had entered the skies and the heavens would return to the earth as rain.

Over the next thousands of years, the trillions of rocks, large and small, that had left the earth would be pulled back to their home, lighting up the sky upon their return.

Billions of massive trees that had been uprooted by the flood would end up gathered together in floating masses all over the world. As the water from the flood receded, many of these masses, covered by earth and debris, would form into what would become a blessing for man in the future: coal deposits, the fuel of freedom. This stored energy would enable man to produce the steel that would be needed to carry out the new dispensation God had envisioned, a dispensation of law.

The giant boulders that had impacted the moon's surface had done so with enough force to speed its rotation around the earth from thirty days to twenty eight days. The rotation of the moon on its axis changed by a similar rate so that the scarring on its face would always be visible on earth.

Forevermore, the rainbows in the sky, the craters on the moon, and the falling stars at night would bear witness to the destruction that had come with the deluge and would forever be a reminder of God's promise that He would never again flood the earth.

As the water escaped from beneath the earth's firmament, the firmament sank to its lower foundation, and the gigantic ark was subjected to its first test as the water rapidly surrounded it.

The ark swayed this way and that way, and then the motion gradually became violent.

At first, Noah thought this motion was just the waters attacking the sides of the ark, but then he heard pounding. Then, after the pounding, he heard screaming and wailing.

He was hearing the Nephilim——the giants who had built the ark were now demanding to be allowed on the boat. They were like rats in a flood, clinging to the ark as to a lifeline, but to no avail. Even the great strength of these giants was no match for the powerful waves and mighty winds that buffeted the boat about as if it was a small toy. As the waves proved to be too much for the giants, and one by one, their grips loosened, and they fell into the violent seas. The last one to go was Anak, whose distinct cry could be heard well into the night and even the next day.

The sinking firmament gained enough momentum that its impact on the earth's inner core actually changed the angle of the earth's rotation. The surface of the earth broke apart and sank down to its lower foundation. This changed the circumference of the earth making it smaller, which in turn changed its rotational velocity. Now each year would consist of three hundred and sixty-five and one quarter days, just as the prophet Enoch had predicted.

God looked away from the destruction that was underway and recalled the decision to show mercy to Cain. The Godhead talked among Themselves and affirmed an earlier decision——from that day forward, whoever shed the blood of man, by man his blood would be shed. The new foundation upon which man would now be instructed to build society would be the death penalty: this would be the lone foundation for the dispensation of law.

If not for the pure generations of Noah's family, their hard work, Meth's wisdom, and God's decision to try again to help His children, all of mankind would have perished on that day.

— 15 —

THE PLEASANT MYSTERY

The final few days in Heaven awaiting the first corporate Judgment of men on earth, brought much reflection into the events that had transpired since Adam. In the light of all that had come to pass the Godhead made plans to honor one special person.

The final few days on earth before the judgment were very different, very chaotic for all, from the eight in the ark who were filled with nervous anticipation, to the hordes of men, giants, and behemoths gathered at the base of the now giant tree of knowledge.

The mob at the tree were as angry as they were thirsty for water and for answers, while the future of the Godhead's entire creation was vested in a massive wooden boat built by four men and a crew of low-bred man-angel creatures.

The drought, which had lasted for three years, had taken its toll on the Square of Adam and on the City of Enoch. Pretty much everyone was now fleeing the City and the Square, and they spread out far and wide in search of food and water. The parched fields came to be littered with hundreds of thousands of dead. Though some had fared better than others, at least for a while, no one outside of Noah and his family would escape the effects of the drought.

Those who were best at wielding the sword were better off than those who were not, and the strongest would manage to survive to the end. Those who had water but not a sword had their water taken from them by the sword.

The water all but gone, yet some still refused to acknowledge that the prophecy of Enoch was at hand. But to most, it was obvious.

A primary objective of the long drought had been accomplished——many people had repented. Few had the means to offer a worthy sacrifice from their meager possessions. The meagerness of their payments would not affect their judgments, though. It was not the value of the sacrifice itself but the value of the sacrifice in the heart of the man that God was judging, and all but the eight in the ark would soon be coming to His judgment bar.

These final events on earth would end up being the stories of legend that would be foundational to every culture to come. The people who lived on earth at this time had no idea that they were to be characters in the story of a cataclysmic event——one that was now unstoppable——that would be recounted for all of eternity in Heaven. And for thousands of years, the story of the ark would be retold on earth.

Life on earth was tough and had become even tougher with the onslaught of the drought. But existence *inside* the earth would be far drier and hotter than even the very worst day on the drought-stricken earth——and dark as well. For many, the place of the dead would become their eternal dwelling because they had failed to open their eyes and humble themselves to what, clearly, only God could have made. God didn't want or desire these outcomes; these outcomes were just an unavoidable consequence of His decision to become a Father. Once procreated, a spirit's freedom was irrevocable, as is life itself.

As difficult as it was for God to contemplate condemning any man to eternal torment in the depths of the earth, He could not even consider allowing a faithful man to be forced to suffer the everlasting fellowship of an eternal evil spirit.

The latter would most assuredly destroy the former. It would be unthinkable for God to punish His first spirit of faith, Abel, by allowing an unrepentant Cain to reside alongside him in eternity.

Man had been given ample time and opportunity to repent but only one chance to do so——only one life to live. This was the practical nature of mercy, and this opportunity could be delayed no more. Three classes of people remained: those who sacrificed, those who did not sacrifice——both would be judged accordingly——and the children. Children were not accountable for their actions and would be granted time in Heaven to make their choice, for they were not yet mature.

While the Godhead were not bystanders, They had been severely limited by the decisions that each man had freely made. Man's choices would, more than any other one thing, limit God's choices going forward. There would be no more trees to guide man; instead there would be law. Cain's obsession with the tree had shown God just how much an unrepentant man needs law. The law of Cain would be the new tree, and all laws would branch out of that single law——whoever sheds the blood of man, by man his blood shall be shed. (KJV Gen. 9:6)

Noah would soon enough know of that one major change that was directly related to Cain and the mercy that Cain had been shown. God's mercy would continue on earth while man lived, but with that mercy comes limitations. Limitations to be set generally by God and then specifically by man in the form of law. These would be added, by man and by God as they saw fit. This would in many ways limit those who were obsessed by the tree——limit them with laws that would feed their obsession. Men were to set up institutions to judge men on earth with these laws. Man would be asked to, with the sword, limit men's mercy while they lived on earth. Then, man's eternal destination would be determined after death in a final righteous judgment.

The law of Cain, capital punishment, would be the cornerstone and foundation for all law in the post diluvian world. Going forward it would be the single most important change God would make. Capital punishment, if swiftly enacted, would add a dynamic that would generally guide man into self-correction, long before their ultimate punishment.

God spoke, "If used as designed, man will seldom need to carry out the punishment that Cain's life has inspired." The Son, "Father what shall We do when men condemn the innocent?" The Father knew of His self-concern, "Son, man's judgment will at times be misguided and wrong, but man can only condemn others to Us where We will judge with a righteous and eternal judgment that will correct the errors made on earth." The Father's words comforted the Son but then the Father added, "Son, all debts will have to come into balance, all payments will have to be made in full to satiate Our thirst for justice." His words sobered the Son . . . And He now contemplated the unavoidable collision course that the death penalty and He were on.

Adam and all of his children had known that they could live for a thousand years, this created a sense of immortality amongst men. A thousand years for man seemed like an eternity to them and that feeling was terribly misguided and led to destructive behavior. God saw a long life as a blessing and a long life was needed in the beginning, but things had changed.

The Godhead could now see, with the wisdom They had acquired watching man, that a thousand years was too long for a human to live on earth. They would move to limit a human life on earth to a more manageable length of time.

The life spans of the people to come could in large part be limited by narrowing the gene pool——there would only be descendants of Noah going forward——and then adjusting as required. Post deluge would also change the earth in many ways as to limit the age of the prodigy of Noah.

God's sixteen hundred years of watching, listening, and learning from the interaction of men and women in every imaginable circumstance had led to this culmination of events that was now unstoppable. God would take the events He found to be foundational, including the changes He had made, and condense them into His story as a guide for those who would come next. It would be a foundation for life that would not be easily broken——one of hard rock, not easily undermined by false science or foolish philosophy. It would be a foundation neither so large as to be divisible, nor so small as to be ignored, but just the right size upon which a man could build a personal foundation of trust, hope, and love.

From above, God looked on, and while He pondered the meaning of all that had transpired on earth, He recalled Abel, His first son of faith born by man.

Abel had been the first spirit being with no place to dwell, and God still held him close. Abel was a good son and more importantly, a faithful one. Abel was now in a special place where he was content. He was with other brothers and sisters who had also perished and who had also sacrificed to God in the way Adam had taught all of them.

Abel was only spirit now, no longer of flesh. He could not see the events that were transpiring on earth, nor did he want to. He was content with his spirit life. On occasion, God would express to Abel and the other faithful spirits His hopes about how they would fit in with His future plans. The inhabitants of Heaven were all content and happy with their eternal lives.

With the events on earth changing in such a big way, God decided that this would be a good time to fellowship with the faithful who were being held close to Him in Heaven. God would take this opportunity to inform the occupants of the Heavens about the millions of earthly beings who would soon be brought to judgment. The Godhead thought it timely, appropriate, and just to invite Abel as a personal and special guest to join Them in viewing the earth as one land mass, as Pangea, for the very last time.

For Abel, this was a new type of meeting with God; this was a very personal encounter. Abel's fellowship with God had always been more like a group event, like a corporate type of meeting. This was very different. He was more in the moment than he had ever been before, and it was very special. One thing that Abel was sure of was that this was a very high honor——he felt extremely humbled.

He could feel that he was in the presence of the Son. He could not see Him clearly, but he thought he understood the reason for this. It was because he was looking through the blood of the sacrifices he himself had made some sixteen hundred years earlier. Now he was as close to the Godhead as could ever be possible, and They were acknowledging his presence. Suddenly he saw creation, mercy, and sacrifice in a new light——the light of the Son.

Abel could see the earth clearly. It made him dizzy at first as he struggled to take it all in. He marveled at this incredible ability given to him by the Son, to see the entire earth. He was curious on so many levels and wanted to see so many things. He looked humbly towards the Son again to thank Him, but still he could not see Him clearly. The Son acknowledged Abel's humility and encouraged him to freely satisfy his curiosity.

What Abel was seeing through his new eyes both amazed and overwhelmed him. He could pan left to right and zoom in and out as quickly as he chose to, as if the whole earth were in his lap. *Is this how God sees things? Is this how They look down upon the earth?* he wondered. Abel continued to explore his new abilities as he sought out each thing that came to his mind.

Abel's first desire was to see the place where he had grown up and to look for familiar places such as the Square and the once beautiful altar Adam had built to the Father, in whose home he now dwelled. He had surmised that things on earth were very bad right now, but actually seeing it firsthand was very different than just knowing about it.

What he saw was in many ways depressing to Abel, so he was thankful that he hadn't been able to see all these events unfold day by day.

The once beautiful Square of Adam was barely recognizable. Where people had once watched their children playing in the Square, they were now cursing the Square. Where people had once bent their knees to give thanks to God at Adam's altar, they were now worshipping the dying trees and begging them for food. It was a horrible and depressing view of what had once been a paradise to Abel.

Where is Father's altar? Abel wondered. But the altar was gone. Every stone of this once great altar had been cast down. This was inconceivable to Abel. How could the earth have come to this? It seemed to him that every thought and every deed of man was evil.

As Abel explored further with his new temporary abilities, he wanted to see the garden. He had never been there himself, but his memories of Adam's tales were still very much a part of his spirit.

The garden he had heard so much about was now what he most wanted to see.

If I can find the Tigris, will it lead me to the garden?

He looked for the Tigris River that had once flowed so mightily, in which he and his brother had swum for hours, but which they had never been able to navigate very far upstream. *This must be the Tigris, but it is all but dry?* He allowed his eyes to continue following it.

As his eyes followed the path of the once mighty river, he saw a horde of men and behemoths traveling along the dry riverbed towards the garden.

Who are those strange creatures and where are they heading? He could then see the hills surrounding the once beautiful garden, and in the garden he could see a giant tree.

The tree of knowledge? he wondered. It was much bigger than he had ever imagined it could be, and it was surrounded by a mob.

Then something else caught Abel's eye. It was another tree, not far from the tree of knowledge, but much smaller. Standing in what seemed to be the center of the garden it was like a beacon of shimmering light, but it was alone. *Is this the other tree I heard so much about as a child? Is this the tree that gives life? Those people who are gathered at the base of the massive tree of knowledge, why are they ignoring the smaller tree that gives life?*

The smaller tree was dwarfed by the tree of knowledge. The tree where Adam and Eve had rebelled had grown to a height of two thousand arm-lengths, and its branches were so large that they could be used to build a wide bridge across a giant river. At midday, the shade of this tree caused night to fall below its canopy. It cast a giant shadow which fully shaded the distant hills in the mornings and evenings. The water that had once flowed from the garden——that had once fed the four mighty rivers and watered the entire earth——was now being restrained by the roots of this one truly massive tree.

Abel wanted to see the tree of life next. Instantly it was as though he were standing right at its base, looking up at its amazing golden fruit.

The tree of life? Yes, this is it. It seems remarkably healthy, given the severe drought on earth. Adam had spoken of the tree of life many times, but Adam had never really looked upon it as Abel was looking upon it now. As Abel looked at it, he came to understand it. These visions even had sound, and he could hear the grunts and groans of the thousands who were beating on the base of the tree of knowledge. *This is amazing. But why don't they notice the tree of life?* Abel realized that to gain wisdom he must look back (it was the same as when he was alive) through the Holy Spirit, and as he did so he received a partial answer——yes that was indeed the tree of life that he was looking at.

Then Abel looked to the Son for an answer as to why nobody was looking to the tree of life. *Have none of these people ever heard of the tree that gives life?*

He received no immediate answer, so he was even more intrigued. With all his humility, he looked directly at the Son and asked, "They are very close to the tree of life. Isn't that extremely dangerous?"

Though Abel's question had not specified this, the Son knew that Abel was concerned for His wellbeing should any of these evil men eat from the tree of life, partaking from the tree would be a type of fellowship with the Son and would have unknown consequences to all creation.

The Son looked at Abel through the sacrificial blood that constrained His intense glory and said, "My brother, no one there is looking for life, so they will never see that tree. We have learned that men will only see what they are looking for. In order to find eternal life, you have to first seek it out. Yes, men have the ability to find eternal life; but they must first have the desire to look for it. You are here because you looked and you saw, just as you now see."

Abel understood these words. He was satisfied and at peace with this answer.

With the wisdom he had received by looking back through the Holy Spirit, and after his now sixteen hundred years of being content and feeling close to God, Abel suddenly had a whole new appreciation of the Trinity. He now saw the Father as the Life, he saw the Son as the Truth, and he saw the Spirit as the Way. He thought about how powerful those three concepts are when put together——the way, the truth, and the life.

God made existence possible. The Son made Abel's presence there with God possible, and the Spirit filled all of eternity with wisdom from the past and eternal hope for the future.

It fit together very nicely in Abel's understanding. While the eternal nature of God would always be a mystery to him on one level——and perhaps to all——it was a pleasant mystery, one to be embraced and relished. Abel understood it as so,

God = Existence = Time. All three were mutually inclusive. They could not exist separately.

The Son = The present = Life. As life is only lived in the present and again all three are mutually inclusive.

Spirit being = The past and the future. The past and the future do not exist except in the spiritual world within the minds of spiritual beings. The past, the future, and Spiritual beings, and all three are mutually inclusive.

Existence (God) with no Son = no life, no movement, only cold darkness.

Existence (God) with a Son but no Spirit, leaves life with no knowledge of a past and no hope for a future, no wisdom, only the present moment nothing else.

No existence (no God) = nothing.

Abel believed that it would be necessary for God to remain a mystery in some ways, partly because man was not capable of understanding the full nature of God, but more importantly because understanding God was beside the point. The point was simply God Himself. God is eternal, and in His eternity we find mystery . . . that will always be the most pleasant of all mysteries.

Abel's curiosity now turned to his father, Adam, and his mother, Eve. *Where are they? Certainly Father must be here and Mother as well, and Eva. I hope so . . . and my brother Cain?* As a roster of his family members passed swiftly through his mind, he felt no inkling of any of them being held close to the Son, and this concerned him. *Could they have fallen? Certainly Cain could have but not Adam——Adam has to be here. Yes, he was guilty at the tree, but he offered so many sacrifices in repentance after that.*

As these thoughts filled Abel's wondering mind, the Son took it upon Himself to comfort him.

"Rise and look back," said the Son, "Look back as the Holy Spirit enables you."

Abel slowly rose, but he sensed that he was still far below the Son. As he turned around, what he saw amazed him. Because he was with the Holy Spirit, he had the ability to look back at things that had happened many years ago. He could see the Square of Adam as it had been in the distant past.

Abel stopped thinking about the amazing new abilities he had and turned his mind to the Square and to wondering about the current status of his mother and father, Eva, and Cain.

His next vision was of Cain——his brother, his murderer. Abel saw immediately that Cain was not now the same man he remembered. *This man, is it indeed Cain? He is very old and in no way strong as he once was.* This was a much weaker Cain than the brother he had once fought. *I feel as if I have not aged a single day, but Cain is now a pathetic shadow of what he once was.* Abel was shocked at the deterioration he could see in Cain's appearance.

In this vision, Cain was leading a group of men, and they seemed to be near the Garden of Eden——this must have been within the past few days. Leading the group along with Cain were Lamech and the Nephilim. Abel didn't know anything about Lamech or the Nephilim, but it was obvious that they were all of one mind and that their common destination was the garden.

Interested though Abel was in Cain's activities, his mind drifted back to his father. Now he was looking at events from eight hundred years ago. The Holy Spirit had deduced what he yearned to see and had put it all before him.

It's Father in his Square, Abel realized. Abel began reminiscing about the times they had spent together there. *I don't know exactly how, but I now know that my mother and father are fine.* The Holy Spirit confirmed this with him and brought him to understand that Adam and Eve were with the Son. He also discerned that both of them had literally millions of grandchildren that desired their attention and he would be meeting with them as Time permitted.

He was comforted by this knowledge . . . And then his mind turned again to Cain. Abel still had received no assurance from the Holy Spirit about his brother Cain.

Then he wondered, *Eva, my wife, is she also among us?* As his thoughts turned to his beautiful young sister and wife, Eva, so did his vision turn to her.

As he panned the Square for Eva, the Holy Spirit allowed him a quick glimpse of her but little more, as there was no need to burden Abel with knowledge of all of the sad events of Eva's life. But there she was——Eva. She was a very elderly woman, a very sad lady, and a person carrying a lot of grief. Abel was immediately saddened by this, but that would quickly change.

The Holy Spirit gave Abel the bare bones of Eva's story. Abel could now see Eva——once his young and beautiful bride——at what looked to be very close to the end of her life. She had carefully stacked a few stones from the ground on top of each other to form a small altar. She had caught a small dove and was sacrificing the dove to God. Then the vision suddenly ceased. Though Abel knew that these events had transpired in the past, he had no idea how long ago that might have been.

This vision had been given to Abel to assure him that Eva was among them and that she was okay. But he would not be allowed to see any more about her life for now, as it had been so full of pain and Abel would not be allowed to witness those events, those events were private.

Abel was thrilled that Eva was among the faithful and that Eva would tell her story, if she wanted to, at a time of her choosing. It would be Eva's choice whether to share the painful events of her life with him, but, regardless of her decision, they would have eternity to sort everything out together. He then had hope that she would contact him soon.

Finally, his brother Cain came back into sight, and again what Abel could see of Cain didn't look good. Abel didn't know how old Cain was, and at first it didn't seem odd to him that Cain was still living.

The Holy Spirit thought it important to inform Abel: "You are seeing Cain as he is this very day; he has lived one thousand, five hundred, and ninety-six years." As Abel watched his brother walking slowly below the tree of knowledge, he was overcome with emotion. Abel closed his eyes and pondered what had transpired in his own very short earthly life.

It had been one thousand, five hundred, and sixty-six years since Abel had received the blow to his head that had dramatically changed all of history forever. But at this moment Abel was dwelling on his own loss and not on the loss of the world.

Abel's first thought was, *I have no children; for all of eternity I will not be a father. Whom shall I love, whom shall I cherish? I will have no grandchildren to care for, all because of my brother Cain! Perhaps, that is why the Holy Spirit had shown me Eva first, as that has comforted me——the knowledge that at least I still have Eva to love.*

Abel once again turned his mind to Cain, the person to blame for all that he had lost. After all these years of not having given Cain much thought at all, Abel could now see his brother, and feelings of vengeance stirred deep inside him. *There he is, the man responsible for my demise. Has he repented?* Abel again looked back to gain wisdom. He received no indication that Cain had repented, and Abel wanted vengeance for what Cain had taken from him.

Abel again looked down upon the events that were occurring now on earth. With the help of the Holy Spirit, he came to understand that Cain's long life had hardened Cain's heart so that it was like a stone. His long life, in his mind, had indeed been a curse, albeit a curse designed to bring repentance.

Abel's desire for vengeance mellowed as wisdom took its place, and with the understanding that Cain would soon be judged. Abel believed that where there was life there was always hope, but he also knew that the chances of Cain's heart softening enough so that he would repent and offer a sacrifice were extremely slim.

Cain had never felt any need to offer a sacrifice, and it was unlikely that he would change now. His final destination, Abel believed, was not in question.

Confident in Cain's imminent judgment, Abel was mildly amused by the irony that Cain was currently in his cherished Garden in Eden. The Spirit had made it known to Abel that Cain had never before made it to the place that he had so yearned to visit. Now Cain finally had made it to the tree of knowledge, and that was where his journey would come to an end.

For more than fifteen hundred years, the tree had exerted a pull on Cain that he was never able to shake. Now the tree was pulling not only Cain but thousands of others who had chosen to live in the way of Cain. The crowds of men, giants and beasts at the tree were enormous.

Abel kept watching as the tree of knowledge took on a new life of its own. The change was subtle at first but it slowly was becoming more apparent. The serpent Lucifer was there, but this time he was not trying to deceive anyone. This time he was there to welcome those who were being pulled down by the tree to his eternal home——and Lucifer was not alone. The earth's hold on the demons below was weak at the base of this tree, and the dead in the earth broke free and scattered into the tree's branches.

The tree of knowledge had millions of branches, and now each and every branch was occupied by demons and the dead. Cain had no idea Abel was watching him; and Abel had no idea what Cain was thinking. Cain, for perhaps the first time in his very long life, suddenly had a strong sense of his mortality and just what that meant. No other man would be given the time and opportunity that Cain had been afforded. The only question now was whether his newfound understanding was strong enough that he would indeed repent.

As the tragedies of his life ran through his memory, Cain sensed, with gratitude, that his time was finally at an end. Cain knew full well that his slaying of his brother was a direct cause of the current situation on earth. He fully owned that burden now, and he also now knew what he would have to do to live eternally with the good brother he had executed.

Cain had never been one to sacrifice because it just didn't make sense to him——but now he was rethinking this stance. *Could it be that easy?* he wondered. He even thought of his brief encounter with Noah as he looked deep inside himself for an answer. He understood clearly the principles of sacrifice, but still he wondered, *Does my sacrifice have to be sincere in order to work? Isn't it worth at least a try? Do I want to live on in Heaven? Do I?*

Cain was old, he was tired, he was guilty, and he had changed his mind about his long life. With his newfound sense of mortality, he finally had a full grasp of the meaning of mercy, and in his own perverted way he acknowledged and thanked God. *Father, I now believe my long and painful life has indeed been a . . . blessing. Thank You.* He had now come to believe that his curse was a blessing——he had been given all this time to repent——all this time and mercy to change as he must. But would he? Abel was now forefront in Cain's mind as he pondered his——final——decision. *I . . . will have to face my innocent brother once again——I . . . will once again be face to face with his goodness——if I repent and offer a heartfelt sacrifice.*

Abel looked on, not knowing that Cain was thinking of him. Abel still carried some need for the vengeance that was due Cain and was not obligated to forgive his brother unless Cain repented. Abel watched as Cain wept for only the second time in his life——engaging in his final act of rebellion, refusing to do what he knew needed to be done. He just could not grasp the concept of forgiveness. Unable to reconcile that someone else could pay for his actions, and not wanting to humble himself before his brother, he chose a spot close to the tree that had consumed so much of his attention for sixteen hundred years and lay down on the ground.

The tree seemed to become a sentient being as it turned its focus to Cain. The millions of demons scrambled down the trunk and into the root system of the mighty tree——a root system that had a far larger span than the tree's canopy and dominated a large portion of Eden. The ground rumbled as the demons found pathways up via the tree roots that Cain was lying on. The demons desperately wanted their prize. The earth beneath Cain began to weaken.

The dead, from the deep and dark abyss of hell, in a massive effort to grab onto one of their own, pushed their hands through the mantle of the earth and the ground broke open to claim Cain.

God would not be judging Cain after all.

Cain bypassed that event, where he would have had to face his good brother Abel, with his final earthly decision to go straight——to——hell.

The tree of knowledge, already weakened, was pulled down as the earth swallowed the garden whole, and the fountains of the deep began an uncontrollable eruption as they broke open. (CEV Gen. 7:11, Eze. 31:14–18)

Just as Lucifer and his demons were satiating themselves with the blood of Cain, Lucifer perceived a flash of light from far away. The light could not be seen by Lucifer but it was felt by him. The Godly light that was sealing the deal with Noah caused Lucifer excruciating torment. Abel could see the light in the distance but kept his focus on the tree and heard Lucifer speak.

"No. No! NO!" Lucifer's penetrating screams were as loud around the garden as the light was bright around the ark. His pain and agony were horrific. The minimal relief he had enjoyed from receiving the blood of Cain only made this new anguish far worse, as he realized that his rebellion was in dire straits. "We had a deal," Lucifer wailed to his Creator, but he was doomed to remain where he belonged——in the earth and out of the Heavens——far away from the powerful and comforting light that was causing him such agony.

Abel again looked back to understand the "deal" of which he spoke, the Spirit quickly informed him. Lucifer had plans of inheriting the earth, plans that were mostly made in his evil mind apart from any agreement that was made between him and God. By ensuring Noah's safe voyage, Lucifer's hopes of returning to an above ground rebellion were put down even deeper into the earth.

Abel had been a young man when he had perished on earth, and thus he had been protected from knowing what the earth had become. But, thanks to the Father's invitation to witness the final current events as they took place on earth, Abel began to understand all things anew. With his new understanding of the world, he could now more clearly grasp——who he was, and, far more importantly appreciate——where he was.

While the Spirit had been helping Abel to look back on these events, Abel had begun to weep. He wept ever harder as each new revelation brought him closer to understanding what he had not until now realized——he was in the Heaven and this peace would be eternal.

With tears rolling down his face, Abel felt thankful for the temporary gift that God had so graciously bestowed upon him during Pangea's final day and for the new perspective that he now had. Then the Father, for the first time ever, wiped away the tears of one of His beloved children in Heaven.

As Abel returned to the present with the Son, he sensed that the time had come, that the judgment of God had begun——millions would be judged.

Some would enter heaven and many would not. Moments before, Abel had lamented the fact that his life had been cut short before he'd had a chance to be a father. Now he realized that there would be many fatherless children arriving in Heaven, and he joyfully anticipated adopting as many of them as possible. They would be his treasures in Heaven.

Now the earth was groaning——it sounded like a woman giving birth or a man dying forever. As the intense pressure of the constrained rivers of the garden ruptured the earth——that had been foreseen by Noah——the water exploded thousands of man-lengths into the sky and was a sight to behold.

As the firmament sank down onto its foundation, it slid in all directions away from the garden. As its momentum increased, so did the resistance underneath it, until a thick front of molten rock had built up, which eased its path. This caused its speed to increase even more until it surpassed the speed of sound.

As the surface of the earth broke apart and began its journey down and away to form separate land masses, the ark was slowly lifted off the ground——with Noah and his family safely aboard. Sealed inside——they began their journey above the waters that were now swallowing the land.

While a new world order was just beginning for the eight on the ark, outside the ark there was nothing but wailing and death, as life was ending for so many.

Within about a day, the continents were already great distances apart as their sliding came to a stop. Below the surface of the earth, the immense amount of energy that had been released by the collapse of the firmament——now deep underground——would become a curse to man in the form of volcanoes in a ring of fire. However, it would also become a blessing to man in the form of potential energy provided by a mature earth.

Vast pools of carbon, the size of the earth itself, would now be available to be tapped into as needed. Carbon would be the fuel of freedom in the postdiluvian world. Oil and gas would propel the gardens of the new world into abundant life for the wise.

God had learned from Lamech and others that steel was the foundation of liberty and carbon was the foundation of steel, so coal would be the source of abundant life in the new, far harsher environment on earth.

The solar energy received from the light of the sun in the sixteen hundred years since creation, stored in the trees and the seas from the now mature earth, would be available for men to use on the surface of the earth. This now potential energy above and below the ground, if used wisely, would nourish manmade gardens where man could live and prosper with abundant life.

As the leading edges of the seven continents settled into formation, kinetic energy pushed up mountains on their trailing edges, thousands of arm-lengths into the sky.

These mountain ranges would be a crucial component in the formation of weather patterns, creating winds that would in turn create clouds full of rain to comfort those who would work the fields.

Creation hadn't gone down the way that God would have preferred, but with time and a proper foundation mankind would have the choice and the chance to find a way back to their Creator——choice was always the greatest part of the gift of life, and the prayer of the Son was that mankind would make better choices from this point on.

And God remembered Noah . . . The End. (KJV Gen. 8:8)

AUTHOR'S POSTSCRIPT

MY FOUNDATION

Of all the things that I have to be thankful for——which are countless——I consider two of them to constitute a major portion of my foundation. First, my mother and father were good parents. I don't recall my father ever telling me he loved me but it was impossible not to feel his obvious love, so I am very thankful to have had loving parents. The other thing that I am most thankful for is that I have never blamed God for my failures or my problems. I don't know where I got the idea that God was in no way to blame for these things——I guess it had to have come from my parents——but I have never blamed God for anything; I have always known that the source of my problems was me and me alone. Of the countless times that I have tried to blame others for my circumstances before eventually bringing the blame home to where it belonged, I am proud to say that I don't ever recall naming God, even once, as the One to blame.

MY WISH

I wish that people would look back before they react. Ignoring history in the pursuit of a particular course of action that has been repeatedly seen to have failed in the past is the essence of arrogance. Albert Einstein defined insanity as, "doing the same thing over and over again and expecting different results." I strongly disagree with his definition. It is not insanity. It is vanity. It is human nature. Indeed it is our own arrogance that leads us to believe that we will succeed where people for generations before us have failed, and it is our vanity and arrogance that lead us to believe that we are far more talented or that our ideas must be far superior to those of whose shoulder we stand upon.

It is arrogance to try yet again, and guilt soon follows to justify the predictable failure with false altruism. "At least we tried," we say, as the ones we "helped" are punished further by our *good* intentions.

We all stand on our fathers' shoulders, and we are obligated by where we stand——upon the billions who have preceded us——to simply look to our fathers and to accept their guidance. We might avoid many mistakes if we would only look to what has come before, look at our place in history, make decisions based on what is known, and then give our ancestors the credit due them——good and bad——for the history they gave us. If we would only look back and then think anew, the world would be a much better place.

What is the opposite of arrogance and vanity? That is humility. All we need to do is to humble ourselves against the background of history, placing ourselves justly, and then, with humility, look forward and reason anew. Wow, the world would be a much better place if just a few of us were to bend a knee before we act and humbly look back to those who tried before us. That we may begin to do so is my wish.

MY PRAYER

Father, I love you; I have for a long time now. I am so sorry that I haven't been a better son, and I would promise You now to be a good son, but I have done that so many times only to let You down. Only my tears of humility allow me to come to You yet again to ask for Your guidance. I wrote this book in an attempt to honor You and to guide my children, and I hope that I, at least in part, have achieved that goal. With all my heart, if I have offended You in any way in writing this book, please give me the wisdom, strength, and courage to acknowledge those mistakes and to change what I have written. I love You, Father.

Amen and amen.